CROSSROAD BLUES

Steve

Malley

Cover by Rebecca K Sterling
http://sterlingdesignstudios.com

For my Dad

ACKNOWLEDGMENTS

Special thanks go out to Kate Sterling for the wonderful new cover. To Candice Proctor and Charles Gramlich, Avery DeBow, Angie Miller and others, for their advice and support as the manuscript slowly took shape. To Clifford Freycinet and all of my other First Readers who caught plot holes and factual errors. To Rick Fey of the Minnesota Kali Group and all my other martial arts teachers over the years. And of course, to Holly Young, for putting up with the madness that is life with a writer.

I owe you all so much.

Also by Steve Malley

Poison Door

Blood and Skin

and coming soon

Buried

CROSSROAD BLUES

ONE

Kane picked his note and held it, long and wailing. The sound echoed off the stone faces of the buildings around him. Right at the moment the song could take no more, Kane fanned the reeds of his Oskar. The airtight cup of his two hands was broken, and the harmonica responded, transforming the single sustained note into a wild tremolo.

He bent that tremolo down into a chord change and picked up the chorus of *Black Cat Blues.* Nobody much played Jack Terrabonne's songs anymore, but that one was perfect for the night: a tale of bad luck and bad women, with plenty of humor and bounce. Early drinkers and late shoppers responded. A small crowd gathered, and Kane was rewarded with the clink and jingle of coins.

Christchurch was good to Kane. His hostel bed was thirty-five a night, and every one of the four days he'd busked had earned him at least a hundred and fifty. Another week, Kane would have enough for a plane ticket.

Cathedral Square was where the best action was. The square was a constant churning mass of office workers, tourists and partiers, and every one of the city's musicians, jugglers, and magicians knew it. It was the only part of the city where buskers needed a permit, and the cops kept up a heavy and visible presence to protect the tourists from drug dealers, junkie thieves and pickpockets.

Kane kept to Cashel Mall. The competition was more relaxed here, and since the street was closed to vehicle traffic, every shopper and worker passing was on foot. Kane played to the crowd. Lunchtime, he played a lot of Delta blues, working the harmonica through flashy bent notes and chord changes. Evenings and nights, the offices and stores were closed, and the people on the street were moving from bar to bar. For them, Kane played roadhouse blues and swamp boogie.

A fiddle joined in on another Terrabonne favorite: *Backdoor Boogie*. Kane looked past his scarred knuckles on the harmonica. The kid was back. Kane dipped his head in greeting, and across the street, the kid's fiddle dipped a little salute in reply. His bow danced over the strings, and a quick little riff echoed in the cold air.

They took turns with the lead. Two junkies watched the performance from a doorway down the block, hollow-eyed and twitching. Four sleek young drunks stopped to applaud at the end of the song and left without dropping any change.

Kane dumped the contents of his hat into a Ziploc bag and dropped both bag and hat into his backpack. The boy was already playing again, some generic bluegrass tune that could have been any of four different songs. Kane waited until the end and dropped a wrinkled orange five.

"Still here, hey Yank?"

Kane shrugged.

"I would've thought you'd be gone by now." The kid was maybe thirteen or fourteen, with thin wrists and a shy smile.

"Aren't you out kind of late?" Kane said.

"Mum's picking me up later."

"I don't like you being out here alone."

"Relax, mate. It's not like you're in Los Angeles or anything. And besides, I've been doing this for over two years now. You've only been out here a few days."

Down the block, the two junkies looked back at Kane, put their heads together and whispered.

"Can I ask you something," the kid said, "What's America really like?"

"Mighty big, that's for sure."

Kane stuck his hands in his pockets. He'd picked the heavy coat up in a thrift shop two days earlier.

"Ever been to L.A.?"

"No."

"I want to go there, when I'm older and do my Big O.E. I'll get a record contract and buy a mansion."

"Keep practicing. You want to play the big stages, you need to be tight."

"You ever play any big stages?"

Kane pushed his backpack with the side of his foot.

"I reckon this suits me."

"You *reckon*?" The boy's voice slipped from New Zealand's clipped consonants and trilling vowels into an imitation American accent.

"You make me sound too much like John Wayne."

"That right, punk?"

"No, that one's Clint Eastwood."

"Whatever. You playing or what?"

Kane smiled. "One more number before I call it a night?"

"Mate, the punters are just getting started."

"They're all yours."

"Can we do Wayfaring Stranger?"

"Again?"

"This time save your harp for the bridge and take the vocals instead."

They played, soft and soulful. The boy's fingers were crisp and accurate on the strings, his face serious, almost grim. It was plain the kid had classical training, but he had a feel for this music too. The boy took his time, tried to capture the eerie beauty of its chord changes.

The two junkies were gone from the darkened doorway.

The song was one of Kane's favorites. It took him back to when he was a little boy, memories of church choirs and afternoons helping his father in the fields. It took Kane back to being a hungry and unwanted teenager, busking on the streets.

Kane closed his eyes and sang. His voice was deep and mournful. Every word was the truth.

I'm just a poor, wayfaring stranger

Traveling through this world alone

TWO

"Why are you *doing* this to me?"

The girl's face was a puffy tear-streaked mask. A foot and a half above the top of her head, the black shape of Harlan Winters blotted out the moonlight.

"Shut up."

Harlan wrenched the rope. The girl cried out as rough braided nylon tore soft flesh.

Harlan Winters loved Mexico, especially Jack's ranch in the Yucatan. The night air smelled of stagnant water, wet leaves and vegetable decay.

Somewhere in the trees nearby, an animal was decomposing. The odor carried to Harlan on a shift in the breeze. He closed his eyes and tilted his head back. His tongue flickered gently behind his teeth as he tasted that faint scent of death.

"*Please* mister," the girl said. "Pleasepleaseplease, you can let me go. I won't tell anyone. *Please*..."

"I'll let you go, just not yet." Harlan showed his teeth. A blade of moonlight fell across his face. It lit his eyes, pale and silvery.

"You still smell too much like soap."

"Couldn't you at least loosen the ropes?" she said. Her voice was wet and choked. "Please? They *hurt*..."

Harlan hauled on the rope. The girl stumbled behind him, crying. She tried falling down and staying there, but Harlan wrapped one big fist in the girl's hair and dragged.

A lightning-struck cottonwood stood in the center of the clearing. Harlan raised his arm until the girl hung with her heels kicking in the air. He pulled her higher, until her arms passed over and circled the tree's blasted trunk.

Once the girl's feet touched solid ground, Harlan walked away. She struggled and thrashed and screamed.

Like it mattered.

Jack Terrabonne's Mexican ranch was over a thousand acres in the middle of nowhere. The nearest neighbors were none of them closer than an hour's drive. The only answer to the girl's screams was the guttural cough of a jaguar, hunting in the dark.

Harlan threw his head back and roared, exultant. Branches thrashed further and further away as the jaguar beat a hasty retreat.

This little piece of land was beautiful. Scrub oak and cottonwood, turtles and fish and birds, wild cats and poisonous snakes. The jungle was dotted with the rocky wet shafts of sinkholes, gateways to vast caverns of black water under the earth.

Harlan loved Jack's Yucatan ranch.

Mexico was perfect. For an American, especially a rich and famous one like Harlan's boss, this place was paradise. Jack's money went a long way here. So did his pull with the local cops.

And backpackers came here from all over the world. They came to Mexico for the beaches, the drugs, the Mayan ruins, a thousand things. Sometimes, they found what was left of Boogie Jack Terrabonne.

A few of those found Harlan Winters.

Harlan and Jack both loved the same women, though maybe for different reasons. Even when he'd been married to that movie star, Jack had never stopped chasing the hitchhiker girls, the drifters and runaways and trashy women just passing through. As long as Harlan had known him, Jack had a thing for anonymous women at the edges of society.

Harlan's thing was for women nobody'd miss.

This one was small and pale, junkie-lean. Her hair was shot through with streaks of purple and blue, and her face and body were full of winking pieces of metal. She'd come to Jack's bed with a bad attitude, staring at Harlan like he was some kind of circus freak, treating him like the hired help.

Now she wept and thrashed, staked out in the middle of a jungle.

Harlan stepped into the tree line. He circled around the back of the jeep, with its still-pinging engine, its smells of motor oil and hot metal. The keys were in his pocket, jingling around with the bullets from the gun.

He felt good under the trees. Small animals scurried and skittered, night birds called and owls hunted in silence. The moon was bright and full, throwing silver light through the wind-rattled leaves.

The girl struggled against her bonds. No way she was able to reach the knot. She scraped all hell out of the soft flesh inside her arms. Harlan walked up behind her. The smell of her fear carried to him on the night breeze.

Harlan flared his nostrils and growled. The girl jumped and whimpered. Her hair was still wet from Jack's endless showers. Sweat streaked her flanks and slicked her limbs. Mosquitoes clustered on her neck and face, at the backs of her knees and in the tender hollows behind her ankles.

She no longer smelled like soap.

Harlan leaned in. His breath curled warm and rank along the girl's cheek. His lips brushed the fine wisps of hair that floated loose, just behind her ear.

"It's time. You can go."

The girl trembled at the touch of Harlan's fingers on her skin. Three pulls and the knot was loose. One more, and the rope fell at the base of the charred and blasted tree trunk.

The girl fell shaking to her knees, rubbing at her bloody wrists. She looked up at Harlan with big wet eyes, shimmering puddles showing him twin reflections of the moon.

"I promise, I swear, IswearIswear*Iswear* I won't tell anybody about this. I--"

Harlan lowered his face to hers and roared.

"RUN!"

She ran.

Harlan watched her white legs scissor in the moonlight. He dug his fingers into the hard dark earth and waited for her to reach the trees. His lips curled away from his teeth in a tight savage smile, and the blood thundered in his wrists and throat.

The girl looked back over her shoulder. The great hulk of Harlan Winters sat crouched at the base of the lightning-struck tree, waiting.

She ran gasping for the safety of the trees. In seconds, her legs were pale flashes in the shadows under the dark leaves.

Harlan gave chase.

THREE

Jack Terrabonne woke to *Black Cat Blues* playing on his cell. He fumbled in the dark until his fingers found the flashing blue screen.

He looked at the name on the screen. *Black Cat Blues* started a second chorus. Jack sat up and rubbed his face with one hand. As his phone started to play through a third time, Jack cleared his throat and answered.

"Delton Adams, you old dog! How'n hell are you?" Jack heard his own voice, rolling, golden and musical. He smoothed his hair back with one hand, scarcely aware of the gesture.

"Delton old son, you get them latest files I sent through on that email?"

"They came through fine, Jack. Did you get a chance to look at that itinerary I sent?"

"That email sure is something, ain't it?" Jack shrugged into a silk robe and stood in front of the mirror. Jack Terrabonne loved mirrors.

"You know," he said, "I remember a day, I wanted to whip up a little track or two at home, I had to drop a big old magnetic tape in the mail. Why, this one time--"

"Jack did you actually *read* the itinerary?"

"I glanced at it."

"Those tour dates start in under a month. And with *The Old Time Country Gospel Hour* going into production in September, this tour's important."

"Not much of a tour, you ask me. Just a heckuva lot of itty bitty shows."

"Nothing small about the Iowa State Fair, Jack."

"I'm headlining in Iowa?"

"Not headlining, exactly..."

Funny, Jack remembered a time when a phone call from Mexico to the States meant scratchy crackling static. Now he was able to hear every little bit of the discomfort in his manager's voice.

Terrabonne couldn't resist the urge to twist the knife.

"And what about some of them other dates? *Shotkickers? Bob's County Bunker?* You booking me into *bars* now, son?"

At the other end of the line, where it was still half past nine in Los Angeles, Delton sighed.

"Look if you don't want to do that summer circuit, would you at least think about--"

"You can just stop right there. Branson is not an option."

"Lots of stars play Branson, Jack. Instead of chasing your audience down, a few dozen here and there all over the country, they'd be able to come to you. And as far as the *Gospel Hour's* concerned, you just opening a club there would be great publicity."

"Branson's where old guitar pickers go to die. Nothing doing." Jack hated the way his voice came out. It sounded whiny, peevish and old.

"It'd be a money maker," Delton said.

"Money I got. What I need's a new hit. Something to get me some radio play, put some butts in some seats. That's what I need."

"Jack..."

"You listen to them tracks I sent?" Jack Terrabonne cast a fond glance at the big round bed, its sheets twisted and stained. "I got me a good feeling about those songs."

"You always have a good feeling."

Terrabonne's eyes narrowed.

"What you trying to say, Delt?"

"You really want me to be honest, Jack?"

"Just say it."

Delton took a deep breath and fired in.

"*Mandy's Song* is just a warmed-over version of *Pussyfootin' Heart*, and those others you sent along are just more of that same good-time bubblegum honky tonk you've been selling for the last thirty years."

"Well hell's sakes, man, don't beat around the bush."

"Look, there's nothing wrong with fluff and schmaltz, but that stuff's just not the current market."

"You even *listen* to them lyrics?"

"Jack, will you at least think about Branson?"

Jack's phone shattered against the wall. By the time his temper was spent, Jack's voice was hoarse and strained and much of the furniture in the room broken."

***

Kane checked back on the kid at midnight. He found the boy sitting a sidewalk with his violin case shut between his feet. Waiting for his ride.

The two junkies waited in the dark. They huddled together in an alley behind the kid, watching the boy and whispering. Their postures were tight, agitated and intent.

Predatory.

Kane circled the building and stepped up behind them.

"Nice night," he said. "Cold."

Both men jumped. Their faces and hands were a mass of ticks and twitches. Their eyes were bright shards of broken glass set deep in their skulls.

Kane shifted his pack on his shoulder. Behind the junkies, the kid sat waiting on the curb.

The junkies looked Kane up and down. He stood with his feet apart and his hands away from his sides. A naked bulb burning in an upper story window threw hard planes of light and shadow across his face. His eyes burned with amber light.

"We weren't–"

"I'm sure you weren't."

The junkies looked at each other and at Kane. One licked at dry cracked lips. The other swallowed twice, hard.

The junkies might have been fiending, but they weren't stupid. They were desperate enough to think about robbing a child, but not desperate enough to tangle with Kane.

"So," one said, "what are you gonna do?"

"I thought we'd all stand right here til the boy's mother picks him up."

"There's two of us..."

"Yup." Kane shifted slightly on his feet.

"It's your call," he said.

The three men stood facing each other in the urban dark.

***

The broken red yolk of the sun had just begun to climb the horizon when Harlan Winters dragged his ass back to Jack's hacienda. The summer heat was like a living thing only just beginning to rouse and stir. Soon, it would devour every trace of the cool wet night.

Harlan was covered in mud, blood and darker fluids. No way he wanted to track this kind of mess over Jack Terrabonne's clean terracotta tile floors.

A sinkhole lay a couple hundred yards behind the hacienda. In the first light of morning, the surface of the water was bright green with slime. In the shadows, the water was so dark it was almost black. Its rock walls, chalky and white in the day, glowed with a bloody light in the first rays of the new sun.

Harlan dived into the sinkhole. His body made a huge and ugly splash, and he sank beneath the surface. The water was like ice. No one knew how deep this shaft was, or how far it traveled below the ground. Divers sometimes explored underwater caves like these for hundreds of miles. For Harlan, the thought of miles and miles of black water trapped beneath the earth exerted a powerful pull.

The green water grew dim as Harlan's body sank further from light.

The water around him was almost black before Harlan resisted its temptation. He kicked hard against the dark until his head broke the slime on the water's surface.

Harlan treaded water and scraped at his big hairy limbs. By the time his shovel-sized hands clawed their way up the rocky shaft, Harlan's skin was red and raw.

The house was still asleep. No one saw Harlan enter, or tracked his dripping progress through the halls to his room. He dropped his wet clothes on the floor of his room and fell into bed. The morning heat soon dried his puddled trail, and Jack Terrabonne's maid staff cleaned every other trace of him from the halls.

His room they left alone. The maids knew better than to disturb Harlan Winters in his lair.

FOUR

Golden light slanted low through the western windows by the time Harlan woke. He shook himself like a bear, pulled on his boots and hunted the dusty twilight halls.

Harlan found Jack in the study. The strains of a twelve-bar blues walk led Harlan to the right room. The missed notes, botches and restarts told him just how drunk the old man was.

Terrabonne did his most serious drinking in his study. It was his favorite room in the hacienda. Whole lot of knotty pine paneling in there, dark leather furniture and a couple of heads mounted on the walls. The deer were both ten point bucks, shot there on the estate, though not by Jack. It was Harlan pulled the trigger on both of those particular animals.

Harlan stopped in the doorway. Terrabonne waved him in without looking up. The famous man's thousand dollar dressing gown hung open. The gown was spotted with wet brown stains, and the man's chest was plumed with long silver hairs. The skin underneath was saggy and tanning-lamp brown. Only the six-string Dobro across Jack's knees saved Harlan from seeing a whole lot more.

The room was dark, stifling in the summer heat. Flies buzzed in the corners, and an eye-watering fog of alcohol fumes filled the room.

The dying sun was a great red eye, almost closed. The sky outside the windows shifted from the color of bleached bone to that of a blood-filled bruise. A single lamp burned on Terrabonne's desk. Its green shade threw underwater shadows across the upper half of the room.

Harlan dropped his bulk into one of the wood and leather easy chairs. The furniture groaned under Harlan's weight, but it held. Despite over twelve hours' sleep, Harlan still felt tired and drained, hellish.

"You weren't here last night."

Harlan gave his boss a narrow-eyed look and growled. Terrabonne was a damn mess. That world famous hair hung limp in his eyes, and the man's tanned and pampered skin looked bloated and gray.

"I needed you, and you weren't here. Where were you?"

Harlan said nothing. In the deep gloaming of the room, his eyes were bright with a feral and dangerous light.

"I mean it, hoss. Where were you?"

Terrabonne looked up. His face caught the light, and his eyes were puffy and red.

"Taking care of your business."

"Not all night, you weren't."

"You didn't expect me to drop your girl at that little bitty airstrip in Ticul, did you? I ran that gal on out to Chetumal, sent her on back home."

"Still..."

Harlan chuckled, raspy behind the liquor. "All right, you caught me. After I got that pretty little gal's butt on a plane, I stayed awhile in town, took care of a little business of my own. That okay with you?"

Terrabonne leaned forward, suddenly earnest. Small batch single malt splashed out of a cut crystal tumbler. Brown spatters stained the hand-braided Navaho rug.

"Harlan? I ask you something, old hoss?"

Terrabonne's mouth flapped open and closed. In that moment, his real age showed through despite all the botox, face lifts and chemical peels. The flesh hung slack from the bones of his skull, ancient, brown and deeply lined. His neck and jowls wobbled yellow in the light, and the upper half of his face was lost in green shadows. Flies turned buzzing little spirals over the spilled liquor.

"Hoss, you didn't...?"

A low rumbling rose from Harlan's throat.

"Didn't what, Jack? Just what is it you're worried about?"

Terrabonne licked his lips and looked to one side. Saliva gleamed at the corners of his mouth.

Harlan's nostrils flared. On the other side of the study window, the earth still carried the scents of dust and of the last trapped heat of the vanished day. Here in this air-conditioned room, Harlan smelled only water and mold and, under the mechanical chill, a faint scent of rot.

Harlan scratched the hair at the side of his neck. He looked Terrabonne straight in the eye and smiled. Terrabonne was drunk, but not so drunk he didn't flinch.

"Lord, Jack. How far back we go, you'n me? All this time, you think I'm about to start selling what I know to one of them scandal sheets? Maybe let a couple of them paparazzi in to take a few pictures?" Harlan threw his head and snorted. Terrabonne relaxed his hunched-up shoulders.

"I know, hoss. I know. It's just, you didn't come back last night, and the boys didn't come back either, and..."

"And you started to worrying."

"I trust you, hoss. You gotta know I trust you, but some of these boys--"

"The boys don't know shit. I make sure of that."

"A lot of folks'd pay good money to hear about, you know, about my visitors. It could really screw things up for me."

"I know it," Harlan said. It was Jack's old fear, worse than ever since his last divorce. Lord knew the tabloids had raked Jack over the coals a good few times, but Harlan doubted anyone still gave a rat's ass.

Of course, word got out about Harlan's shallow graves back in those hills, Jack Terrabonne's face would be all over every channel, though not in the way he wanted. Jack didn't know it, but they were both better off with Harlan fanning those fears.

"What's that?"

"I said that girl, that Mandy? She's gone, right?"

"Yup." Harlan licked his lips and said, "I sent her home."

"You don't think...?"

"She ain't gonna talk on you none. Wasn't cheap, but I'm sure she'll keep her mouth shut."

Wasn't cheap, either. Jack's household cash was lighter by over eight thousand bucks. Not that it was doing the girl much good.

Terrabonne plucked a few strings on the Dobro. Drunk and sloppy, the man was still better than most would ever be. The tune sounded kind of like *Pussyfootin' Heart*, only different.

"I been thinking, hoss..." Jack slapped the guitar's strings into discordant silence.

He reached for the tumbler on his desk. Scotch sloshed wild against the sides, and the rim of the glass rattled against his teeth as he drank. After the last brown streaks had swirled down the sides of the glass, Terrabonne wiped his mouth with the back of one wrist.

Harlan watched in silence. His employer's eyes watered, and his lips were red and wet, like a girl's.

"We go out on tour this summer, it's gonna mean a lot of crowds, lot of fans, whole lot of panties thrown up on the stage."

"You say so."

"Hoss, we don't need that kind of publicity. The *Old Time Country Gospel Hour*'s my ticket to a comeback, but you know my reputation. One little whiff of scandal, those polyester assholes'll pull the plug."

Harlan shifted in the too-small seat. The chair groaned in protest.

"You want to lay low for the summer. I gotcha."

Terrabonne stared out the window for a spell, drunk and quiet. The last glowing red cinder of sunlight disappeared over the horizon.

"I'm sick of this place." he said.

"You want--"

"It's too hot here, and too close to the States. Any damn journalist with half a notion's just a charter flight away. I tell you, it's too damn close."

Jack Terrabonne sneered at imaginary enemies and threw his tumbler at the wall. Liquor flew and glass shattered.

"I want Whispering Pines, goddammit!"

Harlan pulled himself up out of that chair.

"Hell are you still standing there for, you useless pile of crap?" Jack shouted. "Get movin', you damn freak!"

Harlan's boots echoed on the floorboards as he thundered from the room.

FIVE

The next morning Kane spotted a group of Germans in the hostel lobby, checking out. Two men and two women, all carrying enormous aluminum-framed packs and wearing sturdy shoes. Kane spoke to them for a few minutes and caught a ride into a pretty little town named Geraldine.

He spent the next couple of nights staying in the local backpackers. Days, he busked in the park for passing tourists, and the second night he sat in with a country band at the local pub. Icy teeth were just beginning to nip at the edges of the plain, but the peaks of the nearest mountains were already scumbled with snow.

The morning of the third day, Kane climbed into a battered blue campervan with three other Americans. They were rich college kids, soft and smooth, turned loose on the world for a summer vacation. None of them had figured on New Zealand just coming into winter.

Kane split gas costs and played a few songs for them on the way. Mid-afternoon, they drove through a mountain pass where the snow was already falling, thick and fast. An hour later, the campervan came down into raw and solitary country. Isolated vineyards and orchards were surrounded by high craggy mountains and misted dark lakes. The free map from the tourist center called this place the Southern Otago.

***

Whispering Pines was one hundred six years old. The timbers and stones of the main house were smooth, gray and weathered.

The original farmhouse had grown over the generations. A spare room here, a new wing or an extra story there, until the house stood rambling and misshapen. What began as a three-room home eventually grew into fourteen different bedrooms and eight bathrooms scattered through a maze of dark and twisting halls.

The old sheep station sat vacant for years before the rich American came along. True to form, the first thing he had done was to tear off the roof and build a third story penthouse. The new addition looked tacked-on, fragile and modern, all blond woods and glass. Lots of glass. People who could afford the heating wanted their view.

Some sort of musician, the second thing the American had done was to rename the house after some old song.

A lot of actors and musicians owned spreads in the Otago. Like the others, Jack Terrabonne's New Zealand property spent most of its days empty.

Today, Whispering Pines hummed with activity. In the grounds outside, a team of gardeners hired out from the landscaping company placed beds of hothouse flowers on display in the cold earth. Their colors were beautiful in the golden autumn light. In days, the flowers would be dead.

Jack Terrabonne's baby blue Porsche Boxster and the two new Range Rovers were inspected and tuned. His prize white Arabian horses were curried, groomed and freshly shod. Fresh gravel was laid along half a kilometer of curving driveway and carefully raked.

Inside the house, the four maids assigned by the agency were hard at work.

Shutters opened in the main house. Furniture was dusted, the boiler stoked, towels and fresh linen laid. In the front hall, remodeled by the rich American, the imported Italian marble floor and Austrian crystal chandelier were polished until they shined. In all fourteen guest bedrooms and the master suite, white sheets billowed in the light.

Whispering Pines was returning to life.

***

Harlan Winters hated New Zealand.

The Gulfstream IV started its descent. Harlan squirmed in his seat and growled.

He'd been cooped up in this upholstered metal tube a damn long time. The Gulfstream's cabin was a little over six feet tall, a good seven or eight inches shy of the top of Harlan's head and nowhere near enough room to stand up straight. The jet stopped three times to refuel: San Francisco, Hawaii and American Samoa. Not one of those stops did Harlan get a half-decent chance to stretch his legs.

Jack Terrabonne was a spoiled child at heart. Whispering Pines he'd decided on, and Whispering Pines it would be. Once the decision was made, every mile they put between Jack and his latest indiscretion lifted the man's spirits.

Inside the Gulfstream, the house was rocking. Jack Terrabonne in a good mood meant life was one big party. Jack sat stretched out on the plush couch across from Harlan, picking out tunes on his guitar. The boys punched each other's arms and helped themselves to the open bar at the back of the cabin. Dollar bills flew thick and fast in a pickup poker game, and explosions of rough laughter echoed through the cabin every time Jack changed one of his songs to a dirty lyric.

Harlan sat alone. He stroked the fresh lock of hair in his shirt pocket and breathed the cold recycled air. He fought the urge to lift the dry dark braid to his nostrils and breath in that Mexican summer night.

The ocean grew distant in the porthole window. Soon the mountains were visible from both sides of the plane, and the blood surged in the top of Harlan's head as the jet slowly lost altitude.

Terrabonne leaned over and bounced the tips of his fingers on Harlan's knee.

"You all right over there, old hoss?"

Harlan stirred in his seat. "Jet's pretty good."

"Pretty good? They've got this damn thing fitted out like a Vegas whorehouse."

"Still a rental."

Terrabonne laughed. His mouth opened wide, and his teeth were big and white and shiny.

"Hoss, I swear sometimes you don't know how good you got it. I ever tell you how it was back when I started? We had this big old diesel bus, scraps of yellow paint still showing through here and there and--"

"Bout a thousand times, Jack."

Terrabonne's lips pressed together. He plucked an angry little riff on the Dobro and slapped the strings silent.

"I think I know what's biting you," Terrabonne said. He flashed that trademark aw-shucks grin and winked. "You're missing Mexico. I bet you had a little gal back there in the hills."

Harlan had a few back in those hills. More than a few.

"Mexico's sweet," was all he said.

Jack let out a loud wicked cackle. Only hearing what he wanted to, same as usual.

Harlan's eyes shifted to the round porthole window.

Harlan ignored the buildings. His eyes and his thoughts were on the land: sixty-three hundred acres of ridgeline and valley and thick old-growth pines. One big square fingertip returned to the lock of the girl's hair.

"Ain't right," Harlan said. "Perfectly good summer going to waste north of the equator, and we come back here when it ain't even ski season."

"Don't you worry on it too much, hoss. I know you miss those senoritas, but I'm sure you'll find some pretty little filly to keep you busy while we're here."

Harlan nodded and wiped his palms on the leg of his jeans. That was exactly what he was afraid of.

Mexico, Harlan was safe enough. But cops in New Zealand took their jobs seriously. No telling what might break loose if Harlan ever let himself go under those dark and hissing pines.

SIX

Mid-afternoon, the American kids pulled off the road. A dirt track curving off into the distance marked the turnoff for their farmstay, and Kane got out.

The main highway was two lanes of well-worn blacktop. Every time Kane heard the hiss of approaching tires he put his thumb out, but no luck. He walked. The road took Kane past amber fields thrashing in the wind, long stretches of wire fence that hummed and moaned and silent mountain lakes, their waters still and dark. On every side, high craggy mountains held close to their secrets.

The place called out for words and music. Kane wondered if he had it in him to write that song.

After a couple of hours Kane crossed the Shotover River. He stood a moment at the edge of the concrete span, watching the choppy patterns of pale froth on the surface of the raging black water.

A short distance upstream, bungee jumpers dove from a narrow bridge of rusted iron. Their screams were quickly lost in the river's deep-throated roar.

It was gorgeous country: rugged, austere and beautiful.

***

24

The Gulfstream came down low and did one last turn around that enormous damn S-curve of water before it touched down at Queenstown International Airport.

To Harlan, that seemed a big name for such an itty-bitty airstrip. One runway, and that only just about big enough for charters and regionals and private jets like this one. The Gulfstream might just as well have been landing at the airstrip back in Chetumal.

The jet taxied to a stop and the pilots opened the door. It folded out into steps down onto the tarmac. The air that came rushing into the cabin was clean and cold.

One advantage to travel by private jet: Customs was a joke. Two jerkoffs in blue uniforms came on board and flipped through the stack of passports with little more than a headcount. Declaration cards were squared up in a neat little stack without so much as a single piece of baggage being opened, and the Customs agents filed off the plane. Harlan looked around at the scruffy bunch of low-rent carny-types in Jack's entourage and imagined flying commercial. The thought made him shudder.

Jack shifted the guitar off his knee. Harlan gestured and the boys hopped up, got themselves busy with everybody's bags. Terrabonne leaned back, his fingertips against the point of his cheek, his blue eyes flat and expressionless.

Harlan grabbed the box from the cabinet beside him. The box was walnut, with pieces of brass at the corners and the hinges. Wherever Jack Terrabonne went, Harlan Winters was never far behind. And wherever Harlan traveled, the walnut box was close at hand.

He unsnapped the latches and raised the lid. The .44 sat nestled in its dark velvet bed, next to its tooled leather holster and two orderly little rows of ammunition. The smells of gun oil and saddle soap mingled in the air.

That was one other, major, advantage to travel by private jet. Poor bastards flying commercial had to take off their shoes and give up their liquor and hand cream. Rich people, it was like they got to run around on some kind of honor system.

Harlan picked the gun up, flipped open the gate and loaded the weapon. Jack moved in his seat and shifted his gaze out the round porthole of glass. The boys noted that single restless movement and began to scurry faster.

Harlan clipped the leather holster onto his belt and shuffled through the envelope of cards until he found the carry-permit for New Zealand. This wasn't the Yucatan, but Jack Terrabonne's name and money did at least have that much pull.

Down on the tarmac, planes were scattered like some kind of parking lot. Tourists going home, hunters and fishermen taking puddle-jump charters out to the backwoods, fat cats like Jack with private jets: They all had to use the one small terminal, then run across a crazy maze of painted lines to get to their planes without some propeller-driven antique turning them into cat food.

It was even colder out in the open. The mountains were close and purple and capped with snow, and the wind had a definite bite to it. For Harlan, it felt good to stand up straight again, never mind the stares and whispers from the other travelers.

Jack Terrabonne posed on the tarmac, that icy wind ruffling his perfect silver hair. He squinted heroically and angled his face into the sunlight, until he realized there were no photographers to care. Harlan grabbed the nearest of Jack's boys, a lean and mean-eyed man named JD, and hauled him around.

"Harl? I--"

"The hold. You don't want one of them airport fellahs to drop something, now do you?"

"I'll get to it. I just gotta..." JD looked up into Harlan's eyes and swallowed. The thin man's voice trailed off to nothing, and he wiped his mouth with the brown-stained tips of his fingers.

Harlan didn't have to tell him twice. JD started cursing out the others, and they were all on it double-quick.

Ten minutes later, three gleaming limos pulled out of the lot. Jack and Harlan sat alone in the lead car. Harlan poured a bourbon on the rocks from the limo's wet bar and handed it to Jack. Terrabonne sipped and stared out the window. Neither man spoke.

A lone dark figure stood at the crossroads. The drifter wore a black coat and a three-day beard, and his eyes seemed to burn right through the dark mirror-tinted glass.

Jack Terrabonne's fingers slipped on his glass. Liquor spilled, staining his pants. The three cars made the turn onto the main road into Queenstown, and the drifter faded back into the distance and the dust.

Without him being conscious of it, Harlan's nostrils flared and his tongue flickered between his teeth, tasting the fan-blasted warm air.

**

Kane watched the three black limousines grow small in the distance. He waited until they were lost from sight before he hitched his pack up on his shoulder and got back to walking.

For some reason, an old Robert Johnson song flashed through Kane's head. The one about the Devil waiting in the crossroads at sundown.

A single red ember burned just below the horizon by the time he made it into Queenstown.

SEVEN

The hostel foyer was beat to hell. A dark threadbare track was worn down the center of the stained orange carpet. The front desk was scarred and cigarette-burned, most of its useable area taken up with racks of pamphlets and fliers, tourist orientation magazines and other free handouts.

The air in the lobby was hot and stifling. For Kane, those backpacker hostel smells of boiled noodles and wet socks were comforting and familiar. The girl at the desk sat huddled in her coat, a steaming mug cupped in her hands. Dreadlocks like cords of soft black wool hung in her eyes, and she had three small steel rings in the left-hand corner of her lower lip.

Kane stepped in close to the counter, and the girl looked up from her magazine. Her eyes were a vivid and poisonous green: burning, fevered and intense. Pale purple smudges shadowed the hollows of her eyes.

There was something wild and feral about her. Kane's first thoughts were of Celtic war goddesses and blood-drenched shield maidens. He took a half-step back without noticing.

As quickly as it came, that dangerous light faded from her face. Iron door slammed shut, and a careful bland mask was cemented in place.

"Single's eighty-eight fifty, double's one-forty." Her voice was rough and smoky, her accent soft and Irish. "If it's one with an en suite you're wanting, those are twenty dollars more. Otherwise, toilets are just down the hall."

"Dorm bed'll be fine," Kane said.

"That's fifty-five."

"Sign out front says beds from sixteen dollars."

The girl's mouth twisted up at one end. The steel rings danced.

"What can I say? The owner rents two beds at that rate, just so he can hang that sign up."

Kane pulled a Ziploc bag out of his coat pocket. It was heavy with bronze one- and two-dollar coins and smaller silver twenty- and fifty-cent pieces. The bag made a sound like sleigh bells when he dropped it on the counter.

"That's fifty," Kane said, and fished a crumpled five out of the front pocket of his jeans. The Irish girl made a soft noise through her nose and started separating the coins into piles.

"Feck you do, rob a parking meter on the way in here?" Her dreads rustled softy against the shoulders of her coat as she shook her head.

"When I play, it's mostly coins people throw in the hat."

"Busker, eh?" The girl looked at him, her gaze as sharp as a welder's flame. "Then what sort of music do you play?

"The blues," Kane said. "I play the blues."

***

Maeve watched the tall stranger out of sight. American backpackers came through the hostel all the time, mostly milk-fed college students whinging at the tops of their voices about prices and poverty while paying their rooms with platinum and gold cards.

This new stranger was different. He wore a three-day beard and a three-month haircut, a big black coat and clothes that would shame a scarecrow.

He also carried himself with a loose lazy grace that Maeve associated with hard and truly dangerous men. In Maeve's experience it wasn't the loud blustery types you had to watch out for. When the wheels came off, it was always the ones with that sleepy-eyed confidence who turned the most frightening.

Pity. The stranger had those sharp high cheekbones Maeve fancied and amber eyes a shade lighter than melted caramel. Long fingers, strong hands and that broad heavy-lipped mouth. It was almost enough to make her overlook the scars on his knuckles and the fact that he lied about being a musician.

Still, for Maeve it had been a long and lonesome time. She had the knife in her boot if the article got out of hand, and it wasn't like she had anything else to do, not with her rightful quarry still among the missing.

Maeve tapped the edge of the American's registration card on the counter, speculating. Bridey's shade, dead and brittle, watched from the shadows nearby, her expression remote and unreadable.

***

They said you never forgot your first. Harlan was never quite sure what that meant in his case. For him, only one thing mattered worth a damn, and Harlan didn't know how to do the math.

Lots of folks didn't count animals. Harlan wasn't sure himself. All he knew as a boy was that they made the right noises and the light still faded in their eyes.

Harlan never knew the first human he killed either. Just eight years old, no dad at home to teach him right, he was already saddled with a reputation as a bad seed. Nobody would've believed him, but Harlan honestly hadn't known the bum was sleeping in that shed when he set it on fire. He hadn't even known until he heard the grown-ups talking about the bones they found in the ashes and debris.

It hadn't stopped him from burning. Small as he was back then, arson and animals were all Harlan had. Something inside him had found its voice in the crackle and snap of dancing flames.

Imagining a human trapped inside just added to the rush.

***

Kane's room had peeling green paint and flickering lights. There were six bunks, four of them taken. Kane pocketed his harmonica case, ditched his pack in the locker along with the hostel's cheap brass padlock and key and shut the door. The padlock Kane used was his own: steel, heavy and solid.

Kane stopped back at the front desk. No one sat there now. The counter was notched and stained and scarred, its surface piled high with stacks of tourist leaflets, fliers and free handout booklets. A fresh greasy smell of boiled noodles hung in the air. Kane surveyed the handouts, stuck a booklet in one pocket and headed out into the cold autumn night.

"Off to see the sights, eh?"

The girl from the front desk stood out front. A cigarette burned between her fingers, smoke curling blue in the autumn air. She held a red-and-white pack of Marlboros out to Kane. He raised one palm and shook his head, and she tucked the box back in her pocket.

"Kane," he said and stuck out his hand.

The girl took his outstretched hand. Her grip was firm, warm and dry. Her fingertips lingered on his palm as her hand came away.

"Maeve."

"Any good places to eat around here, Maeve?"

She waved one hand in a vague circle. Her cigarette's burning cherry took in the spill of lit windows and neon down the hill.

"Good, *cheap* places."

"You'll be a Yank, eh?"

"American, yeah."

"Well, there's your Subway and McDonald's and that over on Shotover Street, or you might fancy the Jetburger, up on Register. It's Kiwi... You'll get a proper feed there, and they won't mind your bags of coin so much, either."

"You off the clock now?"

Maeve raised one eyebrow and flicked her glowing filter into the darkness.

"Not till midnight. And you can't handle me, Yank."

The rings at the corner of her lip flickered in the faint light, and she looked back over her shoulder at Kane as she turned away.

He watched her walk inside, and she knew he watched. The black cutout of her shape swayed against the soft buttery light coming through the doorway.

Maeve stopped at the open doorway. She looked back at Kane. The thick fall of her hair hooded her face from sight. Only her eyeshine was visible: twin points of cold green flame.

***

In the Ruckus Room at Whispering Pines, the party was raging. Farrel, Turk and Callum played pool with a some of the local boys. Poker chips and folding money went back and forth across the green felt table at the far end of the room. A basketball game played on the flatscreen in the corner, and songs by Jack Terrabonne blasted on the juke.

Harlan hated Jack's music. An endless loop of Boogie Jack Terrabonne hits had played in the background the whole of Harlan's adult life. Jack wouldn't allow anything else in his presence.

The bar was self-serve that night. Nobody seemed to mind. Harlan Winters rattled the ice around in his glass and raised it to his lips. Lynchburg, Tennessee was halfway around the world, but no matter where they were, good old Jack Daniels still left the same sour mash burn down his throat.

It wasn't what he wanted, but it would have to do.

Harlan stood at the window, his back to the crowd. His silhouette in the glass was a black hole cut in the party reflected behind him.

Harlan looked out through that man-shaped hole at the night beyond. The frost on the grass showed pale and ghostly, but the moonlight didn't touch the black heart of the forest beyond.

Gruff voices exploded in laughter. Harlan heard Terrabonne's sawtoothed bray among them, looked to find the man himself in a cloud of cigar smoke, surrounded by local politicos. 'Greasing the wheels', Jack called it.

Terrabonne had the civic-types eating out of his hand. No mean feat, considering some of the other, more famous folks they got in this town.

But then, maybe it wasn't so crazy after all. Taking care of Boogie Jack Terrabonne, Harlan had rubbed up against more than his share of Hollywood types. In person, most of those rock and movie stars were a bunch of fussy old men, spoiled brat kids or flat-out junkies. Terrabonne came off smooth: good-humored, boyish and just-folks. With that deep brown tan and headful of wavy silver hair, the man looked the part too.

And when he wanted to, Jack Terrabonne still had that old-time star power. A star in a long slow eclipse, but Jack had the knack for making people forget, making them feel the magic.

Harlan turned back to the window. Nothing moved on the frost-stubbled field stretching back into the treeline.

Jack was right: Mexico was sweet. All it took there was money, and Terrabonne still had plenty of that. And Mexicans understood the power of the man behind the man.

Back at the hacienda, Harlan pretty much did as he pleased. Same for Jack's place in Jamaica. Even the ranches in Tennessee and Aspen, there were ways. New Zealand was different.

Harlan never let himself go here. Not really. He hoped he never would. Not unless he found the perfect opportunity.

Maybe not even then. Safest to steer clear of temptation. It was an act of will for Harlan to keep his fingers from the lock of hair in his pocket. He tried not to think about what he'd do when the hair's scent faded.

Up at the bar, neighboring ranchers and the area's top cops clustered around Jack Terrabonne. The locals all towered over Jack, warm basking expressions on their faces. Jack was smiling, back-thumping and laughing like he'd just heard a particularly fine dirty joke.

It was a familiar scene.

Harlan Winters remembered the glass in his hand. He knocked back the last of the melted ice and bourbon and let the empty fall. Nobody noticed the sound of breaking glass.

Harlan stood inches from the cold surface of the picture window. The party roared louder than ever behind him.

His thoughts were focused through the black shape of his own reflection, into the night beyond.

EIGHT

Queenstown had a reputation as a party town. New Zealand was a pretty quiet place in general, But this little crescent of streets clustered between the lake and the mountains reminded Kane of Amsterdam made over with a western theme.

The town center was three long curved streets and maybe half a dozen cross-streets. Kane walked the whole of it without much trouble, trying to get a feel for the place.

Queenstown smelled like money. Too much money. The 1800's Gold Rush buildings were all gift-shop clean. The cars, trucks and Hummers parked in the street were all new and expensive. There were a lot of high-end restaurants and exclusive boutiques. And bars. It seemed like every other building was a bar, some of them advertising twenty-four hour a day open times. The town looked like one big party.

Kane found some low-end stuff too. Down one end of Shotover there were a couple of internet cafes and a laundry place, a single tattoo parlor and a combination strip club and brothel with the word *Diamonds* scrawled across the front in purple neon. Just like the boutiques and restaurants, these too operated out of historical buildings with an Old West look.

What Kane didn't find was a good place to busk. He told himself things might look different after a good meal and turned his steps toward the blue and white sign for Jetburger.

Maeve hadn't lied. The place was clean and cheap, its burgers the size of hubcaps. Kane sat with his glossy tourist booklet and ate two of the burgers. After half a day walking, he needed the fuel.

He wasn't the only one. The restaurant saw a steady stream of young people, well-scrubbed and healthy and chatting in at least four different languages. All had wide bright smiles and sleek expensive electronics. Their conversations were loud and laughing and full of references to bungee jumps, whitewater rafting, mountain biking and jetboating.

The adventure-seekers almost all paid with plastic. Not a lot of loose change in a crowd like that. Kane wandered up the slope of the street, looking for a bar. Faint strains of rap and pop carried from open pubs, and groups of rolling drunks moved from door to door. Not a single sign or flier advertised live music. Only one bar looked like any sort of prospect.

The Bunker was smoky and dark. Southern rock and country played on the juke, and faux-Western junk hung from the walls. Autographed photos of movie and rock stars hung behind the bar, a group of Germans dressed like cowboys played pool in the side room, and two Israeli girls sang along with Johnny Cash in heavily accented English.

What the place didn't have was a stage. Or a dance floor. Or any place for a live band to set up, much less any sign one actually played there. Kane's fingers brushed his harmonica's leather case, and he headed to the bar with a fistful of coins.

***

"I can't believe they lock us in at night," Beth said.

"I guess."

"Don't you think it's kind of creepy?"

"Creepy's that big walking haystack. He smells like cat pee." Tanya took a generous swallow from her wineglass and wiped her mouth with the tip of one finger.

"So being locked in doesn't seem weird?"

Tanya shrugged. "Sure it's weird, but it beats making the drive out from town every day. And where *else* are you going to make this much money?"

Beth Fairman sat on one corner of Tanya's bed. Out in the hall, three different songs played in three different rooms. Beth figured they'd all end up in one room sooner or later. It felt good to be out of that drab blue frock, and the other girls in the house did seem to be okay.

"What about all those nondisclosure agreements and stuff?"

"I know! This guy is, like, *insane* about the press." Tanya gestured with her glass, and Beth passed the wine bottle over. There was a cellar full of the stuff, and the staff had their own section they were allowed to take from. The staff section was all cheap Australian plonk, but it was more than most employers allowed. The girls could drink as much after hours as they wanted, just as long as they brought the bottles into the quarters before nine.

"You ever clean for rich people before?" Beth said.

"Sure. You?"

"Couple of times. Back in Auckland, I worked this waterfront condo thing. They were all rich there, but you never really saw them, you know?" Beth stopped to sip wine from a juice glass. "And I worked for this one couple, they were like attorneys or something. At least, I think that's what they said, I never saw them actually *do* anything. This is different, though."

"That's because the old guy's famous. Famous people are different from rich ones."

"Mister Terrabonne? What'd he do?"

"He used to be some kind of singer or something. Mum knew who he was. She got more excited about *him* than she did when I was on staff at Shania Twain's place, out by Glenorchy."

"You worked for Shania Twain?"

Tanya shrugged. "Sure. Most of one season, anyway."

"What was she like?"

"Oh, you know." Tanya tipped the wine bottle up and poured the last dribble into her glass. She dropped the empty on the carpet and pulled an unopened one from under her bed.

"No free wine at *her* house, that's for sure."

The two girls clicked glasses. Beth hoped she'd like it here. She'd never seen anything like Whispering Pines.

***

Midnight, the hookers showed. The owner of the local skin joint brought them, and for once that asshole Lasker got it right. Harlan looked the girls over as they came in: they were just about believable.

The six women stood together, shuffling and giggling, while Harlan laid down the law.

"All right, listen up. It's a party in there, everybody go on have a good time. Whatever. But if Jack seems even a little bit partial, you are fucking *into* him. Got it?"

Whatever the whores saw in Harlan's face quieted them down right quick. Big eyes and nodding heads and not one single goddamn giggle between them.

"Good," Harlan said. "Any questions?"

"Um, how are we supposed to know which one's Jack?"

"Jack Terrabonne? The country star?" Harlan searched the girl's face for a flicker of recognition. Nothing but blank looks.

"Jack's got a big white pompadour and a dark tan, y'all can't miss him. Now get."

The clicking of heels echoed down the hall. A safe distance away, feminine talk and laughter started up again.

"They great or what?" Lasker said.

The pimp was shaved-and-shiny bald, average height and gym-weight solid. Harlan towered over him.

"You only brought six."

"Bloody hell, man. How easy do you think this is? The Southern Otago's not exactly chocker with part-time models don't mind turning the occasional trick. As it was, I had to fly that lot in from Auckland and Wellington!"

"Maybe it'll work. We'll see."

"Christ, you're a picky bastard."

"You don't know the half of it," Harlan said. He fished a thick roll of bills out of his pocket, made sure the .44 showed under the flap of his jacket. The hundreds in this country were pink and red. They had pictures of some guy with a mustache on the front, some kind of duck or something on the back. Goddamned fruity. Harlan counted out a stack a quarter of an inch thick and slapped the bills into the pimp's greasy palm.

"Now get the fuck out of here." Harlan leaned in and showed his teeth. The pimp turned the color of wax and ashes.

***

Kane sat at the bar with a pint of beer going warm between his palms.

There was a lot of hooking up going on around the room. Vacation towns were always like that. A few young women around the room kept looking his way, maybe prepared to take a chance. It was something to think about.

Here and there, he saw a few other stateless gypsies like himself. Kane knew them by their pinched looks and wary eyes, by the way they put their heads together to count out enough change to split a beer. Most would just want something to do that night besides sitting in the common areas at their twelve-to-a-room hostels. Some would be hustling the affluent ones. A few would end up ground up in the gears.

A soft-faced young man with short scruffy dreadlocks waited for a lull in the action to approach the rail. He ordered a single glass of the house red in a quiet voice. He had a soft French accent.

Against his better judgment, Kane looked over. The young man held a thin piece of gleaming black plastic in his fingers. The dark LCD screen took up the entire face of the device and flared to bright life at the faintest touch. Above a graphic marked 'Slide to Unlock', the screensaver was a photo of the young man next to a fine-boned striking woman about his age. He slid one fingertip across the graphic, and the menu danced across the screen.

The young man's eyes met Kane's.

"Two hundred gigabyte," the young man said. "Music, video, movies... Very good, yes?" He used his fingertips to push the iPod toward Kane. Kane left it on the bar without touching it.

"Je suis désolé," Kane said in French, *"I'm sorry, but I cannot. I have not the money for a thing so beautiful."*

"We do not need much," the young man said. *"Please."*

Kane hesitated. The young man's eyes shifted off to one side, where the fine-boned young woman sat in the shadows near the wall. She had chin-length black hair, a small mole at the corner of her mouth and large dark eyes. She sat watching: small, pale and nervous.

"We only wish to return home," the young man said. The French rolled quickly off his tongue, easy and fluent. His accent was country, somewhere in the Languedoc.

"This town, it's expensive, no?" Kane's French was Parisian, quick and clipped, with no more than a ghost of his native accent.

"Our tickets home are not for one more month." The boy looked back at the young woman and dropped his eyes. The bartender set the glass of red wine in front of him. The young man looked down at the coins in his hand. Kane held up one palm and paid the bill out of his own pocket.

"*Back on the North Island,*" he said. "*In Napier, in Hastings, there are many orchards and few workers. The work is difficult, but the pay is good. In two weeks you will have enough to enjoy the rest of your holiday.*"

The young man nodded and frowned. He put the iPod back in his pocket and took the glass away with him.

"Ya daft fooker, yeh could've had that flash gadget for cheap," the bartender said. Kane wondered how many Irish people worked in this town.

"Wouldn't have been right."

"A man of principle, is it? Yeh won't last long in Queenstown."

"Not meaning to last long," Kane said. "I don't figure I'll stay more than a couple of days."

"Probably best." The bartender gestured with his chin to the young French couple sitting together in the shadows. "Don't want to end up like that lot-- no money and no place to go. Taking that gadget off their hands might've been a mercy."

Kane stepped away from the stool and rapped his knuckles on top of the bar. It was time to go.

"I'm not the kind to take advantage."

NINE

After the sound and the fury of the bar, Kane wanted quiet. For all the intensity of Queenstown's streets, peace was never far. A hundred steps uphill, and the lights of town lay behind him. Another hundred and Kane stood above the rooftops. The stars of the Southern Cross and the great wild spill of the Milky Way sparkled overhead.

Kane moved deeper into the woods. Before long, he was surrounded by the good clean smells of dark earth and fresh pine.

He stood in the darkness, allowing his eyes to adjust. Coronet Peak was a great black mass before him. The restaurant lights at the peak glowed faintly through the trees, and the moon was a swollen yellow ball on the horizon. His frosted breath hung in the night air, pale and ghostly.

A gray shape streaked from a branch overhead. Kane caught a brief flash of the owl's wings as the night bird hunted.

The air carried a distant scent of snow.

***

Harlan stood in the doorway and watched the party. The Ruckus Room had devolved into Jack's vision of rock and roll.

Jack sat in his big old leather chair with a little blonde slip of a thing curled up in his lap. Whatever the whore whispered to him, old

Jack was lapping it up. Harlan rolled his head on the column of his neck and wiped his palms on the front of his jeans.

"Man, is this the life or what?" Farrel swayed along in an eye-watering halo of whiskey and bumped Harlan's elbow. "I can't believe JD's missing out."

"Yeah, sucks to be him."

"Where'n hell is he?" Farrel grinned, loose and sloppy. "You know?"

"I sent JD on into town, check something out."

Over by the fire, the blonde on Jack's lap was nuzzling his neck. Farrel laughed and spilled whiskey.

"Man, he sure must've pissed you off."

"Son of a bitch shouldn't have sassed me."

The blonde got up and led Jack by the hand. Terrabonne stopped on his way out the door and put three damp fingers on Harlan's arm. Farrel hunched his shoulders and did a fade. Harlan bent low so that Jack could speak close to his ear.

"That little girl, where'd you find her?"

Harlan shrugged.

"Always plenty of women want to meet a real-life star," he said.

Jack burst out laughing and slapped Harlan on the back.

"Tell you what old son, you oughta talk to one of these little gals your own self." Jack swayed and pointed out one of the women passing by. "I bet this one here'd like you just fine," he said, "Might be her lucky night!"

Terrabonne slapped the blonde's rump and chased her out of the room. A cheer rose from over on the couch, where a woman poured an entire bottle of champagne over her bare breasts. Back in the corner Queenstown's top cop, a hard type named Hollings, looked to be getting mighty friendly with a young woman in a very small dress.

The girl Jack had pointed out stood frozen on the spot. Her eyes flickered, her knees trembled and she had bitten the lipstick from the inside of her lips.

Harlan took in the hollows of her collarbones, the soft skin of her shoulders and the frightened little shape of her mouth.

Her throat was white and soft. The rapid shadow of a faint blue pulse beat in the soft flesh at the side of her neck. Harlan's mouth went dry.

"So," she said, "You... You want to?"

Harlan touched his tongue to his lips. Everybody here was drunk, but too many might remember seeing the two of them together.

"Jack must've been right. This really is your lucky night."

Without another word, Harlan pushed past her and stalked out into the autumn night.

***

It was a night for Americans. Another one stood in the hostel foyer, out of place and uncomfortable and smelling of whiskey. He was tall and wiry and cadaver-thin. His boots and coat were expensive, but his skin and teeth were poor.

"Y'all don't remember me, do you?" The thin Yank said. His eyes were glassy and bloodshot, swimming with poisonous green lights. "Name's JD. Maybe you remember, we met last year here, down to The Bunker?"

"I'm afraid I don't--"

"There was this girl you was asking about...

"Bridey?"

"That's the one." JD's remaining teeth were long and brown and twisted in his mouth. He seemed to think his smile was charming. "I reckon that gal's been on my mind a fair bit. I couldn't stop thinking about what you told me, and well, I got something here I think you ought to see."

"Show it to me."

"Not here," he said. "It's outside, in the truck. Brand-new Rover."

Maeve eyed JD and weighed her options. Under other circumstances, there was no way she'd let him get her anywhere near a truck or van. But for the chance he actually had something about Bridey, the risk was worth it. And if nothing else, Maeve had the knife in her boot.

**

Kane walked back down the mountain, calm and centered. The rising moon was hidden behind a screen of black and rustling leaves. Kane didn't miss its light.

The hostel was easy to find. Its lights glowed downslope, alone at the place where the streetlamps ended.

The windows on that side of the building were dark. As Kane approached, a square of buttery light opened in the side wall.

Low slanting moonlight bleached the hostel wall silver and gray. Two figures stood tightly grouped in silhouette: one male and one female. They argued with their voices low, so that only the hisses carried.

The male was tall and lean. Moonlight gleamed off thin greasy hair and threw black shadows into the hollows of his skull. The wind carried in Kane's direction, bringing a strong smell of liquor.

From his body language, the man was trying to coax the woman into a gleaming new SUV. The woman hesitated.

The tall man grabbed her by the shoulders. By that time, Kane was close enough to see the black tumble of Maeve's dreads as she stepped back out of his grasp.

The two stood facing each other. Suddenly, Maeve ducked low, reaching for her boot. The tall man lashed out. The sharp sound of the slap echoed off the face of the building.

It was followed quick and hard by the muffled thump of fists and boots striking flesh.

Maeve fell.

The tall man reached for her.

Kane stepped out of the treeline.

TEN

Maeve spat blood and dirt and struggled to breathe. JD's boot slammed into her stomach, shoulders and back, and Maeve wanted more than anything else in the world that moment to reach her knife.

If Maeve could just reach her blade, she'd be more than happy to gut the bastard and dance in the spattering red rain. Instead, all she was able to do was crawl and struggle and take the beating.

JD froze where he stood. His head whipped around, and Maeve lifted her face to see the new American, this man Kane, step out of the trees.

"This here ain't none of your affair, buddy," JD said, his voice thin and nasal. "Just you get along now."

Kane said nothing. He walked into the side lot like he owned it, one of those free tourist magazines rolled tight in his fist.

His face was hard. His eyes in the moonlight were cold and terrible.

"I mean it now, stranger," JD said. "You're messing in private business."

Kane stepped closer.

"Last chance... Y'ain't gonna get another warning." JD's words were tough enough, but he spoke them backing away.

When he stood between Maeve and his countryman, Kane stopped.

"Can you walk?"

Maeve tried to tell Kane that she had everything under control. She tried to tell him what a devious and nasty little shite-weasel JD was. She tried to warn Kane about JD's knife.

What came out was a thin faint squeak and a long retching cough.

JD raised his hands and grinned. Fecking bollix acted like he thought it was charming and disarming, didn't realize it made him look like a child-molester.

"All right friend, have it your way, fine. No problem."

Maeve knew what came next. Back in the lighted hostel, she'd seen the shape of the knife sheath on JD's belt. Here in the dark, Kane had no chance. Maeve felt trapped in a slow-motion nightmare.

JD's hand swept down, a bony pale blur suddenly bright with the sharp hidden blade.

The rest of the move was simple and lethal. At the bottom of his arc JD lunged, the knife slashing from low to high, guts to gullet in a deadly whooshing hiss.

Kane stood his ground.

The rolled-up magazine flashed, swift and white. The knife flew. The butt of the magazine struck JD's face with a loud crunch. JD fell away screaming.

Kane kicked the knife back into the treeline. He seemed relaxed, unconcerned.

JD reeled, bent over double. His hands clawed at his face, and his blood was black in the moonlight.

Maeve pushed onto her back. JD met her eyes and let out a loud snarling curse.

He surged at her, bloody hands reaching for her throat. Maeve scrabbled for the blade in her boot.

Kane's arm slashed out. The rolled magazine slapped JD's broken nose, and the bastard fell, screaming like a girl.

Just like that, it was over.

JD lay face down in the lot, crying into his hands. Kane helped Maeve to her feet and walked her back inside.

She didn't even get her chance to kick JD where it hurts.

As they passed through the hostel entrance, Kane unrolled the magazine and put it back in his pocket.

ELEVEN

Maeve had her own room in the hostel. Her relief was nowhere in sight, so she simply hung a sign up and left the desk unattended for the night.

Kane followed her down the dim narrow hall. That easy rhythmic sway of her hips was gone now. She moved like an angry cat, curled around her stomach where she'd been hit.

Maeve's room was spare, but private. There was space enough for a bed and a chair, a stand-up closet and a sink. Loud drunken snoring and loud drunken sex sounds filtered from behind most of the doors in the hall. In the toilets next door, someone was violently ill.

Kane sat on the edge of the bed. Springs creaked, and the edge of his shoe rattled a cup and saucer on the floor.

Maeve dropped her coat and looked herself over in the mirror. She had a split lip, a few scrapes and bruises.

"Could have been worse," she said, holding a tissue under the running tap. "Where'd you learn to fight like that?"

"Just got lucky is all."

She caught his eye in the mirror and said nothing.

"Who was that guy?"

"Some arsehole is all." Maeve dabbed at her cut lip.

"That was a clever trick you did back there," she said. "Hiding a weapon in that magazine. I never saw it, and neither did JD."

"No weapon." Kane showed her the magazine. "Rolled tight like this, the ends do a lot of damage. The sides not so much, but even a little bit was plenty to open that broken nose back up again."

"And that's what you do, run around with a rolled-up magazine playing hero?"

"I'm no hero."

"Yeah?"

"Nope. Just passing through."

One seam of Maeve's tee shirt was torn below the armpit. She noticed, and stripped the shirt up over her head. Her bra was black and simple, her skin the color of milk.

Luminous silver ghosts of childhood scar tissue traced across her back and ribs. Black tattoos swirled patterns across her upper arms and shoulders. Faint pink lines, more recent than the tattoos, striped the outer surfaces of her bare arms. Kane knew them for what they were: knife-fighter's scars.

"That guy back there..." Kane said. "He seemed to know you."

"JD. We've seen each other once or twice on the road." Maeve wet a washcloth under the tap, used it to clean the scrapes at her elbow and ribs. "Must confess, tonight was a bloody surprise."

"So what happened?"

Maeve looked at Kane over her shoulder.

"He was a Yank," she said. "He couldn't handle me, either."

The joke fell flat. Her green eyes flared, hard and intense.

"That damned JD. I wasn't sure about him at first, but tonight the bastard showed his true colors, nasty and foul."

"Are you--"

"Look, Yank, I'm appreciating what you did for me tonight, and you won't find me ungrateful. But can we please leave off with the questions?"

Maeve was smaller without her boots. As she bent to unzip them, Kane was aware of the tops of her breasts and the muscles in her arms.

He was also aware of the knife she placed on the edge of the sink. Maeve followed his eyes and twisted her mouth up at one side.

"Dangerous world out there for a girl alone," she said.

She sat at the other end of the bed. Her skin gave off a scent like copper and gunpowder. The springs bobbed with their combined weight, and there was a lull in the noises from the other rooms.

"Bloody hell," Maeve said in the silence.

She reached under the bed and came up with a half-full bottle of vodka, some no-name brand made in Singapore. Her lip rings clinked against the glass, and Kane watched the motion of her throat as she swallowed.

"Welcome to Queenstown," she said and passed him the vodka. Kane looked at her bloody mouth and wiped the bottle on his sleeve before he drank.

The warm liquor smelled like rubbing alcohol and burned on the way down. Behind the blue-black fall of her dreads, tiny points of light danced in Maeve's eyes.

"So how was your first night? Apart from this business, I mean."

"All right. Doesn't look like this is the best town for musicians."

Maeve snorted through her nose. "Sure and you're the quick one. The only musos we get here are the ones building mansions. Anything else, you'd need to be local, or better still, a DJ."

"That's messed up." Kane took another slug of vodka, passed the bottle back. Maeve rolled the glass rim along her lower lip.

"So, music man, I don't see an instrument..."

Kane pulled the leather case from his inside coat pocket. Maeve spread her arms across the rail at the base of the bed and leaned back. Her dreads fell black and soft around her face, and her shoulders were smooth and white.

"What's in there then?"

"Harmonica," Kane said. He cradled the leather case in his palms.

"You're bloody kidding." Maeve's green eyes danced.

"Not so many instruments you can just stick in a pocket and go. Besides, some really great bluesmen played harp."

"Go on, then. Give us a wee show."

"Little late..."

Maeve cocked her head. Two voices could be heard vomiting, and somewhere in the hostel, a woman reached a very loud and vocal sexual climax.

"Feck em."

Kane nodded. He took his harp out of its case, licked his lips and started to play. He started easy, with a couple of simple blues walks. The old Oskar's tone was sweet and true. Before long, Kane closed his eyes and thought about his day and played.

After the last note faded in the air, silence followed. Kane opened his eyes and found himself once again in the small hot room, a young Irishwoman watching him, her face unreadable.

"What was that?"

"It's by Robert Johnson, usually done with a guitar. It's called Crossroad Blues."

"Spooky. What's it about?"

"The usual blues stuff: Being in the wrong place at the wrong time. The love of a woman lost. Evil stalking a traveler alone."

Maeve said nothing. Her eyes were unreadable and strange.

Kane tapped the Oskar against his knee. When the instrument was clean, he put it back in its case and tucked the case away.

Maeve shifted on the bed. Kane moved closer. Her eyes were bright and vivid, her lashes black and long. Kane tried not to stare at the soft swell of her breasts.

"Get to your bed," Maeve said. She put one palm against his chest, flat and firm.

"I wouldn't want you to catch me germs."

TWELVE

The party finally collapsed in the first faint light of dawn. Harlan put the last couple of hookers in an unmarked cruiser with the town's top cop, a balding hardass name of Hollings. As the tires crunched down the gravel drive, Harlan scraped one hand over his face. His calloused palm came away covered in oil and dead skin.

The night sky leached out to the color of gunmetal. White frost lay on the grass and ice cracked in the branches of the trees.

Harlan didn't care about the cold. His jetlagged thoughts were still in Mexico, back in the summer night of three days ago. Back with the heat and the bugs. With the sounds of snapping branches, quick panting breath and, later, shrill desperate screams.

Harlan lifted the lock of hair to his nostrils. He could still smell the girl's panic and fear, still feel the thrill of the chase.

The sound of the cop's motor had long since faded to nothing. A new sound carried thin and faint through the hills. Harlan lifted his head and closed his eyes. In the space of a dozen heartbeats, he recognized the big diesel engine sound of one of Jack's leased Range Rovers.

Minutes later, the Rover cleared the mountain pass. Headlights threaded their way down through the treacherous curves until their light was lost on the forest floor.

Harlan stepped out into the center of the gravel. His breath curled away in slow rhythmic plumes of billowing frost. Down at his sides, his big hands flexed.

The engine grew louder. A wash of light swung through the trees, and the engine's rumbling was joined by the sounds of tires hissing on gravel and branches lashing against the Rover's sides and roof. Harlan stood impassive in the big truck's path. Gravel flew as the Rover skidded to a stop.

Harlan stared past the glare of the headlights. Finally, he stepped to one side and waited for the Rover to crawl forward. The sight of JD's pale birdfaced profile behind the wheel made Harlan's lips curl away from his teeth.

The Rover almost rolled past, until JD saw Harlan's eyes and lost his nerve.

"Didn't hurt nuthin," JD said. The sound of his voice worked at Harlan's nerves like the screeching bite of a sawmill blade.

"Didn't have permission, either. Perfectly good old pickup sitting out in the car barn, and you had to take the Rover. You know what a truck like this costs?" Harlan said. "You got any idea how many hundred years it'd take your broke ass to pay off even one tiny little scratch? And anyway, what the hell happened to your face?"

JD looked at the empty seat beside him and chewed his lip.

"I was jumped."

Harlan eyed JD's nose, the metal splint and strips of crisp white bandage.

"I kinda figured."

"There was four of em, big fuckers. Jumped me from behind."

Harlan thrust his big head into the open window. The truck's interior smelled of sweat and bad breath, liquor and antiseptic and fresh bandages.

And just the faintest trace of scent, clinging to JD's clothes. A scent like copper and gunpowder.

"You found her, though, didn't you." Way Harlan said it, it wasn't a question.

"I started out hitting the cheap spots, found her working back of the counter." JD's eyes were bright and glassy in the dashboard lights. "Just like you said, Harl, five minutes with her and first thing you know, she's asking about that Bridey Martin."

"And you went and did something stupid."

"I--"

"Yeah, got jumped. I heard."

"I--"

"Probably nothing, anyway. Put the damn truck in the barn. Go on upstairs and get some sleep." Harlan pulled his head back out of the truck. JD visibly relaxed.

"One thing," Harlan said. JD froze.

"Take one of Jack's trucks again without asking, I'll break your goddamned legs."

***

Alone in the dark, Maeve sharpened her knife. She worked patiently, stroke after stroke, one side of the blade and the other, the motion of wrist and arm smooth and practiced.

From time to time she paused. To dribble more water on the sharpening stone's surface, to drink from the plastic bottle of vodka beside her bed, to test the blade's edge against the ball of her thumb.

Bridey looked on: mute and dead and disapproving.

The knife itself was a piece of shite: four for twelve dollars at a discount shop, barely fit to carve a steak. Maeve had been through too many border crossings, police shakedowns and bad moments to carry any weapon she couldn't dump in the nearest rubbish bin, storm drain or river. There was simply no point investing in a quality blade.

The stone was another matter. Top of the line Japanese waterstone, that was, the grain so fine it was almost translucent. Well capable of bringing even that cheap steel to a murderous edge.

The knife Maeve kept in her boot was already razor-sharp. The blade she prepared now was meant for a backup, something she could bring out in case of another time like tonight.

Maeve wasn't going to let any of Jack Terrabonne's bastards get the drop on her again.

If it hadn't been for that Kane, things might have turned bad fast. Maeve paused in her labors, looking at the narrow empty bed with its rumpled sheets. Pity she couldn't risk bringing him on side. A few hours ago he might have been a fun distraction, but Maeve had gone too long, sacrificed too much, to risk it all opening up to some stranger.

Instead, Maeve tipped lukewarm vodka down her throat. The more she drank, the clearer she saw Bridey's shade, standing at the foot of the bed. The sight was like a wire twisted around her heart.

Maeve bent closer to her work.

The cheap Pakastani knife blade was slow to take an edge. For a long time that night, the only sound in Maeve's room was the soft slow rasp of steel on stone.

***

Bridey Martin. The name didn't mean a damn thing to Harlan.

First time he'd heard it was two years ago, back in Mexico. This scruffy Irish backpacker showed up, asking in the village. She had that kind of trashy-sexy look Jack was a sucker for, but Harlan didn't trust the way the girl was keen to get next to the famous man. Last thing Harlan needed was some stalker messing up his meal-ticket.

Harlan didn't think twice. A word to the cops and she disappeared from their lives. He thought no more about it.

Until a year ago, here in New Zealand. Back at Whispering Pines for the ski season, Jack already getting bored, Harlan champing at the bit but staying on his best behavior. JD rolled in one night, bragging on some gal in town digging on him. Harlan figured it was just the usual bullshit, except those same two words came up again.

Bridey Martin. By the time Harlan remembered where he'd heard that name before, by the time he sensed danger, they were already on another Gulfstream, this time for a benefit concert in Colorado. Lot of runaways there, kids passing through from nowhere to nowhere. Harlan smiled at the memory.

At the time, there was nothing for it. Harlan marked the thing with the name as unfinished business. Twenty-odd years traveling the world with Jack Terrabonne, Harlan had left behind one hell of a lot of unfinished business.

Sending JD into town tonight had been a long shot. People came here to raft or ski or bungee jump. Sometimes they came to see all that *Lord of the Rings* stuff. What they didn't do was stick around a whole year, waiting for a chance to bring up that same damn name.

Assuming JD wasn't lying. Assuming he even found that same girl at all. Assuming he didn't just spend the night tucked up in some damn bar, or ogling the naked ladies up at Diamonds. Assuming that dipshit getting his ass kicked had even one little thing to do with a trashy-sexy Irish girl asking about someone named Bridey.

JD was a liar, a liar and a weasel. But if there was any truth in his story tonight, it might mean trouble.

Harlan bared his teeth in the darkness. One thing he loved, it was trouble.

THIRTEEN

Most nights, Kane dreamed of home. No matter where in the world he was, Kane was never far from red clay and piney woods, the smell of woodsmoke and the soft cry of the whippoorwill. Those dreams were both his greatest comfort and a deep wound that refused to heal.

That night, Kane dreamed of his father. He dreamed of burning trees and blood, and he dreamed of his father's deep hoarse voice shouting for Kane to RUN.

Kane dreamed of the last touch of his father's rough and calloused hand on his cheek. He woke with his cheeks wet and a ragged aching hole in his heart.

**

Harlan woke in the dark, dreaming of his first chase. Dreaming about Louisa May Jameson.

Growing up, Louisa May had been about the closest thing Harlan had to a friend. Barefoot and tangle-haired, she showed Harlan what was under her skirt when they were both five. At seven or eight she showed him what to do with it. Harlan liked that no matter what he did to Louisa May, she always came back.

Until that day they found the kitten. Harlan had just wanted to show her how much fun animals could be, but Louisa May ran off crying, swore never to talk to him again.

By the time Harlan chased her down, his blood was up.

It had almost been an accident. Twelve years old, Harlan was already bigger than some adults, and he'd always been strong. For a little while after, Harlan had felt dirty and soiled and sorry. He might have been caught if he hadn't forced himself to stop his blubbering.

Harlan sat up in bed and scratched at the hair on his back and shoulders. Jetlag had his internal clock trashed to hell, felt like gears shearing loose in his head.

Cold moonlight sliced the dark walls of his bedroom in Whispering Pines. In that single waking moment, the membrane between

present and past was razor-thin. Harlan smelled the ghosts of sweat and oil in Louisa May's hair. He remembered her flesh in the sun, the summer heat and buzzing flies.

The sounds of tearing meat and cracking bone.

Harlan was still a kid then. His last moments with Louisa May Jameson had been ugly. Ugly and scared and hot and rushed.

Sometimes, Harlan wished he had her back. He could show her how much he'd learned.

Harlan knew if he had her again, he could make his time with her perfect.

***

Kane was up before dawn. Hostel dorm beds were the same the world over. Thin mattresses and loud bedsprings, other backpackers turning lights on and off or else stumbling in the dark. Between the loud wet snoring from the bunk below him, the sour smells of spilled beer and vomit in the room and his own dreams of youth and home, Kane's sleep was fitful.

Finally, he quit trying. Kane climbed down from his bunk, took his pack out of its locker and dressed in the dark. At a small twenty-four hour market on Frankton, he paid too much for apples and cheese, nuts and bread and a bottle of water. The mountain air was still and watery and gray when Kane walked into the hills.

Queenstown didn't offer much to a poor musician, but the scenery was spectacular.

An hour after sunrise, Kane stopped. He took his rest on a flat rock, warm in the new day's sun and sheltered from the wind. The cheese was sharp and strong, the apples crisp and tart.

Overhead, hawks circled. They rode the thermals, hunting.

After a time, Kane moved deeper into the autumn forest. Leaves were turning all around: yellow and gold and orange and brown and splashes of deep brilliant red.

He came across a sapling as thick as his arm, the bark on one side rough and torn. Soon Kane found other trees and shrubs where deer had rubbed the velvet from their antlers. He found places where the plants had been torn by browsing, and he found teardrop-shaped indentations where small hooves planted in soft earth.

Kane tracked the deer trail across the ridgeline.

Bright leaves and dappled trunks gave way to stunted alpine scrub and harsh cold sunlight. Up high near the top of the ridge, Kane found a faint dark depression in the earth, the last vestiges of what once had been a hard-beaten footpath. The faint remaining trace of the path descended into the forest shadows.

***

Jack Terrabonne had a hangover. The maids cleaning up that morning learned quick to walk soft and stay out of his way. The man was unpredictable under any circumstances. Hung over, Jack was mean as a snake.

It wouldn't be so bad if he'd just stay in bed. Man could stay up in that room all day, wash Oxycontin down with his morning tomato juice or crumble Valium over his eggs. Hell, the man could shoot Vitamin E into the veins in his eye. Any damn thing he wanted, and no one but Harlan would suffer.

But Jack Terrabonne didn't care to suffer in silence. Jack had a hangover, and that meant everyone around him had to feel his pain. Harlan found the man in the lodge room down on the first floor, stomping around in his dressing robe and hand-tooled high-heeled boots, yelling at no one in particular. At the sound of Harlan's steps on the slate floor, Jack turned.

"Hell's wrong with you, you got to walk so loud for? And where in hell is that damned JD? I got up this morning, not a stitch of clothing laid out for me! That old boy ain't got but the one job, and he ain't even done that!"

"It's early yet.."

"Never too early to do your goddamned job right! I tell you..."

"You're preaching to the choir there." Harlan crossed to the sideboard, threw ice and vodka, tomato juice and Tabasco in a pitcher. He knew he was supposed to keep his voice light, play the old game. But the truth was, Harlan's heart just wasn't in it that morning.

He kept thinking about that hooker last night. She'd been small and dark and terrified. Just looking at him had made her tremble. The thought made his skin itch.

Harlan stirred the pitcher and poured two glasses. He splashed steak sauce across the tops of both and extra Tabasco in Jack's. Terrabonne accepted his without a word. He drank it half down, shook his head and made a loud hoarse sound.

Jack's face turned a red so dark it was almost purple. Bullets of sweat popped out across his cheeks and nose. When the worst of it passed, Jack rested the cool glass against his forehead.

"Old hair of the dog. Bout all you're good for ain't it, mixing my drinks?" Jack drank until there was nothing in the glass but ice and blood-colored slime.

"You should've been a bartender," he said. "You sure ain't worth shit as a pimp."

"Beg pardon?"

"Oh come off it, hoss. I ain't got a single song this morning. That little old girl you brought me last night was a pro."

Harlan spread his hands wide. "Far as I know, she was just one of them party girls, you know the kind. Always want to see the big mansion, meet the famous music star."

"You telling me I don't know pro when I see it?"

Harlan turned his face to the window. The whole of one wall was small squares of glass showing the garden and the forest beyond. Harlan crunched ice in his teeth and watched small animals move back in the treeline.

"You know what'd happen to this network deal if you get me caught in some kind of hooker scandal?" Jack said. "The papers'd love to catch me in that kind of dirt."

Harlan said nothing. There was no talking to the man anyway, and Harlan needed Jack's fear.

"Where'd you find those gals, anyway?" Jack said.

"First I saw em was when they showed up at the door."

Harlan set his glass down and started mixing another pitcher of Bloody Marys. Jack let out a low snickering laugh.

"Makes sense, I suppose." He set his empty glass on the bar top and adjusted the lapels of his big fluffy robe. "Sweet young things always do like the big dog."

Harlan rattled the melting ice in the pitcher and eyed the hot sauce.

FOURTEEN

The trail ended among the graves. If you didn't know what to look for, they were easy to miss. The clearing was shadowed and cool, surrounded by ancient pines hissing in the wind. Only a couple of markers remained: fallen pieces of rotted wood, completely unreadable. But Kane saw the sunken earth and the wildflowers, and he knew the truth.

The ghost town lay deeper in the trees. Slanted bolts of sunlight lit the forest floor in a blaze of light and color, and the weathered shacks in the clearing glowed as though lit from within.

Kane hitched his pack on his shoulders and moved closer.

This had been Gold Rush country once. The rolled and crumpled tourist handout told the usual story. Some prospector in the 1860's struck gold. A few got rich, most went broke, and only the shopkeepers were sure of making money. Within a few years, the gold gave out and so did most of the settlements. Only a few towns remained, and only Queenstown prospered.

Kane wandered through knee-high scrub. The sounds of fast-moving water echoed somewhere nearby. The shacks were little more than ruins: a couple of walls here, a warped doorway there. Kane counted nine old dwellings, scattered among fruit trees gone feral with neglect. He imagined the men who lived here panning for gold, hoping to make a strike before the creek flowed down into the Shotover.

A few of the larger ghost towns like Macetown and Bullendale were in Kane's booklet, but the region was dotted with smaller places like this one. A few guys trying to get rich. The men in these nine huts had lived and worked here, months or years. They'd buried their dead. And in the end, the survivors just left. It hadn't been worth staying.

Right next to his feet, a rabbit bolted. Its rump was a white flash zipping through the brush. Standing still, it had been all but invisible. Kane wouldn't have seen the animal if it hadn't lost its nerve and run for the safety of the trees.

***

Maeve dozed fitfully for a couple of hours that morning. She woke bruised, stiff and sore.

She staggered and stretched and avoided the mirror. She felt like shite, and it had been a long time since the mirror showed her anything she wanted to see. Maeve wrapped a towel around her and headed down the hall.

The shower never got hot. But it wasn't cold either, and that was enough for her. Maeve stood under the spit-warm spray and rubbed soap over stiff and aching muscles.

Gary lingered outside the women's toilets. Maeve stepped out into the hallway and found him lounging against the opposite wall. He watched her with eyelids lowered and a twisting little smirk on his face.

Maeve's fist tightened on the towel clutched against her chest.

"Missed you on the desk this morning," Gary said. "I had to check in all the new talent myself.."

"I slept in."

Gary's smirk deepened.

"Funny, I didn't think you slept at all." The look on his face did not at all match his wholesome Kiwi clothes, haircut and accent. The hostel carpet was sticky against Maeve's bare feet.

"You're a sleazy little git and a bloody arse," Maeve said. Her knuckles were white on the towel.

"You really do need to be nicer to me, you know."

"Feck off."

Maeve stomped down the hall and back to her room. Gary called after her, his voice mocking.

"I love it when you play hard to get."

***

Jack Terrabonne spent the afternoon locked away in his recording studio. He hadn't had a new album since mullets were in fashion. Harlan figured it was just a way to blow off steam.

And Jack had some steam to blow off. As if the hangover wasn't bad enough, his third wife was stealing the spotlight. She had a new album climbing the charts and a twenty-two year old boyfriend. Soon as the news broke that day that she was going to show up in some fashion magazine next month with no clothes on, Jack'd found himself on the receiving end of a conference call from the producers at the Gospel Network.

That call lasted over forty-five minutes. Harlan tried to imagine what the good folks behind the Old Time Country Gospel Hour would have to say if they knew about Jack's little escapades. Harlan smiled at the thought and licked the rough stubs of his teeth.

One of the maids was alone in the hall. She stood outside the door to Harlan's room, the vacuum running and her back turned. Harlan watched her step and dance to some private tune only she could hear.

He stepped closer. The maid was small and dark. The staff uniforms hid all the good stuff, but when she pushed the vacuum stick Harlan could see the line of her flank, imagine the neat fragile little ribs in a graceful and ordered row. His eyes tracked the soft flesh inside her moving elbow. Her neck was thin, the bones small.

The maid backed into the front of Harlan's jeans. She jumped and let out a little scream.

"Just me, darlin."

Her eyes were wild, uncomprehending. Thin white wires trailed from her ears to a little metal square clipped to her sleeve. Her fingers fumbled for the square.

Harlan closed his fist around the wires and pulled.

The maid jumped back. Harlan grabbed her wrist, and she winced.

"Beth? Beth!" Quick shadows on the carpet just past the hallway. Harlan pulled his hand away like it was scorched.

Two maids stood together in the hall. One was tall and blonde, the other short and dark like the one in front of Harlan. For some reason, they always seemed to be in pairs.

"Beth, you're supposed to be helping us downstairs. You know we can't turn all those beds without you."

The maid started to reel in the vacuum cord, but the other two took over. She all but ran from the spot.

Harlan stood alone. His face felt hot and tight, as though he stood too close to an open fire.

FIFTEEN

Kane didn't stay long. Another time of year, he might have spent the night in the ghost town, but not now. A cool southerly gave the air an icy crisp taste. In less than an hour, the afternoon light lost its color and its warmth.

An hour later, Kane crossed the ridgeline heading back. He found himself looking out onto a sea of dark gray mist. As he followed his own backtrail, Kane realized he was descending through a blanket of cloud.

Several hours of falling leaves had already hidden his footprints. Kane didn't need them. There were bent and broken branches, muddy scrapes on fallen logs, and crescent-shaped marks left by heels and toes on flat rocks.

He made good time. Downhill was easier than uphill, and this time Kane had a destination in mind. For now, anyway. Queenstown came into sight late that afternoon, its low flat rooftops gray in the weak and cloud-shrouded light.

The lake was a vast dark presence veiled in pale mist. The mountains on the far shore were enormous and hidden, felt but not seen.

Kane thought of the Irish girl, Maeve. There was an awful lot about her that was veiled and hidden. An awful lot that Kane would probably never know.

Life on the road was like that. Moving over the surface of things, never going deep. Like swimming in night waters, you felt only the brush of others' lives. A brief glimpse of texture and velocity passing in the submerged darkness.

Ten years Kane had been on the road, a wanderer the whole of his adult life. Every year it got harder to accept that inevitable cycle of movement and loss, even though getting closer always meant trouble. Too often, what swam in dark waters had very sharp teeth.

The youth hostel stood sad and shabby in the failing light. Kane thought of Maeve's burning green eyes, the bright steel rings gleaming at the corner of her lip.

He hitched his pack on his shoulders and passed through the hostel door.

**

The cold dim day laid a heavy pall on the backpackers. There was no heat in the lobby but what could be gained from a mug of cooling tea, and every time the front door opened the lobby was further invaded by the biting cold and the cruel wind.

Maeve hated this weather. It weighed down her spirits and clouded her mind. It was hard to think in the cold, harder still to care. Damn pity Maeve hadn't been able to do the business in Mexico.

When this was finally over, Maeve swore that she would stay somewhere warm for the rest of her life.

A gust of wind tore the hostel's front door open. It slapped and banged against the wall, and the wind scattered flyers and leaflets in its twisting icy grip.

Maeve was halfway around the counter when the door shut. The icy wind died straight away. Kane stood in the entry, his eyes like points of amber flame.

"Yank," Maeve said. "You left your key behind this morning. Checked out."

"Guess I could use another night."

The man had good hands, hard-boned and long-fingered. Maeve hated that she gave a damn.

"I thought sure you'd gone."

"I left it too late. Not much chance of a ride now."

Maeve crossed back behind the counter, put the reassuring width of the desk between them.

"Tell me you weren't out busking in this weather."

"I went for a walk."

"All day? You're mad."

That earned her a smile. One thing, the man had a nice smile. It softened the hard planes of Kane's face and seemed to light him from within. Maeve fought the urge to touch her hair.

"I was back up in the ridgeline," he said. "Beautiful country." Kane reached into his pack, started putting bags of change on the counter. "I don't suppose one of those sixteen dollar rooms is open?"

"Don't see how," Maeve said. "There's not but the one and that's mine. The rate comes out of me wages."

Maeve looked at the plastic bags full of coins. On impulse, she pulled a key off its hook and dropped it on the counter in front of Kane.

"You'll stay in nineteen. Private single, still shares a bathroom in the hall but it beats all hell out of the dorm beds."

"Maeve, I can't--"

She pushed the bags back across the scarred wood counter.

"Save your coins, Yank. This one's my treat."

Kane thanked her, his eyes warm as melted butterscotch.

"Have dinner with me."

"Not a chance. Now, go have a shower, get yourself into some clean kit. You're getting mud all over me floor."

***

At sunset, Harlan Winters found Jack Terrabonne out back, near the corral. With both elbows propped on the top fence rail and one high-heeled boot on the bottom, Terrabonne looked awkward and ill at ease in the dim purple light. His prize Arabians clustered around him, white and ghostly.

Terrabonne made no sign as Winters approached. The horses tossed their heads and stamped their hooves and ran shrieking into the gloaming.

"Fine animals," Harlan said.

"Half a million dollars' worth." Terrabonne spit into the dirt. The horses made vague and agitated shapes at the far end of the corral. Harlan felt the drumming of their hoofbeats through the soles of his boots.

"Three months," Jack said. He rested his forehead on the fence rail a moment before continuing. "We start shooting in Nashville in three months."

Harlan rolled the toothpick around in his mouth with the flat of his tongue. In the distant gloaming, Jack's prize horses screamed.

"I told you it wouldn't be no problem..."

"Goddammit you dumbass, don't give me that. That bunch of nervous nellies wanted to shut the show right down, *indefinite hiatus* they called it. Took me a whole lot of shucking and jiving to get them back on board."

Harlan stood in close to the boss man. He could smell Jack's expensive aftershave and moisturizers, his desperation and panic and raw animal fear. Harlan wondered what Terrabonne smelled.

"We need this, hoss." Jack's eyes jittered over Harlan's face. "We need this."

At the far end of the corral, a white horse threw its mane, rearing and crying in the gathering dark. A chorus of whinnying cries rose from the herd and the agitated animals started running in circles around the edges of the corral.

Terrabonne smacked one palm against the fence rail as the horses thundered past. His eyes were like stones in the dusk.

"Beautiful animals, aren't they?" he said. "They'll outlive you'n me both."

"Didn't think horses lived all that long," Harlan said.

"They don't."

Terrabonne walked away without another word. Harlan Winters stood in the newborn night, chewing his toothpick and smiling out at the panicked shapes stampeding in the darkness.

SIXTEEN

Kane passed Maeve outside the hostel's front entrance. She stood huddled in a big hooded parka, a cigarette burning between her fingers. The black plastic knife handle still rested, almost invisible, in the top of her boot.

"Oi, Yank." Maeve blew a smoky blue plume into the air above her head. "Off again already?"

"Just thought I'd wander, maybe stop and play a few songs."

The cherry of her cigarette rose to Maeve's lips, flared and faded in the darkness.

"That's your life then, is it? Wander around, play a few songs?"

"Pretty much."

"Give the odd bastard a bloody hiding?" Maeve grinned and blew more smoke.

"Sometimes," Kane said, "it can't be helped."

"I bet."

Kane looked at her torn black tights and the tartan miniskirt peeking out from under the hem of her parka. He wondered if her legs were cold.

"You must get lonely," she said.

"Yeah. Sometimes."

The two stood facing each other in the gravel lot, the silence stretching, growing awkward.

"Alone all the time, unfamiliar places, don't you ever worry about something happening to you?"

"Lots of good folks in this world, lots of great stuff to see. It'd be a shame to let the fear of a few bad apples keep me from seeing all that good."

And evil was just as easy to find at home as out on the road. Kane did not say that out loud, but all the same, Maeve eyed him over the burning end of her cigarette as though able to see the nature of his thoughts.

"But evil does exist." Her voice was rough, charged with emotion. "Evil's threaded deep in the blood of our race, and going back to the time of Theseus, evil's waited in the road, stalking the victim no one will miss."

Maeve's eyes had gone fierce and wild. Her teeth gleamed, wet and sharp in the faint wash of light from the front windows. Kane met her gaze, his own eyes steady.

"I know that story. Ancient Greek serial killer, kept a hotel had some kind of iron bed and murdered the ones passed through alone." Kane rolled his head on the column of his neck. "Way I remember it, that guy met a pretty messy end."

"That's the part they want you to remember, the end of the tale. No one likes to remember all the ones stayed in that bed before Theseus, or the families never knew what happened. No one likes to think about the earth around that bed, soaked wet with blood."

Maeve's eyes were bright in the darkness. Her mouth made a flat dark shape.

"Good night, Yank. Go play your songs."

Her cigarette threw bouncing sparks across the gravel. Her back made an angry black shape against the lighted doorway.

***

By nightfall, Jack Terrabonne was climbing the walls at Whispering Pines. He stormed through the halls, his hair all over the place and the knot of muscle at the corner of his jaw twitching and jumping. Harlan Winters didn't ask, just loaded Jack and the boys up into the trucks and got everyone rolling down the mountain into Queenstown.

Jack was silent on the ride down. He sat alone, sunk low in the plush leather back seat of the Range Rover, his *Live from Hammersmith* album playing on the sound system. Harlan gnashed his teeth and scraped the ridged calluses of his palm across his knuckles.

There was only one place in Queenstown Jack would drink. He always said it was because The Bunker played the kind of music he liked. Harlan figured it was on account of they were the only place had his picture up on the wall.

They took their usual booth in the back of the main room. There were a few Germans sitting at the table when Jack and Harlan and the boys showed up. Not like it mattered. Harlan barely had to speak, just put his knuckles on the table and stood blocking out the light. The Germans cleared out.

Jack was manic. He knocked shots back and told dirty jokes and abused the boys in a loud voice. JD mostly took the worst of it, with his bandages and injuries, his bruised and swollen face. The boys all acted like Jack was the funniest thing they'd ever heard. Harlan stood apart, back in the shadows.

A couple of hours in, Jack was red as a boiled crab. The Bunker was louder and more crowded, and Harlan was on his last nerve. Taking a piss, some drunk kid with a scraggly beard and hair like a girl bumped into Harlan at the urinal. There was no one around to see, so Harlan slammed the guy's face into the bathroom mirror a couple of times and called it even.

Back at the table, Harlan wiped blood and broken glass from his hands with a paper towel. Jack had just sent drinks over to a couple of girls standing up at the bar.

The two were young enough to be Jack's grandkids. The girls brought their drinks over and stood in front of the table, all short skirts and long legs and soft firm skin. Jack stretched back in his seat, acting like their attention was the least he deserved. A small tuft of gray chest hair stuck out of the top of his shirt. The boys all traded sideways looks and elbowed each other. Their leader, the ladies man.

"You gals know who I am?" Jack's line sounded old, well-oiled and well rehearsed. His eyes traveled up and down the women's bodies, never rising above their breasts.

Harlan didn't give a damn. Both had that kind of cared-for and expensive look, the type folks noticed they went missing.

"See," one of them said, "I *told* you it was him."

Jack swelled. He made a strange shape with his lips and tapped Farrel's knee beside him.

"Why is it always the creepy old men?"

The two girls' laughter was cutting. They flounced off and Jack's boys all looked away.

Their leader's face burned with fury and shame.

SEVENTEEN

Maeve slashed on dark lipstick and pulled on her boots. She prayed that tonight might be the night.

It had been a long road, and hard. But Maeve wasn't sure she was ready for it to end.

The Bunker was her best bet. Dermott, the owner, was a fellow countrymen and a good sort. And outside of that remote country estate, Jack bloody Terrabonne and his crony thugs practically lived in The Bunker.

Maeve adjusted her top in the mirror. Once she was certain the knife did not show, she adjusted the second blade tucked into the top of her boot.

Gary sat night duty behind the hostel's front desk. He leaned forward on his elbows to get a better view of Maeve's arse as she passed through the lobby.

"Out trolling again tonight?" Gary's laughter was wet and dirty. His breath filled the air with the smells of marijuana and onions.

"Beg pardon?" Maeve said.

"I see you got your skank on."

Maeve leaned in, poisonously close. Bridey's shade looked on over Gary's shoulder. Her face wore an eager and blood-hungry look it had never known in life.

"Choose your next words carefully, me boyo. They may be your last."

Gary smirked and flipped a pink guest card onto the counter. Maeve caught a brief flash of Kane's name. Gary scratched at his neck with dirty nails and sneered.

"Don't know why you're messing with a guy's got no arse in his trousers."

Maeve left the lobby without bothering to reply. She thought of Bridey's ghost and tried to remember when last she'd slept.

The night air was like a sharp slap against her cheeks and chest.

***

It was late.

Terrabonne's stare was glassy and hard. A small muscle jumped under his left eye. It had been several hard-drinking hours, and the girls' rejection still cut like jagged shrapnel under his skin.

JD opened his mouth to speak, and Jack rounded on him.

"Fuck you. Fuck. You."

He gave the rest of his boys the stink eye. "Any y'all want to clear out, well you just get the fuck out right now. But you better not expect any fuckin--"

Terrabonne's lowball glass struck JD square in the chest. Twenty year old Scotch splashed into JD's eyes and the raw scraped places on his cheek. Some of it hit Turk and Farrel and Callum.

"Bunch of goddamned freeloaders anyway. Who needs you? Who needs any of you?"

Jack threw himself back against the cushions with his arms crossed, muttering. JD sat low in his seat, liquor dripping from his hair and beard. Small wet points glittered in his eyes, and his bruised and bandaged face was like that of a car crash victim.

Harlan eased out of the booth and bought a roll of change up at the bar. The juke only had four of Jack's songs in its playlist, two A-sides and two B-sides, but at least it did have those four. Harlan fed fifty bucks' worth of coins into the slot and punched those same four songs, one after the other, over and over.

By the second time they'd heard *Mansions Within*, Jack was calm again. By the third run-through of *Pussyfootin Heart*, Jack bought a round for the house.

Black Cat Blues was playing when Jack saw her.

Harlan saw Jack's eyes lock, his body stiffen. Harlan's hand brushed the flap of his coat away from the butt of the gun before he saw what Jack was looking at. Off in the shadows, a couple sat alone.

The girl was small and dark. Scruffy and underfed, but still luminous and beautiful. The boy had delicate features, a mop of short twisty dreads and that same scruffy and underfed look. The boy was trying to sell anyone passing their table something small and electronic. No one was buying.

The girl felt Harlan's eyes on her. She turned. Her eyes were wide and full of light, her mouth red and wet. Her black hair fell soft and wild around her face.

Harlan fought the growl rising in his throat.

Jack gestured. Harlan bent low until Jack's lips brushed his ear.

"I want that."

Harlan tore his eyes away.

"Jack, you really think that's..."

"I said... I want that." Terrabonne licked his lips. His eyes were bright, wet and hungry. "Now get."

There was no talking to the man.

Harlan sighed. He rose and shook himself like a bear in cold water and lumbered over to make the deal.

EIGHTEEN

The French kids were hungry, poor and desperate. Harlan wasn't surprised. It was a combination Jack could sense from across the room.

Closing this deal was a little harder than usual. The girl, Chloe, was some kind of prude and not even a little bit interested in meeting the famous man. Top it off, her boyfriend was the only one spoke any English.

Course, they both understood the sight of a thick roll of hundred dollar bills. And with Harlan promising the boyfriend could come along as chaperone and lying through his teeth about every everything else, those hundreds started looking mighty tempting. Jack was in for one hell of a surprise.

Harlan wished he could see Jack's face. This little two for one deal was necessary, though. Left here alone, the boyfriend was a loose end hanging. Near as Harlan could tell, nobody'd much miss the pair of them both.

And something about this French girl touched Harlan. Something he wanted.

***

JD grabbed Harlan's arm. *Black Cat Blues* played on the juke in the background for the fifth or sixth time, and the bar-sign neon flared in

Harlan's cold blue eyes. He stared down at the hand on his arm until it fell away.

"You can't just leave us," JD said.

"It's one night." Harlan peeled a few bills off his roll and pressed them into JD's sweat-slimed hand. "Stay here and keep drinking. Hit the titty bar. Hell, just check into a hotel and call up an escort service. I don't give a damn."

"But we was counting on you."

Harlan's only answer was a low wordless rumble. Over his shoulder, he was aware of the young French couple leaving. In a few minutes, he'd collect them outside their shithole hotel.

JD leaned way over to see around Harlan's arms. He licked his lips as the French girl walked away, moving sort of slow and stunned, numb. The light in JD's face was lean and hungry.

"Look, you already done struck out," he said as the French girl vanished from sight. "I figure you can come along. Me'n the others are going to find that, I mean *those* guys and get our own back."

"Rest of the boys know this?"

"*They* ain't afraid to stand by their own."

Harlan's eyes narrowed.

"Say again?"

"I didn't mean nothing, Harl, I swear." JD raised both hands and stepped back. "I only, I just figured you'd want to help is all. Chance to kick a little ass?"

Harlan eyed JD's broken nose. He fought the urge to grind his thumbs down into the strips of grubby bandage.

***

Maeve hit The Bunker a little before eleven. Even in the slow season, Queenstown was an all-night party town. Maeve didn't sleep much anyway, and when Jack Terrabonne rolled in, she wanted to be ready.

Tartan skirt, corset top and torn black tights: except for the jacket over the top of it all, it was the same outfit Bridey'd had on. Maeve had seen photos from the cantina that night, and she was dressed to kill.

Thirsty punters were piled three deep at the bar. It didn't stop Dermott from catching her eye and nodding her over. Maeve got her elbows up on the bar and leaned in until their foreheads almost touched.

"He here yet?" She said over the music.

"Been and gone." Dermott's face was grave. "Yeh're too late."

"Then why the bloody hell didn't you ring?"

"It's madness girl. Yeh'd be locked up, or worse. I want no part of it."

"But you *know*--"

"I know what yeh've told me," Dermott said. "It's the believing that's the trouble."

"I *told* you how--"

"Yeh're no killer, Maeve Kelly."

Maeve wanted to argue. It was too late. Dermott was already halfway down the bar, drawing beers from the tap. She was left with the jostling crowd pressing on every side of her, utterly alone.

NINETEEN

"JD? Hey, JD?"

JD opened his eyes.

"Goddammit, Turk. What?"

"Hey JD, weren't we gonna kick that guy's ass?"

"Them guys. How many times--"

"I know, four of em. You told me. But weren't we gonna find at least *one* of em and kick his ass?"

A whip of blonde hair brushed across JD's forehead. He forced himself to look past the double-D's gyrating in front of his face.

The stripper giving Turk his dance looked pissed-off and bored. Of course, with Turk to dance for, it was hard to blame her.

Farrel stared at the girl dancing on him. His mouth was wet, and that weird light was bright in his eyes. Right then, the dancer looked like she'd rather be just about anywhere else in the world. Which was actually pretty common when women were close to Farrel.

He and Callum weren't paying any mind to Turk.

"I don't remember nothing about that."

"But you said--"

"Y'know, for a fat ugly dumbass with a naked woman on his lap, you sure are full of complaints."

"What I'm tryin to say," Turk bumped the dancer off to the side with one meaty forearm. "If we ain't gonna kick ass, can't we at least get laid?"

Callum's ears picked up. The woman dancing on him frowned.

"Yeah," Farrel said without taking his eyes off the girl in front of him. "No offense, darlin, but this here ain't quite doing it for me."

The girl shivered. Farrel smiled slow.

JD climbed out from under his own lapdance. The stripper let him up without much more than a token protest. Her pout was halfhearted and fake, gone before JD finished turning away.

Outside the VIP lounge, the music was skull-splitting loud. JD had a word with one of the bouncers posted in the hallway and followed the width of the man's back through the club.

Lasker sat at his usual table in the back. Way the acoustics in the club were set up, a man could just about hear himself think in that one corner. Lasker sat under the purple neon, arms and shoulders bulked out with muscle, looking like some kind of pirate with his gleaming bald head and gold earring.

He had a couple of girls drinking at the table with him. A puffy-looking junky with acne scars in the hollows of her cheeks, and a hard-faced blonde with lines around her mouth and eyes like stones.

Lasker nodded. The bouncer showed JD into a chair and stood behind him. The guy was almost as big as Harlan Winters: over six and a half feet tall and more than half that wide. For JD, it was like having a mountain loom over his head.

"JD... Always a pleasure." Lasker splashed clear liquor into a glass and pushed it across the table. The liquid glowed blue under the lights. JD watched it with one eye squinted shut.

"Thanks, but good old Jack Daniels'll do me fine if you're offering."

"Drink. It's good."

JD drank. The liquor tasted like licorice and burned like fire. Lasker laughed as JD coughed and sputtered. The two women looked on, hard-eyed and dead-faced.

JD wiped his eyes. Lasker was still laughing.

"Good one," he finally said. "Now... how can I help?" "Me'n the boys was looking to go upstairs."

"So go." Lasker gestured with a single sweeping hand. The blonde shifted her arms against her stomach. Behind those big fake knockers, her body was hard and brown.

JD didn't move, didn't answer. Behind him, the bouncer shifted his weight. Light disappeared behind him as the bouncer shifted.

"Is it money?" Lasker said. "You lot are good customers. If you've spent all your cash, we can always send the bill up to the house."

"Oh, no. No can do. I do believe a bill at the house from *Diamonds*'d be more than my job's worth."

That licorice booze made JD's face want to slide right off the front of his skull.

"Fact is, my boss is crazy-weird about having his name linked to places like this. He's all afraid it'll mess up some big deal he's got cooking."

"I see."

Lasker stared. Tiny blue points of light gleamed deep in shadowed black sockets.

"Money ain't the problem," JD said. " Thing is, we go on upstairs, you know as well as I do they're just gonna give us any three girls ain't busy."

"And you want... something special." Lasker touched the center of his lips with one finger. "Special may be possible, but you do understand that special... costs."

The hard-faced blonde leaned in. Her lips were parted, her teeth small and sharp. JD wondered if he knew how a bird feels, looking at a snake.

JD looked down at his hands, big clumsy balloons, blurring at the edges.

"Any of them girls you got upstairs Irish?"

Lasker laughed, harsh and cutting. The blonde turned her face away, no longer interested.

"I look like what to you, the United Nations?"

"Well then, can you at least give me one with green eyes?" JD said. "Black hair and green eyes?"

***

The young couple huddled close together, holding each other across the gravel lot. The night was still, mist off the lake lying heavy on the ground, but the two walked bent over as though caught in a heavy gale. They stood outside the Rover's open rear door, glassy-eyed and colorless, murmuring to each other in French.

Harlan looked over his shoulder at the hostel's windows and shifted to block anyone might be watching. His shadow fell wide and black over the young couple.

The boy was sweet-faced, with skin like a woman's. He stood with one arm around the girl, protecting her or sheltering behind her, it was hard to say.

The girl, Chloe, was ivory-skinned and soft as a peach under the grime. She bit her lips and knotted her jaw, and her skin smelled sweaty, metallic and afraid.

Her coat was too light for the weather. The girl stood with her fingers dug into the flesh of her upper arms, and her shoulders shook with every gust of windblown rain.

Harlan wondered if she would tremble like that all over.

"You came."

Harlan meant it to sound friendly. It pissed him off the way they both jumped and cringed when he said it.

The boy whispered to the girl. She responded in a quick little hiss of French, sounded like somebody having trouble with a zipper. The boy swallowed hard, looked up at Harlan towering over them.

"Please, we may have our money, yes?"

"You two got your passports?" The boy fumbled them out of the bag on his shoulder.

"Got to make sure you're legal, you understand." Except instead of handing them back, Harlan put them in his back pocket.

"We are paid now?"

"Sure, kid. Sure."

Harlan pulled the roll out of his jeans. A little lighter after what he'd given JD, but still plenty fat.

He unrolled the hundreds out into a stack, separated twelve bills off the top.

"That there's for just what we agreed on. Course, you decide you're up for any extras..."

Harlan made sure the rest of the stack was a little bit fanned out. Misty drops glittered like diamonds on the surface of the bills. The French kids' eyes were glued to the cash.

The sight of all that extra money started a brief whisper storm. Harlan didn't catch a word, couldn't even figure out who was on which side.

Not that it mattered.

"Please," the boy said, "We are doing the... just as we agree. We are doing this only."

"No problem." Harlan flashed a big smile, brown and meaty.

He gestured, and the French couple climbed into the Range Rover. They sat together on the back seat, practically in each other's lap.

Harlan handed the bills across. The girl's hand snapped out, and she held them crumpled against her stomach with both fists.

An uncomfortable silence followed. Both of the French kids looked like they might be sick.

Harlan's lips parted and his nostrils flared. His tongue flickered at the backs of his teeth.

He slammed the Rover's rear door. It shut with a heavy thunk, like a vault door closing. Two pale faces stared out from behind the tinted glass.

Harlan thought of souls, frightened and lost, trapped under black ice.

TWENTY

"Goddammit JD, you asshole."

JD kicked a loose pile of dead leaves out of the gutter.

"Wasn't my fault."

"Bullshit, it wasn't your fault. This town ain't got but the one whorehouse, and you're the asshole just got us thrown out."

"Don't start with me, Farrel. You got us thrown out of that same place plenty of times before now."

"Yeah, but tonight it was you."

JD blew on his hands. His fingers ached with cold, and his palms stung where they'd scraped the sidewalk.

"I got half a mind to kick that bouncer's ass."

"Who'n hell you kidding?" Farrell spoke with his head back and his nose pinched, trying to stop the bleeding. "That big old Samoan'd break you in half."

Turk and Callum laughed. They were scraped up too, but not so bad.

"I tell you, that bouncer's just lucky I didn't open up the old whup-ass on him. I might've had to show him some of my Green Beret moves."

"Green Beret my ass. You couldn't even--"

"I was jumped, I tell you."

It was about to come to blows. Lord knows it had often enough, sometimes a night in the drunk tank on the back of it. It was Turk got between JD and Farrell, called their attention to the sounds of blues harmonica, playing in the near distance.

"It just me, or is that *Black Cat Blues*?"

Last few years, JD had come to hate that goddamn song. No way to admit that in front of the others, though. Not without having to eat some serious shit, maybe even find a brand-new job.

"Whoever it is," Callum said, "They can play."

JD led the boys down the street and around the corner, looking for the source of the music. He'd already half-decided whoever that poor freezing bastard was, he was gonna get to sample some of JD's Green Beret moves.

For a little while the music stopped. No sound to follow, the boys were starting to whine about finding another bar when right on time, the music started up again.

"Hey, that's Sonny Terry now. His stuff ain't easy."

"Hell are you now, Callum, Mister Music or something?" JD moved off in the direction of the music.

The musician played, sheltering in a corner. Fog creeping up all over town made it hard to see, just some tall guy in a big black coat, big bony hands held up in front of his face.

A few steps closer, JD felt his lips stretch tight across his teeth. That same goddamn stranger, one snuck up on him and sucker-punched him last night.

Except this time the stranger was alone, and JD had three buddies with him. Looked like they were gonna get to kick a little ass after all.

CROSSROAD BLUES

Jack Terrabonne paced the length of his penthouse suite. He made sure the door between the rear lounge and the back stairs was unlocked and that the magazines all showed his picture on the covers.

He sailed through the shower room and gave the door a little kick to shut it behind him. A couple dozen rapid steps across the room and Jack plopped his butt down on one side of his big old feather-stuffed super-king and rummaged in the top drawer of his bedside table. Brown plastic pill bottles rattled against the maple.

Jack shook out a couple of Ritalin for the energy. And after a bit of thought a single Diazepam, to take off the worst of the Ritalin's edge.

Harlan wouldn't be long now. Jack put a couple of his own albums on the CD changer, ballads and love songs mostly, to set the mood.

It was a good few years now since groupies had thrown themselves at him. Even so, Jack didn't mind paying for it, long as the girl wasn't a pro.

Jack didn't have much use for whores. Look at how many back in the 80's and 90's sold their ass to famous men and turned around and sold their stories to the papers. Much better to take some sweet thing down on her luck, help her out with a few extra bucks and a ticket someplace far away.

Way Jack looked at it, he was practically doing a good deed. Those little old gals ought to be grateful, and he figured they were too. All these years, not one of them'd ever tried to blackmail him or sell her story to the media.

He thought about his treat for tonight. She had those dark liquid eyes and big pouty lips, somehow European looking in that way that they had, and that down-and-out look that put the itch in Jack's pants. He tongued two little blue lozenges of Viagra off his palm. Making sure that little black-haired gal would find him up and ready.

Last thing Jack did was shut the drapes. He loved the view from his penthouse by daylight, but at night the darkness out here was complete.

The window walls showed Jack nothing but his own reflection. While the thought of endless images of himself with that little gal was tempting, it would also be a tempting target for any reporters camped in those woods.

Too tempting. No way Jack was going to take that risk.

Drapes shut, Jack boogied on over to the wet bar to fix himself a drink and wait for the sound of showers.

He wondered what songs this one might inspire.

TWENTY-ONE

Kane let the final notes of *Black Cat Blues* trail off. When the song was over, he blew the harmonica's reeds clear and stuck his hands in his pockets to warm them.

Queenstown was no town for musicians. Playing off and on for over three hours, Kane had less than twenty dollars to show for it. He wouldn't even have that if not for one middle-aged drunk's ten dollar bill.

But tonight wasn't about money. Tonight was about the tendrils of white fog creeping up the street, the moon rising fat and yellow in the night sky. Tonight was about playing for its own sake.

The chill and stiffness soon left Kane's fingers. He took the harp out of his pocket and fanned a quick dancing arpeggio across the reeds. He was ten bars into a Sonny Terry blues riff, fun and breezy, when he saw them: JD and three others.

JD's stringy hair still fell in his face. He had two black eyes and a busted lip, his broken nose smeared across the front of his face and strapped down with a wide strip of grubby white tape.

He stood at the point of a ragged triangle. The man on one side of him was short and heavy, with his hair in a single thick braid down the back of his head. On JD's other side was another nothing carny type with a shaggy black beard and arms like boiled hams. A moon-faced man with a balding head hung toward the back of the crowd.

All four of them were scraped and bruised. The heavy one's left eye was swelling shut, and the bearded man was trying to pinch shut a bloody nose.

Kane dropped the harp back in his coat pocket. He stood with his weight low and his arms loose at his sides.

"Hey now," JD said, "don't stop on account of us."

JD swayed on his feet. Behind all the bruising his eyes had a bright alcoholic shine. But he was still careful to stand outside Kane's reach.

"This fellah plays real good, don't he boys?"

Two men laughed. The heavy one and the one with the bushy black beard. They crowded in close behind JD, egging him on. The man with the moon face crossed his arms in front of his body and turned his face away. He stood as far apart as he could and still be some tenuous part of the group.

Kane didn't have to worry about that one. Three on one then, with heavy one and the bearded one outweighing him by a wide margin.

"Seems to me," JD said, "we was never properly introduced. This here's Turk and Farrel, and that pussy over there's Callum. I'm--"

"Your name's JD. I know."

"What about you, stranger? What do they call you?"

Kane held his arms away from his sides.

"Just a harmonica player, about ready to call it a night."

"Tell you what." JD fished a wet and crumpled bill from the front of his jeans and threw it in the hat at Kane's feet. "Why don't you play us a little something? You know any songs about guys got their ass kicked for getting in other people's business?"

Kane didn't answer. The corner he stood in made it impossible for them to get behind him. It also meant that to get any room to maneuver, he'd have to punch straight through.

"Tell me something, stranger." JD wiped his mouth with the back of one wrist. "That Irish bitch really worth all this hurt you're about to receive?"

"What is it between you and her anyway?" Kane said.

"Bridey Martin, that's what. The Irish bitch'd just told us what the deal was with this Martin woman, I wouldn't a had to get all unpleasant." JD checked over his shoulders for his friends. "You, stranger... I reckon for you, it's a little too late.

JD was the loudest and possibly armed, but Kane figured the third one, Farrel, for the most dangerous. Above that blood-flecked black beard, the man's danced with an oily and sadistic glee.

"Sucker-punching a man in the dark's one thing." JD crowded in close. "Standing face to face in a fair fight, you ain't so tough now, are you stranger?"

JD's fist came up. Kane caught the arm at wrist and elbow and snapped the limb.

The other two tried to surge around their screaming friend. Kane drove a quick strike into the soft tissue behind the black beard and shot under that man's flailing arms.

Their positions were now reversed. Kane on the outside with his three attackers caught in the corner.

JD writhed on the ground. Farrel was bent over coughing, his bloody nose reopened, but he was still on his feet, his fists up.

Turk danced back. Impossible to tell if he was about to break and run or looking for an opening to charge.

Farrel surged up, swinging. Fists glanced off Kane's elbows and shoulders as he slipped the punches. He locked on, forced Farrel's head down and drove four hard knee strikes into the man's solar plexus. The force of the impact was comparable to a thirty-five mile per hour car crash.

For such a heavy man, Turk was fast. He turned and ran.

Kane dropped Farrel to the sidewalk and turned back to the corner.

JD scrabbled backwards, eyes wild with fear. Kane reached down past JD's head to pick up the hat full of change.

"Don't make me see you again," Kane said, his face inches from JD's. "Next time, I won't go so easy."

He walked away before the running coward or the moon-faced man had a chance to bring the cops.

TWENTY-TWO

Maeve paced along the waterfront. Deep in her pockets, her hands were balled into fists. She'd missed her chance, and now she was going to have to wait another day, maybe more. It was enough to drive a body mad.

There were few enough people about this night. On Maeve's part of the pier there was no one. The thick white fog rolling off the lake was enough to make those few who were out keep to the brightly lit bistros and neon-lit bars further up the slope of the street.

Maeve walked alone, her only company the smacking echoes of her boots on the concrete dock and her own troubled thoughts.

She barely heard the second set of steps until they were nearly on top of her. Maeve crouched, one hand on the grip of her newly-sharpened knife.

The shape that emerged through the swirling mist was tall and dark. It was also oddly familiar. Maeve relaxed her grip on the blade and straightened.

"Don't you know better than to sneak up on a girl that way, Yank?"

Kane's face was grim. His eyes were wild, dark and glittering.

"Walk with me."

Kane put one arm around her shoulders. They set off at a leisurely pace. Maeve caught herself breathing in the scents of clean warm male, excitement and danger.

"How'd you know to find me here?" she said.

"I didn't. Just walking in random directions." Kane shifted his arm on Maeve's shoulder. "Hope you don't mind, it's just the cops're less likely to look at a couple strolling than one man alone."

"You daft bastard, what've you done?"

Kane watched her in silence. His amber eyes captured the light, for all the world like the lions in those nature shows. They were bright and pitiless: predator's eyes.

"I'm no friend of the Guard," Maeve said. "Whatever you've done, the razzers won't hear it from me."

"I had another little run in with JD."

"That all? Last time, you beat him with a rolled-up newspaper."

"This time he brought more friends. The ones who stayed got hurt worse."

They started walking again. Maeve slipped one hand around Kane's waist. The deepening fog curled around their legs, and the sounds of water slapping against concrete pilings echoed up from below.

"What're you doing out here?" Kane said.

"I was supposed to meet someone, back in town. They left without me." Steel rings clinked as Maeve bit her lip. "I suppose now I'm at loose ends."

"Can't imagine anyone standing you up."

"Maybe tomorrow..."

Sounds came at them out of the fog: the heavy measured slap of footsteps, the creak and jingle of leather harness and the squawk and crackle of a two-way radio.

Kane stopped, tense. Maeve pulled his head down to her and kissed him before the cop arrived.

The kiss surprised her. Rough and brutal as she knew the man to be, and the agitated state he was in, Maeve was prepared for a cold distracted nothing. Or the kind of front-on facial assault leaves a girl with bruised lips and razor burn.

Kane's kiss was soft, gentle. His lips were strong but tender, his tongue the barest electric flicker.

Maeve's toes curled. She was barely aware of the cop barking into his radio, or of the sound of running feet fading in the distance.

Finally, they broke away, Maeve stood close, her fingers hooked in his belt loops. Kane's eyes were different now, that cold and pitiless light replaced by something softer, more urgent.

They stood watching each other for a moment. At the first sound of a siren, both turned in the direction the cop had run.

A light show played up the hill. In among the twinkling orange streetlamps, red and blue fairy lights pulsed, gathering quickly in one spot. "I'm guessing that's for you?"

"Those others, yeah."

Maeve looked up at Kane from under her lashes. She tugged his belt loops so that the front of his jeans thumped against her belly.

"Best we're getting you home, then."

**

The French kids didn't speak a word the whole drive up the mountain. That suited Harlan fine. He snuck a few quick peeks into the back seat, but those two just sat knotted in on themselves, alone with their thoughts. Once he caught a look at his own eye staring back at him in the rearview mirror. Broken blood vessels threaded through the white, and the iris was an eerie toxic blue-green in the dashboard's poison light.

That eye burned with terrible and unsettling lights. He shuddered and afterward kept his attention on the road ahead.

The Range Rover threaded its way through the pass. Coming down through the mountains, Harlan drove with both hands on the wheel. Knuckles stood out like pieces of stone on his massive fists. Safe on the valley floor, Harlan hit the gas. The phosphorous-white high beams carved a rushing tunnel of bleached-out color through the night-dark pines.

Within minutes, Harlan spotted the turn. Gravel sprayed under the Rover's tires, and branches whipped and slashed at the windows.

Whispering Pines came into view. The house was dark. Only thin cracks of light burned at the edges of the dark-curtained top floor. The wide white oval of gravel drive glowed in the moonlight, and the clipped wet lawn was a ghostly gray.

The other Rover sat five steps from the front door. The parking angle was careless, and the driver's door and the house's front door both stood wide open. Jack Terrabonne didn't bother closing his own doors.

Harlan rolled to a stop. The French kids climbed out. The great gray pile of the main house loomed above them. Its wide and rambling shape seemed to blot out the landscape.

The boy looked up at the dark face of Whispering Pines and shivered.

TWENTY-THREE

Kane wondered if they would ever make it back to the hostel. Maeve didn't make it easy. The woman kissed like she was dying of fever.

In the dark and the sheltering fog, they stopped often. Maeve's throat was scalding against his lips, and her skin tasted of gunpowder and freshly sheared copper. They rummaged under each other's clothes like a couple of teenagers. At the first brush of Kane's thumb against her nipple, Maeve arched into him and moaned. She bit his lip and raked her nails across the unprotected flesh at the small of his back.

Coming up to the hostel's entrance, Kane saw two young people coming out. The French couple from the night before, walking arm in arm as though sheltering from some unseen storm. They headed toward a late-model SUV parked around the side of the building, almost out of sight.

Kane watched them a moment, then followed the rhythmic flick of Maeve's miniskirt in through the open door.

***

Harlan led them across the threshold. They crossed the foyer, high and narrow and tiled in glossy Italian marble. The French couple's footsteps sent shuffling echoes hissing off the tiles, and the room's upper reaches were lost in shadow.

The back hall was narrow and dim. Harlan marched them through twists and turns, past dark wood doors, closed against them, and onto the service stairs. They began to climb.

At the top of the stairs, Harlan stood aside to let them pass.

A sour odor rose from the boy's limbs, and the girl's cheeks were wet. Harlan was able to smell the salt.

The sitting room wasn't much. A couch and a couple of chairs, a low table and a couple of magazines with Jack Terrabonne on the cover. The magazines' pages were yellowing, the covers brittle and faded.

Harlan licked his lips and locked the door.

Music played nearby. Jack in the 70's, covering some old song about teenagers in love. Harlan watched the girl Chloe pace the room, out of sync with the music. Her legs were smooth, with tender blue veins in the hollows behind her ankles.

Drops of sweat beaded on Harlan's cheeks and upper lip and slicked the sides of his face.

The room beyond the sitting room was brightly lit, warm and tiled. There were showerheads and faucets in the wall and a wide drain in the floor. Harlan gestured the two through. As they passed, his lips parted and his nostrils flared.

The girl's skin smelled delicious.

"Man wants you washed. Not like I think you need it, but I ain't the one paying the bills," Harlan said. "After, you just go through that door over there. Make sure you wash your hair real good, too. Jack-- um, the gentleman is freakin crazy about clean hair."

The two stood in the shower room together. The wall opposite the showerheads had chrome hooks with fluffy robes hanging from them and a glossy wood bench. They both kicked off their shoes in front of the bench but stayed standing.

"You don't got to worry about your clothes, either. You'll put on those robes there, and you can pick your own stuff up after you're done."

Another quick burst of French from the girl. Harlan reckoned he could just about spend all damn day watching the muscles in her back move. The boy spoke up again.

"Please, if these extras..."

"I'll be waiting downstairs after you're done. You go for anything extra, the gentleman'll let me know and you'll get it then."

"*Merci.*"

"My pleasure, buddy."

The kid turned away to shuck out of his shirt. His bare back was pale and delicate. The girl sat on the bench with her legs crossed, glaring. No way she was gonna give Harlan even a little peek.

Like it mattered.

Harlan pulled the door shut, heard the lock click in the latch.

TWENTY-FOUR

Late that night, Kane and Maeve lay together, in the darkness. Smoke from her cigarette rolled in lazy blue coils along the ceiling, and a pattering rain made faint sounds against the window. The glow from the bar heater was the only light in the room. It painted their flesh in soft red tones and deep warm shadows.

Kane was exhausted and sore. Maeve was a passionate and violent lover, full of strange and fevered intensity. His skin was welted with stinging red stripes from her nails and lamprey-puckered rings from her teeth.

Maeve lifted her cigarette from the saucer laying on her belly. Her breasts rose as she inhaled. The cherry flared in the darkness.

Kane, propped on one elbow, ran the backs of two fingers idly down the length of her bare flank. Maeve's body was white and hard, tattooed and scarred. He felt her finger traced the billowing flag inked into Kane's chest. Faded red and blue, trapped beneath his skin

"Tell me about your tattoo."

"What do you want to know?"

"Well..." Her fingernail drifted in lazy patterns over the design. "What is it with you Yanks and your flag, anyway? I mean, I'm proud as hell I'm Irish, but you won't catch me inking the green and gold in me skin."

"I don't know what to tell you," Kane said. "Last time I saw the States, I was fifteen years old. This way, no matter where I am, I've got a little piece of home."

"Bloody daft, y'ask me." Maeve's lips were soft against the hard muscle of his chest. The cigarette burned close to the filter between her fingers. "Then again, for me, growing up's about the last thing I want to remember."

Maeve dragged at her cigarette. The momentary flare cast a crisp black shadow along the shaft of her nipple. She exhaled a stream of smoke, and her body was once more soft in the heater's light.

Kane wrapped one arm around her. Maeve stubbed her cigarette out in the saucer and curled in close to his body. Her skin was warm, and Kane felt the quick hot beat of her heart against his chest.

"Fifteen..." Maeve said. "How'd you manage?"

Kane shrugged. "I jumped a boat, container ship out of Manilla. Ended up about a year later in Paris. Not a word of French and not a centime in my pocket."

"Tch." Maeve's cigarette smoke roiled in the air, and shadows slid across her body as her shoulders rose and fell.

"It wasn't so bad," Kane said. "I started busking, in tourist spots, on the Metro, stuff like that. People like how you play, they drop a few coins. Nobody cares where you're from, or what it says on your passport."

Kane stroked her body, one thumb traveling the furrow of her spine and the arch of her rump. Maeve curled, sheltered in the crook of Kane's arm. He felt her, warm and slick against his thigh.

"Maeve, can I ask you something?"

She stretched, arms straight above her head like a cat.

"Who's Bridey Martin?

Maeve's eyes narrowed, green and glittering. In the dim red light, the points of her teeth were white and sharp.

"Where did you hear that name?"

"JD. When I asked him why he attacked you."

Maeve sat up in bed. Her nostrils and mouth were pinched, her eyes hot and bright and wild.

Kane felt the heat of her across the narrow bed. Crouched among the twisted sheets, dark ropy dreads falling in her eyes, Maeve looked feral and dangerous.

She regarded him for a long moment. Despite the heater throwing its buzzing warmth into the room, an icy chill snapped along Kane's skin. Suddenly, she dove past him, leaning down to the floor to rummage in a pile of dirty clothes for her backpack. Knots of muscle made crawling black shadows across her arms and back.

The photo she handed Kane was creased and faded. It might have been in color, but the heater's red light cast the picture in darkroom monochrome.

Two children smiled out at the camera, arms around each other's necks. They might have been fifteen or sixteen, certainly no older. The one on the left had spiky blonde hair, baby-fat softness around her lower jaw and a heartbreaking smile: at once fragile and brave. The one on the right wore her hair shaved into a black mohawk. Her face hadn't yet grown into the size of her ears or her mouth. Her eyes were wide and slanted, like those of a cat.

Kane felt a sudden twist of shame at the look that passed between the other girl and Maeve, as though he was intruding into an intimate moment best left private.

"This is her? Bridey?"

Maeve's hands shook as she lifted a fresh cigarette to her lips. The wheel of the lighter rasped, and paper and leaf crackled at the first touch of the flame.

"That's us in London, '99 that was. Couple of runaways in the Big Smoke, ringside seats for the end of civilization." Maeve wiped at her eyes. "Couple of bloody eejits."

"What happened?"

"You ever love someone like they're a part of you? Ever care so deeply it hurts to breathe?"

"I see."

"We'd been thick as thieves from the time we were just little." Maeve's voice was soft and far away. She no longer made any effort to halt the tears tracking down her cheeks. "We had our troubles, same as anyone, but we always patched it up before long."

Kane dropped his eyes. The two girls in the photograph shared their timeless and tender moment, and Kane once again looked away.

"I told her not to go. Time and again I told her. But Bridey always was a bit of a fool, thinking something better waited further on down the road and only too happy to believe the lies of rich men."

Maeve seemed to remember Kane, though she lay beside him in the darkness. She looked him full in the face, her voice gravelly and choked.

"Twas a rich man dropped her in Mexico, left her penniless and alone with no more thought than you'd throw a piece of rubbish. And 'twas a rich man a year later, stole my Bridey's very life."

"She was murdered?"

"I felt it," Maeve said. "the moment it happened. There I was, middle of the street at ten o'clock in the morning, screaming and crying and carrying on. Completely losing my shite."

She went quiet, her eyes far away.

"Sometimes, it's like I still see her."

"I'm sorry."

Maeve brushed Kane's words away like so many cobwebs.

"Six months it was before I was able to scrounge the fare. In Mexico, I retraced her steps, talked to those as remembered her."

"Cops?"

Maeve snorted and crushed out her smoke. "I did even go to the Guard, for all the good it did me. Penniless backpacker on the one hand, wealthy landowner on the other. I was lucky to even get out of Mexico."

Kane laid his palm on Maeve's flank. The skin felt warm and tight, as though she stood too close to an open fire or a hot stove.

"I still don't get how JD and that bunch fit in."

Maeve slid the length of her body along Kane's. The dark spill of her dreadlocks fell around him, shadowing her face.

"Their boss has a place in these mountains. Now they're back in town, JD is that bastard's way of sending a message." Her fingertips slid down the flat of Kane's belly, and her breath curled along the side of his throat.

Maeve's fingers worked in slow, almost lazy movements. Kane's heart raced.

"Of course.."she said, "you took care of that little problem, didn't you."

Maeve's mouth was wet on Kane's palm. Her teeth were small and sharp, the pain thrilling.

"JD won't bother you again." Kane curled his fingers in Maeve's dreads and kissed the top of her head. Copper currents stirred in the air.

She tossed her hair out of the way and looked down at him. She slid one thigh over Kane's legs, her lips curled slightly at the corners, her eyes bright and unreadable.

"Maeve, wait. Wait. Tell me..."

She sank back against him, slick and scalding. Her smile was dark and wicked.

Scarred hands gripped her hips. Maeve arched and hissed. The sight of her body in the ruby light was like a brushfire under Kane's skin.

"What do you want from me, Maeve?"

"Not one damn thing." Her mouth softened and her eyes closed. A low moan rose from her throat and blended with the rain sounds outside.

"I'm grateful," she said, moving against him. "For the company, for JD, and for one night of peace."

Her face was transported. In the dim red light from the heater Maeve looked like an angel, of a sort.

"You've made it that much easier," she said, "to get my hands on that rich bastard took my Bridey so I can slit his fecking throat."

TWENTY-FIVE

The night wasn't much more than a ragged wet wisp by the time Terrabonne was finally done. Harlan was there waiting for the French kids.

The boy was wide-eyed and shivering. The girl's nose and eyes were red and swollen. She held her arms tight against her torso, as though some part of her body might break.

Jack's suite was a wreck. Harlan got a quick flash of the room as the door swung shut behind them. Bedsheets knotted, wadded and twisted. Stains on the carpet and wet towels wadded up all over the place.

No sign of Terrabonne, of course. The lock clicked behind the French kids, and they were Harlan's problem. Jack would sleep like a baby.

Mister Boogie Jack Terrabonne never once had to clean up his own mess. Not since he got Harlan Winters looking out for him.

Harlan touched the boy, gently, on the shoulder. The kid swayed on his feet and shuffled in the general direction of the only open door. Harlan's fingers hovered over the top of the girl's head. She was skittish as a colt, shaking and flinching at even that little bit of movement.

He stood behind her, spread his hands out a little bit from his sides. She smelled of cheap bar soap and that godawful strawberry shampoo

Jack kept in the shower. The stink of it made Harlan gnash his teeth. The girl lurched to her feet and staggered after her boyfriend.

Harlan watched them both through the doorway.

He didn't give much hope for that relationship.

***

In her small and grubby hostel room, Maeve watched the first gray shift in the light. The bar heater still buzzed, its warmth and glow and sound like that of an animal's den.

Maeve stared at patterns in the room's sole window. Sheets of ice spread crystalline fingers across the window glass, brilliant as diamonds in the growing dawn.

The big American slept beside her. In sleep, his skin was soft and yielding, the long cords and flat planes of muscle now slack and flaccid. His eyelashes lay black and long above the broad curve of his cheek, and his mouth was full and sensuous, almost gentle. His chest rose and fell, slow, steady, and she was able to see the pulse of his big heart beating just below the skin.

Maeve smoothed Kane's ruffled black hair and tried not to hate the man for the quality of his sleep.

Maeve couldn't remember her last good night's sleep. Nor could she recall the last time she'd shared her bed. Losing Bridey, not in a small way but *really* losing her, totally and forever, had changed everything. For close to two years now, a dark veil clouded the sun and all pleasures tasted of ashes.

In a way, Maeve was surprised at the way she let herself go last night. And with a stranger.

Maybe it shouldn't have been such a surprise. Even after a year staked out and waiting in this place, Maeve knew almost no one. Anyone she chose was bound to be a stranger. And now, with Jack Terrabonne finally back in town and the end so close, Maeve craved nothing more than one night of warmth and pleasure. Especially in the face of what might come after.

Quiet as she could, Maeve kissed Kane on the brow and slid out from under the shelter of his circling arm. She dressed in silence and left him sleeping in her own narrow bed.

It was a couple of hours before the white-water rafters, first of the day, were due to leave. Maeve used the time to get ahead on her work. This time of year there were precious few hours of daylight, and Maeve wanted to be staked out early, in case Jack Terrabonne showed.

She stood in the hostel foyer. Weak pale light filtered through the windows and pushed the shadows into the corners. Maeve fingered the hilt of her knife and counted the hours until darkness.

***

Dawn was still a little way off yet. The Rover's headlights still bleached the old logging road the colors of bone and soot, but the upper branches of the trees could be seen, black and scrabbling against the lightening night sky.

The access road was deserted. Thick dark pines crowded the edges of the packed-earth road, pressing close at every bend and curve. Harlan tapped the brake and let the Range Rover coast to a halt.

He checked the rear view mirror. The two French kids didn't look up. Neither of them seemed to notice they weren't on the road back to town.

Harlan pulled the key out of the ignition. Without the noise of the truck's tires over the unpaved road or the bass thrum of the Rover's big diesel engine, the wind in the pines was loud, thrashing and hissing.

The French kids finally did look around. They found themselves staring down the barrel of Harlan's gun.

After that it was almost pitiful, it was so easy. The girl started crying in the back seat. The sniffly little weeps seemed to bubble up out of her. The boy tried to hold her, but Chloe wouldn't let him touch her. He ended up hovering over her, stroking the girl's hair and whispering to her in French.

They were real quiet after that. Harlan could see it in their eyes. Somewhere under the hope and the terror, but still close enough to the surface, those kids knew they were doomed.

TWENTY-SIX

The mud-splattered Range Rover crested the ridge. It carved long dark curves in the brown and brittle grass as it plunged down the other side of the hill. Seconds later, the four-by-four slid to a halt. Harlan turned off the ignition and pocketed the keys.

The sun glowed watery and red, burning on the horizon. The vast sky overhead was a streaked riot of reds and purples. A bruised darkness to the south threatened bad weather, but so far the new day was dawning clear, and cold.

A stand of trees clustered on the valley floor. An acre or so of beech, birch and maple and a pond this time of the year wasn't much more than an ice-crusted mudhole.

Here at the edge of the treeline were saplings, gray and silver. Some were thin little whippets, waist-high or smaller. Most were as thick as Harlan's wrist and two or three times his own height. Irregular patterns of shadow and sunlight danced across his windshield, and yellow leaves spiraled down on every side.

It was quiet here. The only sounds were the ticking of the cooling engine, the soft sound of fallen leaves on the hood and the quiet weeping of the two French backpackers handcuffed in back.

Harlan stepped out of the Rover and stood with his arms out wide and his eyes closed. The autumn sunlight on his face was a blessing, a covenant and a promise.

Harlan grinned like a child.

When he was damn good and ready, and only then, Harlan opened the truck's tailgate. He hauled the boy out by his stubby little dreadlocks and dragged him to the nearest strong sapling.

The kid was out of it. He didn't even put up much of a fight when Harlan unlocked the handcuffs and recuffed him around the tree. The cuffs were good strong American steel. The kid wasn't going anywhere.

Harlan looked his captive over. Whatever Jack had been up to, he hadn't left too many bruises.

A thrashing in the leaves caught Harlan's attention. The girl was out of the truck and running for all she was worth. Hands cuffed behind her and Lord knew the poor thing had been through a hard night, but damned if she wasn't giving it everything she had.

Harlan cheered her on with a big old rebel yell. They were on thirty-six hundred acres of private land: a little bit of noise wasn't going to hurt.

In fact, Harlan decided to let her know just how he felt about noise. He pulled the .44 from its leather holster and pressed the muzzle against French boy's thin and bony chest. The barrel dimpled the soft skin and caught milky reflections in its chromed metal length.

Harlan pulled the trigger.

The thunderclap of the blast echoed off the surrounding hills. The French girl staggered, looked behind her and screamed.

The boy lay dead at Harlan's feet. A powder burn in the shape of a great gray flower lay across his chest, and splinters of raw white wood were thrown from the trunk of the tree to the wet and dark-frosted grass.

Harlan smudged one thumb across the flower pattern and licked the tip of his thumb. He tasted gunpowder and sweat, and that damn cheap soap.

The girl got back to her feet, crying as she ran.

Harlan watched her seek safety deeper in the trees. Her legs were thin white flashes in the leafy darkness. Harlan felt the stub of his tongue flicker against his lips.

She'd be sweating now. Sweating and afraid. That godawful strawberry shampoo would be worn away in no time.

Harlan thumbed the release on the gun. He flicked open the gate and dropped the bullets, brass and twinkling, on the flat of his palm. One time a teen runaway had got Harlan's gun away from him. Ever since, he'd learned his lesson.

Birds sang in the trees. An icy wind brushed the dry and brittle grass, and the sun was warm on Harlan's face. Deep in the treeline, he could hear the French girl thrashing.

Soon Harlan would run. Right now, he wanted to savor the moment.

It was perfect.

TWENTY-SEVEN

Kane woke late and alone. In daylight, the room was cramped and messy and unfamiliar. Bedsprings squealed as he sat up in the narrow bed. Memory stirred in the air with the scent of freshly-sheared copper.

There was no sign of Maeve. Kane washed his face in the room's sink, dressed and went down the hall to the bathroom. He took his pack with him in case her door locked when it swung shut.

Maeve was working. Kane found her in the lobby, behind the big scarred front desk. He stood in front of a rack of color brochures for bungee jumping and jetboating and watched Maeve check in three young Japanese men.

They filled out their cards and paid for their bunks and tried not to be too obvious about sneaking looks down her shirt. After the three took their keys and left, Kane stood at the desk where they had been. The air smelled faintly of a medicinal and unfamiliar aftershave.

Maeve leaned across with both elbows on the counter. Her eyes were slanted and green, merry and wicked.

"So the sleeper awakens after all. I was starting to worry I'd killed you."

"For a while there I thought you had."

"The cheek of it." Maeve traced a pattern on the scarred wooden countertop. "So, if I remember right, today you're after moving on, yeah?"

Kane didn't reply. Maeve's look darkened.

"Don't be getting too far ahead of yourself, Yank," she said. "You're a fine ride. That doesn't give you a claim."

"I keep thinking about what you said last night." He placed one hand, big and brown and scarred, over Maeve's, small and white and just as scarred. "I can't get Bridey out of my head."

"Me either."

Maeve pulled her hand away. Kane tried to reconcile the tender and loving look in that old photo with the burning gaze facing him now.

A scrap of tune played in his head. A slow backbeat, weird chord changes in a minor key. Kane realized it wasn't one he knew.

"I have to stay," he said. "At least one more day."

***

Whispering Pines had fourteen bedrooms and eight baths. At first, the house's sheer size was intimidating to Beth, especially those endless, dark and twisting halls. But it turned out there wasn't actually that much cleaning. Those dark old halls didn't need as much work as those bright new places that showed every speck of dust. Also, most of those fourteen beds were in empty rooms. Beth wondered if anyone had ever slept in half of them. At any rate, there was not much to do in those rooms but dust and change the sheets once a week.

Mister Terrabonne's entourage was another story. Those four all stayed together on second east, and each one made enough mess for any three normal people. Cleaning those four rooms every day was work enough for twice as many maids.

Beth figured they got it from their boss. The man did not know how to pick up after himself. Didn't know, or didn't care. He was like a spoiled child. Any given morning, Mister Terrabonne's suite of rooms at the top of the house were a minefield of discarded clothes, wet towels and empty liquor bottles.

Terrabonne's man, that scary giant Mister Winters, wouldn't let any of the maids into his room. That was fine with Beth. The room was at the other end of the house, and the hallway outside had a lingering smell that reminded her of cat urine. The memory alone of his touch on her wrist made Beth shudder.

That morning was a strange one. Not one of those rooms in second east had been slept in, and there was no sign of that frightening Harlan Winters. For a change, the four girls were able to clean their scheduled rooms in less than an hour. That left vacuuming the halls and the master suite up on three, Mister Terrabonne's bedroom.

Today was Rebecca and Chrissy's turn to do the suite. Beth caught up with them in the hall.

"Hey, you guys want to switch?"

"Why, what've you got?"

"Halls."

"You serious, you want to trade hoovering for diaper duty?"

Beth's face burned, and she looked down at her shoes. From behind her, she heard Tanya's voice.

"I'll help her. I mean, if you two don't mind switching."

Rebecca and Chrissy looked at each other and shrugged. Tanya opened the wood panel that hid the entrance to the service stairs.

The panel opened silently and shut with a soft click. The inside of the stairwell was all hush and echoes. The steps were narrow, twisting and dark. The air smelled like strawberry perfume and cat musk.

"Winters really scared you that bad?" Tanya said when they were alone.

"I don't know what you mean."

"Come on, Beth. You haven't hoovered even once since he grabbed you in the hall the other day. Plus, I've seen you walk halfway round the house to keep from passing near his room."

Beth said nothing. Their footsteps scuffed on the bare concrete steps. Her fingers shook as she pressed the latch to open the panel at the top of the stairwell.

The two peeked out into the master suite.

"Bloody hell, Beth..." Tanya whispered. "What have you got us into?"

***

Kane ate at the Subway on Shotover. Two meatball subs got his energy back up, and by the time he was done eating Kane was certain: He was onto a new song.

He took the gondola up the face of Coronet Peak. At the summit, Kane bought a coffee at the lunchroom and took it to one of the outside tables. Not many tourists chose to sit out in the cold weather, even with the outdoor heaters. There was privacy, and unlike the interior of the sandwich shop, no threat of Kei$ha or Lady Gaga on the radio spoiling his concentration.

Kane sat at the far edge of the deck. The nearest tourists were a British family five tables away. Kane opened his pack, took out his Oskar, a tattered spiral notebook and a pencil. On the other side of the railing, people raced wheeled sleds down a concrete toboggan run. They seemed to be having fun.

Kane hummed a little under his breath. A scrap of tune, a couple of words. Definitely something. He flipped through his notebook until he found a blank page, hummed a little more, looked off into the distance and began to write.

TWENTY-EIGHT

Nothing good ever lasted.

Harlan sat with his back to the trunk of a tree. His legs lay out before him, wet and sticky. His arms hung heavy and sore and slick at his sides, and his stomach was unaccountably full and tight. The autumn sun streamed through the branches overhead, raking in at an angle that colored the air in thin shafts of golden light.

That angle changed as Harlan watched. Where the sunlight touched his jeans, the dark spattered patterns showed the brilliant color of dark ripe cherries.

The forest floor around him was churned, jagged scars of black earth showing through the leaves, immune to the dancing patterns of shadows and light.

Falling leaves hung in the air, flared like slow-moving sparks as they drifted through the spears of light. A scattering of beech leaves stuck to the wet legs of his jeans, gold coins on a bed of crimson.

Harlan had missed his moment. It had all been over too fast, the French girl gone before he knew it. It hadn't stopped anything, and there was still plenty of fun to be had with the broken rubber doll she became. But Harlan hated missing that one special moment when the light died in her eyes.

It had always been the same. Even as a little kid, it happened every time Harlan stole a candy bar from the little store at the four corners, or filched enough out of his grandmother's purse to buy one. He'd always meant to make it last, but somehow it never worked out that way. He'd be hunkered down in his special place, hidden among the cattails and cypress and rusted engine parts.

Harlan's jaw ached. When he raised a hand to wipe his mouth, it came away sticky.

One minute, he'd be looking down at his Snickers, or Hershey, or Baby Ruth. Whatever. Snickers were always Harlan's favorite. The wrapper would crinkle in his fingers, waxy and beautiful and full of promise. Next thing Harlan knew, he'd be lying there with that brown goo smeared all over his hands and mouth and the worst fucking stomach ache you ever imagined.

Then there was that one time. That first time Harlan found a kitten.

Shadows gathered around the roots of the trees. The spears of light faded, and vanished. Soon, the crooked shafts of the beeches were pale smudges in a thin and purple gloaming.

Pattering drops of rain began to rattle the leaves in the trees.

In the past, Harlan had always been so careful. He waited, sometimes for years, until the time was right. This time he had taken a terrible risk. This time he may have made a mistake.

Mexico was one thing. This time, Harlan had done it in a country where the cops were actually on top of things. The thought of life in a cage crackled like ice across Harlan's skin.

Nausea overtook him. Harlan had only a moment to feel his gorge rise before a cascade of butcher-shop liquid struck his shirt and belly. He fell over on his side and retched until he was empty.

In the end, it was that moment of panic that spurred Harlan into action. He meant to keep breathing free air. That meant getting those bodies buried by nightfall.

***

124

That afternoon, Kane rode the gondola back down the side of the mountain. The cables overhead groaned and keened and the little car rocked in the wind.

The song wasn't what Kane had expected. He looked down at what he'd written.

The lyrics told of love and loss, of loneliness and the terrible cost of vengeance to the human soul.

The song was unlike anything Kane had ever written. He called it *Bad Angel Blues.*

The tune wasn't his normal stuff either. Normally, Sonny Terry's influence was strong in Kane's work. This song had none of Terry's breezy riffs. Its rhythms were closer to Robert Johnson or Leadbelly, and Kane had struggled for almost two hours trying to nail down the weird, almost eerie chord changes he heard in his head.

Mist-shrouded pine trees passed under the floor of the gondola. The rooftops of Queenstown weren't even in sight yet. Kane used the time and the privacy to take out his harmonica and run through the new song a couple more times. The inflections on the chord changes came out just the way Kane wanted. That was the thing about the blues: what was hard to set down on paper was sometimes easy to do by feel.

The gondola descended into the cloud. Queenstown's buildings came closer, darker gray in the swirling pale mist. Icy drops spit against the heated glass.

Kane put away his notebook and his harp. It wasn't long before the gondola car was level with those rooftops, then down among them. A great wheeled engine took the car, brought it level with the deck and moved it through the building at the speed of a slow walk.

The doors slid open. Kane stepped out and followed the yellow lines. Up ahead, the two young Japanese men from that morning got into the empty car. Its doors slid shut again, and the car was drawn back up the side of the mountain.

It was nowhere near four yet. Kane was feeling good, and he had time to kill.

TWENTY-NINE

"I can't believe you, Beth. We could have been vacuuming the halls."

"It's not that bad."

"No, it's worse."

The master suite was a bomb site. Tanya and Beth stepped fully into the room. Beth snapped open a black plastic rubbish sack and began to fill it with trash.

Tanya bit down a rush of anger and resentment. Any normal day, they knew to expect clothes, discarded towels and empty bottles, sometimes the stub ends of cigars, wet and chewed. This was worse.

For one thing, there were twice as many bottles and towels. Empties and half-empties stood on every horizontal surface and lay discarded on the floor. The towels were sopping wet, often streaked and stained. The bed linen was all but destroyed.

"Looks like somebody had a serious party."

"Tanya--"

"Relax. It's not like there's anyone around to hear."

"I need this job," Beth said. She dropped empty bottles into the rubbish sack. They hit with a sound like a TV car crash.

Tanya didn't answer. She shook a cotton laundry bag open and stuffed it with soiled towels.

The two worked in silence for a time. Tanya filled two laundry bags, and Beth packed three black plastic sacks. "Hey, hold up a minute?"

Tanya grabbed the handful of finger-length metal cylinders before Beth got a chance to biff them out.

"What're those, nitrous?"

"Better... Amyl nitrate." Tanya shook the cylinders, one at a time, next to her ear. "All empty, though. Worse luck."

She threw the amyls into Beth's rubbish bag. They landed ringing.

Tanya figured it was a damn shame their uniforms had no pockets.

They worked together to strip Terrabonne's bed. Neither commented on the smells, or the stains on the sheets.

The master suite had two bathrooms. They took the main one first: wide white marble counters and a great sunken hot tub. They did the shower room second. The big tiled cube was larger than Tanya's entire room downstairs. Six shower heads were set high in the white tile.

A lone towel hung from its hook next to the door on the bedroom side. Three more sat folded in the rack. Tanya used the one on the hook to help Beth wipe down the wet tiles and threw it into the laundry sack. She left Beth to finish the shower room and headed into the lounge.

The lounge room was neat. Poison neat. Not a thing was out of place, and the air smelled faintly sour, chemical and toxic.

Tanya hesitated. There was nothing to do in this room, but the alternative was helping Beth pull long black hair out of the shower drains. Tanya adjusted the spines of some of the magazines on the coffee table and plumped the cushions on the couches.

Her fingers brushed metal. Tanya reached further down between the cushions. Whatever was wedged down there was smooth and thin, plastic and metal. She got it between her fingers and pulled.

The MP3 player was state of the art. It was the new generation one, with movie downloads and web browsing and everything. A player like this one went for close to a thousand dollars.

Tanya looked over her shoulder and bit her lip. Beth was still on her knees in the shower room, fussing with the drains. Tanya lifted the hem of her uniform, tucked the MP3 player under the waistband of her panties.

The cool metal warmed quickly against her skin. Tanya stood and looked down at herself, pushed the player further down so that nothing showed.

That done, she straightened her uniform and went to help her friend.

**

Maeve spotted Kane on Brecon Street, down the hill from the gondola. The Yank had a range of leg on him, and he made good time with those long strides.

She idled at the curb for a time, watching the man walk. When he looked like cutting through the woods, Maeve pulled up alongside and blipped the horn.

"It's me, ya bollix," she called into the empty treeline. He'd been right there not a moment before. Maeve tapped the horn again and laughed.

Kane stepped back out of the trees.

"Don't just stand there, man. It's bloody freezing!"

Kane climbed in and pulled the door shut. He set his pack on the floor between his feet. Maeve dropped the truck into gear and let out the clutch. The 4x4 pulled away in a low diesel rumble.

They rolled down the street. Maeve sat tall behind the wheel, watching Kane out of the corner of her eye. She answered his unvoiced question.

"The truck's Dermott's. That old baggage behind the bar at The Bunker?"

"Yeah?" The Yank wasn't able to keep the tightness out of his voice. Kind of charming, really.

"Feck off. Not only is the old bugger practically a fossil, it'd be like incest."

Kane turned in his seat. The man had a silence about him, a deep quiet way that invited a body to fill it with talk.

"Dermott's about the only friend I have in this place. He thinks I'm every bit as crazy as you do, mind, but he's a good man, and kind."

"Hell of a truck." Kane bounced one palm on the doorsill.

"Aye. Something of a hobby with the old man. Dermott lets me borrow his baby every now and again, mostly as he knows I'll treat her right."

It was warm in the cab, and isolated. The look Kane gave her made Maeve warmer. It felt good to take her mind off bad business.

"Good day?" he said.

"Ah, the worst. Busy at the front desk all morning, and I had a couple do a runner on their bill."

"Weren't French by any chance, were they?"

Maeve looked across the cab of the truck at Kane. "Couple in a bar tried to sell me an MP3 player, I got the impression they were down on their luck. Coming out of the hostel last night, they looked totally miserable."

"I can imagine. They owed over four hundred dollars." Maeve flicked the wheel to avoid a couple of laughing young drunks staggering into the street.

"My own fault, of course. They were paid up ahead for a time, and after that I was the one as let them slide."

"Think you might lose your job?"

Maeve's look was answer enough.

The big public carparks, the backpacker hostel where they stayed and the buildings and fields at the local school, all slid past like phantoms on the far side of the truck's fogged windows. Maeve adjusted the vents, warm air channeled against the glass and the windows began to clear.

Seconds later, downtown Queenstown lay behind them. The businesses along the sides of the road sold cars and boats and scuba tank refills. A supermarket called New World slid past on their right.

"You've been on the road a while, yeah Yank?"

"Ten years."

"That was young. Runaway, or just keen to be seeing the world?"

"Something like that."

Maeve waited for Kane to say more. After a time, she spoke again.

"Close to your family?"

"Reckon I was, once."

"Not me. Fourteen I was. Bridey and I left the place where they kept us and ran as far as we could. Told those as asked we were eighteen. No one believed us for a minute, but it was still the right answer."

"Maeve--"

"Don't, Yank. Just don't." She flicked on her turn signal, and the logging truck ahead crowded to the side so that she could pass.

"My point is, I know you don't believe me about Bridey, but for most of me life, she's been the closest to family I've ever had. All the love I've ever known."

Kane sat back in his seat. His mouth was set and grim, his amber eyes fixed on a point in the far distance.

After that, the truck rumbled along a curving two-lane. Maeve dropped the hammer and smiled as Dermott's truck surged on the open highway. Autumn woods surrounding them flew past in a blur of brown and gray, a blaze of green and gold.

Frost clung blue-white in the shadows. Melting ice sparkled in the sunlight, dripped from the branches of trees and filled the air with a lively wet shimmer.

It was nothing like Ireland. Maeve was glad for that.

The road twisted, dipped and climbed. Maeve took the curves with grace and skill, showing off a little. The Yank sat with white-knuckled hands gripped tight on the dashboard. His eyes were on the sheer granite rockface and the empty space where the edge of the road fell away. He seemed blind to those moments when twists in the road opened onto sudden and breathtaking visions of snow-capped peaks and vast dark forested gorges.

***

Arrowtown's buildings glittered like tiny stones in its autumn bed of reds and golds. Maeve engine-braked as they came out of the mountains, and Kane breathed a sigh of relief.

They parked in a leafy open area between the river and the town's single parking lot. Leaves crunched underfoot and drifted down in slow lazy spirals. Three large tour buses sat on the asphalt, diesel fumes shimmering in the bright cold sun. A young family panned for gold at the water's edge.

The town itself was a single main street, closed to vehicle traffic, heavy on the cafes and galleries.

Kane and Maeve walked along the main drag, the Wild West feel even stronger than in Queenstown, same with the upscale boutique atmosphere. A lot of the places to eat had menus posted out front, or specials chalked on sidewalk blackboards.

The street was filled with tourists, most gray-haired and overweight. Even the younger people milling around looked nothing like Kane and Maeve.

The town was built in a small flat notch between the Remarkables and a quick, twisting river. Under all the cafes and art galleries and souvenir shops, the town still wore its Old West bones: a single main street of low, false-fronted buildings complete with hitching rings, hand pumps and water troughs, and another, residential street running parallel to the main drag. Two thirds of the length of that second street, the homes were tidy, bright and dollhouse-neat. Maeve was more interested in the farther end of the street, where faded paint peeled away from warped boards and dead leaves lay in heavy drifts right up to the walls. Those homes were still uninhabited: cobwebs and dust stood thick and gray in the remaining window glass.

At its far end, the town butted into the foothills of the Remarkables. The single straight street gave way to a twisted maze of modern asphalt climbing into the hills. The houses there had cars in the driveway and satellite dishes on the roofs. Pale trunks rose into the autumn sky: beech, elm, birch and oak, and the hills were carpeted in fallen leaves: brown and scarlet and gold. There were four churches on the tops of the tallest hills.

The town churchyard lay on the exposed face of a bare hill. Twisted trees and wind-blasted grass clustered among the sunken graves. A low iron fence rusted at crazy angles on the three sides of the graveyard.

Maeve raised the latch and the gate screeched on its hinges. The shrieking metal cry was torn away by the voice of the winter wind.

They walked a while among the graves. The markers ranged from simple slabs of stone or wood, worn, weathered and unreadable, to elaborate Victorian cenotaphs, crosses and veiled urns and praying angels all shrouded in lichen and moss.

"I've been thinking about what you said last night."

"Aye?" Maeve studied the gravestone in front of her, five infants dead in the same year.

"I can't get Bridey's face out of my mind."

The skin tightened around Maeve's eyes, but she said nothing.

"I keep thinking about her, about what happened." Kane didn't mention the song he'd written. His palm touched the weathered corner of the tombstone, cold, mossy and rough.

"I have a few questions."

Maeve thrust her fists into her pockets and kicked at a piece of loose turf.

"How did Bridey die?"

"I don't know."

"No autopsy in Mexico? Or wouldn't they let you see the report?"

"No body." Maeve spoke around an unlit cigarette. Her lighter kept blowing out in the wind. "Whatever that bastard did with my Bridey, her body's never been found."

"Then--"

"Because I fecking *felt* it, that's how. Half a world away, I felt the pain and terror of my best friend's death."

"And you haven't heard from her since?"

Maeve shot him a filthy look over the top of her cigarette.

"I mean," Kane said, "There's no chance she just hasn't been in touch, maybe avoiding you or something?"

She snapped the wheel of her lighter several more times. No matter how she turned her body or cupped her hands, Maeve was unable to shelter the flame.

"You said yourself the two of you had been fighting."

"Fecking Jaysus, you sound like the bloody Mexican razzers. Don't believe me, see what I care." Maeve threw her unlit cigarette on the ground. Her coat, her dreadlocks, made black flapping shapes against the winter sky.

"Look," Kane said, "If Bridey was murdered like you say, we need to find the killer, *whoever* he might be, and bring him to justice."

"And you're going to help me, is that it?"

"Well..."

"Just ride in on your white horse and rescue the damsel in distress. And did it ever once occur to you that I might not *want* your help?"

"Maeve--"

"No! You've no part in this, Yank. Stay out."

Kane stood up.

"What are you going to do, kill a man because you *suspect* he might have been involved in your friend's disappearance?"

Maeve glared at Kane. Her skin was bone-white and stretched tight across her skull. The flesh around her eye sockets was dark and sunken.

"Look, we all know how enough money can make people feel like they're above the law." Kane kept his voice deep and soft. "If you had proof it'd be one thing. But all you have is intuition and suspicion."

Kane took a step closer. Maeve didn't give an inch.

"Taking your revenge on the wrong man would be bad enough," he said. "And if you're wrong, the real killer gets away."

The two faced each other among the moss-crusted graves. A blistering wind howled through the stones, and Maeve's breath hissed through her teeth. Her shoulders heaved as her breath came, short and sharp and ragged.

THIRTY

Harlan straightened from his work and shivered. The day hadn't been warm to start with. With the dying of the light, the temperature dropped below freezing.

Out under the open sky, a thin line of flame lit the western sky. The ridgeline and the forest were towering black presences, and the first dim stars were already visible overhead.

The earth was frozen, the mud like concrete. Half an hour slashing and hacking with the camp shovel, and all Harlan had to show for it was an ankle-deep trench no wider than a dinner plate.

By the time Harlan got that hole dug, he'd have nothing but bones to drop in it.

Even on thirty-eight hundred acres of private land, there was no guarantee some bunch of hikers or trampers, quad bikers or horse trampers, wouldn't wander past.

In the end, Harlan dumped the bodies in a steep low gully. He laid the two French kids out on the ribbon of gravel at the bottom and used the camp shovel to drop the wet clay walls on top of them. In no time at all, the sharp-sided ditch was little more than a wide shallow dent in the soggy green hillside.

Harlan staggered back to his four wheel drive. He felt flat and empty and sad. He felt like he might sleep for a week.

***

Jack Terrabonne spent the afternoon in his recording studio. Every one of his houses, everywhere in the world, had full facilities. After all, there was no way to tell when inspiration might strike.

That little old French gal, that Chloe, was one hell of an inspiration. Didn't speak a damn word of English, but what a firecracker. Her and that fellah of hers, Emil. Today, Jack was on fire. Bit hung over, sure, but he hadn't had a writing day like this in years. Not since that one gal, back in '77. Her name escaped him for a moment.

Skeeter. That was it. Only name Jack ever had for her. Truth be told, Jack never knew too much at all about Skeeter, but he could remember his time with her like it was yesterday.

Scabby knees and a crooked smile. Denim cutoffs and cowboy boots. That kind of saucy and dangerous look, daring the big dog to step into her yard. She had Jack from the moment their eyes locked.

Couple weeks later, Jack finally woke up sober. Skeet was missing, along with all of Jack's cash and a ten thousand dollar Rolex. What he was left with was a dose of clap and three spools of magnetic tape.

Little shot of penicillin got rid of the dose. What was on those masters paid for three of Jack's houses and two of his divorces.

It was the stuff of legend: Jack Terrabonne calling his band into the studio one afternoon, illegible scribbled notes in one hand, bombed out of his mind. That one single session, the band tried to keep up as Jack laid down track after track, hit after hit. In just five hours, Jack recorded the masters to *Backdoor Boogie, Fishin' Down* and his biggest hit, *Black Cat Blues.*

Jack didn't remember a damn thing about that session. He didn't need to: he had the legend and the royalties. And he had his memories of Skeeter.

Jack picked a quick riff on the Les Paul. He stopped, backed up and played a different version. Later on, in the mixing booth, he'd pick out the one he liked best.

The studio door opened. Some damn fool couldn't see the light on over the door. Jack flicked the switch to stop recording. Too much background noise from the hall, and a pretty little maid standing in the doorway.

"Wow. Mister Terrabonne... that was really neat."

Jack flashed his teeth. Those Kiwi accents he could just listen to all day. He shifted the sling of his guitar and hitched one foot on a rung of the stool. What Jack thought of as his musical genius pose.

"Sir, you wanted something?"

"I was just wondering," he said. "Y'all know if Harlan's around? Big old boy, runs my errands for me?"

The maid jumped back like something bit her.

"No sir. We haven't seen him today, or any of your-- your others, either."

Poor little thing was nervous. Hard to blame her, walking down that long hall with all those golds and platinums hanging in frames. Gals always loved the big dog, even if it did make em a little bit nervous.

"Don't worry darling, that's fine." He shot the cuff of his pants leg over his boots. Custom-made hand-stitched ostrich leather, over five thousand dollars.

"So," he said, "liked that song, did you?"

"Sure." The maid dropped her eyes and blushed. Jack swelled with pride.

"Some of that old music still sounds all right."

Jack's smile snapped shut. "What took you so long? I musta rung over an hour ago."

"I only just--"

"And where'd everybody run off to, anyway? You know when I got up I had to make my own damn tomato juice?"

"I--"

"Just hand over my aspirin and let me get back to work."

"But... you didn't--"

The little thing was about ready to cry. Jack looked her up and down, from trembling lip to shaking knees. He couldn't resist the urge to punish the girl for making him feel bad.

"No excuses. Shut your mouth and fetch my damn aspirin. And don't you know better than to walk in when that light's on? These here recordings pay your damn salary."

When the girl didn't move fast enough, Jack brought his hands together in a single explosive clap.

"Today!"

Watching her scoot out of the room, Jack was reminded of the cute little ass on that Chloe. The maid wasn't quite so round or pert, though it was hard to tell with those godawful uniforms the agency made them wear. Still, it was something to think about: he was the big dog, and she was right there in his back yard.

Come on in the Big Dog's yard. Yeah, Jack liked the sound of that. Drop a bouncy little beat behind it, maybe something scorchy and dark in the melody...

Jack shifted his guitar back onto his knee. He flicked the switch back to record.

That first riff was red-hot magic. These songs were going to be hits. Jack had a good feeling.

He wondered if the maid had a boyfriend. Somebody frail and pale.

***

Back in Queenstown, Maeve and Kane wandered the botanical gardens. Most of the flowers had gone dormant for the winter, but the roses still hung like heavy drops of blood in the deepening red light.

The gloaming did little to soften Kane's features. Instead, the sunset light called attention to the hard planes in his face and the dark hollows of his eyes. Maeve curled her fingers inside the curve of Kane's scarred and muscled hand.

The air was biting and cold. Kane's hand was dry and warm.

"Stay with me tonight," he said.

Maeve stopped walking. Kane's face stood above her in deepening shadow, and she breathed in the clean warm smell of the man's skin. Her mouth twisted into a brittle painful shape.

"I can't. There's work to be getting on with."

Kane touched her hair. "Not the hostel?"

"No. Not the hostel."

"You have a plan?"

"Not so much. The bastard drinks most nights in The Bunker, and he's got an eye for the women. I figure I can work the rest out as I go."

Kane was silent. Behind him, the lake reflected the black jagged teeth of the mountains and the burning sky.

A lick of wind shrilled in off the lake. Black hair blew wild around Kane's face, and Maeve thought of the tattered shreds of some dead knight's banner.

"You never mention the man's name."

"It took me two years to get this close. I can't have you warning him off."

Deep in the shadowed planes of his face, Kane's amber eyes seemed to hold the last glowing sparks of the now-vanished sun.

"I could go there tonight. Be waiting when you make your move."

Maeve eyed him sideways.

"That you could. Don't suppose a body could do much with you following her about."

"No."

Maeve bit her lip. The deep red of the roses around them was almost black in the gloaming.

"Might as well call it a night then."

She hooked one arm around Kane's waist and bumped him with her hip. The wind off the lake was stinging her eyes.

"One last night."

THIRTY-ONE

Harlan brought the muddy Range Rover out of the hills. Off-roading in the dark and over muddy wet ridgeline was tricky business, even with the GPS and the racks of halogen floods to light his way. Without them, it would have been damn near suicidal.

Sensible thing to do would have been to stay the night. There was an old hunting lodge off in that part of the hills. It wasn't much more than a shack. Four walls, cobwebs and canned goods, damn thing hadn't been used since sometime in the eighties. Harlan would have been warm enough there, and safe from prying eyes. But that also would have meant spending the night less than a quarter mile from the French kids' graves.

Harlan gripped the steering wheel and shuddered.

Normally, the thought of his girls was a comfort. Jamaica or Tennessee, Nevada or Mexico , Harlan knew they were tucked away and waiting for him. Revisiting them, looking at the places they were buried and seeing what had grown there was deeply satisfying.

But that was in daylight. After dark was a different story. No way in hell Harlan Winters wanted his little darlings anywhere near him at night.

A knot loosened in his chest when Harlan finally saw the lights of Whispering Pines.

He guided the Range Rover around a large stand of old-growth pine and followed the lights of the main house back to the courtyard. The south wing was lit up like the deck of a cruise ship. Jack was in his studio, burning the midnight oil.

Perfect.

He didn't bother to pull inside the car barn. The truck was going to need a serious scrubdown in the morning anyway, and Harlan's thoughts were of warm showers and soft beds.

Until he saw the police cars.

Two units sat on the oval of white gravel at the front of the main house. White, with blue and orange checkerboards painted down their sides and racks of red and blue lights on the roof. Neither unit had its lights on, and there was no sign of the drivers.

Harlan's hand went to the butt of his gun. The Rover had less than half a tank, and it was too damn slow anyway. He thought about Jack's Porsche in the garage, wondered if it would outhandle those zippy little Jap police cars on these mountain roads.

Harlan thought about how far he might get. He thought about how much more of a head start he might have if the cops in those two cars were dead.

"Winters!" The voice came from inside the open front door. It was deep and authoritative, and also familiar. Harlan had just seen the man a couple nights ago, drunk and fondling an out-of-town hooker.

Of course, it only seemed fitting that District Superintendent Hollings would want to be the one to take Harlan down.

"That is Winters, isn't it?"

Hollings came down the steps onto the drive. Harlan turned, the flap of his coat casually tucked back over the butt of the gun. For this man, Harlan wanted to use his hands.

"That maid staff of yours is bloody useless."

"Yeah?"

"Nobody seems to know where that boss of yours is. That, or they don't want to tell me. Bloody stupid, either way."

Harlan didn't move.

"Don't suppose you know where Mister Jack is, then?"

"Sorry. Fact is, I just got here myself."

"That so?" The cop flicked his chin the direction the Range Rover. In the faint wash of light from the mansion's windows, the truck showed a spattered muddy two-tone, all the way to the doorsills.

"You weren't out four-wheeling in these hills at night? Mucking around like that, you're lucky you didn't break your bloody neck."

Harlan's eyes narrowed and his nostrils flared, but the cop didn't smell like violence.

"Wasn't my idea to stay out after dark," Harlan said. "I got stuck."

"Explains the wardrobe, I suppose."

Harlan's face tightened. He'd been covered in dark mud and clay for so long, he'd completely forgotten how he must look. He hoped the black dirt spattered, caked and drying on his skin and clothes hid the blood.

If not, the cop would have to die.

"What brings you out, officer? Come for a couple of drinks, shoot a little pool?"

The cop hard-eyed Harlan.

"Business." The cop hitched a thumb back in the direction of the house. "Returning four of your own. You'll want to have a talk with those lads."

Harlan let out a soft curse.

"Two of them were badly beaten last night. Up until a couple of hours ago they were still in hospital."

"Yeah?" Harlan's first thought was of JD asking after Bridey Murphy and coming home with a broken nose.

"The owner of that strip club, *Diamonds,* said they'd been thrown out earlier that night. Sound of things, they should have spent the night in jail."

"Goddammit." Harlan wiped his face. "Of all the dumb-ass..."

"Look, that security staff of Lasker's are a bunch of rough bastards, but they swear up and down they weren't the ones gave your lads such a thrashing."

"How bad?"

"Two of them, cuts and scrapes, nothing serious. About what you'd expect. But you've got one man with a spiral fracture to the right arm and another with cracked ribs, whiplash and head injuries. The hospital staff thought he'd been hit by a car."

Harlan looked at the lighted face of Whispering Pines and gnashed his teeth.

"Some of those bouncers are ex-cons, violent offenders. I asked your lads if they wanted to press charges."

"Yeah?"

"They said they slipped on some ice. All four of them."

"Not one of them was able to identify their attackers, or even willing to sign a complaint."

"Yeah?"

"According to them, they all slipped on the same icy sidewalk."

"I see." Harlan used the toe of his boot to dig a dark scar in the frosted ground.

"Listen, Winters--" The cop raised a hand to touch Harlan, thought better of it and let the hand drop. "Mister Terrabonne's not the wealthiest, or the most famous person in this community. But he *is* one of my favorites, and God knows that poor man's been through enough in the press. I'll keep his name out of this, but you need to put a leash on those lads."

"One night off..." Harlan muttered under his breath.

"Petty theft, drunken brawls, the odd lost hiker. That's most of what we deal with here in Queenstown. There's no room in this town for anyone, *anyone*, setting out to pursue a private vendetta."

The knot in Harlan's chest eased. The cop's words had the flavor of a well-worn lecture, and it was a lecture he delivered on his way back to the squad car.

"Don't worry," Harlan said. "I'll have them on their best behavior." He thought about smiling, but he knew the effect his smiles had on people. The cop stopped with his car door open and one hand on the sill. The interior light burned behind him, cheery and bright.

"You said you got stuck? You mean bogged down?"

"Ground looked a lot more solid than it was."

"While you were digging yourself out, did you cut yourself with the shovel or something?"

"Tree branch." Harlan's lie was quick and reflexive. "Why?"

"You might want to get that looked at," the cop said. "You've got blood all over your face."

THIRTY-TWO

A skin of ice floated on the surface of the horse trough. Harlan broke the ice with his fists. The cold bit deep.

The water burned his face. Clouds of red and muddy brown spread from Harlan's hands when he put them back in the trough. By the time his face was clean, Harlan felt like he was wearing thick leather gloves. He closed his clumsy fists on his wet hair, found it already icy and stiff.

An iron cowbell hung from a nail by the water trough. The striker, a rusted lump of pig iron that might once have been a tool, hung next to it on a weathered piece of cord. Harlan grabbed the striker and banged it into the bell over and over. The sound echoed through the pine forest and throughout the house.

The boys came shuffling outside. They followed the light, found Harlan standing in the center of the horse barn. Steam rose from his arms and shoulders, and on every side of him horses screeched and kicked in their stalls.

They were a sorry-looking bunch. Bumps and bruises and bandages all over the place. JD stood in the center of them, one arm bulked out huge in a fresh plaster cast, looking the worse for wear and guilty as hell.

"Well? Who wants to start talking?"

Nobody spoke.

Harlan pulled his piece and those four pains in his ass shrunk back. For the second time in twenty-four hours, Harlan flipped open the gate on the .44 and dumped the shells into his palm.

"I'm not sure I trust myself not to shoot one of you assholes. You, Farrel. Start talking."

Farrel scratched his beard, his hand pale and shaking. He had a white foam collar around his neck, and the whites of his eyes had gone unnaturally dark with broken blood vessels.

"Well, see, it was like this..." Harlan cut him off with a chop of his hand.

"Last time I talked to old JD here, he was going on and on about how y'all were gonna get back at them three guys from the night before. It *was* three, right? Or was it four?"

"Four," Turk said. "I think he said four." JD kicked him in the ankle.

"So you geniuses went out on the town looking for trouble and got your asses handed to you. Again."

Turk made an indistinct noise deep in his throat. Callum stared at the floor and kept silent.

"What," Harlan said, "this damn feud you got with this local gang ain't enough, you got to get into it with the staff at this town's one titty bar?"

"Wasn't Lasker." Farrel scratched at his beard where it met the foam collar. "It was one of that bunch jumped JD."

JD shot Farrel a filthy look. Farrel didn't seem notice.

"Me'n Farrel did fine til the guy's friends showed up," JD said. "Buncha sneaky bastards, crept up on us with a sneak attack."

"So much for your revenge."

JD's reply was muttered underneath his breath.

Harlan flicked his wrist. The gate of the .44 snapped closed with a loud steel crack.

"This shit ends here. It ends now. I don't give a damn this other bunch march the lot of you naked down the middle of a public street, y'all go against me and they'll never find your goddamned bodies!"

Harlan stopped short. The boys were looking at him funny. He looked down at the gun in his hand and slapped it back in its holster.

He was bone-tired. There was mud and blood and all kinds of stuff Harlan didn't want to think about crusting his clothes and his skin. The barn was full of body-heat and horse-smell and screaming, thumping, pounding noises from the stalls around him. And every time he closed his eyes, Harlan saw that sweet little French girl, her nostrils and mouth plugged with wet clay.

Harlan got in JD's face. It felt good to see the man flinch.

"I won't have Jack Terrabonne's name dragged through the gutter on account of your personal grudge." Harlan's voice was thick and heavy, a low growl. "That is the one and only reason your sorry asses aren't out on the side of the highway right now. Now y'all can kick your own asses, I'm taking a shower."

Harlan shouldered JD out of the way. He stalked out of the barn, away from the noise of the screaming horses.

As he went, Harlan thumbed the bullets back into his gun.

***

Some damn fool was banging on a cowbell. In the engineering booth, Jack Terrabonne looked up in annoyance. Whoever the hell was making that racket was just lucky he was done recording.

Jack wondered what happened to his band. Used to be a day, he never went anywhere without his full band in tow. Back in the 80's, he even hauled his entire horn section along with him, just in case he thought up something for those guys to play.

Not that he did. Nothing worthwhile, anyway. After that one magic afternoon in '77, Jack pretty much fell off the charts until the mid-90's, when Callum played fiddle on a string of country ballads and bluegrass gospel.

That was all years ago. There was no one big event. The guys just sort of dropped off, a little bit at a time. An argument here, a better gig there. Even Callum finally decided he'd rather drive and cook Jack's meals than play in his band.

Now, those rare times he did have a live gig or short tour, Jack hired studio players. Rest of the time, he was alone.

Better that way. No one to interfere in his genius. In the studio, Jack covered his own keyboards, and the synth showed the hired boys what their parts ought to sound like. And mixing tracks on the computer, that wasn't much more than a few mouseclicks.

Talent Jack could hire. Inspiration like those French kids'd given him, that was rare. He wondered if he ought to see about putting Chloe and Emil on staff.

THIRTY-THREE

Maeve shifted her hips, caught her rhythm and let it build. Beneath her, Kane's eyes were full of tender and liquid lights. The American looked for all the world like some sort of love-struck puppy.

She raked her nails across the half-healed scratches on his chest. Kane hissed and arched against her, all hint of softness gone from his face. Deep inside the black hood of her dreads, Maeve's lips curled away from her teeth.

The puppy she didn't need. She liked her men rough.

Later, as the sweat cooled, Maeve curled in on herself, biting the edge of one thumb. Kane was like some kind of big dumb dog, warm against her back and running one leathery hand over her arm in long clumsy strokes.

There was no sign of Bridey in the room. Hadn't been since last night, when Kane first came to her bed.

Maeve tried to imagine life without even the ghost of her friend.

"This was a mistake."

Her voice sounded low and faint, as though it came from the mouth of a faraway stranger. Kane's hand stopped moving.

"I should be at The Bunker right now. Instead, here I am lying in bed with the likes of you."

"That so bad?"

Maeve turned over. The silent hurt look on his face was like a punch in the chest.

"It was just supposed to be the one night. One last chance to cut loose before the hard times to come." Maeve shook her head. "Bloody eejit I was."

"So this is one more night."

"You just don't get it, do you?" She drew the bedsheet close against her body. "Once I knew what I had to do, I set myself to it. I've no talent for a bare-handed killer, and it's not like I'd be able to get me hands on a gun. So I found the best knife-men I could, and I learned every single bloody thing they had to teach."

Maeve's fingertips unconsciously traced the glossy stripes of scar tissue on her other arm.

"I paid what it cost," she said. "Now all I have to do is get close enough, and I'll send that bastard where he sent my Bridey."

"You know you won't get away with it." Kane's mouth was flat and set, his face dark and grim.

"The thought *had* occurred." Maeve twisted her mouth halfway close to a smile. "Before, with all those rough types in his entourage, it would've been suicide. Thanks to you, I figure now it's just nine chances in ten I get to grow old in prison."

Maeve ran one palm, small and white, over the broad length of Kane's thigh, the sturdy heft of the man's upper arms.

"I went into this with me eyes open, Yank. Every day for nearly two years, I've hardened my soul to what I had to do. I've stayed strong, stayed focused. For Bridey."

Maeve struggled to bite back her tears. Kane's fingers brushed her elbow, and she threatened to lose it entirely.

"Now here I am, almost at the finish, and all I can think is *Not yet, please God, just one more night.*"

Kane's arms folded around her. He pulled her to him, held her against his chest. The tears did come then, hot and ugly and gasping and raw. Grief came roaring out of her, every tear Maeve hadn't shed since that one terrible afternoon, screaming Bridey's death on a street crowded with uncaring strangers.

The man's arms were strong. The skin on his chest was warm and tough. Maeve wept until there was nothing left.

"Tomorrow," she said, "in the morning..."

"Yeah?"

"You have to go."

THIRTY-FOUR

"Hey, Beth?"

Beth hit pause on her Shuffle and took out her earbuds. Tanya stood in the doorway to her room.

"Hey yourself. You notice they didn't lock us in tonight?"

"Yeah..."

"You think they just forgot, or do you think we're going to have some kind of night duties on later, like a function or something. They'd have told us though, right?"

"I don't know, probably." Tanya said. She moved around Beth's room, fingertips gliding over brushes and makeup and clothes.

"Hey, if they do leave us unlocked tonight, you wanna sneak out, maybe do a little exploring?"

"Sure," Tanya said. "But first, can I use your charger?"

"What for?"

"To charge my MP3 player, silly." Tanya pulled a thin square of black plastic from the pocket of her jeans, totally nonchalant. The screen lit up bright blue when she rubbed one finger across its face.

Two unfamiliar people smiled out from the screensaver. Tanya toggled over to the music menu before Beth got a good look at their faces.

"I didn't think you had an MP3. You always listen to CDs."

"I've had this a while now, but I didn't bring my charger with me, so I was stuck with that boring old CD player for backup. So can I use your charger?"

"Sure, I guess. It's over there plugged into the wall."

"Cool! Um, Beth? One other thing..."

"Sure, what?"

"Do you have any spare headphones?"

***

Jack Terrabonne couldn't sleep. Some nights, it wasn't in the cards. Especially not when his manager had his newest song.

By 2AM, Jack was fed up waiting for a reply on the email. He yanked the phone cord out of the laptop and dialed direct.

Delton Adams picked up on the fourth ring. His voice was muzzy and slurred.

"Jesus, Jack. You have any idea what time it is?"

"Never mind that. You listen to that song I sent?"

A long muffled sound from the other end of the line. "Can't this wait until morning?"

"You mean it ain't light out in L.A.?" Jack tapped a guitar pick against the polished surface of his desktop. "Did you listen to it or didn't you?"

"As a matter of fact, I did." Jack heard the shush and thump of a sliding door followed by the cry of seagulls. "I wanted to give the files another listen at the office before I emailed my notes."

"C'mon, hoss. Short version."

"It was pretty good, Jack. You're definitely getting closer."

Jack Terrabonne silently punched the air.

"You're still overproducing," Delton said. "But at least the lyrics are better, more heartfelt."

"Heartfelt, sure. You got that one right, hoss." Jack closed his eyes, pictured California at dawn, silver water running over hammered-steel sand.

"So..." he said. "We talking single, album, what?"

"Jack, listen. You're on the right track, but this is still..."

"Rough?"

"No." The ocean sounds vanished as Adams stepped back inside. "The song's not rough at all. That's the problem."

"Come again?" The guitar pick snapped in Jack's fingers.

"*Sweetback Baby* is still too slick. You know what I liked best in those files you sent? That little scrap of *Tobacco Road* you tucked in with the guitar track."

"Look, hoss, I'm sorry about that. That was just a little warm-up is all. I ain't had a whole lot of sleep the last couple nights, must of left that one in by accident."

"But that's what I'm trying to tell you, Jack. You and your guitar and a little heartfelt pain, *that's* the Jack Terrabonne I can sell."

"So *Sweetback* ain't worth a damn neither."

"I didn't say that." Jack heard a refrigerator open and close. "I've got a guy, very hot right now. He's going to take a look, see what he thinks."

"You wouldn't kid an old man now, would you?"

"What can I tell you. Whatever it is you're doing Down Under, it's working."

Jack Terrabonne hung up, feeling like the king of the world. He'd be back at the top of the charts again in no time.

He couldn't wait until the next time he saw Chloe and Emil.

***

Harlan stepped out of the shower. He stood dripping on the tiles, breathing the steam. His skin was swollen and tight on his body, red and raw from hard scrubbing.

The French girl haunted him.

She was there every time Harlan closed his eyes. He saw her fine bones, her tender swollen mouth. He saw the wet clay plugging her nostrils, the loose dirt on the surface of her eye.

No one since Louisa May had bothered him like this. Harlan told himself that sooner or later, this French girl would fade like all the others. He wondered if it was true.

Harlan's clothes lay in a heap on the floor, muddy, bloody and greasy. The biggest loss was his heavy ram's leather coat, with its warm fleece lining. The towel and washcloth he'd used to clean up were a total write-off too. Harlan scooped them all into a trash bag and tied it shut at the neck. Soon as he got a little shuteye, he'd burn them.

Long as he was at it, he'd have to pour a bottle of bleach or something down the drain, probably scrub the floorboards down too. He figured he'd find something he wanted on those little carts the maids pushed around.

But all that could damn well wait until he got a good few hours sleep under his belt. Of course, the way Harlan felt right then, he'd need a week under the blankets to feel right again.

Trouble was, Harlan never did sleep too well after one of his own wild nights. Terrabonne, he'd do his ridiculous little business, spend a day or two messing around in the recording studio and come up with some dumb reason to leave. He put himself through that same little act, every damn time.

Harlan wouldn't sleep good for another couple of days yet. About that time, Terrabonne would start to getting itchy feet again. There'd be an invitation to Monterey or Aspen, Montreaux or Berne. Or he'd want to be off to the estate in Jamaica, or the ranch in Tennessee.

Where they went hardly mattered to Harlan. Once the landing

gear lifted, he'd curl right up and sleep like a baby.

He just had to make it through tonight.

Harlan reached under the bed. Just touching the smooth steel lines of the box, he felt a little better. It still took him a couple of tries to fit his key into the lock.

His fingers barely brushed the stacks of currency inside.

Harlan's hands went straight for his envelope full of hair.

THIRTY-FIVE

Harlan woke hard. The loud shrill blare of the household intercom unit tore him out of sleep and threw him onto his feet before he was properly awake. Shreds of nightmare still clung as Harlan shoveled his old hair into its envelope, locked the envelope in its box and chucked on some fresh clothes. He grabbed the fresh lock of hair from his stained and dirty jeans and headed for Terrabonne's bedroom.

This was what Harlan had been waiting for. Jack always got drunk as a skunk after a big night in the studio. Today, he'd be hung over as hell. He'd also be ready for a change of scene.

Harlan came out onto the second floor gallery and caught a flash of bare calves, scissoring legs vanishing around the corner. Just one of the maids, but Harlan couldn't help seeing the French girl, Chloe, in those movements. He thought of the lock of hair in his pocket and hissed behind his teeth.

The wallpaper in the boys' wing was a dark and swirling blue, that kind of Texas-whorehouse pattern Jack thought was classy. The air in that hall always smelled of tobacco, bad breath and body odor.

Harlan heard movement behind a door and stopped. A fist the size of a human head and the weight of a sledgehammer pounded on the wood, and a muffled voice called out from inside.

"Who's that in there?" Harlan said. "Callum? Good, I want you boys up and started on packing us all up."

There was a soft thump and a sound like dishes crashing to the floor. The muffled voice on the other side of the door replied.

"Fuck do I know where we're headed?" Harlan called. "That's up to Jack, ain't it. I want this house ready to roll up by tonight, and y'all are already short-handed as it is."

Harlan turned away with a growl. His steps thumped away down the hall, and the main stairs up to Jack's suite on the third floor shook under Harlan's boots.

Once those wheels left the runway, Harlan would be safe again.

Terrabonne was up and dressed. That world-famous hair was piled high and perfect as ever, and the man's cheeks glowed with a fresh shave.

"There you are, old hoss. I was startin' to wonder."

"I guess you're feeling all right then, Jack."

"All right? Hell, I feel like a new man! I gotta tell you, when I saw them two kids come in together, I about had to pick my jaw up off the ground." Jack shot Harlan a wink and a grin.

"Now I can't believe I never tried it before."

Terrabonne clapped his hands together and waved Harlan over. Though they were alone in the room, Terrabonne cast an involuntary look left and right before speaking.

"Tell me something, hoss. Them French kids, Chloe and Emil..." He leaned in closer and lowered his voice. "Any chance of a return engagement?"

Harlan's lips went numb. Black spots crowded the edges of his vision. He fought the urge to touch the hair in his pocket.

"Hoss? You all right?"

"Huh? Um, yeah, sorry. Hard night last night's all."

"So how about it? We get them two back here, maybe keep em around a little while?"

"I don't know about that."

"Offer more money. Hell, double it, just get them two kids on back in here. Put em on the goddamn payroll!" Terrabonne looked around his bedroom. The hot tub bubbled and steamed in the corner.

"Ain't that easy, Jack." Harlan ran his palm over the knots forming at the back of his neck. "You know those kids just wanted a grubstake to them out of town and on their way."

"Another night'll take em even further..."

"That's what I'm trying to tell you. Them two're already in the wind."

"You'll check though, won't you hoss?" Terrabonne's hand was damp on Harlan's arm. "Just one more night."

"Jack, I drove them to the airport my own self."

Terrabonne cursed and kicked the furniture. Harlan waited him out. Soon enough, Jack lost interest in his tantrum and started tucking his shirt back in.

"Fine then. But next time I want another couple, y'hear? Much like them two as you can get."

"I'll get right on it, soon as we get there."

"Get where?"

"Hell, I don't know-- Aspen, Jamaica, back to Yucatan? Wherever we're headed next. I already got the boys started on the packing."

Terrabonne stopped in the middle of smoothing his hair back down.

"Why on earth would you do a thing like that?"

"I just figured..."

"We ain't going nowhere." Terrabonne's voice was like stone. "When my one-day-I-hope-to-God-ex-wife wanted us to buy a spread in New Zealand, I honestly thought she was out of her cotton-picking mind. But I've found something here I never found nowhere else, and I mean to stay put until I at least get me another little taste."

Small drops of spittle clung unnoticed to Terrabonne's mouth. His eyes were glassy and fevered.

Harlan turned his face away and hissed.

THIRTY-SIX

"What the goddamned hell are you two doing?" Harlan said.

"Packing."

JD didn't stop throwing Jack's clothes into trunks and cases. In another part of the room, Turk did the same thing, but a whole lot more gently, with one of Jack's guitars.

"Well quit it."

"But you're the one just told us to start."

Harlan's hand flashed out. The sound of the slap rang off the plaster walls.

Turk lay on the ground looking up at Harlan. There were tears in his eyes and blood running from his nose. JD stood mute and still, a pile of custom-made Western-embroidered shirts draped over his cast.

"Y'all put everything back now, y'hear? You got fifteen minutes, tell Callum and Farrel to bring the Rovers around front. And for God's sake, Turk, clean yourself up. Mister Boogie Jack Terrabonne his own self is taking us all into town."

Harlan cut his eyes to where JD stood and snarled. JD flinched but held his ground.

"We go out," Harlan said, "Y'all are gonna eat your lunch and drink your goddamned beer. Most of all, *behave.*"

***

The American stopped in lobby on the way out. Maeve stopped what she was doing, came around from behind the desk to where the tattered black scarecrow waited.

"You'll be off then."

Kane looked at her. His mouth was sad, his eyes soft and golden, the color of burnt butterscotch.

"Look," Maeve said. "Another time, another life, things might have been different."

"I wasn't thinking about that."

"Ah." Maeve shifted her weight and resisted the urge to touch the hilt of the knife tucked in her boot. Kane saw, and his mouth curved slightly at the corners.

"Yeah."

"And?"

Maeve silently cursed herself for a damn fool. The Yank couldn't prove a thing against her, but she had no business telling him anything in the first place.

Kane curled his fingers around hers. The ball of his thumb traced patterns in the skin on the back of her hand.

"I was thinking," he said, "about some of the stuff I've done over the years. Lots of times I might have died, and there would've been nobody to care. Let alone avenge me."

Maeve reached up, standing high on tiptoes. Their last kiss was bitter, tender and heartbreakingly sweet.

"Tell you what, Yank." Maeve wiped at the corner of his mouth with her thumb. "I finish this, you can have my next one."

Kane's eyes danced. The lights were sparkling and golden. He gave her hand a final squeeze, hitched his pack on one shoulder and headed for the exit.

He stopped in the open doorway, framed in bright winter light. The silhouetted black shape turned, looking back over its shoulder.

"I was also thinking, it'd be a terrible dishonor to Bridey's memory if you were wrong."

The only answer to Maeve's curse was the rapid banging of the open door against the wall and the lonesome howl of the winter wind.

***

Harlan found it on the downstairs table. The plastic envelope stood out, bright red and yellow against the dark oak planks. Damn near as garish as Jack's framed Elvis display up on the wall.

The envelope was local. Written on the front was Harlan's own name.

He looked side to side. There was no one else in the room. The damn thing might've been left any time in the last day or so, no way of knowing.

Harlan tore the plastic open with his thumb. As he read the single sheet of paper inside, his lips moved.

The skin tightened against his face. Harlan's neck burned against his collar, and his eyes blazed with a poisonous light.

THIRTY-SEVEN

Queenstown only had the one skin joint. It was a bright purple storefront on the downscale end of Shotover, down by the internet cafes, coin laundry and tattoo shop. Harlan left Terrabonne and the boys drinking in The Bunker and walked the three blocks down to the storefront with its scrolling purple neon.

With any luck, he'd be back before Jack noticed he was gone.

The strip club had a bouncer on the door. Big damn fucker, Samoan or something like it, and near about as large as Harlan himself.

The bouncer took himself too seriously. Ten o'clock in the morning, and he was out on the sidewalk with his suit and shades and little white wire earpiece, probably thought he looked like some kind of secret agent. Harlan thought the bouncer looked like somebody hung a necktie on a haystack.

The Samoan put one hand across Harlan's path.

"Shoes, mate."

Harlan looked down at his feet and back at the bouncer's sunglasses. The red and yellow plastic envelope in his hand tapped against the side of his leg. He kept his coat buttoned over the .44, and his reflection in the dark lenses looked pissed.

"Those boots are steelcaps, hey?" the bouncer said. "Club doesn't allow steelcaps."

Harlan restrained himself. Air hissed through his teeth. He leaned in close, until he could smell his own breath curling off the bouncer's cheek.

"Lasker."

The bouncer's bland hard look slipped. Harlan pressed harder.

He waved the plastic envelope in front of the bouncer's face.

"That greasy little pimp wants to see me."

"Mister Lasker didn't mention any appointments."

"There so many jobs in this town you want to lose this one?"

That wire in the Samoan's ear must have connected to something. Two more bouncers stepped out onto the sidewalk in front of the entrance. Hollings was right: they were rough looking characters, with notched ears, dead eyes and scarred faces. The Samoan's lips curled, tight and triumphant.

"Right this way. Sir."

Inside, the strip club was dark and low and insanely loud. The air was perfumed and moldy and chill. At a waist-high stage in the center of the room, a naked woman shuffled inside an island of light, looking like she didn't give a damn.

Harlan wondered what kind of tips she expected to make before eleven o'clock in the morning. Then he spotted the pimp and quit thinking about the dancer.

Lasker sat at a table in the back. Purple neon reflected off the waxed surface of his head and sent bright slick highlights crawling over the bottle of Ouzo in front of him. Lasker nodded and the women with him left the table.

They moved past Harlan on their way to the bar. The lead one wore silicone implants, a leathery brown tan and hot pants that exposed the bottom half of her ass cheeks. Her face was lined beneath its makeup, her gaze cold and hostile. Trailing behind her like some kind of pet was a puffy-looking brunette with a dark bruise in the hollow of her hip. She had bad teeth and acne scars, and her eyes were dark and glittering, fiending and addicted.

They were nothing like the French girl.

Harlan dropped the red and yellow Courier Post envelope on the table. Lasker lifted the flap with the tips of two fingers, glanced inside and let it fall.

"Drink?" The pimp gestured to the bottle and the empty glass.

"Fuck do I look like, you think I'd touch that pussy shit?"

Lasker shrugged and folded his hands across his stomach. Harlan felt the bouncers behind him shift positions.

"So you have my invoice," the pimp said. "How would you like to pay? I thought you would want to use cash, but a credit card is fine. We can run it at the bar."

"You must be plumb crazy. Twenty grand's way too much for half a dozen whores, and you already been paid. Hell are you thinking, sending this thing up to the house, anyway?"

Lasker rubbed his stomach and yawned. "I did not think you would want to leave this with your employer's accountants. This way," he waved a hand in the air, "seems more discreet."

Harlan growled. Behind him, the bouncers leaned closer. Cheap aftershave and musk stirred the chilled air.

" I googled your Jack Terrabonne last night. Know what I found?"

"That he shared a stage with Elvis one time in '73?"

"That your employer is in negotiations for a one-hour variety show on that Christian network back in the United States."

Harlan flexed his hands, open and closed.

"A terrible tragedy if anything were to queer that deal," the pimp said.

"Like, say, word getting out that Boogie Jack parties with hookers?"

Lasker winked and showed his teeth.

"But I pay this here 'invoice' you give me," Harlan said, "you're just gonna shut up about that little party the other night."

"And all those other nights before. After all, we go back quite a few years, you and I."

"Reckon so. And here all this time I figured you for civilized."

"Nothing is more civilized than to accept payment for a service."

The pimp crossed his arms over his chest. The purple light shifted over the gym weight-machine muscles. Harlan shook his head.

"Don't reckon you give me much choice."

Lasker's laughter was a series of quick sharp barks.

"You see gentlemen, I told you Americans are capable of listening. You have only to use short words and have plenty of patience."

The three bouncers laughed. Mostly, they did it because their boss did. They never had a chance.

Harlan lashed out. The blade of his hand caught the bouncer on his left in the throat. A stomping kick turned the man on his right into a cripple. Harlan palmed the head of the big Samoan behind him and swung it over his shoulder in a tight circle. The man's body followed, crashing the Samoan down spine first and smashing Lasker's table to splinters.

All three bouncers were out. The pimp fumbled in his belt, going for some kind of weapon. Harlan kicked him in the chest and heard ribs crack. Just to be sure, he broke Lasker's wrist and three of his fingers.

Harlan bent low over Lasker's face. The pimp smelled of raw animal terror.

"You'n me do go back a ways," Harlan said, "And I want you to know on account of that, I'm going easy on you now."

Harlan's left thumb pressed deep into the soft flesh just below Lasker's eye.

"Jack Terrabonne is, he's like a father to me. You ever *dream* of fucking with him, I won't be this nice. You dumb, greedy fuck."

Lasker's only reply was a frenzied high-pitched mewling.

Harlan's right fist was the size and weight of the average human head. It crashed into the pimp's face with a sound like thunder.

Harlan wiped blood from his knuckles onto the leg of his jeans. It was time to get back to Jack and the boys at The Bunker. His work here was done.

On his way out, he paused to stomp on the Samoan's spine.

THIRTY-EIGHT

Kane stood at the side of the road. The scene before him was postcard perfect: snow-capped mountains against an impossible blue sky, the cold clean wind riffing the surface of the lake. In the distance, a steamboat packed with tourists appeared no bigger than a child's toy.

To his right, the road curved around past the wharf and up into the trees. Glenorchy and the Fox Glacier lay beyond. To the left lay plains and orchards and a concrete bridge over raging black water. It was the same road Kane had walked in on three days ago.

He wasn't ready to walk back out.

Maeve had a good heart. The loss of a loved one may have made her a little crazy, but there was a wide and terrible gap between comforting fantasies of revenge and crossing the line to take a human life.

And something about her scenario didn't add up. No matter how he looked at it, Kane couldn't shake the nagging feeling that Maeve was making a mistake.

The street up the hill behind him was crowded with neon bar signs. Looking back over his shoulder, Kane could just make out the one he needed.

He had promised Maeve he'd leave. He hadn't said when.

***

Time didn't touch The Bunker. Eleven o'clock in the morning, the bar looked the same as midnight: a low and windowless box, lit by bar-sign neon and jangling with old-school country.

The Bunker was a timeless, airless space. Kane was able to close his eyes and almost believe that he was back home, in the honky tonks of his boyhood. With his eyes open, it was too easy to be distracted by the longhorn skull over the mirrored bar, the single-malt scotches on the top shelf and the autographed photos of country music stars and other celebrities hanging on the walls.

But with his eyes closed, it was a different story. Kane could smell the spilled beer and sawdust, hear Patsy Cline and Johnny Cash play on the juke. He could imagine the plywood and tarpaper walls, the beaten square of raw red clay that served as the lot, even the rusted trailer out back where it was rumored that twenty dollars or a small amount of meth bought things a teenaged boy could barely imagine.

With his eyes closed, The Bunker was the kind of place where Saturday nights and check days meant gunshots or knife wounds.

Kane suspected it was no accident. For people who hadn't grown up as he had, the atmosphere in this place was as exciting, and as real, as a theme park ride. And for someone like Kane, it was important sometimes to return to the past, and the truth.

Kane searched the room. Without knowing what their boss looked like, he looked for JD, and his three friends or any other low rent carny-types.

He didn't search long. A broad back wheeled away from the bar and into Kane's shoulder. Liquor splashed and fell. Eyes dark with burst blood vessels went wide, and the curse died in the man's throat.

The man sputtered and spit. The black beard rasped against the white foam collar. In the end, his swollen and busted lips were able to form but a single word.

"You!"

***

"Anybody know where the hell Harlan's gone off to?" Jack Terrabonne rattled the ice in his glass. "And where in hell's that goddamn Farrel with my drink?"

Jack looked around the table. Three faces looked back at him, uncomfortable and clueless. Turk tugged at his shirt collar and smacked his lips, trying to find the words.

"Don't waste your breath on some lame-ass excuse," Jack said. "Just get your fat ass off that bench and bring me my drink."

Turk sighed and levered himself out of his seat. He muttered something under his breath Jack didn't quite catch, probably another half-assed apology. It was always that way: ask a simple question, make a simple request any idiot ought to be able to do, and instead get nothing but excuses and apologies.

The fat boy hadn't taken two steps when he froze. Turk fell back against the bench, his face the color of bad cheese.

On the bench next to him, JD was lowered down halfway under the edge of the table. That one looked about ready to wet his pants.

The stranger drifted like gunsmoke, and he stood like a coiled trap. Jack liked that phrase, thought it might work right in a song. The whole time Jack sat there trying to remember it, the stranger stood in front of the table, tall and shaggy and dark. His steady amber eyes put Jack in mind of mountain lions and timberwolves, or the kinds of animals usually seen on safari.

Jack looked from the stranger to JD and back again.

"You know this fellah?"

JD looked like a pig choked.

"This-- he's, this is one of the ones jumped me'n Farrel in town that other night."

"You said that was the same bunch busted your nose."

"I, yeah, that's right. Him and his buddies."

"No others," the stranger said. "Just me alone."

"Looking at you, son, I'd just about believe it." Jack scanned the room. No sign of Harlan Winters. Farrel either.

"Now why don't you tell me what you're doing here?"

"Bridey Martin."

"Beg pardon?"

"Bridey Martin. Irish, couple years ago in Mexico, she would've been twenty-two, twenty-three years old."

Jack grinned his aw-shucks grin.

"What's this, son? You don't look like no reporter I ever seen."

"I'm not."

"And you really stomped two of my boys, all on your own?"

"Didn't have much choice."

Forty-seven years in the entertainment industry, concert promoters, record executives and corporate lawyers, Jack figured he knew when he was being lied to. The stranger's words had the ring of truth.

"This Irish gal, you her husband?" Jack said. "Boyfriend? Brother maybe?"

"Friend of a friend, that's all."

"Sorry, son. I just had to ask." Jack touched the silver cowskull clasp on his string tie. "You know who I am?"

"Sure. I just about wore out your concert tape when I was a kid. Everybody goes on about that duet you did with Bonny Rait, but I was always partial to your take on *Wayfaring Stranger*, just you alone with the spotlight and that steel-stringed slide guitar. You put some soul into that one."

Jack looked around at the boys. He couldn't quite keep the smile off his face.

"You got a name, son?"

"Kane. My name's Kane."

Jack shook the hand the stranger held out. It felt like some kind of old-time tool, sculpted out of leather, bone and blocks of wood.

"And is that a little bit of down-home I hear in your voice?"

"Yup. Tiny little town south of Atlanta, name of Zebulon, Georgia."

"Easy to see y'ain't been back in a while."

The man named Kane tilted his head to one side. Jack Terrabonne gave a brief flash of his most famous and dazzling smile.

"Zebulon's not so little no more. I did a little TV work there once, back when they were shooting 'Heat of the Night' in the 80's. Went back to shoot a movie a couple of years ago, you wouldn't recognize it."

Jack went on talking about small-town Georgia. After a couple of minutes, he kicked his heels back and stretched out in his seat.

"Son, you mind if I ask you a question?"

The young fellah Kane said nothing. That old boy had a spooky kind of silence to him. He was like the space between notes.

"Messing with you..." Jack's mouth twisted at one corner. "Was JD out of his cotton-picking mind?"

JD's lips worked like he had something sour stuck to his gums. Jack and Kane both paid him no mind.

"He struck a woman. I got between them and JD took it personal."

The twist in Jack's mouth deepened.

"Son, why don't you come on over here and have a seat?"

THIRTY-NINE

Harlan Winters headed back up Shotover, rubbing his knuckles. Now his new coat was also a wreck. One sleeve was torn at the seam, and there were flecks of blood on the cuffs. Blood was a real son of a bitch to wash away.

Teaching the pimp a lesson had taken no more than a few seconds. Even walking there and back, the whole visit had taken less than twenty minutes. Doubtful Jack would know he'd been gone.

The Queenstown air was crisp and smelled of snow. Harlan couldn't tell if it was his imagination, or if there was more of the white stuff up on those mountains than there had been yesterday.

He was halfway up the steps to The Bunker when blades of shadow fell across his path.

"Hell you been, old hoss?"

Jack Terrabonne stood at the top of the steps. In the cold winter light, his blue sharkskin suit shimmered and gleamed. Callum stood on his left, and at Jack's right hand was a man Harlan had seen once before: the drifter standing at the crossroads.

The stranger was tall and lean. His eyes were intelligent and calm, but the stranger's hands and the way he stood told a different story. This man was rough and capable.

Like woodsmoke in a forest, Harlan smelled danger.

Jack's voice cut across the growl rolling unconscious from Harlan's throat.

"This here's Kane. I'm having him back up to the house."

Harlan's eyes narrowed, and his hands flexed.

"Callum'll take us back to Whispering Pines," Jack said. "Hoss, you want to get over to the hospital. The other boys already took Farrel on over, seems he got himself busted up back in the bar."

Jack brushed past Harlan. Little runt ignoring him like he wasn't even there, playing up in front of the stranger, acting the part of the rich and famous asshole.

The other two followed Jack down. Callum looked stricken. The stranger, this man Kane, kept his body angled toward Harlan and his hands away from his sides.

"You get that Farrel patched up," Jack called over his shoulder. "After that, tell JD and all them they're fired."

Just like that, the three walked off down the sidewalk. Callum ran ahead to fetch one of the Rovers. Jack, tiny and bright blue, strutted alongside the tall dark stranger. A scrap of laughter drifted to Harlan: Boogie Jack Terrabonne telling one of his stories.

Twenty minutes. Harlan had been gone less than twenty minutes.

***

Kane froze. No way Maeve could have known that the 'rich bastard' she intended to murder was one of Kane's childhood heroes. Walking out of The Bunker next to Jack Terrabonne himself, Kane came face to face with one of the largest and most frightening men he'd ever seen in his life.

Harlan Winters was huge: six-six or six-seven and covered in light gingery body hair and thick slabs of rubbery muscle. His new leather coat was torn and bloody, and more blood was spattered across the lower half of his face. A powerful sting of eye-watering testosterone surrounded the man. Beneath it, Kane smelled deeper, more organic scents of raw meat and decay.

Winters fixed Kane with a junkyard stare. His eyes were a blue so pale they were almost colorless: intense, alien and dangerous.

Jack Terrabonne acted like nothing was wrong. His tone was arrogant, patronizing. His words were borderline insults. Despite the difference in size and build, facing each other Winters and Terrabonne had very similar bone structure.

Winters never took his eyes off Kane. Terrabonne didn't seem to notice that Winters bared the brown stumps of his teeth at Kane and made a deep noise, low in his throat.

Terrabonne brushed past Winters, completely oblivious. Kane stayed out of arm's reach as he edged past.

He was certain, right in the marrow of his bones, that to be alone with Harlan Winters would mean his death.

***

It was a busy morning for Maeve at the hostel. German, Belgian, Chinese and Israeli backpackers checked in and checked out, all of them needing help of one sort or another. There were rafting trips and bungee jumps, Lord of the Rings tours and jetboat rides to book, often for people who didn't altogether speak English. There were handout maps to draw routes on in ballpoint pen, and the phone never stopped ringing.

It seemed like forever before Maeve was able to nip off to the loo.

"Ah, brilliant." The voice was low and lazy and male, with a distinct New Zealand accent.

Maeve stopped just inside the bathroom door. Gary stepped out of one of the stalls.

"And what is it you think you're doing in the women's?"

"Cleaning?"

"You're kidding."

"Well, I figured you'd be too tired." He tossed his head to throw the hair out of his eyes. The gesture, affected and rehearsed, worked Maeve's nerves like nails on a chalkboard. "Awfully glad I ran into you, though."

"I've been up front all morning. You could've stopped by the desk any time."

Gary's tanned face split. His teeth were long and white, his eyes hungry.

"Giving a room away free of charge, then keeping the guest in your own room all night. That's not the kind of thing you'd want me talking about up at the desk. Or to the owners."

Maeve's eyes narrowed. "Do tell?"

"Come on now, it's not that big a deal." He eased a little closer and lowered his voice. "It's not like I'm asking you to fall in love."

"I've told you before, what you want's never going to happen."

"Fine then." Gary tossed his hair. "It's your job, not mine."

"You'd really do it too, you fecking bastard."

Gary's white smile was his only answer.

"I suppose you're after going back to your room?"

Gary shook his head. His smile vanished.

Maeve looked back over her shoulder and bit her lip. She pitched her voice low and quiet.

"What, here?"

"I'll put out the cleaning sign. Nobody'll come in." The backs of his fingers brushed her cheek.

Maeve's blade flashed. She laid it hard against the flesh of his cheek and ran the bastard back until his skull clacked against the wall.

Gary's eyes were glassy and wild. His mouth gobbled, a high-pitched wordless sound. His breath was thin, reeking and sour.

"Big mistake." Maeve's voice was soft, low and dangerous. Blood welled over the face of the blade where the edge bit skin. She shifted the knife so that the point hovered just in front of the center of his eye.

"Your sleaze has gone on long enough. I don't give a tinker's damn about this job, but you'll die before if I let the likes of you put your hands on me."

Tears and sweat slicked Gary's face. The tip of Maeve's blade brushed his eyelashes as her hand shook.

Maeve's knee shot up. It caught the bastard between his legs. Maeve pumped hard and kneed him twice more.

Gary howled. His knees buckled and he let out a wild howl. Maeve stayed in close and kept kneeing his balls until he went down.

He screamed and tried to rise.

Maeve took a half-step back and swung her foot. Her boot caught him in the back of the thigh, and Gary collapsed face first into the tile floor. For a hot reckless moment, Maeve felt the temptation to finish things with her knife.

Instead, she stayed with the boot. She kicked him in the arse and the ribs, the back and the legs. She stayed away from his face. Maeve kept the boot in until Gary lay curled in a ball, sobbing.

Only then did Maeve bend low to whisper in the shell of Gary's ear.

"Touch me, so much as *look* at me that way again, and I'll tear strips out of your fecking hide."

Maeve hung the 'Closed for Cleaning' sign on the door and stalked out of the bathroom.

Gary lay on the tile, bleeding, whimpering and quivering.

FORTY

"What're we gonna do, Harl?"

Harlan shot Turk a filthy look and kicked a dark scar in the raked white gravel. The bare dirt beneath was the color of a muddy riverbank. The French girl's mud-smeared lips and teeth jumped behind Harlan's eyes.

"You think it means anything Jack left us all back here?"

"Somebody had to wait and get Farrel out the hospital. Again." Harlan eyed Turk's fat neck and spit on the sidewalk.

"But Harl, ain't you worried? Jack--"

"Jack gets notions in his head sometimes," Harlan said. "Yoga. Religion. That girl with no eyebrows told fortunes with cards. He always changes his mind again, just as quick."

"But what if he--"

"Come on, goddammit. It's time."

Harlan brushed past Turk and headed up the walk to the hospital entrance.

The nurses knew him by sight. He was the head of the rich American's accident-prone staff. They were brisk and polite and sort of British-sounding, and they tried not to stare. They waved Harlan through, and he nodded on his way past. His boot heels rolled like thunder down the tile hallway.

Farrel sat on a paper-wrapped table in the Accident and Emergency. He held a kidney-shaped steel dish under his chin in one hand and a fistful of paper towels up next to his cheek. His own shirt and jacket had been replaced by one of those blue paper gown-things and a fresh foam collar had been fitted to his neck, but there were still wet red stains in the waist of his jeans and parts of his beard. A large scrape on the front of his forehead had been swabbed, disinfected and bandaged.

The smell of iodine mingled with the room's background scents of bleach, floor wax and blood.

Farrel raised his eyes to Harlan without moving his head.

"Fell is all, caught a barstool on my way down," he said. "They wanna take some X-Rays yet and check me out for concussion, but the doc's pretty sure ain't nothing broke."

JD leaned against the bench next to Farrel. His black eyes were glassy and darting, and large beads of sweat stood out on his upper lip. As they came in, Turk came around from behind Harlan to take up a post on Farrel's other side.

Harlan stood in front of them with his hands on his hips, shaking his head. JD and Farrel wore identical hangdog expressions. Turk looked hurt and confused.

"Y'all ain't the best listeners, are you? Or maybe there was some part of 'knock this shit off' y'all didn't understand?"

"Didn't do nothing," Farrel said. "Those bastards what jumped us came into the bar. I didn't start nothing, but I must've tripped coming to find you."

"Trying to run away, you mean." Harlan kept his voice low when he said it, didn't care how gruff it sounded. "This was one of that gang. What was it, three, four people?"

"Something like that," Farrel said. He didn't see Turk and JD, trying to signal him. "I told you, there was a bunch."

"You sure it wasn't just one? Another American, maybe?"

Farrel's eyes shifted from side to side before he answered. "One of em might have been American. Yeah sure, maybe..."

"Good old boy name of Kane?"

"You seen him? At the bar?"

Harlan nodded. "More important, Jack saw him."

"Walked right up to the table," JD said, "and asked Jack himself about Bridey Martin."

Harlan's fists tightened. Knuckles the size of walnuts cracked.

"You didn't mention that part," he said. His eyes were cold and hard. "Anything else you left out?"

Turk turned a dark red color. He hung his head and kept his mouth shut.

"I was only doing what you told me to," JD said. His eyes were black and hot and burning.

"What's so special about this Bridey woman anyhow?" he said.

Harlan leaned in. The tissue paper crackled under the weight of his fists.

"You fucked up. You fucked up, and now this same American kicked your asses, he's up to the house on the personal invitation of none other than Jack Terrabonne his own self."

JD stared. A muscle jumped in his cheek. It was Farrel, his nose blocked with clotted blood, who spoke first.

"What do you want us to do?"

Harlan scratched at the side of his neck, thinking.

"Jack'll get tired quick enough. He always does, right?"

Harlan saw the funny way Farrel and JD and Turk were looking at him.

"What?"

Turk shuffled from foot to foot.

"This guy... back at the table, I heard him tell Jack that he's a musician."

A rumbling growl escaped Harlan's throat, and he dug in his pocket for his money clip. He threw a wad of bills at the three of them. Pink and red hundreds fluttered to the linoleum.

"Pay your damn bill and make your own damn way home. You assholes have already done enough."

Harlan stormed through the hospital corridors. His boots echoed like thunderclaps, and his face burned in the antiseptic air.

FORTY-ONE

Whispering Pines. That was the name Jack Terrabonne gave his ranch.

"She ain't the biggest spread in these hills," Jack said. "Sam Neill and Charlie Boyd both have fair-sized places, and Shania Twain must own half this damn country. No, sir, Whispering Pines ain't the biggest, but she sure is the prettiest."

The Range Rover twisted north and west out of Queenstown. The moon-faced man drove, fast and nervous. Kane rested his weight in the soft leather seats and watched mountains slide past out the window. One of Jack's old concerts was loaded on the DVD player. A tiny four-inch Jack Terrabonne, thirty years younger, strutted across the screen. *Backdoor Boogie, Pussyfootin Heart* and *Back of the Barn,* played softly in the background. Jack ignored the songs and told stories about sharing the stage at the Opry with Carl Perkins and Porter Waggoner, about partying in Sydney with the Rolling Stones and his famous early-nineties fistfight with Mickey Rourke.

Kane had never heard most of those stories. He listened.

Black Cat Blues started playing. Jack Terrabonne trailed off in the middle of what he was saying. His eyes went misty and faraway, and a tiny smile played at the corners of his mouth.

"You ever been to France, Kane?"

"Sure."

"I tell you, some of the prettiest little gals come out of there. Why..." Terrabonne leaned forward in his seat and slapped the moon-faced man in the back of the head. "Get Harlan on the phone, find out where he's at on that thing for me."

The moon-faced man tapped a fingertip against the touch screen in the center of the dash. The word 'telephone' lit up. Kane shifted in his seat and rubbed one thumb across his knuckles. He heard a faint electronic tone and the sound of a rough low voice on the other end of the line.

"Harl? It's Callum. Jack wanted me to ask-- Harl?"

The screen's light muted. Callum looked back at Jack in the rearview mirror.

"Must've passed out of the service area. You want I should try again later, or maybe wait til we're back at the house?"

Terrabonne snorted. His jaw was clenched too tight to answer. He thumped his small brown fist on one bony knee and said nothing for several long seconds. In the background, *Black Cat Blues* trailed off to its ending, Jack Terrabonne's smoky and soulful voice mourning his bad luck and lost love.

Kane turned his face to the rain-streaked window. The Rover followed a bend in the road, sheer mountain granite on the right and below on the left, a twisted finger of mountain lake. Shreds of mist hung over the surface of the black and icy water.

***

Tanya found Beth in her room after work. It had been an easy day, all things considered, and they were done early. Tanya stood in the doorway with two bottles of wine in each hand.

"Hey," she said. "Saw your door open and thought I'd stick my head in. Got extra wine for tonight."

Beth laid back on her bed, comfortable now in regular clothes.

"Seems like all we ever do is drink," she said to the ceiling. "It's getting boring."

"We've got a day off soon, we can go into town or something. Meantime, what else is there?"

"I guess..."

Tanya set the wine bottles on Beth's dresser. She still wore her uniform and wiped her hands on the front of her skirt.

"You have your laptop here, right?"

"Sure." Beth made a face. There was nothing exciting about her laptop in this house.

"Help me load some new songs on my MP3?"

Beth sat up and nodded. Tanya thanked her and popped across the hall. By the time she came back, dressed in jeans and a top and waving her MP3 player, the laptop was booted up and ready.

"So can you like, download new songs off the internet and stuff?"

"I could," Beth said and shook her head, "if I had a connection. Big expensive house, and they don't even have a cable modem, much less wireless. No downloads or email, no MySpace or Facebook or Bebo. Nothing."

"Know what I think?" Tanya said.

"What?"

"I know Mister Terrabonne's got email in his study. I've seen him on that computer. And I bet old Cat Pee Winters has the internet up in his room. He probably uses it to watch porn and wank off."

"Porn," Beth said. "I bet he watches *Animals Attack* clips on youTube."

"Shark porn!" the two said together, and laughed.

Beth plugged Tanya's player into a USB port and waited for the laptop to sort itself out. Her machine was three years old, practically an antique and getting sluggish in its old age.

"God, can you imagine the woman who'd sleep with Cat Pee Winters?" Tanya said and wrinkled her nose. "You'd smell for, like, a week!"

The new device popped up on screen. Beth mouse-clicked her way inside it, thinking Tanya might have some songs she'd want.

"Ton?"

"Yeah babes?"

"Why do you have so much French pop on here? It's like everywhere."

Tanya scratched the side of her lip and twirled her hair around one finger.

"Oh, that. This guy, he was a French guy, and he set it up for me. That's why I wanted to get some new music from you." She paused a moment and twirled her hair some more. "And that's why you didn't see me with my MP3 player before. I thought I was stuck with all that French *amour-amour* bollocks, it was driving me mad!"

188

Beth clicked and dragged some of her music onto Tanya's player. While she was there, she looked in a couple of the other folders.

"Did you know you have sound recordings on this?" Beth said.

Tanya gave her a blank look. Before she could reply, Chrissy stuck her head in the doorway.

"Suit back up, girls. Mister Terrabonne's driver just called ahead, and they're headed back for dinner."

*****

The Rover blasted down a lane and a half of mountain road. At the bottom of the twisting mountain pass, the road cut straight across the valley floor. The weathered asphalt was slick with rain and treacherous with fallen pine needles. Up front, Callum stabbed the brake and palmed the wheel.

Tires hissed. The Rover turned and passed through high iron gates. The drive was gravel: white, raked and immaculate. Rows of beeches lined the drive. The trees were stunted and twisted, their trunks black and furred.

"Some kind of mold," Jack said. "Landscapers can't seem to do a damn thing about it." Behind the wheel, Callum turned up the wipers. Falling leaves clung to the windshield, wet, brown and diseased.

A teenaged girl with a New Zealand accent opened the front door. She was small and dark, her dress navy blue and modest, the cut and material vaguely industrial. She had a dark band-shaped bruise inside her left wrist and three others the size of large coins stretching high up, almost to the inside of her elbow.

"C'mon, Kane. Let me give you the ten cent tour." Jack Terrabonne blew through the front door like there was no one

189

there. Kane apologized to the girl and followed in his wake.

"House itself is over a hundred years old," Jack said. "Original three rooms are back thataways somewhere, but this place has been added to plenty over the years. And of course, I added a few of my own touches."

The room they stood in was larger than most houses. Paintings hung on the walls, and two broad staircases swept up to a long balcony. A crystal chandelier the size of a small car tinkled softly in the distance overhead. It was a vast cavern of a room, without enough light to fill it. Sounds were easily lost in that space, left to wander lonely, isolated and confused.

"Sure is something, ain't it?" Jack's voice cast strange warbling echoes, and the click of his boot heels on the marble floor was small and thready. "Every one of them paintings? From Europe. German crystal in that there chandelier, I don't even want to think about what it cost. Weighs over half a damn ton."

Kane stood under the crystal monstrosity. In the shadows above his head, the chandelier groaned on its chain, and each crystal was the color of rain.

"Come on, son."Jack flashed a bright smile. "I got lots better to show you yet."

FORTY-TWO

Jack Terrabonne escorted Kane around Whispering Pines. The house and grounds were stunning, but everything Terrabonne pointed out came back to his own history and career.

After a time, Kane found himself following the man down a dark red hallway lined with gold and platinum records. None of the dates on the plaques was less than twenty years old.

At the far end of the hall were two doors. One opened onto a dark narrow room with mixing boards running along a glass wall. Kane waited while Terrabonne flipped switches and pushed buttons on the boards. It was dark on the other side of the wall, and Kane saw only his own reflection in the glass.

Behind the other door was Jack Terrabonne's private studio. It had a black rubber floor and black eggcrate-shaped foam lining the walls. There were microphones covered in big foam sleeves and microphones with gauzy disks mounted in front. There were guitars propped on stands in the corner, and a long glass wall with the mixing boards beyond. There were couches and easy chairs and a couple of waist-high plain wooden bar stools.

It was the first time Kane had ever been in a recording studio.

"Don't worry, son. Ain't none of this stuff going to bite."

The walls and floor trapped echoes and deadened sound. Kane touched the edges of one barstool with the tips of his fingers.

"You know who sat in that stool right there? Mister Willy Nelson himself." Terrabonne shook his head at Kane and winked. "I bought em off him, back when he was having that old tax thing."

Terrabonne laughed and hitched himself up onto the other stool. His blue sharkskin suit was the brightest thing in the room.

"You know why I brought you here, don't you son?"

"No sir."

Jack Terrabonne gave Kane a long and calculating look.

"You do play, right?"

Kane shrugged. "Street music, I guess."

"What, like rap?"

"No, like busking. Put out the hat and play for change."

Terrabonne chuckled. "Now that makes sense. Cause you know, you don't exactly look like any hip-hopper I ever seen. You any good?"

"Enough people walk past, I do okay." Kane stuck his hands in his pockets and looked at the eggcrate walls.

"What kind of music you play?"

"Country and blues, mostly. A little gospel sometimes."

"Been playing long?"

"Bout ten years."

Terrabonne swung one small booted foot back and forth in the air. "Pick a little guitar?"

"Not much. I can play a chord or two, but a guitar doesn't travel too well."

Terrabonne let out a low scraping laugh. "Lord Jesus, son. It's like pulling teeth with you. I was your age, I already had ten gold records, and you know why? Because every damn time anyone so much as *hinted* they might want to hear me, I played. Hell," he said, "I'd play just on the off-chance they wouldn't go running off in the opposite direction!"

Kane felt his neck and wrists grow hot.

"Now look," Terrabonne said. "What you got here, if you don't mind me saying, is a certified country music superstar asking questions about your music. *In* a recording studio! And you're too dumb, or too pussy, to grab the chance that's right in front of you."

Kane took the Oskar's leather case out of his pocket. He put it on the seat in front of him and ditched out of his coat. He stripped down the layers until he was in his tee shirt. The studio air was cool on Kane's bare arms.

He thumbed the latch and opened the case. The harmonica gleamed, tiny points of reflected light moving in its metal surface like trapped sparks.

Kane tapped the reeds clear, fitted the harp to his mouth and began to play.

Minutes later, the room returned to its weird echoless silence. Jack Terrabonne clapped, the sound sharp and clean and instantly gone.

"Son, you weren't lying, were you? I do believe you really did just about wear out that tape when you was little. You got *Black Cat Blues* note for note, and that was one damn fine take on

Wayfaring Stranger. What was that other one you took it into? Sounded a little something like Clapton, or that old fellah, Robert Johnson. Those chord changes are downright creepy."

"Just a little something I wrote this morning."

"You wrote that? Damn, son." Terrabonne shook his head. "Play it one more time?"

Kane played *Bad Angel Blues* again. The Oskar was as warm as a living thing in his hands as he chased those chord changes, slow and eerie.

The last note faded. Terrabonne hopped off his stool and shucked out of his shiny blue jacket. He dropped it over the arm of the nearest couch, rolled up his sleeves and grabbed his old steel-stringed Dobro by the neck.

Terrabonne climbed back up on his stool, less than a meter away from Kane. Terrabonne fiddled with the frets for a few seconds until he was happy with the guitar's tune. Kane blew the reeds clean on his Oskar.

"That song got words, son?"

"Sure," Kane said.

"Tell you what, you take me through that blues walk again, see if I can get the hang of those chord changes. Then we'll get you to put that Mississippi saxophone down, see if you can sing."

FORTY-THREE

The second Rover roared through the black iron gates of Whispering Pines. It was early yet, but the autumn sky was already the color of a bone-deep bruise.

The Rover skidded to a stop in front of the main house. Gravel flew as the oversized tires carved swift crescents in the immaculate white drive and laid bare the wet dark earth.

Harlan Winters stormed up the steps and through the front door. The little thing running to answer it, Harlan's favorite maid, like to have peed herself. She screamed and jumped and ran back in the other direction. Harlan stood in the center of the hall, under Jack's big damned German crystal chandelier. He spread his arms and threw his head and sniffed.

Dried sweat and cheap aftershave hung in the dry dead air. Harlan followed the scent and burst into the Ruckus Room. Callum leapt up out of Harlan's chair and flicked the channel on the flatscreen TV away from the Asian porn.

He was alone.

"Fuck are they?"

"I-I don't know, Harl. Last I seen the others was all back in town, when they took Farrel to the hospital. Ain't they with you?"

"Not Turk and JD, dumbass. Jack. Him and that other one."

"Oh." Callum's eyes lost focus and his mouth made a small weak shape. "Where's Farrel and them?"

Harlan forced air deep into his lungs. He held it for a count of three and let it out in a long flat hiss.

"I expect they'll be along. What's bothering me is that a country music icon, not to mention the man signs your paycheck and mine, is off alone with some no-account drifter already put two of those boys in the hospital. Now, where's Jack and the stranger?"

Callum's lips were wet and red. He looked from side to side, searching for a way out. Harlan leaned in close. The gun hung heavy on his belt. His palms itched, and it took real force of will to keep from fitting his hands to the sides of Callum's head.

Harlan leaned in closer. Stale sweat and the ghosts of bar soap and aftershave rose from Callum's clothes, and the heat from the man's forehead burned against Harlan's throat.

"Where."

Callum wiped his hands on his shirt. "Last I saw, they was headed down Jack's hall, the red one."

Callum said something else. It was lost in the steady drumming thunder of Harlan's boot heels.

***

Gary snuck out that afternoon. Maeve was busy at the front desk. It was a couple of hours before she got a chance to check back into the ladies' to make sure she hadn't killed the little shite.

There were spatters and drops of blood drying on the tiles, but of the man himself, no sign.

Maeve never saw him pass by the front desk, but that was hardly a surprise. The fire exit at the end of the hall stood open more or less 24-7.

She only hoped he was gone for good. On a bit of an impulse, Maeve crossed the hall and used her passkey.

Gary had cleared out. His room was trashed, but it was the kind of trashed looked like he'd done it himself. There were no clothes in the closet, and the gaming console he used to bang away at for hours at a time was also missing.

There were a lot of magazines still scattered about. Everything from FHM and Ralph to bondage stuff with Japanese writing on the covers.

Maeve flicked one open with the tip of one finger. The cover was hardly like paper at all. The photo inside showed a trussed woman, lines of clothespins pinching the soft flesh of her breasts. Tears ran down the woman's face, and she seemed to be screaming into her gag.

Maeve stepped back, wiping her fingers on the hem of her skirt.

No matter how many times she washed her hands that day, the feel of that paper stayed with her, a limp and greasy ghost clinging to her fingertips.

FORTY-FOUR

She let the darkness enter,

> *Now she calls the darkness home.*

> *Bad Angel far from Heaven,*

> *Bad Angel calling me on...*

Jack Terrabonne's voice faded to silence. The man's sound was whiskey, leather and a sadness dark as smoke.

Terrabonne's guitar strings fluttered, a faint and haunting glissando. Kane held his final note, soft and sure, to the very last moment. He let it fade, and Terrabonne's fingers fluttered over the strings in a final flourish. His palm fell flat across the strings, and the room was silent.

The two men looked at each other. Jack Terrabonne shook his head and slid into that famous aw-shucks country boy grin.

"You're a damn sight better'n you said you were, son."

Kane tapped the reeds clear on his Oskar and put it back in its velvet case. Terrabonne shifted his guitar to a more comfortable position on his knee. The Dobro gleamed waxy and golden in the light.

"You sure you never had any training?"

"Just listening to the great ones," Kane said. Two weeks at the Sorbonne didn't seem worth mentioning. "And when you play in public, people drop you money or they don't. Keeps you honest."

"I hear that, I hear that." Terrabonne's fingers played over his knees. "So you really liked that concert tape I did? What am I saying, course you did. You know, one leg of that tour, Hamburg Germany that was, you know who joined me up on stage? None other than--"

"Jack, I'm sorry, but I really do need to hit you up for that ride back to town. I'm already late as it is."

"Woman?" Terrabonne's eyes were knowing, bright and merry. "I thought so. You ought to call her, tell that gal who you're with and that you'll be a little late."

Kane's reply was cut off by the door slamming against the studio wall. An eye-watering sting of testosterone curled in the air. Harlan Winters looked down from the top of the doorway. His eyes were red and wild, the muscles in his face hard and white.

Kane snapped the Oskar's case shut and held it ready. Jack Terrabonne looked up from plucking on his Dobro.

"Oh, hey old hoss, there you are," Jack said. "I wanted to ask you bout that thing you were looking into for me. That French thing. How you going?"

Harlan's eyes darted from Jack to Kane and back again. Hands the size of shovels curled and uncurled. A low rumbling growl rose from his throat.

Jack noticed Harlan's look and plucked out a quick little honkytonk riff on the Dobro's strings.

"Did you know old Kane here's also a musician?"

***

Four-thirty that afternoon, Maeve felt like a thousand ants crawled under her skin. Kane was gone. The last obstacle standing between her and that murdering rich bastard Jack Terrabonne had been removed.

Tonight, tomorrow at the latest, Bridey would have her revenge.

Maeve tried to imagine what came after, but her thoughts skittered away from that place like drops of oil on a hot grill. Her mouth went dry, her stomach knotted tight, and her palms left damp stains on the front of her jeans.

In that moment, the phone ringing in the hostel lobby was both distraction and relief. Maeve picked up, forcing bright and chipper notes into her voice.

"It's me," Kane said. Maeve closed her eyes and cursed. Softly, and with feeling.

"What's wrong? Where are you?"

"I'm on a phone in Jack Terrabonne's study. He's--"

"You son of a bitch."

You're wrong about him, Maeve."

Knuckles stood out, small and white, across the back of Maeve's hand. She reached for her cigarettes.

"And *you* don't know what you're talking about, you two-faced fecking bastard." She shook a Marlboro out of the deck and lit up, blew a plume of blue smoke at the plastic 'Clean Indoor Act' sign.

"I talked to him, asked him about Bridey. He had no idea who she was."

Maeve blew a plume of blue smoke at the ceiling.

"And you were expecting, what, he'd confess?"

"I grew up with this guy's music, Maeve. He's no killer."

"He's the man, the *rich* man, surrounds himself with JD and all the rest of those bloody animals."

"We played a few songs together. He likes my stuff."

Maeve's breath hissed over the phone line as she dragged on her cigarette.

"Jack invited me to stay over," Kane said. "We're going to play some more after dinner."

Two German backpackers came into the lobby and made sour sniffing faces. One made a big show of coughing and the other waved his hand in front of his nose.

Maeve blew a stream of smoke at them and turned her chair away.

"I wouldn't have thought it. You laid down with the vipers."

Kane made a soft and inarticulate sound into the phone.

"You'll have told the bastard about me then?"

"I want to talk to you first. Tomorrow."

"Give me chance to see the error of my ways?" Maeve stubbed her smoke out in the center of the desk.

"Look, I can't talk right now, but I think I might have an idea. About Bridey." He paused, clothes rustling as he leaned in closer to the phone. "Let's talk tomorrow."

Maeve's only answer was to slam down the phone. She dropped her head on her folded arms. Not a chance in hell Bridey's killer would be coming back into town tonight.

There were a lot of empty hours until the dawn. And nothing but Bridey's shade for company.

FORTY-FIVE

Kane set the phone back in its cradle. Down the hall, Harlan and Jack still shot fierce whispers at each other from behind the recording studio door. Kane looked around the study walls. The room was plastered with memorabilia, mostly photos of Jack Terrabonne with other famous people.

Footsteps sounded out in the hall, Jack's clicking little heels and Harlan's heavy boots. Both faded away quickly in the distance, muffled by the wood paneling and the thick carpet.

After a time, Kane got restless waiting for the steps to return. There was nothing to do in the study but think about Bridey and Maeve, and wonder what a man like Jack Terrabonne was doing with a creature like Harlan Winters.

Kane didn't get it.

He pulled his coat back on, dropped his harmonica case in one pocket and left to wander.

The floorplan to Whispering Pines was a nightmare. It reminded Kane of an African souk crossed with the House of Usher. The house was dark timber, dry and dusty. The decoration was ornate and lush, too expensive. The halls were long and twisting, dark and quiet, the air too warm and too still.

A side door let out onto a deserted garden. Kane left the main house for the cleaner air outside. White paths threaded through thickets of dormant brown rose bushes. The shallow scallops left by Kane's feet were the only steps tracked in the raked gravel. Flowers were bedded on either side of the paths: mums and begonias and geraniums, all bright spring blooms thrust in the frozen ground far out of season.

Kane knelt on the path. Rain had beaten the fragile blossoms into the soil. Brightly colored petals lay like bloodstains on the dark earth. Kane rubbed a petal between his fingers. It was brittle and stiff, already dead from frost.

Beyond the garden was a wide stretch of grassy lawn, maybe two acres. On its far side, a treeline beckoned. Black pines, swaying and hissing in the wind.

Kane thought of Bridey, the painful innocence in that single creased photo. He tried to imagine her somewhere now, telling fortunes on a beach in Brazil or drinking Mad Dog margaritas in a bar in Texas. Too busy, too angry, maybe too ashamed to contact her best friend.

No matter how hard he tried, Kane was unable to convince himself that Maeve's friend was still alive.

The sky was clear. The rising moon wore a bright crystal halo. Snow, and soon.

His feet carried him to the center of the lawn. Close enough to smell the coming cold and the sharp sting of good clean pine.

Close enough to see the long dark marks in the wet grass. Tire tracks, gouged into the soft dark earth.

Behind him, the main house's timber walls glowed purple in the gloaming. A few lights shone buttery and yellow. Most of the windows were black and empty and silent.

Kane stared after the place where the tire tracks curved around the trees and out of sight. Tempting as they were, he turned instead and followed them across the lawn. They led past a large empty horse corral to a group of outbuildings, sheds and enormous wooden barns.

There was a broad muddy area where the earth was churned. A bare electric bulb burned on the side of the barn. Below it stood a brass tap and a coiled green hose with a spray nozzle. Water dripped into a stone trough crusted over with dark ice. Dripping marks in the dirt all seemed to lead from the muddy area into different slots in a single barn: some sort of converted garage.

Something about that patch of dark wet earth bothered Kane. In the dim and uncertain light, the scene did little more than whisper its story. After a moment, he turned his back and followed a lively and interesting set of smells and sounds.

Jack Terrabonne kept horses. The stable was full of Arabians, beautiful animals nickering and moving in their stalls at the sound of Kane's approach. It felt good to be surrounded by the warmth, sounds and smells of hay and horses. Kane wandered the central aisle, giving each animal a welcoming pet and a handful of feed from his palm.

He was still doing it when Jack Terrabonne entered the barn.

"See you found your way around all right." Terrabonne gently pulled one shiny blue pantsleg up and perched an elaborately worked ostrich-skin boot on a rail. He shot his cuffs and leaned forward to rest one elbow on his raised knee.

"They're beautiful," Kane said.

"They oughta be. Damn things cost me enough."

Kane turned away from the mare he was scratching. She reached out of her stall to bump him with her muzzle.

"Son, I just talked to Harlan. JD's racked up pretty bad, ain't going to be able to work til that busted arm heals."

Kane stood firm, his feet a shoulder's width apart. He made no reply.

"Looks like I need a little extra help," Terrabonne said. "Pay's eight-fifty a week as long as I keep you, and a fair few fringe benefits on the side, if you know what I mean. Who knows? Way you blow that harp you got there, I just might know a couple industry types'd like to hear you. Could be a foot in the door."

Jack Terrabonne flashed his world-famous smile. The gleaming white crescent was dazzling in his sunlamp-brown face.

"What do you say, son?"

Kane stood motionless for a long moment before replying.

"I'll have to think about it," he said. "And if you're serious, first I'll need a favor."

FORTY-SIX

"Not a chance, mate." The bouncer crossed his arms over his chest.

"You're new here, ain't you?" JD said. He had Farrel and Turk at his back, big solid men even if they were banged up a little and swaying some on their feet. "We're regulars. *VIP* regulars."

"And you're from Whispering Pines, yeah?"

"That's right. We work for Mister Jack Terrabonne his own self, and we come in here all the time. You just ask that boss of yours, that Lasker."

"It was Mister Lasker left the orders you lot were eighty-sixed." Pulsing lights danced across the bouncer's shoulders and the sides of his head. From the open doorway behind him came the canned sounds of electric guitars and a thumping bassline. "None of you's named Harlan, are you?"

JD and Turk and Farrel all looked at each other. Bouncers started filing out of the open doorway, until the sidewalk in front of the strip club was full of shoulders, chests and arms. JD took a step back.

"You see, if one of you is Harlan," the bouncer said, "we're supposed to give him the bash, good and proper."

JD snorted. "Y'all want to take down Harlan Winters, you're gonna need a damn sight more'n you got there."

"Not so much for you though, hey Yank?"

"Hey wait a minute!" JD raised one hand and stepped back further, right into Turk's big solid belly. "I know my rights, you can't touch me long as I stay out here on the sidewalk!"

"I thought you wanted to come in the club, mate." The bouncer grinned and cracked his knuckles.

"We was just leaving," JD said. "Come on boys."

Turk fell in line behind JD, but Farrel lingered on the sidewalk. JD's first thought was trouble, but Farrel's voice when he spoke was thin and wheedling.

"If we can't look at the strippers, can we at least go upstairs, to the whores?"

The bouncer flashed his teeth.

"Not a chance in hell. Now, you gentlemen have a nice night."

***

Harlan Winters raged. There was no one in the other rooms on his hall to hear him yell and curse.

Harlan swung at the wall. Plaster bit into his knuckles, and the crater in the wall was the size of a dinner plate.

This new stranger could spoil everything. Jack didn't even see it, or if he did, he was having too much fun playing everyone off each other to care.

Course, Jack didn't care about much. The man believed what he wanted to believe. Hell, he was happy enough thinking all those runaways and junkies and backpackers were safe and snug somewhere. Far as Jack knew, his biggest worry was a bit of bad press, maybe something messing up his deal with that Christian network.

Poor damn sumbitch had no idea what Harlan had at risk. Or what Harlan would do to protect himself and stay free.

A straight-backed chair splintered in Harlan's fists. What was left wasn't good for much more than kindling.

Harlan grabbed the side of his bed. The frame leapt in his hand, and the mattress flew. The box was steel, heavy and strong. For the second time in two days, Harlan hauled it up and dropped it on the messed-up bed.

Money had a smell all its own. There was nothing else like it. Most of the bills in the box were good old-fashioned American dollars, hundreds and fifties. A little less than five thousand in this stupid country's money lay loose across the top of the banded stacks. Harlan hadn't had a chance to change it over to US currency yet.

Harlan sat on the floor rubbing the red and pink hundreds in his palms. These bills were special. This was the money Jack thought he'd spent on the French kids. The sweetness of those kids' deaths fizzed like the best champagne against the walls of Harlan's heart. He told himself he'd never spend those ridiculous red hundreds.

One corner of plastic had peeled back on Harlan's fake passport. He'd bought it off a guy in Singapore four or five years back. The passport wasn't fake, exactly. It was the genuine article, it just wasn't Harlan's name on the paper. But the photo looked close enough, and the signature was a wild squiggle any damn fool could duplicate. Best of all, the passport was still good for a couple of years, but it was old enough that it didn't have the microchip. It wasn't loaded with any vital statistics, height or weight or any dead giveaway.

Harlan thought of it as his Get Out of Jail Free card.

He had a good thing going with Jack. Twenty years ago, Harlan never would have imagined the rewards of doing dirt for a man like Boogie Jack Terrabonne. Standing in Jack's shadow had given Harlan the freedom to find his true self. But gratitude aside, there was no way Harlan was about to let anyone put him in a cage.

There had to be a way out. Harlan just had to think.

He dropped the passport back in the case. His fingertips brushed the crumpled manila envelope, but its contents held nothing for him now. For the moment, his little keepsakes had lost the power to excite, or to comfort. They were dry, brittle and dead. Harlan's fingers felt too big for the front pocket of his jeans, but the moment he touched the hair he felt an instant surge of relief.

This lock of hair was black and glossy. The braid was wispy and thin, tied at the ends with small bits of ribbon. The French girl had worn her hair short, no longer than Harlan's pinky finger.

Harlan touched it to his cheek. He breathed in the barest traces of that cheap strawberry shampoo from her last shower.

Most of that nasty soap smell had worn off, and Harlan's nostrils flared as he caught other scents: coppery, salty and animal.

Those scents were fading. They didn't take Harlan back as quickly, or as completely, but the memories evoked were still sweet. He closed his eyes and remembered the French girl, Chloe: the way she ran and the way she fought, her skin and hair and eyes, her scents and textures.

Harlan fell asleep curled on the floor. The lock of hair stayed curled in his fist, next to his lips.

He dreamed of trees. Of rustling leaves. Of sunlight falling in thin golden shafts.

Harlan dreamed of the chase, and the sound of screaming.

FORTY-SEVEN

The door to Tanya's room was open. Beth knocked on the doorframe and stuck her head inside. Tanya sat on her bed with her feet up, concentrating on something in her earphones.

"Hey, what's up?" Beth said. "We're starting the movie soon, and everyone's asking about you..."

Tanya thumbed a button on her MP3 player and looked up. "Oh, hey."

"I didn't think those songs I gave you were *that* good."

"Here, listen to this."

Beth sat down on the bed, took the single earbud Tanya handed her and plugged it into her ear.

Tanya hit play. There was a rumble of background noise, and the tiny speaker filled with the sound of a deep and growling voice.

"You two got your passports?" the voice said. "Got to make sure you're legal, you understand."

"Omigod, is that Mister Winters?"

"Old Cat Pee himself. Listen, it gets better."

Beth pressed the earphone closer to her ear. There'd been a quick exchange that she missed, Mister Winters and some guy, he sounded young and foreign, European like. Everything was muffled and distant, like the recording was made from inside a pocket or something. Beth heard the rustle of paper and cloth and that familiar rumbling voice.

"That there's for just what we agreed on," Winters said. "Course, you decide you're up for any extras..."

"Eeww, is he...?"

"Wait," Tanya said. "Listen to this." She fast-forwarded to the right spot, the tip of her tongue touching her upper lip as she concentrated.

"--All cleaned up, you just go through that door over there. Make sure you wash your hair real good, too. Jack-- um, the gentleman is freaking crazy about clean hair."

***

Midnight in New Zealand was 5 AM in Los Angeles. Jack Terrabonne was surprised when the phone in his study rang.

"Jack, buddy! How's things Down Under?"

"Delton Adams, you old dog!" Jack leaned back and put his boots up on his desk. "I figured you'd be asleep."

"Yeah well, you know what they say. No rest for the wicked."

Jack chuckled, warm and rich. "So I'm guessin you got that last file?"

"Three words, Jack: Fab. U. Lous! I can't quit listening to it."

"So it's all right?"

"Seriously, Jack, you give me two more like this, maybe seven or eight business-as-usual, we can move some units, even in this market."

Jack swung forward in his chair. His feet scraped the desk and hit the hand-woven Navajo rug with a soft thump. He pressed the phone to his ear and pumped his fist in the air.

"The cut's rough yet," Delton said, "but the rough edges work. A little bit of post, and this sucker's sure to get plenty of air play. Heavy rotation."

"I'm glad to hear you say that, Delton. Glad to hear."

"This is a new direction for you, Jack. When did you start writing, really writing, again?"

"Well, you know..."

"Seriously, Jack, I like it. I like it a lot, up there with any of your best stuff."

"Hey, I don't know I'd go that far."

"I would. This is what I've been trying to tell you. It's great to see you step away from that slick and polished crap. This new work, it's dark and gritty. It's *real*."

Jack Terrabonne didn't hear the rest of the conversation. His face and ears were burning.

***

"You shittin me?"

"Mate, why would I do that?"

JD watched the local kid through narrowed eyes. One long red cut aside, the guy's face wasn't marked up too bad, but the way he was moving, that damn kid was even more beat to hell than JD. And the way the kid was swaying and slurring, he'd been drinking that pain down. Farrel and Turk looked at JD and each other and shifted on their feet.

They all stood on the sidewalk outside The Bunker. Their breath plumed in frosty clouds, but none of them much felt the cold. Didn't seem right, all the drinking they did in that place, the damn bartender wouldn't even run JD and his buddies a tab. People weren't so beat to hell, or so drunk, or still had money in their pockets brushed past them heading into the bar or leaving, none of them alone.

"Bloody hell, I don't see what the big deal is, anyway," the kid said.

"You don't see the big deal." JD's hand itched inside the cast, and his fingers were unable to form a proper fist.

"I just figured you'd want in on this, after, you know, the way she punked you."

"Watch your mouth, boy."

The kid held his hands up in front of him and shrugged.

"I'm just saying, mate. Everybody knows you came around the other day to talk to her and got your ass handed to you. Of course," he eyed JD's cast, Farrel's foam collar, "I don't know where anyone'd get that idea."

The kid took a long pull from the Early Times and passed the bottle to Farrel. Turk's eyes tracked the sloshing brown liquid, and his tongue wet his lips.

Liquor wouldn't last long between Turk and Farrel. JD rattled the bottle of pills they'd given him back at the hospital, for the pain. It was nearly empty. He scratched at his arm above the cast and wondered what the hell he was going to do next.

Turk and Farrel worked at the whiskey. The local kid zipped up his jacket and winced, like moving even that much hurt.

"Maybe it's best," he said. "I mean, I've got the passkey. She'll be sound asleep right now, nothing she can do. If it's just me, I can keep that bitch quiet. If you guys were there, it'd be a lot worse, and take a lot longer. We'd have to take her off someplace where it wouldn't matter how much she yelled."

JD's eyes slid across the other two. Farrel thrust the whiskey bottle at Turk's chest and wiped his mouth with the back of one fat hand. That weird creepy light was bright in his eyes again.

"She *is* pretty," he said. "You know, for a slut and a whore."

JD scratched the plaster above his broken arm. It did no good at all. He scratched the bare skin higher up his arm and fed his resentment and hate.

"You know a place we could take her?"

The kid nodded.

"Good. I want to hear that bitch scream."

FORTY-EIGHT

"Ssshh."

"But what if someone comes?" Farrel looked more excited than scared. His eyes were bright and glittering. The oils on his skin smelled like burning metal.

"Ain't gonna matter if you wake every damn fool in this place up. Now keep quiet."

"But I bet there's folks staying here, still out at the bars and such. What if one of em comes back?"

JD raised his good hand to Farrel. The local kid, Gary, turned the lock on the front door. The deadbolt fell into place with a loud tumbling clack.

"Seriously, mate, how hard was that? Come on, she's just down this hall."

The surfer snickered like he'd just told himself a dirty joke. JD thought about killing him.

Turk picked that moment to be a weak sister.

"I'm telling y'all, I thought I saw Jack's car," he said. His voice was thin and whiny, and his fingers kept twisting themselves in knots.

"Jack ain't in town," Farrel said. "He was back down from the mountain, We'd all be tucked up in The Bunker, drinking with him right now."

"What about Harlan?"

That stopped them. JD and Farrel looked at each other, and at Turk and back again.

"Hell, Turk," JD said. "Must be two dozen of them Range Rovers parked on the street tonight. Leave it to you to decide that one's got Harlan Winters in it. What're you, trying to drop out?"

"I was just thinking, JD. I mean, Harlan's mad enough at us already, maybe it'd be best if we--"

"Go on then, get the hell out." JD was right in Turk's face. Tiny flecks of spit struck the fat man's cheek. "I never figured you for chicken."

"It's not that. Come on, JD..."

"You're in, or you're out. And I mean if you're out, you *stay* out."

"But if it *is* Harlan..."

"What's it gonna be, *chicken*? In or out."

Turk's shoulders sagged and his head dropped. JD cuffed him over the ear with his one good hand and pushed the larger man in front of him down the hall. Farrel followed, his face full of unpleasant lights.

"Hey, hey mate... who's this Harlan guy anyway? Why're you lot so afraid of him?"

JD struck Gary in the mouth. The kid let out a short high squeal and tumbled to the carpet. JD grabbed the kid's shirt and leaned in, close and low.

"You get this through your head, boy. We ain't afraid of nothing." JD gave the kid a shake for emphasis. "Now get up and get that passkey of yours out, and for God's sakes, keep it quiet, or it just might be *you* we haul off into them woods."

Gary turned a waxy green color. Too ready to believe every hillbilly myth or too dickless to handle his liquor. JD didn't know and didn't care.

"Move it!" JD whispered, but it was Farrel hauled the boy up by his collar and pushed him and Turk both down the hallway.

Somewhere in the fog of painkillers, liquor and anger, JD worried. That weird light burned in Farrel's eyes, and he was breathing hard through his mouth.

It was quiet in the hall. That slack time of night, the only sounds from behind any of the doors was snoring. That kind of quiet made them all a little uneasy. Turk actually walked on tiptoe.

Everyone stopped outside the girl's door. They stood bunched up together in the hall, finally looking to JD for leadership.

"All right, here's what we do." JD dimly wondered if his whisper was a little too drunk and a little too loud in the silent hallway.

"We gotta keep this quiet. You, boy, you're gonna open her door with that passkey. I'll go first, get a good hand on her mouth, then Turk'll grab her arms and Farrel gets her legs. Real quick like, we carry her out that there fire exit. Bitch is sure to kick and scratch, so watch out."

The surfer fished a tarnished brown key on a shoestring from inside his shirt. The key scraped and rattled in the lock, and the bolt made a single loud click.

The kid smiled with bloody lips and turned the knob.

FORTY-NINE

"The fecking bollocks," Maeve whispered in the dark, "You wouldn't think they could make any more noise."

"They're drunk," Kane said quietly. "Makes them sloppy."

"And twice as dangerous." Maeve bounced her weight from foot to foot, the blades of her knives gray and glinting in the half-light.

"Come on," she said. "Open the door."

Knives were messy but effective. The problem was that they only worked at close quarters, too close to keep from being overwhelmed by multiple attackers. Out in the hall or inside the tiny hostel bedroom, with no room for Maeve or Kane to move, JD and the others had all the mass and weight they needed. Unless Maeve did something vivid, terrifying and lethal.

Kane pictured the carnage and held up one hand, palm out.

"I've got an idea," he said.

"What is that you're after doing?"

"Pass me that vodka."

The bottle was mostly empty. Kane held it up to the faint orange glow from the wall heater, saw two or three centimeters of liquid slosh at the bottom.

It was enough.

"What're you going to do?"

Kane searched the floor until he found a scrap of cloth that might have been a tee shirt or a miniskirt and the porcelain saucer Maeve used for an ashtray.

JD's voice carried, thin and nasal, from the other side of the door. Kane's fingers closed on Maeve's lighter, and he unscrewed the cap from the vodka.

The key rattled in the lock. Kane stood at the door and waited. It felt like forever before the last tumbler slotted home.

Kane swigged the vodka. The deadbolt snapped open.

The knob turned, hesitant and slow. Kane grabbed it and tore the door open.

Gary, the other hostel worker, stood in the doorway. Behind him were JD and the two others. All wore identical masks of shock and disbelief.

Kane flicked the wheel on Maeve's lighter and spit vodka.

The liquor left Kane's lips in a fine spray. The widening funnel of droplets crossed the lighter's flame. In a chain reaction that took less than a twentieth of a second, the high-proof vodka ignited.

What hit the men on the other side of the doorway was a burning cone of liquid flame.

Man's reaction to fire is instinctual, primitive. Especially when that fire appears suddenly, and where it's not expected. Suddenly engulfed in flame, the men's reaction was even worse.

Gary and JD screamed. They panicked and flailed, beating at their burning hair and clothes.

Kane wiped his mouth with the cloth. He took another mouthful of vodka, stepped into the hall and blew a second blast.

He kept his lips round and firm and close together, like he was blowing a raspberry. The click of the lighter's flame didn't take much coordination: Any point on the cone of spray would ignite. Kane was careful to shut the spray down before the burn traveled back to his face, and to wipe his mouth clean right away.

The fat carny with the black beard caught the worst of the second blast. His long hair and beard and the collar of his coat went up in a bright flash. The white foam collar sizzled as it melted. The man screamed and ran and blazed like a torch.

The burning men set off the fire alarm. An electronic tone burst out in an ear-splitting shriek, and overhead nozzles sprayed water down into the hall.

Kane shut the door and turned the deadbolt. From out in the hall came the sounds of doors opening and closing and an agitated and confused babble in at least five languages. Kane tipped the bottle a third time and this time swallowed the vodka. The medicinal taste, like warm rubbing alcohol, made him shudder but did help him to ignore the smells of charred meat and burnt hair.

"Jaysus... Suffering... *Fuck!*" Maeve said over the wail of the alarm. The knives were stowed away now. She held one bare white arm out to Kane. He handed her the bottle, watched her throat work as she drank down the last of the dregs.

"You don't half play, do you, Yank?"

"Cops'll be here soon. Fire department too. Probably best we left."

FIFTY

Leaving the scene was no problem. Kane and Maeve were just two more sodden figures filing out of the youth hostel. Many like them were half-dressed, carrying a single pack or bag. The focus was on the fire and the smoke, the old wooden building and what it meant to their vacations.

Kane and Maeve eased to the back of the crowd and just kept walking. By the time the first flashing red lights appeared in front of the hostel, Jack Terrabonne's Range Rover was rolling north and west, up into the hills and out of Queenstown.

They rode in silence for a time. Kane kept both hands on the wheel, intent on the twisting ribbon of blacktop in his headlights. Maeve sat in the passenger seat curled close to the window glass and said nothing. It was twenty minutes before she spoke.

"I thought you were just going to thrash them."

"Odds were against us. I had to think outside the box."

Maeve looked over, searching the side of Kane's face. Kane eased off the gas and steered through a series of switchbacks.

"That with the fire... Where'd you learn to do that?"

"Busker's trick. I can juggle too."

"Aren't you the man of hidden depths."

Kane shrugged. "Like you said, there's not a lot out there for a kid on his own, and most of what there is isn't very pretty. I was lucky."

Maeve's face went distant and private. She bit her lower lip and held her fingers to the vents of the Rover's heater.

"I wasn't so lucky," Maeve said. Her voice was soft and quiet, her face without expression. "To tell you the truth, my life those days was bloody dodgy."

"I know."

"Oh yeah?"

Kane held his breath until he cleared a hairpin turn. The Range Rover gripped the road well enough, but the vehicle was both wide and high, and Kane wasn't a great driver at the best of times.

"It's not so much what you say as what you don't say. You're not shocked or even upset at what I did to those four men. Instead of asking whether they're all right, you ask how I learned to do that."

"The sprinklers put them out quick enough, and they had worse in mind for me, I'm sure. You heard them." Maeve folded her arms across her body. "Besides, if they managed to get out of that hallway under their own steam, the bastards couldn't be too hurt too bad, now could they."

Kane eased further off the gas to negotiate a series of downhill turns. "You don't even seem to care where we're going."

"Come on, that's dead easy. Mister Rich Bastard Music Man records a song with you and offers you a job, it's no mystery who lent you this bloody flash truck you're driving like a nanna." Maeve shook her head. "You'll have to do better than that."

"There's something I need from you."

"Yeah?"

"Your word. That Jack Terrabonne is safe while we're guests under his roof."

Maeve was silent a moment before replying.

"You really think Bridey was killed by this man Winters?"

"I didn't say that. Even assuming she is dead, she could have fallen off a hiking trail or been bit by a snake for all we know, or met her end a hundred different ways. But if I did have to look in Jack Terrabonne's house for a killer, I'd start with Harlan Winters."

"You don't think Bridey fell off a trail, do you?"

"No."

Maeve put one hand on Kane's thigh. It was small and white against the wet denim.

"All right," she said. "You have me word."

Kane's skin warmed in a way that had nothing to do with the Rover's climate control.

Once they'd cleared the pass, the mountain road threaded through great tracts of tall pine. In the daylight, the pines had been shadowed, green and cool. By night the truck's headlights carved an endless tunnel of flashbulb brilliance. Frosted branches and black asphalt slid past, at times punctuated by startled dots of bright green eyeshine.

"You came back for me."

Kane looked over at Maeve and nodded.

Her fingers curled tighter on Kane's thigh, and his breath tightened in his chest.

"Right now I don't really care where we're going, and I don't give a damn whether those others are all right." Maeve's voice was low and thick and rough. "But I think of those men coming after me, and you burning them, and the only damn thing I care about is having you inside me." Her eyes were witchy and green in the dashboard light. "Is that wrong?"

Kane had to swallow twice before his voice would work.

"No."

Maeve's hand moved higher up Kane's thigh. Her palm was like burning ice. The blanket fell away as Maeve leaned over in her seat. Her face and body were sculpted in the faint glow of the dashboard light, and the truck's cab filled with the smells of fresh copper and burnt gunpowder.

"Don't you think you'd better pull over then?"

Tree branches lashed the side of the truck. The Rover's tires hissed over pine needles and slid to a stop. Somewhere in the distance, a night bird screamed.

FIFTY-ONE

Harlan woke the next morning groggy and lying on the floor. He rubbed his face with one hand and was surprised to find the lock of the French girl's hair still lying in his palm. He held the lock to his nostrils and inhaled, gave the hair a little kiss and tucked it back in his front pocket.

The room was a wreck. The mattress was half off its frame, splinters of furniture were all over the floor and a fist-sized crater in the plaster stared back at him. He'd change rooms tonight, after he got rid of the stranger.

Harlan kicked his getaway box out of his way and climbed to his feet. He pulled on his boots and rubbed the sleep out of his eyes with one broad palm and staggered out the door to make his problem go away.

The doorknob locked automatically. And Harlan's room was the only one in Whispering Pines that the maids' passkeys didn't fit. All Harlan had to do to protect his privacy was pull the door closed. Today he thumped down the hallway without listening to make sure it latched.

The thought of his fit last night made Harlan embarrassed and ashamed. There was no need to get so worked up. Especially since Harlan's problem had such a simple and obvious solution. Getting rid of the new stranger would be easy, and it would give the boys a chance to redeem themselves in the process.

Except the boys weren't in their rooms. Callum was there, sure, but he was next to useless. The ones Harlan wanted were missing: Turk and Farrel, and that nasty little shitweasel, JD.

Harlan sighed and lumbered downstairs to the other end of the house. There was no cell service in this valley, and the only landline in Whispering Pines was the one in Jack's study.

The study curtains were closed. The room was a museum of shadows, the only light trapped in the squares of glass hanging on the wall. The framed photos stared back at Harlan like the eyes of dead men.

He flipped open his cell and thumbed through the address book. The landline connection was scratchy and static. It rang twice before Queenstown's top cop, Superintendent Hollings, answered.

"Ah, Mister Winters." The cop's voice was venomous and unpleasant. "I was about to call you."

Harlan shut his eyes and pinched the bridge of his nose.

"What've they done now?"

***

The previous night had taken its toll on Kane. It was already full light by the time he got up. Maeve lay beside him, tangled in the sheets and snoring.

He dressed in silence, all the way up to his heavy black coat. Maeve didn't stir. After a moment's consideration, he reached into the jumbled pile of Maeve's clothes and pulled out her knives.

The weapons weighed almost nothing. The handles were cheap black plastic, but the flimsy steel had been hand-sharpened. Kane touched one edge with the ball of his thumb. The blade's edge was sharp as any razor.

The temptation to drop the knives in his pocket was strong. He had Maeve's word that she wouldn't harm Jack Terrabonne, but taking her weapons would be more certain.

Unless she found the kitchen. Or the stables. Or any of a thousand other places where bladed objects might be found. And for that matter, if Maeve really did decide to kill someone, Kane believed she would not hesitate to use her bare hands.

He replaced the knives where he'd found them and set out to navigate the still and silent halls of Whispering Pines. On his journey down to the front door, Kane passed two pairs of young women, all of them in matching dark blue dresses. They didn't pause in their dusting and cleaning, only watched him pass out of the corners of their eyes.

The air outside was clear and cold. Kane breathed deep and smelled a strong wet promise of snow.

Gravel crunched under Kane's shoes on the driveway. Closer to the barns the gravel drive gave way to packed earth and frozen mud. Kane heard faint birdsong in the trees and saw a solitary rabbit start and leap away in a distant field, its fur the exact color of the dry dead grass.

The trampled area next to the garage was clearer in daylight. The nagging sense that Kane missed something last night was strong. He knelt down close to the dark earth with the watery sun at his back. The low slanting morning light threw small impressions into sharp relief, as clear to Kane as words on a page.

The site was a mess. Four different pairs of boots, two sets of similar tire tracks and water splashed from the hose all complicated the scene. Kane's breath hung frozen in the air as order began to emerge from the chaos.

The rain made it easier. At first glance, the overlapping rings formed by raindrops seemed to complicate the scene, but they had the virtue of washing down older prints. Within moments, Kane was able to see the rain-rings as nothing more than background. It also meant the marks he was looking at were less than two days old.

Tracks circled, overlapped and doubled back again. There were a lot of wide crashing steps and places were the earth had been thrown up at the sides of the foot by a sudden change in direction. At the base of the tap, two deep cupped hollows were the right distance apart to be left by a large man's knees, and dark patterns in the wood told of horsetails of dark mud thrown from a low position.

Kane looked closer. He wondered how much of this scene his subconscious had understood last night. The water tap, the edges of the stone trough and the pipe at the side of the barn had all been wiped clean.

Down at the base of the wall, a finger's width above the mud, dark red stains ground into the bare wood beside the trough looked nothing like dirt.

"Help you?"

Kane turned and stood. It was the driver from the day before. The moon-faced man who had walked away when it was clear the others were going to attack Kane.

"It's Callum, right?"

The driver nodded. Callum had stringy hair and flecks of gray in his beard. He kicked a small vee-shaped notch in the hard mud.

"Jack hire you?"

"He offered."

Callum nodded and walked past Kane. The two men walked together to the horse barn.

It was dark in the barn, and warm. Jack Terrabonne's prize Arabians nickered and bumped in their stalls. Kane breathed in the childhood scents of alfalfa, hay and horseflesh.

Shovels and pitchforks stood propped in a corner. Kane reached for a shovel.

"Don't bother," Callum said. "Jack's breeder has his own team handle the mucking and feeding and suchlike. They get their panties all in a twist if you try to do any little part of their job."

"Sorry. Just thought I'd help."

Callum shuffled over to the nearest stall. A shaggy head reached out, and Callum stroked the horse's muzzle.

"I like to come here sometimes," he said. "Always had horses growing up, and it kinda helps clear my head."

"I understand." Kane picked a handful of feed pellets from a plastic bin and moved to where Callum stood. The horse's nostrils rippled and twitched, and Kane held his palm out. The horse's lips were whiskery and delicate as it ate the alfalfa.

"You have horses when you were little?" Callum said.

"I used to have a little mare named Snap." Kane scratched the Arabian's neck near the corner of its jaw. The horse nickered and stretched his neck.

"This one here," Callum said, "I call him Biscuit but I don't know what the breeder calls him. Jack don't name any of them anything."

"Biscuit's a good name."

"He likes you."

"He knows I don't mean him harm." Kane looked up into the horse's eye, enormous, brown and liquid. "They're pretty good judges of people."

Callum kicked the toe of his boot into the hay.

"These horses don't like Harlan none at all."

"Yeah?"

Callum looked directly at Kane for the first time. Callum's eyes were small and soft, with the first faint traces of crow's feet at the corners.

"Jack say what you'll be doing for him?"

"No. And I haven't decided I'll come on, either."

"You will. Everyone does."

"How long have you been with Jack?"

"Ten, eleven years. Longer'n most, but not as long as Harlan. He's been with Jack best part of twenty years."

"What's it like?" Kane said.

Callum shrugged. "All right, I guess. Jack don't tour so much no more, but he's still got these places here and there round the world." Callum stroked the horse's head, his eyes distant and private. "We travel all the time, but mostly it's like we never go nowhere at all."

Kane watched the man pet the horse. When Callum spoke again, his voice was small, quiet and childlike.

"JD and Turk didn't come back last night. Farrel neither."

"No."

"You hurt them?"

Kane nodded.

"They deserve it?"

"Yeah."

Callum frowned and nodded his head. His hand moved over the horse's muzzle.

"They're not good people, Callum."

"Turk and Farrel ain't so bad, and JD's all right when he's sober. It's drunk he's got a mean streak."

"Wise man once said, expecting bad men not to do wrong is madness."

Callum petted the horse in silence. His mouth turned down at the corners, and his eyes were infinitely sad.

FIFTY-TWO

Harlan stomped into the hospital before the glass doors had a chance to slide all the way open. The glass shuddered but held. This time, the nurses at the front desk gave him a stony stare. Behind his back, there were a lot of stiff faces and sidelong looks and brief hissing whispers. The word 'police' came up a time or two before they told him which painted line to follow.

Harlan followed the painted line to a different part of the hospital. The day before, Harlan had left JD, Turk and Farrel by themselves in the Accident & Emergency. He'd figured he could trust them on their own for once.

Clearly, that had been a mistake. Instead of coming back to the house, those boys had screwed up even worse. Harlan suspected the hospital staff were making their feelings known. The A&E had been streamlined, crisp and efficient. This part of the hospital was older, and darker.

The nurse in this ward had a mole on her mouth and thick black hair on her forearms. She stood up with her arms crossed when Harlan came onto the ward. She made a choking face and gestured wordlessly down the hall.

JD, Turk and Farrel were all bunked together. The room had six beds and scuffed brown linoleum on the floor. Two of the beds were empty. An old man lay in the third. He was still and frail, making wet gobbling noises in time with the hiss and shush of the machine beside his bed. The air around his bed smelled of mucous, urine and death.

Harlan stepped into the room and met wary eyes, sullen and mean. The boys heard him coming before they saw him. Harlan looked at each of them in turn, and took his time about doing it. The thrill of fear that ran through them pleased him no end.

The boys were a mess. Turk and Farrel were bandaged up like mummies. The smell of cortisone cream hung chemical and cold over the deep raw scents of burnt hair and weeping flesh in the air near their beds.

Turk was the less injured of the two. A small square of his face from his eyebrows to his nose had been left open to the air. The skin that Harlan could see looked red and angry and sunburned.

Farrel's head was completely cocooned in gauze. All he had was a thin dark slit to look through. Behind all those thick layers of bandages and swollen burned flesh, Farrel's eyes were small and piggy and filled with blood.

JD was the worst injured. And the most pissed. He sat propped on his pillows with his right arm in the cast from the day before yesterday, the other wrapped thick and immobile with bandages. The left side of JD's head was hairless, cracked and red. He stared hard at a point on the brown lino and looked ready to spit tacks. Maybe he was thinking about how he was going to wipe his ass the next little while.

Harlan paced in front of them. Six beds was supposed to mean space for twelve or more bedside visitors, but Harlan filled the room. His sheer size made the space feel small and hot and suffocating.

His boots drummed across the floor, echoed off the walls, grew louder and louder.

When the drumming suddenly stopped, the boys jumped.

"Something y'all want to tell me? Far?"

Farrel's piggy red eyes jinked from side to side behind the slit, but he didn't say a word. Not so much as a murmur rose from under the gauze.

Harlan felt the heat rise in his neck. His palms itched, and his lips curled back from his teeth.

"He ain't bein smart," JD said. "His face's burned up pretty bad. He can't talk."

Harlan hitched the front of his coat back with his thumbs. The butt of the gun showed at his hip, and JD saw it.

"Fine. You tell me then." Harlan's shadow fell over JD's bed. "Just what the hell happened?"

"We weren't drinking, if that's what you mean."

Harlan sniffed the air. JD winced.

"Not much anyhow," JD said. His cheeks were tight and pinched where the gauze stopped. "Not that much. And besides, we was just trying to get home. You know, after you left us."

"Don't you lie to me. You remember the last time you lied to me."

A sour odor rose from the hospital bed. Harlan bent down until the heat of his breath crawled over JD's face.

"Talk," Harlan whispered. His fingertips brushed the back of JD's right hand at the open end of the cast. JD's eyes rolled wild in his skull.

"We was jumped."

"And set on fire?"

"It was this local dude. He set us up."

"Set you up. So someone could set y'all on fire."

JD's eyes darted from side to side before he spoke.

"We was going to see a girl."

Harlan chuckled. His breath smelled like bone meal and bad meat. JD tried not to crawl away from it.

"And this girl just happened to be that same one already got you messed up twice. That same one I already told y'all to stay away from. Twice. *That* girl?"

JD's lips pressed into a thin line, like a cut in the lower half of his face. He didn't say anything. He didn't need to.

Harlan straightened. One thick palm bounced on JD's cast, twice. The man in the bed writhed. Knots of muscle at the corners of his jaw spasmed.

"This'd be that same girl's connected somehow with that stranger Kane. That stranger busted your nose and busted your arm. That stranger I wouldn't be surprised set you on fire. That stranger staying up to the house. That stranger who's right now working his way deeper and deeper into Jack's good graces."

Harlan brought his hand crashing down on the cast. Plaster crumbled under his fingers. JD cried out and the stench of urine filled the air.

"Y'all left me one hell of a mess," Harlan said. "Now I'm going to have to go take care of this stranger my own self."

Harlan buttoned his coat and wiped the saliva from his mouth with the back of one hand.

His eyes swam with lights the color of arterial blood.

FIFTY-THREE

Maeve woke in an unfamiliar room, naked and alone. Her left arm was numb where she'd laid across it, her legs were tangled in the sheets and her face felt like it was gummed shut.

She didn't understand it. For some reason, with Kane she slept. Really slept.

And Bridey was nowhere to be found.

Much as she hated to admit it, Maeve felt better than she had in a very long time. She felt strong.

The shower spray was hot and hard and needling. Maeve stood under it until her fingers and toes puckered and every knotted muscle along her spine loosened and dissolved. The towels were thick and soft and plush, so plush it was almost obscene.

The face in the bathroom mirror was less gaunt, the skin no longer pulled so tight against the bone. The bags were less dark, but the eyes were still haunted. Watching her reflection look back out at her, Maeve thought she heard the distant keen of winter winds.

Her knives were where she'd left them. Bit of a surprise that: she'd more than half expected Kane to take them with him, trying to protect that damned rich bastard.

The house was enormous. Maeve wandered the halls for over twenty minutes without running into a single living soul. Once she saw two wheeled trolleys in a second-floor hall, each piled high with towels and linen. Female laughter trilled from the open doorways near those carts, but Maeve passed without entering. She didn't know what to say, or how to explain her presence.

On the first floor, she found a room bright with winter sun. The room was long and low, with gray slate floors and dark wooden timbers. At the far end of the room a dining table sat next to a large stone fireplace, dark and cold. At the near end stood a jumble of great leather couches and chairs. Maeve descended the three short steps and entered.

One long wall was glass. The leaded windows broke the cold morning light into bright cold squares. Two french doors led out onto a slate-floored patio surrounded by gardens. The doors were shut against the cold. The patio was bare of furniture, the garden shriveled and dead.

The opposite wall was hung with pictures. Eight by ten glossies, most of them black and white. Some of the people in them were famous, others Maeve didn't recognize. They stood in ones and twos and sometimes groups, always around a short man with a dark tan, high white hair and a big toothy smile. That man was in every photo.

Maeve looked into those smiling eyes and tried to find something cold, diabolical.

In the center of the wall was an enormous gold frame. Behind the glass, lit by baby spotlights, was a white and gold guitar. It shared its box-frame with a pair of chunky gold sunglasses and an autographed photo of Elvis.

"Man himself give me that." Maeve jumped at the echoing boom of the voice behind her. "Back in seventy-three that was, pulled me right up on stage with him in London. Course, I wasn't much more than a pup back then, but that old hound dog knew talent when he saw it."

It was the man from the photos. There was no doubt, this was Jack Terrabonne: Kane's hero and the last man to see Bridey alive. The bastard was short in person, just a few inches taller than Maeve herself and probably a good deal less than that without those ridiculous boots. He was every bit as handsome as his pictures, but the camera didn't show how bloody large the man's head was on his body.

He was also a lot older than in any of those photos. The bastard's hair was still thick and white and piled high on his head and his skin was still tanned and brown and expensive, but the signs were there, if you knew where to look. The man had faint white scars at his hairline, and he'd been botoxed within an inch of his life. His forehead and cheeks didn't so much as move when he smiled and winked.

"Didn't scare you, did I now?"

Maeve bit down on her natural response. The blades felt like ice against her skin. Instead, she forced her eyes wide and a purr into her voice.

"It's just such a bloody big house. A body starts to wonder she isn't half a ghost."

The old man looked her up and down.

"Sure look like flesh and blood to me. Jack Terrabonne, darlin, at your service."

Maeve braced herself for a big American handshake. This Terrabonne article surprised her. He took her fingers softly and turned up the back of her hand. He didn't go so far as to kiss it. Instead, he folded his other hand over the top of hers, enveloping her in a warm, dry and delicate touch.

She could draw her second blade across the rich bastard's throat. Nothing could be easier. But she had promised and Kane did seem convinced of the man's innocence. The moment passed.

"Maeve Kelly" she said. "Mostly people just call me Maeve."

"Right pretty name, right pretty. That some kind of an accent I hear?"

"Irish, yeah. Hope it's okay, me staying here last night."

"Day a pretty little thing like you ain't welcome under my roof, well, they might as well start pounding nails in my coffin." The bastard had a good laugh. Pity the facial muscles didn't move with his mouth.

Maeve looked down and took her fingers out of Terrabonne's hands. She fought the urge to wipe her hand on her skirt.

Terrabonne caught her eye, gave a slight shake of his head and the barest hint of a wink.

"Twas Kane as brought me," Maeve said.

"I didn't ask, darlin'. I didn't ask..."

***

Harlan stopped short outside the hospital. A police car was pulled across the front of his Range Rover, its blue and orange checkerboard side inches from his grille. He took a couple steps closer, and the cruiser blipped its lights. The driver-side window slid down when Harlan was close enough for the glass to show him his own hulking reflection.

"Winters."

"Hollings."

"Fires now."

Harlan's breath hissed an icy plume between his teeth. "What it's worth, it don't exactly look like they started it."

The cop flat-eyed Harlan for several seconds. Harlan felt the blood swell and burn in his wrists and throat.

"I don't have to tell you this is the last straw."

"Those shitbirds been nothing but trouble lately. Far as I'm concerned, you can throw their candy asses *under* the damn jail."

"Wasn't for your boss, we'd have done just that long before now." Harlan wanted to smack that smug, not-quite-British, not-quite-Australian accent out of the cop's mouth. "As it stands, attacking tourists and burning down hotels, it's like those lads are on a mission to wipe out the whole region's tourism industry."

Harlan's eyes slid from side to side. Over by the hospital entrance, two nurses pointed and whispered.

"You'll keep Jack's name out of it, right?"

The muscles in the cop's jaw flexed and bunched.

"You disgust me." The cop's driver's side window slid up as the cruiser began its slow roll forward.

Harlan was left staring at the glassy face of the police car's window, the black mountain of his reflection blotting out the winter sky.

FIFTY-FOUR

Kane stood at the far edge of the dead garden. The sky was opaque, the color of pearls. The air was wet and cold with a crystalline snap. The great gray pile of Whispering Pines stood just behind him, but the last thing Kane wanted at that moment was another roof closing him in. His eyes traced the twin lines of broken grass and rutted mud across the open field, up to the point where the tire tracks curved out of sight around the far edge of the strand of tall pines.

Something about the sight bothered him. Kane couldn't put his finger on it, but he was sure there was something he was missing in that muddy jumble of prints and tracks at the side of the barn. Like a powerful dream lost on waking, the feeling of missing something important was maddening.

Boot heels ticked on the slate flagstones behind Kane. The step was quick and light, with a little rock-tap of a swagger. The cloud of moisturizers and aftershave smelled leathery and expensive.

"Morning, Jack," Kane said without turning.

"Sure is! I tell you what, I can't remember the last time I was up this early."

Kane shifted to face Terrabonne, his hands in his pockets. Jack was small and elfin, wrapped in an oilskin stockman's duster. The tailored coat looked almost child-sized, and the high collar on the wool liner was like a frame for his big brown head.

"There's something I should tell you," Kane said. Terrabonne cut him off with a wave of his hand.

"About that gal? Don't even mention it."

"You've met her?"

Terrabonne flashed that trademark blinding-white smile.

"Sure did. Breakfast this morning!"

Kane watched Jack closely.

"Everything went all right?"

"We had us a little grapefruit juice, and she told me about your wild night."

"I see..."

"I hate to think of what it sounds like JD had planned."

"He's a bad sort, Jack."

"I know it, son. I do." Terrabonne patted the air between them. The scent of his beauty products roiled in the still and wintry air.

"I knew his momma a long time back, before JD was born even. I promised her I always would look after that boy, and I have. He's been a good worker for me. But this now, I just don't know..."

"I heard them talking," Kane said, "out in the hall. They meant to rape her. Abduct her and rape her."

"Boy was drunk, but that's no excuse." Terrabonne shook his head and spat. "That kind of publicity, it'd ruin me."

Deep in the pockets of his coat, Kane's knuckles stood out against the bone.

"Course, son, I'm grateful to you for stepping in. And I do intend to show my gratitude, don't you worry bout that none. But y'all left one mighty hell of a mess back down there in Queenstown, and Harlan, he'd normally sort this kind of thing out, but I got no idea where the heck that old boy is. He's been running off a lot lately. So I got to go on in to town my own self and straighten all this out, talk to the police and so forth."

Terrabonne's eyes were bright and blue and intent on Kane's face.

"Now, before I go on down there I got to ask-- any reason you might not want to talk to the cops?"

Kane rubbed the back of his neck with one rough palm.

"You wanted for anything, son? Any warrants?"

"Not exactly."

"Just rather steer clear of the cops?"

Kane nodded. Terrabonne clapped his hands together.

"I reckon I ought to be able to swing that. You won't be the first fellah on my staff pulled his hat down low when the police rolled past."

"I don't--"

"Son, don't you worry about it none." Terrabonne chuckled. "Far as I'm concerned, it's all settled."

He looked at Kane out of the sides of his eyes. The corner of Jack's lip twisted into a tight little hook, and his brown and flawless skin resembled leather taken from some ancient reptile.

"You're gonna like working for me, Kane. Good money and plenty of travel, lots of little extras and a foot in the door for your music. Life don't get much sweeter."

"I haven't decided."

One muscle jumped under Terrabonne's left eye. He stuck his hands in the pockets of his duster, turned his face to the pines and the mountains beyond and took a deep breath of fresh air.

"Of course, of course," he said. "Tell you what, we'll talk some more on it tonight. You're up to it, we could play a little more this afternoon, maybe do a few more songs like that *Bad Angel*."

Terrabonne reached up to clap Kane on the shoulder. That flash of teeth was the brightest thing in the wintry landscape.

"Right now I gotta take care of that mess you left, back in town. You got yourself the run of the house, grounds too if you want. Make yourself at home."

Terrabonne's expensive aftershave trailed behind him as he left. Kane turned back to the field, the woods and the mountains. Terrabonne's boot heels beat their ticking little rhythm around to the front of the house. Kane was intent on the sounds of the dark and hissing pines, the secrets whispered by the wind moving through the dry dead grass.

FIFTY-FIVE

Maeve rode back down through the mountains with the rich bastard. Jack took his baby blue Porsche instead of one of those clunky big Range Rovers. The flash little sportscar was fast and low and snug to the ground. Terrabonne drove like a maniac, showing off.

She curled her legs up under her on the warm leather seat. Trees and rocks and wide sheer-dropping cliffs rocketed past. One hard wrench at the wheel and Bridey might be avenged. Or Maeve might end up dead or paralyzed, while the bastard walked away with cuts and scratches, the Devil looking after his own.

Bridey's presence was there in the car with them, sullen and silent.

Maeve understood. She had come too far. Given up too much. She was too close to the end not to be sure.

"My driving make you nervous, darlin?"

"Hm, what's that?"

"You look like a cat swallowed a hard-boiled egg."

Maeve looked away. Green blurs flew past out the window, and the lowering sky was the color of hammered lead. Bad weather coming. Terrabonne downshifted and hummed to himself, pleased and smug. The man had no idea of Maeve's own bloody thoughts.

"What's so funny, darlin?"

"Your driving. Coming up this way last night, Kane drove slow as an old woman. And here's you, taking these curves like a bloody teenager."

"Ain't the only curves I can take like a teenager."

"You really are a dirty old man, aren't you? Every inch of you."

"Guilty as charged, darlin. Guilty as charged."

Jack looked back at the road and flicked the wheel. The Porsche skimmed through a hairpin turn, whipping through just in time not to fly off the bloody side of the mountain.

"Christ, this thing's bloody fast."

Terrabonne smiled. He had that smile all the American celebrities had, white and gleaming, totally self-assured.

"Mm, but I do love that accent!"

"Got a thing for Irish girls, do yeh?"

"Wasn't for that accent," he said, "You'd remind me of my second wife. And my third."

"That's a hell of a thing to say."

Terrabonne cut his eyes over at Maeve again. She wondered if he'd tried these lines with Bridey.

"Darlin', my third wife'd had your accent, there might never have been numbers four and five."

Maeve shifted in her seat, and her fingers brushed the knife in her boot.

"What about wife number two?"

"I'm not so sure even your accent would've helped that one," Terrabonne laughed. "Pretty little gal tried to poison me."

"Watch the road, you dirty old thing, or our deaths'll be a lot quicker than poison."

Jack gunned the engine coming into a rise. They took the top of the hill so fast the Porsche's wheels left the ground.

***

Whispering Pines had a large square kitchen. Two ovens, a gas-ring stove and a restaurant-sized grill stood against one wall. Sinks, stainless steel counters and an upright cooler lined the other. A butcher block counter in the center took up most of the floor space, and the cold winter light gleamed off racks of copper pots and pans.

It was a lot of kitchen for Jack and his small entourage. Like the rest of the manor house it was too large, a room of shadows and echoes, a hollow monument to Jack Terrabonne's vanity.

Kane entered from the empty dining room, its walls crowded with photos and memorabilia. There were three other doors in the kitchen: a walk-in cooler, a short hallway that could only be the maids' quarters and a passage through to the back stairs. Kane picked the stairs and began to climb.

The hallways were dark, narrow and silent. Kane stalked their length back to the room he and Maeve had slept in. A high narrow trolley finished in fake wood-grain stood in the doorway. A cloth sack hung in a metal frame at the front of the cart. Cleaning supplies sat in a tray at the top, and open shelves on the side contained towels and bedding. Kane stepped around the trolley and into the doorway.

Two maids were at work stripping the bed. One was a small brunette, her mouth and jaw still soft with baby fat. The other was a redhead a couple of inches taller and not much older. Both wore identical blue polyester dresses. Neither dress had pockets.

The dark-hair girl looked up and gave a startled little jump.

"Sorry," she said. "We're almost done."

"No problem." Kane looked around the room. No sign of Maeve's clothes and her pack was gone.

"Is something wrong?" A quick look passed from the dark-haired maid to the redhead. There was an element of anxiety in it, and accusation, that Kane could in no way interpret.

"No, just looking for someone is all."

The dark-haired maid seemed about to speak, but the redhead straightened and brushed a strand of hair out of her eyes.

"Looks like you found us," she said. "I'm Tanya, and this is Beth. You're an American, hey?"

"This person you're looking for," Beth put in, "is she an Irish girl, long black dreadlocks?"

"That's her," Kane said. The redhead, Tanya, shot her friend a filthy look. Beth shrugged and stuffed the loose bedsheets into one of the pillowcases.

"She's gone," Tanya said. She took a step closer to Kane and looked up at him from under her lashes. "She left twenty minutes ago with Mister Terrabonne. They seemed real friendly together."

Jack. That damn fool.

"You don't have idea where they might have gone?"

The redhead's laugh was wicked. Beth came out of the bathroom with the other pillowcase full of wet towels.

"I'm sorry, sir." She shot a narrow-eyed look at her friend. "Most of the time we don't even know where Mister Terrabonne's guests are when they're here in the house, and neither of us has any idea what he might do when he's out." She stopped a moment and bit her lip.

"You see, we've only been here four days."

Jack had deliberately hidden the fact that he'd taken Maeve with him. There was nothing Kane could do to save the man from his own folly, especially now he was half an hour gone.

Kane nodded and shouldered his pack. Everything he owned was already inside, neatly packed.

"Pleasure meeting you ladies," he said.

From down the hall, Kane heard their voices rise in argument.

***

"What's wrong with you?" Beth said. "Talking about the boss like that, and to one of his own guests! Are you *trying* to get fired?"

"Yeah, like that'd be so bad?"

"Where are you going to get another job? And without a reference?"

Beth folded her arms across her chest and frowned.

"You realize, one word from Mister Terrabonne to the agency and you'd be finished?"

Tanya shrugged. She raised her eyebrows and made a half-hearted pass at wiping the furniture down with a rag.

"Like I want to be a maid all my life. Besides, it'd get me out of this house, me and my MP3."

"Come on, you can't be serious."

"Mister Terrabonne's always going on about how the tabloids are all out to get him, how they'd pay good money for any dirt they can get. Imagine what they'd pay for that recording..."

"Tanya..."

"For God's sakes, Beth, don't be such a baby! Everyone does it. People like Mister Terrabonne practically expect us to sell our stories..."

FIFTY-SIX

The crew taking care of Jack's horses were all business. Three men and two women, they were from a local ranch, what they called a sheep station. They mucked out the stalls and spread fresh hay and generally ignored Kane. The manure went onto a trailer behind their truck, probably so the rich man wouldn't be offended by its presence.

"Anybody ever ride them?" Kane asked the crew's leader.

"They're horses." The crew leader was short and blocky, with weathered features and short dark hair going gray. He checked that each scoop of pellets was level before it went into a horse's feed trough.

"Any chance I might take one of them out?"

"You're a guest of Mister Terrabonne's, hey?"

"That's right."

"Then it'd probably be all right, you wanted to take a bit of a spin around the corral. We do it a couple times a week, keep them trained to the saddle."

"And outside the corral?"

"Not a chance."

"But--"

The crew leader gave Kane a cold and wary look.

"You think I'm going to give you permission to run off with a prize animal worth a quarter to half a million dollars, mate, you're out of your bloody mind. Because every one of these bloody animals is a bloody pedigreed prizewinner, and Jack bloody Terrabonne's not interested in doing too much else with *but* collecting trophies and selling foals."

The horse in front of them threw its head and nickered, riled by the crew chief's outburst. Kane clicked his tongue and stroked the animal's muzzle to calm it. The crew chief watched, his eyes thoughtful.

"Tell you what," he said after a time, "tack room over there's never locked. Fifteen minutes or so, we'll all be gone. You know how to hang your own saddle, there'd be nobody could do a bloody thing to stop you."

"Thanks."

"Don't go far, though. There's a storm front rolling in, due to hit late today, maybe early tomorrow." The crew chief squinted at the distant horizon. "Sounds like it's going to be a bad one."

***

Maeve had never been in a Porsche. The speed and the fragility of the tiny car were no problem, but she was unprepared for the looks the car got as they rolled into Queenstown. Even in a town full of luxury cars, people on the sidewalk noticed the bright blue Porsche. They looked through the windows at the people inside the car, their expressions at once admiring and envious.

Jack Terrabonne slowed the car right down. He looked over at her, fatuous and proud.

The man had no idea. All Maeve saw in those looks were potential witnesses.

The Porsche cruised past the backpackers. A spray-painted plywood sign out front said the hostel was closed. There were official looking notices stuck to the front door. Close to a year Maeve had lived there, sleepless haunted nights sharpening her knives. Already that time seemed like an artifact of somebody else's life.

Bridey's presence was like ice on the back of Maeve's neck.

Terrabonne flipped open a cell phone and thumbed through the menu. Maeve heard the faint buzz of a ringtone, some corny country song she didn't know. When the ringtone stopped and the voicemail flicked on, Jack Terrabonne swore and thumbed the 'off' switch. He found another number in the directory and called that one.

The same song played, but this time someone picked up.

"That you, Turk?" Terrabonne barely waited for the reply and began talking over the other man's voice. "Fine, fine, but y'all are together, right? Good. Now, here's what you're gonna tell the police."

The guy at the other end listened to what Jack had to say, but the Porsche's interior soon filled with the strident buzz of the other man's voice.

"Calm down, Turk. I say, calm down. You let me deal with old Harlan, just you make sure you and JD, and Farrel soon as he can talk, you boys all give the police the same story. Okay? Now haven't I always looked out for you? All right then. Yup, later."

Terrabonne disconnected and dialed another number. This one had a simple ringtone, all business.

"Bob? Jack here! Yeah, I know, I heard about the boys. Damn shame." He listened for a moment. The voice at the other end was low and full of authority. "Well, Bob, you do what you got to do."

Terrabonne flipped the phone shut and dropped it into the slotted tray in front of the gear shift. He gave another brief flash of those bright Yank teeth and tossed his head.

"All right darlin, let's get you some new clothes."

The Porsche was stopped at one of the town's three stoplights. Maeve could slit the bastard's throat right now. Or she could open the car door and walk away.

Either way, she would never know for sure. And Bridey would never forgive her.

Instead, Maeve crossed her legs and made her voice soft and husky.

"Tell you what... Why don't you get us a room, something private?"

"But, goddammit, we just left a beautiful house in the middle of nowhere with over a dozen goddamned empty bedrooms!"

"And your man Kane, wandering the halls."

The old man's look was arrogant and unsavory.

"I gotta say, darlin', I like the way you think."

FIFTY-SEVEN

Kane found Callum in the converted garage, changing the plugs on an old Harley. The bike's chrome gleamed softly in the dim and dusty light, and the air smelled of sawdust, motor oil and gasoline.

"Nice bike."

"Yup," Callum said. "Jack rode it twice, scared all hell out of himself. Probably won't never touch it again."

Callum set down his ratchet and dropped the used sparkplug in a grease-smeared glass jar.

"Them new cars," he said, "the Rovers, Jack's Porsche and whatnot, they pretty much run their own selves. All the microchips and so on, nothing you could do to em if you wanted. Lease company trades em out every couple years too, so it ain't like they get much chance to break down."

Callum picked up a small cardboard box that rattled when he shook it.

"But every place of Jack's, there's at least one or two old vehicles'll still take a wrench. And I figure they're right grateful for the attention."

"This part of your job?"

Callum shrugged. "More to pass the time, really. Working for Jack, it's go when he says go, but side from drinking with him and laughing at his jokes, there ain't a whole lot Jack needs doing. You'll see."

Kane tucked his thumbs in his belt loops and scuffed the bare dirt floor with his shoe.

"I'm taking one of Jack's horses out for a ride," he said. "I should be back by nightfall, but there's always a chance I'll get caught out after dark. That happens, you'll see me again at first light."

Callum nodded and rattled the cardboard box between his fingers.

"Jack asks, I'll tell him."

"How'd you fall in with Jack, anyway?"

Callum opened the cardboard box and tumbled the new sparkplug out onto his palm. He shifted a disc-shaped gauge into the gap at the tip of the plug and looked Kane full in the face.

"I was a pretty good fiddle player once. Jack caught my act, even recorded a couple songs with me. Running with him was supposed to give me a foot in the door."

***

Terrabonne chose the hotel. It was one of half a dozen places at the bottom of Queenstown, just past the small town's third cross street and jostled up against each other along the lakeshore. The hotel was crisp and upscale but a step or so short of truly posh, the rich bastard's idea of slumming.

Maeve waited in the Porsche while Jack paid for the room. She stayed pushed down low in the seat. Bridey's shade hunched down beside her, looking over with eyes at once sad and alarmed.

It would have been easier if the old man had taken one of the SUVs. In Queenstown, a two year old Range Rover was every bit as common as a twenty year old campervan.

The baby blue Porsche was unbelievably memorable.

Maeve was ashamed at the thought. Bridey's revenge, and the truth that would make her revenge certain, proper and correct was the highest priority.

Escape was second. A distant second.

FIFTY-EIGHT

Kane sat tall in the saddle. From that height, the snaking dark tire tracks were easy to follow. He lifted the reins from his mount's neck and felt the horse begin to move. A quick shake of the reins and the Arabian broke into a trot.

It felt good to have a horse under him again. It had been years. The animal Kane chose from Terrabonne's stable had a deep muscular chest and a rangy loping stride. The hired crew had done a great job. Aside from a slight tendency to lift the head, the Arabian was perfectly trained to the saddle and responded to every command. Kane had to fight the temptation to snap the reins and take the horse to a full gallop.

The dark pines slid past on Kane's left. After an hour more or less, the trail veered away from the tree line. Kane put pressure on the horse's flank with his left leg and laid the reins along the right side of its neck. His mount moved into the pressure and away from the contact, turning to the left and following the tire tracks up into the hills.

As they climbed the grass grew thinner, shorter and more brittle. Now and then Kane stopped, standing high in the stirrups to scan for signs of his next course.

In a way, it was almost too easy. The 4x4 weighed over a ton and a half, and its wheel base was close to six feet wide. Even in hard and barren hills like these, there were only so many courses possible for a vehicle that size.

The hardest part was accounting for the driver's state of mind. Winters, assuming it was Winters, had driven ramshackle and roughshod over the ridgelines. He'd paid no attention to the best course or even the merely practical, and he'd paid the price. Kane found gouges in the earth where the Rover had taken the brow of a hill too fast and gone airborne, and several hillsides had long dark loops carved in their faces where the Rover's tires slid sideways on the slope, fighting for traction the whole way.

Kane's mount followed the Rover's course at an easy and surefooted lope. The horse had an easier time finding its footing than the heavy truck, and Kane made good time. The sun tracked closer to the horizon this time of year, but its position was still shy of noon. The smell of snow was strong in the air, but there was still plenty of daylight left.

Kane thought about the blood stain on the barn. About the scalloped ridges of a partial footprint. About the reckless course of the vehicle he was now backtracking.

Every step filled Kane with a sense of mounting dread.

***

Maeve's boots made faint hollow sounds on the tiled floor. Those sounds echoed among the ceiling's crisp geometries. The room smelled clean and anonymous. The hotel suite was a place of white surfaces and pumped heat, utterly sterile.

"What you think, darlin'?"

"Fabulous," Maeve said without looking over her shoulder.

She needn't have bothered. The old fool was too busy tonguing a little blue pill off the palm of his hand to look for the truth in her face or her voice.

Maeve looked at the little man with the oddly large head. Crazy to think that big handsome head had been famous once. Crazy to think of this foolish little man sharing a stage with Elvis.

But was it crazy to think this rich old man killed Bridey?

Terrabonne stood close to her. His aftershave was smooth and expensive. Maeve saw the facelift scars in his hairline and the age spots the laser treatments didn't quite burn from his wrinkled neck. His palm cupped the curve of her arse.

Maeve went stiff, and the rich bastard gave her a self-satisfied look.

"Wicked thing, yeh. Why don't you make yourself comfortable on the couch." Maeve forced her hands to release their clenched fists. "I'll pour us a wee drop of that wine."

Terrabonne chuckled, low and wordless and endlessly wicked.

"So is that a yes to the wine, then?"

"Darlin', far as I'm concerned, it's a big old yes to *everything* you got on offer."

A small island of glossy countertop marked the kitchen area apart from the rest of the suite. Wine glasses were hung overhead and bottles of red laid in a small rack on the counter. Safe on the far side of that island, Maeve snuck a glance at the old man on the couch: his shiny green cowboy suit, his chunky gold Rolex and his pointy-toed leather boots. She thought of what she meant to do, and was surprised at the way the neck of the bottle rattled against the lip of the glass.

Maeve forced her trembling hands still. The wine, a red so dark it was almost black, jumped and splashed in the glasses as she carried them over to where the old man sat.

Terrabonne accepted his glass as though it were his natural due. He patted the couch cushion beside him, and his eyes were a sticky presence moving over Maeve's body.

"Lord Jesus, gal," the old man said. "Don't go all coy on me now. You're acting like some kind of virgin."

Maeve stood over him, the stem of the wine glass slick and oily in her hand.

"I've never done this before." She didn't recognize the sound of her own voice.

Terrabonne's eyes went hooded and speculative. He opened his mouth to speak, but Maeve never found out what the man had to say. The bowl of her wine glass shattered against the side of his head and her blade flashed in the cold gray light.

FIFTY-NINE

Jack Terrabonne struggled on the couch. Maeve pressed her knee harder into his chest and her hand tighter to his throat.

The blade of her knife stood high behind her, poised to strike.

"I want you to know why you're here now." Here in the moment, her voice was quiet and level and dangerous.

The old man's gaze was scattered and wild. His careful white pompadour was ruined by red wine and broken glass, and beneath the tanning-lamp brown, his skin had gone gray and sweaty.

"My wallet's in my coat," he said, the words spilling out in a babbling rush. "Go on, take it!"

"What makes you think I want your money, you murdering bastard?"

"There's gotta be, I don't know, at least a few hundred in there. Cards, too."

"Look at me, ya git. Look here. At. Me."

Maeve hauled his face around. Terrabonne's chin quivered and his lips trembled, and his wine-soaked shirt was the color of spilled blood.

"Your money won't protect you," she said. "Not anymore. You killed my friend, and for that you'll die."

"What the-- Missy, I never killed nobody in my whole life."

"You're a damned liar. Her name was Bridey Martin, and you were the last on this earth as saw her alive."

At the sound of the name, recognition dawned.

"What, you mean that Irish gal? But that was--"

"Two years ago. At your ranch in Mexico." The knife point wavered. Maeve quickly moved the blade to the wrinkled flesh over the old man's throat. The thick vein throbbed against the press of the steel edge, the pulse beating like the wings of trapped butterflies.

"Hell yeah... I remember her. Little gal, right? Blonde, couple inches shorter than you?"

"So you admit it." A fat drop of blood welled over the flat of Maeve's blade. The old man hissed in pain.

"Please," he said, "Last time I saw your friend, she was fine and happy. Cash money in her pocket and a plane ticket to Peru in her hand."

"Peru?"

"Something about some ruins, up in the mountains." The old man's legs squirmed, one heel making a dragging beat against the carpet. "Macho Pincho, something like that. Lost city, deep in the jungle, she wouldn't shut up about it."

Machu Pichu. For a skinny ten year old orphan, the thought of a lost city high in the Andes had been a dazzling and impossible dream. The nuns had been furious when the crumpled page, torn from the Encyclopedia Britannica, had been discovered. Maeve had claimed the theft, and taken the beating.

She'd been able to protect Bridey then. It was a long time ago.

Maeve had expected Terrabonne to deny his part in Bridey's death. She hadn't expected to believe him.

"You mind letting me up some, darlin? This ain't quite the position I'd hoped to find us in."

Maeve eased back, slow and careful. Her weight stayed tight and coiled, and the blade stayed in line with the bastard's throat.

"Tell it," she said. "All of it."

The old man sat up, coughing and rubbing at the cut on his neck. It was a few seconds before he wiped the sticky red trails of wine from his face. Finally, he brushed the wet wreck of his hair out of his eyes.

"Ain't much to tell," he said. "except I spent four days with this Bridey of yours and at the end of it, that girl was healthy, happy and a damn sight better off. I was damn good to that little thing."

Terrabonne's eyes were bright and cold and blue. Those eyes locked on Maeve's, and his face was shadowed and grave.

"I just want you to know, whatever happened to your friend... It wasn't my responsibility."

Maeve returned her knife to her boot. On the far side of the window, snowflakes spiraled to the ground. Jack Terrabonne dropped his face into his hands, and his shoulders shook.

She left him there. As the door swung shut behind her, she heard Terrabonne's phone ring. A tinny electronic version of his own voice warbled something about black cats, bad luck and sex.

Maeve's eyes were hot with tears. Her mouth tasted like ashes.

SIXTY

Jack Terrabonne loved his *Black Cat Blues* ringtone. It was a little reminder of better days, especially after the insanity of the last few minutes. A couple of choruses had him feeling better, feeling like he could listen to that song all day. In the end, he flipped open his phone anyway. The voice at the other end was rough, male and unfamiliar.

"That's Jack Terrabonne, yeah?"

"Who's this?"

"You should have paid me, arsehole."

"Hang on a second. How'd you get this number?"

"I would have stayed quiet, you know. There was no call to send that bloody big ape of yours after me."

Terrabonne shut his eyes and pinched the bridge of his nose. The Viagra was kicking in. Painfully.

"Son, y'all need to start talking some sense here." Jack stifled a groan. "Who in the hell are you and what on God's green earth are you talking about?"

"I'm your bloody pimp, you dumb fuck."

"I'm afraid you're mistaken, friend." Jack crouched forward on the sofa, curled around the tight pinching between his legs. Red drops spattered on the carpet. Jack couldn't tell if they were drops of wine or blood. "I got nothing to do with that kind of woman... Not in a whole lotta years."

The pimp snorted.

"Very good, you stick with that," he said. "*The Insider* seemed happy enough with the documentation I gave them, but you stick with that story."

Jack's mind flashed to his last big party. *Always girls want to meet a famous man.*

"Fans, my ass. That damn Harlan..."

"You know what, Jack? I was happy to stay quiet for twenty thousand, but you sent that goddamned *animal* Winters after me. The TV people did not give me anywhere near that amount, of course, but by that point I would've trashed you for *free.*"

The phone went dead in Jack's hand. But not for long. It rang again almost immediately.

A producer from *The Insider,* looking for confirmation. In the time it took Jack to chase that jackass off the phone, he had missed three more calls.

His erection was kicking into high gear now. It would've been a real beauty, if that damn girl of Kane's hadn't turned out to be such a goddamned psycho. Instead, Jack was in for one hell of a rough couple of hours. He growled and punched up his voice mail.

Two more reporters, easy to delete. The third call was from his producer at *The Old Time Country Gospel Hour.* Jack listened to the message with screws tightening in the center of his chest.

Black spots danced in front of his eyes and his face felt like it was poured from concrete.

***

Harlan Winters was behind the wheel of the Range Rover when his phone went off. By the ringtone he knew who was calling. He only had to listen to a single chorus of that damned *Black Cat Blues* before he managed to get the phone open and his pitch ready.

"Hey Jack, I wanted to talk with you. With JD and them laid up for awhile, I'm gonna need to hire a few more boys. I can look around here some, but really it'd be better if we went back home."

"Harlan Winters, you goddamned jackass! What in the name of Jesus Suffering Christ is wrong with you?"

Harlan stopped in the middle of the street, forcing traffic to swerve around him. He gnashed his teeth and ignored the drivers hitting their horns.

"You got no call to talk to me that way," he said. "I had about all the disrespect I can take for one day."

"Disrespect!" Jack's voice climbed with every syllable of the word. "Boy, the best part of you ran down your momma's leg, and you wanna whine to me about respect? Sometimes you purely make me wish your momma'd thrown you out and raised the goddamned   afterbirth."
Harlan's only answer was a wordless growl.

"Goddamn it, hoss," Terrabonne said. "You really screwed the pooch this time."

Harlan pressed the phone to his head and wiped his face with one hand. His palm came away covered in oil and dead skin.

"What's going on, Jack?"

"I got some goddamned *pimp* telling me I'm going to be all over goddamned tabloid TV!"

Lasker. Harlan's tongue rasped against the backs of his lips and the blood thundered in his wrists and neck.

"I'll kill him."

Terrabonne's laughter was barking and derisive.

"You'd find a way to make a mess out of that too. Y'know, I do believe you'd screw up a glass of water."

"Look, I can--"

"Thank you very damn much, shit-for-brains, but you already done plenty!"

"Jack..."

Horns blared as cars swerved around the Rover. Harlan didn't give a damn.

"They pulled out," Terrabonne said. Anger deflated out of his voice. What remained was sad and tired and old. "The Country Gospel folks pulled out."

"Aw shit, Jack. I'm sorry." Harlan closed his eyes and shook his shaggy head. "Maybe we can--"

"Hoss, I've had about enough of *we*. You done screwed up for the last time."

"Jack--"

"Harlan, I'll be home in an hour. I get there, I want your shit cleared out and you gone."

"Now goddammit, Jack, hold on a minute... Jack?" Harlan replied, but he was speaking to dead air. Jack had severed the connection.

The cell phone snapped in Harlan's fist. He threw the pieces at the windshield and beat his fists against the steering wheel. The Rover was well insulated. No one passing on the street outside heard his hoarse and savage cries.

SIXTY-ONE

Kane was tempted to turn back. The sky had darkened and a line of pale cloud grew wider on the southern horizon, an army of ghosts marching on the attack.

So far, Kane had found nothing to support his misgivings. There had been no sign that Harlan Winters had done anything more than drive one of his boss's Range Rovers around the estate. It was still early in the afternoon, but if Kane burned any more daylight he risked being caught out in the snow after dark.

One more hill. If the view from the top of the next hill was like every other Kane had seen so far, he would turn around and ride back to Whispering Pines. He clicked his heels against the horse's flanks, and the animal trotted up the slope.

At the top of the ridge, Kane reined his horse to a halt. Ragged clouds of steam rose from the horse's nostrils, and the animal tossed its head and cantered sideways in impatience.

Kane looked down the slope and knew that his ride was at an end.

***

That day at Whispering Pines, the guest beds in two west were due for a half-turn. It seemed a ridiculous waste when the rooms had only been made up for four days, but those were the rules. Twice a week, whether someone had stayed in them or not, the bedrooms got fresh towels and a change of linen. Beth and Tanya trundled their cart down the hall, and they made good progress. It was quick and easy work, without all the scrubbing and vacuuming that went with the full turn for an occupied room.

"Two more and we're done," Tanya said.

"The day does go quicker when Mister Terrabonne isn't throwing one of his parties." Beth sorted a stack of fresh towels from the cart: two bath, two hand, two face and one bathmat.

"And when we don't have to clean that man's bedroom. I mean, really!" Tanya grabbed a clean set of sheets from the cart.

"Careful, Tanya... You never know who might hear."

Beth ran the stack of towels into the bedroom. She came back out with the slightly musty but unused set to dump in the laundry sack. Tanya still stood by the cart, the fresh bedding in her arms.

"What is it?"

"Cat Pee's door is open."

"Mister Winters? You're joking."

"Look."

Sure enough, faint gray sunlight fell into the hall from Harlan Winters's doorway.

"He *never* leaves his door unlocked."

Tanya looked at Beth, sidelong and impish.

"Maybe he wants his room serviced."

"Tanya, no..."

"Are you going to tell me you're not the least bit curious?"

"You're not serious."

"Come on," she said. "What's the worst that can happen?"

***

The Range Rover tore up the blacktop on the way back to Whispering Pines. Harlan drove with his big fists tight on the wheel, muscles popping and twitching up and down his arms.

A beat-up VW van rounded the blind curve coming the other way, damn hippies camping in the hills. Harlan crossed the white line and ignored the weak shrill bleep of the VW's horn.

The van got closer. Two faces in the windshield screamed in shock and terror at the sight of Harlan's big damn 4x4 barreling down at them head-on. He pulled the wheel back at the last second. Brakes screeched and squealed, and sparks flew from grinding metal.

Harlan bared his teeth and mashed down on the gas. The big diesel engine roared. The van disappeared in the rearview as the truck surged around the curve.

Goddamned ungrateful Jack Terrabonne.

Every passing second brought Whispering Pines closer. Harlan's tongue flickered against his teeth. His face glowed with a terrible intensity.

SIXTY-TWO

"What a dump."

"You know," Beth said. "I actually thought he'd be messier than this. It could be worse."

"Are you kidding? Smell that!"

Beth made a face. Her eyes were watering. Tanya's gesture was triumphant.

"Worst part is, you *know* he doesn't have a cat."

The two girls stood in the doorway to Harlan Winters's room. Weak winter light filtered in through the window, relieving the room of some of its layers of soft shadow.

Debris was strewn everywhere. There was a ragged hole in the wall, and two picture frames had been shattered. Tiny motes of white dust powdered every surface and danced in the gray light. The bed lay at crazy angles to its frame, the sheets twisted around the mattress. On the floor, splinters of furniture and pieces of torn cushion glowed in the twilight.

"Must have been some party," Tanya said.

"Alone?"

"Can *you* imagine anyone wanting to have fun with old Cat Pee?"

Beth made a face. "I can't imagine him having fun."

The two shook loose a couple of black plastic rubbish sacks and started bagging up the broken furniture. Jack Terrabonne's entourage always seemed to be destroying something or other, though this was the first time the girls had cleaned up after Mister Winters.

"You think maybe he lives like this all the time?"

"Tanya, that's mean. Besides, if he did there'd be, like a track. You know, between the bed and the door and the bathroom. I think he probably left the door open for us so we'd come in and clean."

"Makes sense I guess. I mean, if you could help it, would *you* want to clean this up?" Tanya held up the ragged remains of a seat cushion. Hanging limp between her fingers, the fabric looked like a dead animal.

Beth shuddered and stuffed more cotton batting and splinters into her bag.

"Hey, look at this." Tanya pointed to a small bare spot on the floor near the bed. "It made itself a little nest."

Beth shook her head and went back to the cart for the whisk broom. She'd need it to sweep up the worst of the broken glass.

She came back in to find Tanya on her knees. She had a dark metal box open in front of her, and gave a guilty start at Beth's entrance.

"You're not going to believe this," Tanya whispered.

Beth peered over her shoulder. Tanya held up her hands, and they were full of money. Beth knelt down beside her friend. A small pile of loose bills sat on top: Fifties and hundreds from both Australia and New Zealand. Beneath them were stacks and stacks of banded money: US hundred dollar bills.

"Isn't this cool?" Tanya said. "There's *thousands* in here."

"More than that..." Beth ran the tip of one finger over the stacks of bills. There were maybe four or five packets in a stack, six stacks total. Around each packet was a little paper band with a bank stamp and a teller's initials. Printed on each band: US$ 10,000.

Tanya looked up. Her hands were full of loose bills and her eyes were full of light.

"Ever wonder what it'd be like to be rich?"

"Ever wonder what it'd be like to go be arrested?"

"You think he even knows how much he's got here?"

"It's not ours, Tanya. Better put it back."

"Spoilsport." Tanya stuck her tongue out. She dropped the bills and picked up a crumpled manila envelope. A soft weight shifted inside when she shook it.

"What do you think's in here? Think it could be jewels?"

"In an envelope like that?"

"Gotta be something valuable to be in with all that money. Hey look, a passport..."

"Come on, Tanya. That's enough." Beth looked back at the open door and the dark and silent hallway beyond. "If anyone sees us we'll be fired."

"Fine, fine." Tanya dropped the passport and envelope back in the metal box. "Let's get this place cleaned up so we can take a break."

"Now you're talking."

Together, they wrestled the mattress back into place. Beth took the bathroom and Tanya changed the bedding. They worked quickly. The sky outside had darkened terribly, and the room's many shadows took on a different and more malevolent cast in the stormy purple light.

Beth ran fresh towels from the cart into the bathroom. Tanya bent down in front of the bed, straightening the bottom edge of the duvet. Beth came out of the bathroom to find Tanya standing, flattening the hem of her skirt against her legs.

"All done?" Tanya said. "Great, let's go!"

SIXTY-THREE

Something was wrong about the clearing below. Something serious. Kane's horse started to skitter and spook as they approached the edge of the treeline. The trees there were hardwood: beeches, birches and maple. All were stunted and twisted, their branches bare of all but the last few tatters of their autumn glory.

Kane brought his mount in a wide circle around the place where the Rover had parked. He dismounted beside a good-sized maple and tied the reins off to a sturdy limb.

A lone beech stood a couple meters from the place where Harlan parked the Rover. A white patch glowed in the center of its silvery gray trunk.

The sight of the torn sapling made Kane's blood run cold. Behind the tree, a cone of splinters in the shape of an arrowhead had been sprayed out onto the grass. in The heartwood of the young tree was embedded with blood and tissue and fragments of bone.

The ground here was soft, the grass brittle and dead. The eerie purple light of the coming storm softened every shadow. Kane stood and headed into the trees.

The birds showed Kane the bodies. His scent carried on the wind, and a murder of crows rose black and screaming into the darkened winter sky.

Winters hadn't buried them deep enough. Parts of the bodies had been exposed when the wet clay slid away. The fingers of one hand, the edge of one foot and the toes of another, the ball of a shoulder. For the crows, a feast.

The corpses' faces were still buried. Kane scraped away less than an inch of wet clay before his fingers brushed cold dead flesh. He shuddered as though a blade of ice had sliced through his body, and it took a force of will to push away another handful of clay. The sight was a powerful and sorrowful weight on Kane's heart.

One smooth cheek and part of a full and pouty mouth. A lock of hair, short and black and fine, was plastered across the curve of that cheek. Waxy lips curled back from small and even white teeth, and the girl's mouth was caked with clay.

Kane threw himself to one side and vomited. In that moment, he would have given anything to go back in time, to empty his wallet in exchange for that damned MP3 player, anything to get the French couple out of town and away from Harlan Winters.

The contents of his stomach steamed on the grass. They soon froze. Kane wiped the tears from his face and stood.

His eyes burned with a hard and dangerous light.

SIXTY-FOUR

The Range Rover turned through the black iron gates of Whispering Pines. Gravel cracked and rattled off the bottom of the truck, and low-hanging branches whipped at the windshield. As the house came into view, it occurred to Harlan that this was the last time he would ever see Whispering Pines.

It wasn't the first time Jack had fired Harlan. Hell, it wasn't the twentieth. But for Harlan, this was the last. Too much had changed: it was time to get in the wind.

Harlan stopped the Rover and got out. He was still some distance from the house. Gravel crunched like small bones under his feet, and the first flakes of snow steamed and melted against his skin.

The house grew larger as Harlan walked. Veils of snow parted, and Whispering Pines stood revealed: a great gray pile of weathered timber, tall and wide, dark and cold.

Money, passports, his special envelope. It was all in the box under Harlan's bed, and it was the only luggage he figured he'd need. Get his shit and get gone, Jack had said. A damn fine idea.

Harlan stood at the end of the drive. Whispering Pines loomed before him, and flakes of snow clung to his jacket. His eyes narrowed and his nostrils flared, scenting the air.

Eight stone steps led up to the front entrance. Harlan's boot left a wet and dirty print on the lowest step.

His lips curled away from his teeth in a red and savage smile.

***

Kane rode hard back to the house. The sky was a color so deep it was almost black. As the storm front rolled ever closer, the colorless clouds piled high and white and angry.

Harlan must have driven back to the house in the dark. The Rover's course had been veering, wild and erratic. Kane rode straight to Whispering Pines.\

Icy winds whipped at Kane's clothing. The cold stung his face and hands. The horse's hooves drummed a hard and powerful beat over the dry dead grass.

Kane rode like a man possessed.

***

Harlan passed through the front door of Whispering Pines. The main hall stood dark, echoing and cold. A chill wind twisted through the room from the open door. In the shadows above his head, crystals in the chandelier rattled and shook, and the chain made a low keening groan.

The wind slammed the door shut. The air inside was still and dead.

Harlan's boots threw clapping echoes off the tiles and walls. The marble floor had been recently polished. Harlan's reflection followed him like a dark spirit trapped under water.

SIXTY-FIVE

Snow had begun to fall. Maeve stomped her way along the muddy roadside, following the curve of the lake shore. At the entrance to one of the hotels lining the road a car pulled into her path, turn signals blinking and wiper blades clacking. The faces behind the snow-stuck glass were swollen and red: squalling kids and grim parents, determined to enjoy the precious family holiday at any price.

Maeve flipped them the fingers and stormed past. Her face was red and swollen, her cheeks rimed with frozen tears.

Further along, the land rose away from the water. The sidewalk started, and the upscale hotels turned into time-share resorts. At the first cross street, the businesses started: the laundromat and internet cafe, the strip club and tattoo parlor giving way to increasingly expensive clothes.

Snow fell in thick wet flakes that clung to hats and arms and sidewalks alike. People on the street avoided Maeve's eye, hunched over and hurrying in the face of the winter storm.

There was no sign of Bridey anywhere.

Maeve began to feel like a ghost herself, haunting her own life. She felt a curious urge to remember everything she passed. Every bar and restaurant and storefront, every face she passed on the street, every single detail from the wet cobblestones to the snow spiraling down out of the dirty white sky, all had a jeweled clarity: precise, bright and sharp-edged.

She knew she was seeing Queenstown for the last time.

***

Harlan's room was the last in a long line of closed doors. The walls of the hall were dark red, the carpets thick, the light dim. Harlan stalked the length of that hall, filling its width with his shoulders and arms and leaving the air as he passed tainted with a trail of his own pungent and eye-watering personal scent.

His door was closed, same as always. Harlan fit his key to the lock, relieved he hadn't forgotten to close it after all.

The locked clicked. The door opened. Harlan's mouth went dry.

The room was clean. The hole in the plaster was still there, but everything else was square and tidy. The plaster dust had been vacuumed, the debris cleared away. The bed was reassembled and made up with fresh sheets.

The room smelled terrible.

Harlan crossed the room in two steps. His getaway box was under the bed. It sat just behind the edge of the blanket, squared and centered and completely unlocked.

Black spots danced in front of Harlan's vision. His hands shook as he lifted the lid.

Harlan threw back his head and roared. The sound was full of rage and pain.

The money wasn't the problem. A banded stack of hundreds was missing, but only one. His fake passport was there too. What was missing was his envelope.

His hair was gone.

Harlan's eyes stung. His chest heaved, and his breath came wet and uneven and ragged.

He could run. Harlan knew he could run now, and still probably get away. But every goddamned lock of hair in that envelope linked him to a different murder. Running now meant running for the rest of his life.

Besides, that hair was *his.*

Harlan lifted his head, moved it from side to side. His nostrils flared, and his tongue flickered behind his teeth.

The air in the room was soapy and sanitized. Fresh linen and that deodorizing stuff they put on the floor when they vacuumed: It was like sticking his head in a goddamned washing machine.

But under all that industrial soap, Harlan found what he wanted. He knew that perfume, knew that skin.

Harlan knew which of those little bitches had stolen his hair.

SIXTY-SIX

Kane was halfway back when the storm caught him. The Arabian ran hard, picking up Kane's urgency, frightened by the smell of death on his hands. Kane put his head down behind the horse's mane and slapped its rump until the horse ran at a full gallop.

He barely noticed the first swirling flakes. Within minutes the snow was falling thick and heavy, stinging Kane's eyes and slicking the hair away from his face.

The horse's hooves tore black divots in the snow-covered earth beneath them. A slip would mean disaster for both man and animal.

Kane rushed on, unrelenting.

***

"Aren't you changed yet?" Beth called in from the doorway. "We're already late as it is. The others are going to start the movie without us if we don't hurry."

"Tell you what," Tanya said. "Why don't you go on? I'll be along."

"Everything okay?"

Tanya made a face and put one hand over her stomach. "I don't know, I'm wondering if maybe that yogurt was a little bit off. Just give me a little while, tell the girls to start without me."

"You sure?"

"Go."

Tanya made what she hoped was a brave-but-pained smile. Beth put one hand on her shoulder and gave it a squeeze. Tanya waited until Beth's footsteps faded down the hall to move.

She took her bag down from the top of her closet and dropped it on the bed. Tanya stripped everything off the hangers in her closet. Shirts and pants, tops and skirts and dresses all got stuffed into the bag. She opened the drawers of the dinky little dresser and started throwing in bras and underwear.

The little French MP3 player she threw on top. Only then did Tanya lift the hem of her uniform and pull the money out of her underwear. She riffled the bills with one thumb. It was more money than she'd ever had in her life, and she wondered how far it would take her. She pulled a handful of bills out of the stack and stuffed the rest down deep in the bottom of the bag.

Ten thousand US was a lot of money. A lot, but not enough to last forever. There were hotels here in Queenstown where that much money wouldn't pay for a whole weekend.

Tanya took the envelope out of her waistband. She hoped whatever was inside hadn't been damaged when she folded up the envelope. She didn't really think it was jewels, but it had to be something valuable to be locked away with all that money.

Tanya stuck her head out into the hall and looked both ways. Empty. The other girls would all be in the servants' lounge watching Titanic for like the fifth time that week. Tanya closed her door again and pressed her back against it as she opened the envelope and stuck her fingers inside.

"Ugh!"

Tanya's shudder was sudden, whole-body and involuntary. When she could force herself to touch the envelope again, she picked it up by the corner with two fingers and dumped the contents on the bed.

Hair. Dried-out braids of hair, some blonde but mostly dark brown or black. There were braids of short hair and braids of long hair but nothing in any way valuable.

"God *damn* it," Tanya said under her breath. She wondered if she could get the money back into the box before its owner came back, or if she should take the ten thousand and run to Australia.

She could totally see herself on the Gold Coast. A funky little apartment right on the beach, designer clothes, the perfect hair and makeup and tan. She'd sit on the beach all day watching hot guys surf, play footie or just lie around. Tanya was just getting into imagining it when she noticed something odd about one of the braids.

She picked it up for a closer look. There, caught in the hair at the end of the braid, a brittle scrap of something brown and leathery.

Except that the scrap wasn't caught in the hair. The roots of the hair were caught in the scrap. It was skin, a dried and leathery piece of scalp.

In spite of herself, Tanya screamed.

SIXTY-SEVEN

Harlan hunted the halls of Whispering Pines for those goddamned thieving maids. They were nowhere to be found. He looked in all fourteen residential bedrooms and all eight goddamned baths. He even looked in Terrabonne's suite on the top floor. If looking meant busting up a bunch of furniture and pissing on the man's bed.

Harlan hit the first floor. The front hall was tall and dark. His footsteps threw thousands of angry echoes from walls and floor and ceiling. The noise of his passage surrounded Harlan, and after he left, echoing ghosts lingered in the empty room.

The hallways on this floor swam with gray shadows. The only light came through the ground-floor windows, and those were already beginning to cake with snow.

Harlan pushed through the doors into the Rumpus Room. Cloth rustled, and something moved in the shadows.

"Jesus, Harlan," Callum said. "You like to scared the life out of me."

Harlan looked down at the other man. Callum sat hunched on the couch, his eyes red, his mouth bright and wet.

"Hell's wrong with you, Callum? You been *crying*?"

Callum shrugged and wiped his face with a small moist palm.

"You seen any of them damn maids?" Harlan said.

"I dunno."

"I want them maids. I got somethin I want to ask em."

Callum shrugged.

Harlan turned away in disgust. Jack's blue-felt pool table stretched silent before him. On the flat-screen plasma on the wall, stock cars raced around a dirt track in silent pointless circles.

Harlan palmed the cue ball. He squeezed it in one big square hand and eyed the plasma screen.

"I been thinking," Callum said behind him.

Harlan looked back over his shoulder. His upper lip curled away from his teeth.

"I been with Jack a long time now." Callum's eyes grew shiny and wet as he spoke. "Maybe it's time I quit."

"Ask me if I give a damn."

"You're looking for the maids," Callum said. "Why don't you try the servants' quarters?"

Harlan chuckled and hung his head.

"Now why didn't I think of that?"

Harlan threw the cue ball. A big green spot burst across one corner of the plasma TV, but the damn stock cars kept up their silent racing.

He stopped in the doorway and took one last look at the Rumpus Room. With just weepy old Callum in it, the room seemed big, dark and lonely. On the damaged screen, a stock car blew a tire and spun out. Other cars crashed into it, flipping and rolling. One car flew into the bleachers.

Harlan sighted down the end of the .44 and pulled the trigger. This time the plasma TV exploded.

**

A large piece of plywood was nailed over the hostel's sign. Letters in black spraypaint, cramped and uneven, told anyone passing that the hostel was SORRY, CLOSED FIRE. Maeve walked past the sign and found the hostel's front door locked.

The fire door around the side still had a broken latch. Maeve let herself in and stepped into the shadowed and dripping hallway. The cheap carpet squelched underfoot, and the air smelled of smoke and chlorine and mold. The only sounds were drops of water dripping from the ceiling and the beating of Maeve's own heart.

The silence was deafening. For the past ten and a half months, Maeve had lived with thin walls and the constant noise of human life. Seeing the place like this was unnerving.

Maeve's room was unlocked. In all the excitement last night, she must have forgotten. She let herself in, prepared for the worst.

The sprinklers had drenched everything. The narrow bed was sodden, the sink was choked with dirty water and an iced-over puddle stood in the seat of her chair.

Maeve looked down at the bed. The sheets were twisted and crusted with ice. Her breath frosted in the air, but in her mind's eye the room still pulsed with heat like a furnace.

Kane was a hard man. And a good man. It was the first time Maeve had ever seen both together. She felt a sour twist of shame at the way she'd betrayed and abandoned him.

It didn't seem right. But then, much in the world wasn't. Maeve would have given her life to protect Bridey. Now, she had lost her one chance at revenge.

Kane was a grown man, and Maeve's time in this place was at an end.

She stood in the wreckage of her old room, her old life, and listened to the soft pat of snow against the window.

Bridey still smiled behind the surface of the creased and battered photo. In that one frozen moment they were still young, still together. Still in love. Maeve's hand closed over the other girl in that picture, crumpling her own foolish youth.

It would be so easy. Maeve had spent so many patient hours honing her blade to a glinting blue edge. There'd be no fussing about with wrists, either. Sharp as her blade was, one quick slash across the throat would likely take her head half off.

It wasn't the use for her knife that she'd dreamed. But there was nothing left now that she'd failed.

If only the room wasn't so cold, wet and miserable. She didn't want to die in the cold.

Maeve hated being cold. The cold brought back memories, and memory was one thing Maeve never cared to entertain. Memory was no friend.

Wherever she went next, Maeve suspected it would be warm.

SIXTY-EIGHT

Tanya stared down at the braided hair and the torn piece of scalp. Three other girls were crowded into her room, talking and pointing and making shrill grossed out sounds.

Tanya forced her legs to move. One small step backward. A second. The others pressed in close around the lock of hair, debating what exactly they were looking at. A couple more steps and Tanya would be able to slip out unnoticed.

Beth caught her at the doorway.

"Where do you think you're going?"

"Just kind of, you know..."

Beth looked at Tanya's quilted jacket and crosstrainers. She looked at the packed bag on the floor, and her mouth made a firm flat line.

"You do realize this thing with the hair could be nothing, yeah?"

"That's just what I was thinking."

"You still have to tell the police."

Tanya looked down at her own feet. Her face burned.

Beth grabbed her friend by both arms.

"Tanya, tell me that envelope was the only thing you stole."

Tanya opened her mouth to speak. The door burst open at the entrance to the servants' hall, and the corridor echoed with a wild and bestial roar.

Tanya grabbed her bag and ran. Harlan Winters shouted again, and the hallway echoed with a sudden deafening explosion.

Wood paneling shattered next to her head. Her bag fell from Tanya's fingers. She skidded around the corner and ran for the back service stairs.

Heavy footsteps pounded down the hall behind her.

Tanya gulped air and ran for her life.

***

Harlan lost the little bitch on the back stairs.

Didn't matter. He had her bag.

Harlan dropped to his knees, grabbed two fistfuls of nylon and ripped. The zipper tore apart, and clothes spilled everywhere. Cloth shredded as Harlan searched, but there was nothing inside but clothes and shoes and ten thousand dollars of his money.

No sign of his envelope.

A couple of girls stuck their heads out into the hall. Harlan rose to his feet, snarling.

The maids screamed and ran. One in particular, small and dark, ran back out of the servants' quarters and into the kitchen. Harlan wanted to have a word with that little girl.

From the open doorway, Harlan heard whimpering. He cocked his head, his tongue flicking against his lower lip.

Another girl tried to hide behind the bed. Dirty blonde hair was plastered to her forehead, and her face was slick with tears. She looked different without the uniform, they all did. Harlan wasn't sure he liked it. Not that it mattered.

Harlan's envelope lay on top of the bed. Locks of hair were scattered around it. *His* hair, that he had earned.

The girl made a little jump, like she might run. Harlan narrowed his eyes at her and growled.

"Please Mister Winters, please. I won't tell anybody. Please..."

Harlan picked up the nearest lock. Little Mexican gal, name of Esperanza. The braid was long and dried and brittle, not much more than a faded specter of Esperanza's black and glossy mane. Harlan sighed and dropped it in his envelope.

"Tell anybody what?"

"About, about the hair. Or the gun, the gunshot! I wouldn't tell anyone about that, either. I, I won't say anything."

Harlan picked up another braid. The maid pressed back against the side of the closet. Harlan didn't pay her much mind. He was trying to remember the girl's name, pretty little hitchhiker from Jack's salad days. She'd been so excited to have her first ride in a limo, and to meet a 'real' star...

"You touch this?" Harlan said. His voice was low and thick and rough with emotion.

"This here braid. You touch it? Any of these?"

"I-I-I..." The maid broke down blubbering.

Harlan lifted the hair to his nostrils and inhaled.

Bleach. Bleach and soap. Industrial cleaners. The maids had been handling his hair with their bleachy little fingers, and now it was ruined.

Harlan faced the crying maid and howled. She put her hands in front of her face and screamed.

She was a fair-sized girl. Tough, too. Harlan was pretty sure she was still alive after the second or even third time he hit her.

Not that it mattered.

SIXTY-NINE

Jack Terrabonne hated his Porsche. Damn thing was crazy-fast, skittish as a cat at the best of times. Worse, it handled like a scalded hog on crack on mountain roads in the snow.

Wasn't for the ladies, Jack wouldn't have bothered. But the ladies, even the crazy ones, loved the big dog, and a Porsche painted to match his eye color was one of the ways they knew which dog was biggest.

Terrabonne drove back up through the mountains at a fraction of the speed he'd come down. That damn little tramp of Kane's had run off, and with no one to impress, Jack would rather not break his fool neck, thank you very much. He kept his speed sensible and drove hunched over the steering wheel, trying to peek past the wipers and through the swirling veils of falling flakes.

The snowstorm was going to be a big one. About a thousand years before Boogie Jack Terrabonne came along, there'd been a little boy name of Andrew Robert Tebberman from New Ulm, Minnesota. Jack liked to think there wasn't much of that awkward kid left now, but damn if he couldn't help knowing a little something about cold weather.

He'd been a fool to stay here so long. Now he just hoped Queenstown's rinky-dink airport wasn't closed.

Jack wanted to get out while he still had a chance.

***

Beth ran out of the servants' wing and into the kitchen. Chrissy stopped in front of the kitchen door, shrieking and crying and arguing.

"Stop it!" Beth said. She grabbed the other girl by the arm, digging in with her nails until she paid attention. "This is what you have to do: Get out of the house. Take one of the cars and head back into town. As soon as you get cell coverage, call the police."

"What about you?" Chrissy's voice and hands shook. Her eyes were jittery and wild.

Beth took a deep breath and swallowed.

"There's a land line in Mister Terrabonne's study. I'm going to try calling 111 from here." She was surprised at how calm and level her voice sounded. "The police have to know that Mister Winters has gone crazy."

Harlan Winters howled. Sandy screamed.

Beth shoved Chrissy ahead of her into the lodge room and yelled.

"RUN!"

***

Jack Terrabonne couldn't get up his own driveway. One of his own goddamned Range Rovers sat blocking the way, snow already starting to crust on the truck's roof and pile up against its windward side.

Jack cursed and pulled off the gravel. He snugged his Porsche up under the trees and headed the rest of the way to the house on foot. That way, he'd be able to take the Rover back down the mountain.

Ten steps later, Jack's feet were freezing. The good folks at Blucher made some damn fine, and expensive, footwear. But hand-stitched ostrich leather wasn't waterproof, and some of the drifts were deep enough that snow seeped in over the top of his boots.

Whispering Pines sure was beautiful. Jack had never seen it in winter before, and it was pretty as a picture. In fact, the main house looked more than a little like the local beer baron's mansion back in New Ulm, but Jack didn't think about that, any more than he thought about most things to do with little Andy Tebberman. Instead, Jack Terrabonne told himself he'd return to Whispering Pines another time, when he had a better bunch of boys and better weather.

The front door flew open. It slapped against the wall with a sound like a gunshot. A young woman ran out into the cold. She wore no coat and ran with her arms flapping, the whole time crying and screaming.

Jack took wide cautious steps through the snow. The woman ran across the courtyard and into the open garage. Jack wanted to reach her, but there was no use hurrying if it meant falling in the snow.

He was still plucking his way through the snow when the second Rover burst out of the shadows at the entrance to the barn.

Jack Terrabonne was sixty-three years old. He nearly broke a hip jumping out of the way of the speeding truck.

SEVENTY

Harlan Winters looked at the lifeless thing at his feet. His breath came in hot ragged gasps, and blood dripped from his knuckles.

Harlan had always had a bad temper. But really, it was her own damn fault.

"Shouldn't of touched my hair," he said, and spat.

The hair was useless now. Just so many brittle strands, smelling of bleach. Those goddamned maids had ruined his hair.

Harlan kicked the corpse. The broken ragdoll flopped and crunched and fell back to the ground. Harlan narrowed his eyes and sneered.

He remembered the lock of hair in his pocket. Harlan's fingers left wet red prints on the front of his shirt, but when they brushed that soft silky braid, his heart soared.

It still smelled perfect. Wet earth and wood and autumn decay. The tiniest ghost of shampoo. The rich scents of sweat and blood and raw animal terror. Harlan closed his eyes and licked the backs of his teeth.

The dead maid was big and blonde. Traces of the chemicals she worked with clung to her skin. She wore too much perfume and washed her hair with something that smelled like coconuts.

Fuck it. It was a start, and Harlan had just lost his whole collection.

He wrapped a hank of her hair in one big fist and ripped.

***

The two Rovers made a single crunched shape across the drive. The wrecked trucks had crashed into one of the beeches lining the drive. A power pole tilted into its branches. Electric and phone lines lay dead in the snow. A hundred and sixty thousand dollars' worth of British steel lay busted and useless, and the tree's cracked and shattered trunk blocked the only way in, or out.

Jack Terrabonne stomped back through the snow to his mangled Rovers. He was cold and wet, and his entire body felt like one big bruise but Jack was too damned angry to feel his own age.

"What in the goddamned hell is wrong with you, girl?" he yelled. "You had to go and wreck *both* my trucks?"

Terrabonne kicked the Rover's rear bumper. The truck's engine still roared under the hood, and white vapor billowed from the exhaust pipe.

Up in the front seat, behind all the exploded airbags, nothing moved.

"Darlin?"

***

The halls of Whispering Pines were dark, silent and still. Beth crept from shadow to shadow with her heart in her mouth.

For the thousandth time in the last few minutes, she cursed Tanya's black and thieving heart.

The door to Mister Terrabonne's study was closed. Beth set her hand to the knob and turned.

Locked.

Beth licked her lips and swallowed. She looked from one end of the hall to the other and reached for her passkey.

The air inside the study was cool, and damp. Beth hustled inside and pulled the door shut behind her. The latch clicked into place, and she let out a breath she didn't know she'd been holding.

The room was dark. The only light was what filtered through the snow-crusted window. The light switch did nothing.

Beth snatched the phone from its cradle and punched in 111. She held the receiver to her ear with both hands.

"Hello? Hello?"

No sound, not even a dial tone.

The phone was dead.

SEVENTY-ONE

Harlan stalked through the kitchen, banging cabinet doors as he went. He didn't bother checking inside the pantry, walk-in freezer or under the gleaming steel counters. He could taste the trails the maids left in the air: perfume and soap, cleaning fluids and sheer terror.

The kitchen let out into the lodge room. The lodge was half dining room and half lounge, gray slate and dark wood and a long glass wall of mullioned windows. Like every other room Jack Terrabonne spent any time in, it was a museum to Jack himself.

Harlan's boots clicked softly on the slate. The room stood deep in shadow. The far wall glowed a bluish white, each individual square of glass crusted with fallen snow. The mingled threads of perfume and fear split in that room, moving off in different directions.

"Harl? That you?"

"What is it Callum?"

"Everything okay, Harl?"

"Shouldn't you be off somewhere crying?"

"I thought I heard a shot..."

Harlan stepped further into the lodge room. Blocks of weak blue light fell across the slate floor, and large parts of the room were wrapped in darkness. The snow- bright windows were blinding in the gloom, too painful to look at directly. Callum was a paler blob among the shadows.

"Did you see which way them maids went?" Harlan said.

"Why?"

"Goddamn it, Callum, what do you care?"

"I ain't gonna let you hurt them, Harlan."

Harlan laughed.

Callum shuffled forward. As he crossed in front of the windows, squares of cold light crawled across his features.

Harlan ignored him. There were four doors from the main hall. The one he'd just come through led back to the kitchen and the servants' wing. The glass double doors in the wall next to him led out into the garden, falling snow piling up and burying the remains of the flowers.

No slush melted on the slate, and the cool air in the lodge carried no trace of the wild outdoors. The maids hadn't gone out that door. That left the main hall and the back hall. The back hall led to the rest of the house. The main hall led to the central stairs, the ballroom and the front door too. Harlan knew if *he* was in their shoes, he'd be running for the trucks and freedom.

Front door it was, then. Harlan took two thundering steps when Callum grabbed his arm.

"Whatever it is, Harl, don't do it."

"Leave me be, Callum."

The smaller man's face was puffy and blotched from crying. His eyes were bright and intense.

"You got no call to hurt those girls."

Harlan shook the other man's hand away from his sleeve. Callum stepped into his path.

"You're really startin to piss me off," Harlan said. "Get out my way."

Callum shook his head.

"I looked the other way too many times while you done wrong," he said. "No more."

Harlan growled. Every second he wasted, the fainter the scent trails grew. And the further the maids might have run.

He put one big hand in the center of Callum's chest and pushed. Callum tumbled into the dining table and hit with a crash.

Harlan stomped away. It was time to put this thing to bed. Some corner of his mind wondered if he'd be able to frame Callum for the maids. Another part wondered why he didn't much care.

Callum tackled Harlan two steps from the door. He scrabbled and clawed up the length of Harlan's back, the whole time making a weird high-pitched sound, hoarse and keening.

Harlan roared. He threw an elbow back and heard bone crunch. Callum's hands became frantic in their scratching search for Harlan's eyes. Harlan twisted under the smaller man and grabbed Callum's wrists.

Blood and tears slicked Callum's cheeks. His nose was smashed flat against his face, but he flailed with all his strength in Harlan's grip. Harlan lunged up, smashing his forehead into the center of the other man's face.

Callum's eyes glazed. His face went slack and his hands fell. Harlan stood and threw the quietly struggling weight of Callum's body halfway across the room.

Harlan drew his gun. Callum spat blood and thrashed on the ground, unable to rise. Harlan's boots struck the slate tiles, each step thunderous, booming and measured. The echoes of his steps were like the tolling of a great dark bell.

"Damn it, Callum," Harlan said. "I actually liked you."

Callum spat blood and tried to speak. The only sound he made was a soft raspy choking. Harlan's upper lip pulled back from his teeth.

He pulled the trigger. The lodge room vanished in a sheet of flame and a sound like thunder. Powder smoke and cordite filled the air.

Harlan pulled the trigger again. And again. He pulled the trigger until the hammer fell on empty chambers and the air was blue with gunsmoke, acrid and bitter.

SEVENTY-TWO

Kane's mount forged through the deepening storm. The Arabian's hooves crunched in the snow, and its breath rumbled like an enormous bellows. Kane's pulse pounded in his throat. Behind him, the tall pines hissed and thrashed in the winter wind. The horse recognized its home fields and pressed harder.

Whispering Pines stood dark and still in the blizzard. Thick white flakes drifted and spiraled and obscured the great gray hulk of the mansion. Not a single light burned. Kane fought the tightening in his heart as he searched the shadowed windows for signs of life.

Nothing moved.

Terrabonne's garden was snowed over. The rose bushes, shrubbery and manicured trees had been transformed by the winter storm into a twisting white abstract sculpture.

On the far side of the garden, the wall was gridded with tiny black half-moons: snow collecting on mullioned windows. Kane's restless eyes immediately caught the bright flash of light behind that glass.

Kane urged his mount harder. The animal shied and spooked at the flat sharp crack that rang out from inside the house. The horse pitched and reared and ran for safety. Kane jumped before he could be thrown and landed rolling in the snow.

He came up on all fours and started running for the house.

Kane knew that light.

A muzzle flash.

***

It was quiet inside The Bunker. The lights were off, the bar was empty and Dermott had the music turned down low. Just as well. Maeve didn't want to listen to the usual country music litany of lost jobs, wasted opportunity and lost loves.

Dermott sat on one of his own barstools. The shadowy gloom was thick around him, and his face was bleak in the cold muted light.

"Body might think you're closed, they didn't try the door."

"Ah, this foul weather. I'm just not in the mood." Dermott set a second shot glass on the rail and poured Bushmills into both without being asked.

"Your rich man's not here."

"I did notice."

"Shame about the fire."

They clicked glasses and drank. Normally, Maeve loved Bushmills, loved that sweet burn.

Today in her mouth, it tasted like ashes.

"Hell of a face you're wearing there, miss."

"Hell of a crowd you've got in."

Dermott smiled and poured another shot. When the bottle passed her way, Maeve put her hand over her own glass. The song on the juke made its quiet complaint about how, sometimes, it was hard to be a woman. The singer's voice was rough with cigarettes, whiskey and bad decisions.

"I saw the plywood," Dermott said. "Got a place to stay yet?"

Maeve looked down at her hands on the bar top and shook her head. Dermott filled her shot glass with an absent flick of the wrist.

"Carol asked me to mention, you're welcome to our home."

"Actually... I just wanted to say goodbye. I'm leaving."

"Roads are closing all over the district." Dermott's chuckle was rumbling and deep. "You'll not be leaving town today. Best take a wee drop and put up the night in our guest room."

Dermott drank off half his whiskey and set the glass back on the counter. The cigarettes-and-whiskey voice wailed softly in the background.

"That old business," Maeve said, "it's over."

"Say?"

"I finally caught up with the man, no thanks to you."

Dermott looked down at his half-full whiskey. He refilled the shot glass but left it untouched.

"Not that way," Maeve said. "Last I saw the old bastard, he was alive and healthy." She heard the echo of Jack Terrabonne's disclaimer in her own words. The thought of Bridey came back, a scab torn from a deep raw wound.

"You're no killer, Maeve Kelly. I've always said as much."

Maeve touched her fingertips to the base of her glass. The surface of the Bushmills wobbled, and a tiny amber drop ran over the edge.

"I'll call Carol, have her make up the room."

Last I saw her... Maeve cursed herself for a damn fool. She looked up, her eyes bright and fierce.

"You're a kind man, Dermott. But I'll have another favor."

"Aye?"

"The keys to your truck."

"The roads--"

"Will be no match for that bloody big four-wheel of yours."

Maeve met Dermott's eye, and held. His gaze was the first to break.

"Bloody hell."

A ring of keys clattered on the bar top. Maeve separated the key and its black plastic electronic fob. Dermott drained his whiskey, and hers.

The woman on the jukebox belted out her final notes, swearing to stand by her man.

Maeve all but ran from the bar.

***

Kane crossed the open ground in a loping run. More flat cracking gunshots sounded from inside the house. Kane stayed low and used the garden for cover.

The french doors would be suicide. Banks of windows ran the length of that room, and the inside was unlit. Kane's dark silhouette against the snow would make a perfect target. He curved his path away from the french doors and around the corner of the house.

***

"Darlin'?"

Jack Terrabonne picked his way over to the Rover's driver side door.

"You okay in there?"

Jack didn't need this. Wet ostrich leather was pinching his feet, and he had water down the neck of his oilskin coat. Now one of his employees, like as not drunk or stoned out of her fool head, was busting up his vehicles and it'd be Jack ended up getting sued.

His hand hovered over the door handle. Jack had heard once how moving an accident victim could hurt them worse, and Jack did not want to end up liable for any part of this mess. Those kids might need help, but it was the kind of help best left to professionals.

Jack pulled out his cell. No damn signal. He never could understand why, just because his house was tucked up behind a couple of tiny little mountains, his cell refused to get a working signal.

"Um, darlin'? You there? Tell you what, I'm just gonna go on in the house. I'll phone for some help for y'all..."

He turned away and took a couple of tiptoe steps toward the house. Blowing snow struck his face and stung his eyes. Jack stopped and looked back over his shoulder.

"This ain't my responsibility!" he shouted to the wrecked trucks.

SEVENTY-THREE

The front hall at Whispering Pines was dark and cold. Snow muted the high narrow windows, and the only direct light streamed in through the open front door. The chandelier jingled softly overhead, and the ceiling was lost in shadow.

Harlan stepped into the hall. The echo of his steps was slow and measured, each footfall cracking and fading in the vast empty space.

The front door stood open. Drifted snow kept the heavy oak door from closing, and blowing flakes were already starting to collect inside the threshold.

Harlan's birds had flown the coop.

He looked down at the gun in his hand. The metal was heavy, the barrel warm and smelling of smoke. Harlan thumbed the release, swung out the cylinder and dropped the cartridges into his palm. None still held their copper-jacketed hollowpoint tips. They were nothing more than hollow brass tubes with a strong smell of gunpowder.

Harlan turned his palm. The spent cartridges bounced ringing from the marble floor. He took a handful of fresh hollowpoints from his jacket pocket and thumbed them into the wheel. When the .44 was once again fully loaded, Harlan snapped the cylinder closed with a practiced flick. The sound was like an axe blow in the space and the silence.

Jack Terrabonne whooped as he came through the front door. He stomped snow from his boots and slapped it away from his two thousand dollar oilskin coat.

"Hoss!" he said. "Just the man! I need a hot bath and some warm clothes, I tell you what."

Terrabonne stripped out of his dripping coat and dropped it on the floor. That famous hair was a wet mess, and the man looked like a drowned rat. There was a clotted cut high on the side of his throat, but the red stains splattered over his clothes were too pale to be blood.

"Oh, and we need to get some folks, fire department or somebody, out to the driveway. One of them little gals, the ones clean up around here, musta got into the liquor cabinet or something. Now both my damn Rovers are wrapped around a tree."

Harlan didn't speak. He didn't move.

"Hell you waiting for, man?" Jack snapped his fingers twice, close together. "That gal might be hurt down there, and I don't want to end up getting sued."

"You fired me, Jack. Remember?"

"Aw hell, you didn't take that serious, now did you?" Terrabonne bent over and ruffled his hair with his fingertips. It didn't help his look any. "You know I always got a place for you, old hoss."

"Yeah," Harlan said. "I know it."

Jack Terrabonne noticed the gun in Harlan's hand for the first time.

"Hell you doing with that thing, hoss? Little indoor target shooting? Or maybe you thought I was a prowler?" Jack laughed at his own jokes.

"You say them trucks're wrecked?" Harlan said.

"Yeah, that little gal plowed one into the other, and now I'm just hoping one of em isn't too banged up to drive. You just know a little snow like this, that itty bitty airport they got here'll close right up. I figure we might need to drive on out to some other town, someplace warmer where the planes still fly."

"How bad you say that girl was hurt?" With his free hand, Harlan scratched the bristles at the side of his neck.

"How'm I supposed to know?" Terrabonne looked all at once guilty, sly and petulant. "I look like a medical professional to you? That's why I said you need to get some folks up here. I swear, hoss, you could at least *try* and keep up."

Harlan looked at his boss with narrowed eyes.

"But you did say she was hurt, right?"

"Ain't jumping or dancing, and that's all I know. Now where's my bath? Aw, forget the bath, just let me get changed into some dry clothes and we'll get out of here. Where you figure the nearest airport for us is?"

"Probably Christchurch," Harlan said. "I been trying for days to get you to leave, Jack. Why now?"

Terrabonne waved his hands over his head. He was always at his most theatrical when he was worried.

"There was this psycho bitch back in town and-- goddammit, what do you care? Just get anybody round here still works for me to start packing, and get on the phone and charter us a jet. You have to, you'n me can leave now and the rest can follow."

"That maid didn't say nothing to you?"

"Hell was there to say? She was busy wrecking my cars, wasn't exactly a lot of time for conversation."

"You *sure*, Jack?"

The wind seemed to go out of Terrabonne. In that moment his shoulders dropped, his face fell and every wrinkle showed. He looked like a sad little old man in a half-drenched shiny green suit.

"I'm having a bad day, hoss. Please, don't give me a lot of grief right now. Just go on make the calls. I want to go someplace warm."

Jack put his hand on Harlan's arm, above the gun. Harlan blew air through his nose and nodded.

Harlan's lips curled up at the edges. Two maids down, two left. He could do this. He could totally do this. He might even go free.

"You just go on up to your room, Jack. I'll take care of everything down here."

"That's my boy."

Terrabonne left a wet trail across the cold marble. At the far end of the room, the main staircase swept up into darkness and off to Jack's penthouse suite. He paused at the bottom step.

"Hoss, how far is Christchurch, anyway?"

"Driving? About five, six hours. More on these roads."

Terrabonne nodded. His face was serious, like he was pondering a big decision.

"Long drive. Might want to look into renting a limo."

Harlan stepped forward. The looming bulk of his shadow fell over the smaller man, and the whites of his eyes were threaded with blood.

"No limo," Harlan said. "I got other plans."

SEVENTY-FOUR

The stairs were shrouded in darkness. Without bulbs burning in the wall sconces the only light bled, soft and blue and cold, from the circular skylight far above. Climbing those steps was like ascending from the bottom of a well.

"What the hell is wrong with everyone today? You don't need to do this, hoss."

Harlan tightened his grip on Jack's shoulder and pressed the barrel of the gun deeper into the man's spine.

"You're wrong about that."

Jack tried to keep going up the stairs. Harlan pulled him off the steps and shoved him down the hall.

It was dark. The hall to Harlan's room was dimly lit at the best of times. With the power off the narrow and twisting passage might as well have been under the earth.

Jack stumbled and squirmed in Harlan's grip. Harlan marched forward, hardly seeming to notice the absence of light.

"Whatever it is, hoss, we can work it out."

"Wrong again."

"Can't we at least talk about it?" Jack said. Harlan pushed him forward and around the final corner.

A cold sliver showed: light from a bedroom window shining through an open door. The sliver of light grew wider, until its faint wash touched the full width of the hall.

Jack made a break for it. One tiny boot kicked Harlan in the shin, and Terrabonne wriggled half out of his oilskin coat.

Harlan barked and lashed out. The barrel of the .44 caught the old man just above the ear.

A dark figure burst through the open door. Harlan caught a quick glimpse of a female silhouette: small and fragile, poised on the edge of flight.

Harlan leveled his arm and pulled the trigger. The gun bucked and roared in his hand, and the dark hallway flashed bright in a gout of flame.

He didn't wait for his vision to clear. He didn't wait for his ears to stop ringing or the smell of gunpowder to clear from his nostrils. Harlan charged down the hall with one big fist knotted in the back of Jack Terrabonne's collar.

"Goddammit!"

Harlan kicked the wall. There was a fist-sized hole in his bedroom door but no body on the ground, not even a little bit of blood.

And Harlan's money was all over the damn floor.

Harlan swung Jack around by the neck and threw him on the bed. On his hands and knees, Harlan scrambled to gather the banded packets and throw them back into his strongbox.

"That's my blood, my own blood!" Terrabonne couldn't stop staring at his slick red palm. He had a pretty good cut on the side of his head. Harlan figured it balanced out the cut on his neck. "Goddammit hoss, what the hell's got into you?"

The money wasn't all there. At least seventy, maybe eighty grand was missing.

"That bitch!"

***

The side door was unlocked. Snow skirled inside as Kane let himself in and fell melting to the floor when the door closed. The back hall was dark and deserted. Kane padded quickly down its course, the only sounds the soft patter of meltwater falling from his clothes and the thumping beat of his own heart.

Kane paused at the entry to the lodge room. The air stank of blood and gunpowder, but the only sound in the room was the pat of snowflakes on glass. Nothing rustled, moved or breathed in the shadows or in the light.

Callum lay dead in the center of the room. Kane found him face down, one arm curled under his body and the other stretched forward, reaching. Bullet holes had torn gouts of white stuffing from the couch behind Callum, and exit wounds had shredded his back to a wet red ruin.

Kane said a brief and silent prayer over the man's body. That done, he rose and moved off in the direction Callum had been headed when he died.

SEVENTY-FIVE

The entrance hall was open to the elements. Kane's breath frosted in the icy air.

Snow drifted in through the open front door. In the darkness overhead, the chandelier groaned on its chain and shuddered with a thousand crystal voices.

Kane stood in that high narrow space. He listened to the wind howl in the corners, through the recesses and along the high shadowy ceiling, and Kane knew that he was alone.

A murdered man lay on the floor of the lodge room. It was time to call the police.

If the phone hadn't been knocked out along with the power. If police cars could even get up these mountains in this storm. And if Kane didn't end up cuffed in the cells himself while Winters got away.

A lot of ifs.

And Kane stood facing an open door, the whole world outside.

***

A single set of tracks led to the front door. The footprints formed a single thin groove, its edges softened and filled by the rapid accumulation of flakes.

Kane followed the trail across the wide open space of the circular drive, around the curving corridor of skeletal trees.

Two SUVs sat crumpled together in the swirling snow. One had broadsided the other. A shattered tree trunk lay on its side, black and crackling power lines tangled in its branches. White exhaust plumed from one tailpipe.

Kane forged through the drifting snow. Its wet and clinging weight fought him at every step. Through the driver's window Kane was able to see the floppy white bulk of partially inflated air bags. And sandwiched between the air bag and the window, a single feminine hand.

The driver's door was crunched in its frame. Kane set one foot against the body of the truck and pulled. The door opened with a loud groaning screech.

The girl was unconscious. Her pulse was thready and weak. Kane took a single heartbeat to weigh the consequences and make a decision. He moved her over as gently as possible and climbed behind the wheel.

The engine made a terrible grinding sound when Kane dropped it in reverse. He worried that the transmission had been damaged in the crash, but the truck rocked slightly on its chassis when Kane touched the gas. He gunned it. All four tires bit the frozen ground and held, but the Rover refused to move.

Kane stamped the pedal down to the floor. The truck crept backward an inch at a time, dragging the second Rover along sideways. The two were mangled together. A tree trunk leaning against the passenger side of the truck's cab shifted and crashed to the ground. The Rovers moved another half a foot.

Metal ground on metal, and something snapped. The sudden loud noise came from the floor beneath Kane's feet, and while the engine still raced, the tires no longer moved.

Kane hopped down out of the truck. He switched off the ignition and gathered the driver into his arms. Moving this girl might make her injuries worse. Leaving her where she was would be fatal.

Right now, this girl needed warmth, blankets and shelter.

Kane knew just the place.

SEVENTY-SIX

Beth crept through the halls of Whispering Pines. She hoped Chrissy had escaped. Without a working phone, the other girl was the only possible source of help.

In the meantime, Beth had to stay hidden.

At the sound of the shots, she jumped. The noise carried through the house, a series of loud sharp BAMs, one after another, that wouldn't have been out of place on a building site, a garage or a highway road crew. Alone in this great dark house, those mechanical explosive sounds were unmistakable. They were the voice of death.

Beth's heart raced. Her mouth was dry, and her cheeks were tracked with tears. She had to find a place where she would be safe until help arrived.

She needed a place to hide.

***

"Is this about money?" Terrabonne said. "Cause if it's about money, I can give you a raise."

"Shut up, and don't you drop that box."

"My head feels like you bust it open. And it's all bloody, too. You know, hoss, I think you mighta hurt me."

Harlan blew air through his nostrils, flat and hissing.

"It's a scalp cut, Jack. They bleed some. You'd know that if you actually did half the things you like to say you did. Now shut up and carry that goddamned box or I will truly make you hurt."

***

Snow swirled in front of the windshield and caked on the wiper blades.

Maeve saw flashing orange lights through the curtains of falling snow. She engine-braked and eased Dermott's truck forward until men in coveralls stood in front of its grille with their arms waving.

"You can't go through here, miss. It's not safe."

"Give me a fecking break. This truck's got four wheel drive and snow tires."

"I'm sorry, miss, I can't let you through."

The man looked up the road into the white flakes swirling in the purple light.

"Nothing much up those mountains anyway," he said. "Some old mining camps and sheep stations're all."

Stray snowflakes blew in through the open window. Each one touched Maeve's face with a small icy sting. Behind the man speaking to her, other highway workers were setting up roadblocks.

"Come on..."

The man shook his head.

"Road's closed."

Maeve powered the window back up. The man in coveralls stepped back away from the truck, and she dropped it into reverse.

One perfect three point turn later, Maeve was rolling back down the mountain.

***

Tanya ran down the stairs for all she was worth. She'd never even seen a real gun before today, and now she'd actually been shot at, twice.

Of course, Tanya had never had her hands on this much money, either. On the whole, she figured it was a fair trade.

The northwest service stairs dropped her out right by the lodge room. Tanya stopped in the doorway, listening. That creepy weirdo Harlan was still upstairs: after all, he'd just shot at her. But Tanya didn't want to run into anybody else right now, either. Not with her arms full of tens of thousands of US dollars.

The coast was clear.

Tanya stepped into the lodge room. She crept past the dining area, moving from the back hall to the kitchen. In the dark she didn't notice the broken furniture, didn't see figure lying on the floor at the far end of the room, too still and too silent.

Her only thoughts were of the money, and of escape.

SEVENTY-SEVEN

Harlan marched Jack Terrabonne up the final flight of stairs and into the master suite. The old man griped the whole time. He complained about the psycho bitch who threatened him over some Irish girl back in Mexico. He complained about the cut in his scalp and about carrying the heavy steel strongbox. He complained about his sore joints from his fall and the wet boots pinching his feet. He complained about Harlan's ingratitude.

Harlan ground his teeth and tuned Jack out. He thought about the rough points of his plan.

"You can put the box down now," Harlan said when they stepped out into Jack's bedroom.

The room was wide and spacious: bigger than the entire house where Harlan had grown up. Truth be told, Jack's closet was larger than Harlan's childhood home. The bed, an enormous damn thing, sat on a raised dais in front of the windows. Up on another platform in the corner, Jack's hot tub bubbled. Glass walls on three sides of the room looked out over the tree tops, the vast panorama of the whole valley made to look like a winter wonderland.

"You really steal all that money from me?" Jack rubbed his shoulder and worked his arm around in circles.

"Lotsa folks did," Harlan said. "You made it easy."

Terrabonne smiled, a full Hollywood special. He finished it with a wink.

"Tell you something, old hoss, I been stealing from my own self too. Keeping it from the tax man more than anything. There's money's been lost in little dribs and drabs over the years, just sitting in accounts: Switzerland, Luxembourg, the Cayman Islands. Tell you what, you and me, let's go get some. We'll split it, fifty-fifty."

Harlan flashed Jack his own smile. There was nothing Hollywood about it.

"That's a kind offer, Jack, but I got other plans. Go on and open up that drawer there for me, the one by your bed."

"Look, hoss... Harlan. I know I lost my temper..."

"Just open the drawer."

Jack sat on the edge of the bed and shot Harlan one last look. Harlan gestured with the gun, and Jack opened the drawer. Among all the condom-wrapper crinkles and lubricant smells, pill bottles rattled and fell on their sides. Without being told, Jack started stacking his private drugstore up on the night stand. There were a lot of brown plastic bottles.

Harlan sighed and sat down. The chair creaked and groaned under his weight.

"You gonna need some water, or you fine popping them dry?"

"I don't--"

"It's called an overdose, Jack. You certified music stars have em all the time. Course if you like, you mighta shot yourself in the head."

Terrabonne's laughter was dry and mirthless, like the scraping of dry stones.

"Son, you must be out of your cotton-pickin--"

Harlan shifted the gun. Looking down the barrel of a .44 Magnum, Jack Terrabonne for once in his life shut up. For at least five seconds.

"Nobody'd ever believe I killed myself," he said.

"Maybe, maybe not." Harlan's left hand scratched the wiry stubble on the side of his neck. His right was steady with the gun. "Little time's all I'm looking for, and I figure when folks get your goodbye note, they just might think on it awhile. After all, what with losing the Gospel Hour and all, you do seem kinda... distraught."

Terrabonne folded his arms, his face glowing in triumph.

"I got you there, hoss. No way in hell I'm writing any suicide note."

"See Jack, that's one thing you never did quite figure out. Email don't care who types it."

Terrabonne came flailing up off the bed. He got three steps into his run for the door before Harlan got in front of him.

Jack swung wild. Harlan ignored the old man's fists and lashed out with an open hand. The sound of the slap was sharp and sudden, like the crack of dry wood.

Terrabonne looked up at Harlan with one hand on his face and tears in his eyes. Harlan's voice was quiet, almost tender.

"Overdose won't hurt a bit, and a gunshot'd be over before you know it. Can't you see I'm trying to be nice?"

"This ain't right, hoss. Harlan. This ain't right."

"It's what we got, Jack. Now take the pills."

"You just hold off a few years more, you're in my will." Jack's hand was damp on Harlan's arm, and his breath was metallic and foul. "You'll get a darn sight more than whatever you got in that box. Or, let's run on out of here together. We'll go empty out those accounts I was talking about, get your hands on some major loot."

Harlan stepped back. Jack's hand clung, and fell away.

"This ain't about money, Jack. This was never about money."

Terrabonne sat back down on the bed. He picked a pill bottle from the night table and rolled it back and forth between his palms.

"Then why don't you tell me what it is about?"

Harlan searched for the words, but all that rose from his chest was a low rumbling growl. The growl rose in pitch, and Harlan dropped his bulk into the chair. This time, something inside the chair cracked.

"I wasn't much more than a kid when you took me out on the road with you." Harlan lifted his feed cap by the bill and scratched the top of his bare scalp with two fingers. "You been, you been like a father to me, Jack, and there's some things a man don't want his daddy to know."

Terrabonne's hands went still. His eyes were solemn and wet.

"This is about that girl Bridey, ain't it? Couple years ago, back in Mexico?"

"Kind of. Yeah."

"Oh no. You didn't"

The gun hit the carpet with a muffled thump. Harlan steadied himself on the chair.

"So that Irish girl today wasn't just some psycho." Jack touched his palm to the sticky wound at the side of his neck.

"Son, you got to tell me the truth here. Was she, was Bridey the only time?"

Whatever Jack saw in Harlan's eyes was the only answer he needed. The old man seemed to visibly deflate. His clothes seemed loose on his body, his skin lined and wrinkled and sagging.

"Reckon I understand why you'd want to run. Tell you what, why don't you get gone and, you need it, I'll wire you money."

"Yeah, right."

"Old-- Harlan, I promised your mamma I'd take care of you. You were just a baby then. Later, I... I knew you had your problems, but a promise is a promise. Sides..." Jack snuck a glance at Harlan, and his lips twisted. "You're my only blood."

"Wait a minute, wait--" Harlan waved a hand in front of his face. "You. Knew. I was yours?"

"Well sure," Jack said. "How else was your mamma gonna get me to look after you?"

"All this time."

"And you know, this thing with the gals aside, I'm right proud of you, hoss."

"All these years. All them tantrums. All that abuse." Harlan felt himself swell.

"What do you say, let's get out of here?" Jack said.

"Treatin me like dirt." The blood pounded in Harlan's wrists, and the collar of his shirt constricted his throat.

"We'll go someplace warm, maybe the house on St. Bart's."

"Puttin me down in front of folks, making me feel like a freak." Veins stood out on the sides of Harlan's skull.

"Now... now hoss..."

"Throwin me your seconds and actin like I oughta be grateful!"

Harlan barely noticed himself rise from the chair. He took the front of Jack's clothes in his fists and hauled him up. Harlan held Jack's face so close that drops of spit appeared on the old man's face with every word.

"And all this time, you *knew* I was your kid. YOU KNEW..."

Jack clawed at Harlan and screamed.

Harlan roared.

Glass shattered.

SEVENTY-EIGHT

Kane staggered through knee-deep snow. The girl in his arms stirred and kicked, weak as a newborn. Her weight burned between his shoulders and down to his elbows.

He pressed on, moving carefully not to disturb her.

Twice he heard his horse moving between the trees. The animal was still spooked. It followed his position but stayed out of sight.

The stable door stood open and beckoning. The air inside was dark and warm, rich with the smells of hay and horseflesh.

Kane put the girl down gently in an unused stall. Horses nickered and chuffed up and down the row. Kane covered the unconscious young woman with horse blankets and hay to keep her warm.

After he pulled the stall door closed, Kane searched the stables. Going up against a killer with a gun, he wanted a weapon.

Leather tack, saddles, crops and whips hung from racks and hooks. None of them offered much promise. A bench in the back held farrier tools.

The tongs were big and heavy and blunt. Clamped in Kane's fist they were concentrated cast-iron mayhem, but the tongs would be slow to swing, awkward at close quarters and useless against a man with a gun.

The hoof knife Kane rejected outright. The little three-inch blade was barely sharp, its tip blunt and curled at the end. The tool was perfectly suited to shaving a horse's hooves, but against what Kane expected to find inside that house, it was worse than useless.

In the end, Kane took the driving hammer and pritchel. The driving hammer had a long head and a short claw, and the pritchel was in essence little more than a pointed iron bar. Both were a foot long, light enough for a good fast swing and heavy enough to strike with authority.

Finally armed, Kane stepped back out into the snow. The barn's warmth soon faded away from him, and thick wet flakes clung to his coat and stuck in his shaggy hair. Already the track he'd worn between the barn and the wrecked trucks was little more than a shallow groove sculpted smooth by the windblown snow.

Whispering Pines stood gray and massive, monolithic in the storm. Snow swirled around it, obscured it, turned the house into a vast dark mountainous shape in the thickening purple light.

Somewhere inside that house was a murderer. Harlan Winters was armed. He'd killed those two French backpackers a couple of days ago, and Callum's blood was still wet on the pine boards in the lodge room. If the maid in the wrecked truck died, her blood too was on Harlan's hands.

Kane tightened his grip on his improvised weapons. He took his first steps into the snow between the barn and the side door of the main house.

The falling snow warped and distorted sound. The sound of breaking glass seemed to come from several directions at once. The same was true of Jack Terrabonne's terrified scream.

The old man flew from the top floor of the house. He flailed his arms and yelled the whole way down and struck with a sick wet crunch. His body made a twisted red shape on the snowy stones of the garden courtyard.

Jack Terrabonne was silent at last.

SEVENTY-NINE

Tanya's bag lay right out in the middle of the hall. Winters had just left it there, clothes scattered all over the floor. The money was gone, but that was no problem.

Tanya dropped to her knees and dumped her armful of cash into the open bag. She'd had the bundled stacks pressed so tight against her body that her arms ached. The cash fit nicely in her bag, and its weight was sweet. What room she had left Tanya stuffed with clothes and knickers from the hallway floor.

Whispering Pines was a big house, dark and creepy. Without lights or power or the company of the other girls, Tanya heard every creak and rumble and groan.

Before she knew it, she was jumping at every sound. It didn't help, knowing any of those noises actually could be a dangerous madman.

"Time to go," she whispered.

Tanya snatched her bag and quick-footed down the hall. She passed by the open door to her old room and stopped short.

Blood was splashed everywhere. The great whipping red arcs went all the way up the walls and even speckled the ceiling.

Tanya's white duvet was rumpled and torn, the spattered stains dark and sticky. Locks of hair were scattered everywhere, and the air was thick with the smells of blood and feces.

Tanya felt her gorge rise. She fought the sensation, her knuckles small and white on the strap of her bag.

She was okay until she saw it. On the far side of her bed, where the duvet was most rumpled and stained. Hanging limp against the blanket, a woman's hand.

Tanya's knees went weak. Jo's hand didn't sit right on the wrist, and not all of the fingers bent in the right direction. Tanya pitched forward, splashing the carpet with her vomit, sour and acid.

Tanya ran then. She ran for all she was worth. She ran through the kitchen without stopping to grab a knife, and she ran through the lodge room without stopping for the dead man lying across the doorway. Tanya ran with her feet skidding on the marble in the entry hall, and she ran with her feet crunching in the snow.

She ran across the open courtyard, terror riding high and choking on her shoulders. She ran past the crashed Range Rovers, one with its door hanging open.

Tanya almost ran past Jack Terrabonne's bright blue Porsche.

At first she stood a few meters away from it, lungs burning for air and her heart in her mouth. The Porsche seemed too good to be true, but she couldn't imagine how it could be a trap.

The keys were even in the ignition. Without another moment's hesitation, Tanya threw her bag into the passenger seat and hopped in behind the wheel.

The engine started first try. Warm air flooded in from the heater, and the wiper blades cleared twin arcing windows in the snow on the windscreen. Tanya listened to the deep powerful purr of the motor and wanted to both laugh and cry with relief.

The gear shift was on the floor. Tanya put the car into reverse and tapped the gas. The powerful little car growled in the snow and leapt backward down the drive.

There was no room to turn around. Tanya backed down the long and twisting drive, steering by her mirrors. The Porsche was quick and responsive. More than once she overcompensated and put the car halfway off the gravel, or left scraps of blue paint on the tree trunks on either side of the drive.

Tanya didn't care. She just wanted out of that hell house. It occurred to her that she might want to call Whispering Pines that in interviews. *I Escaped From the Hell House* had a nice ring. She wondered who would play her in the movie.

Finally, she reached the end of the drive. Trees no longer pressed in on all sides of the Porsche, and the open road stretched away down the mountain, a snowy white ribbon leading to freedom and safety.

Tanya reached inside her bag to touch the cash. The money was real, and it was hers. She let out a loud whoop, put the Porsche in gear and punched the gas.

EIGHTY

Harlan Winters prowled the lightless halls of Whispering Pines, muttering and growling.

He'd taken a lot of shit from Jack Terrabonne over the years. Sixteen years old, Harlan had started out carrying the famous man's bags and hauling his guitars. It wasn't long before Harlan was lining up the man's parties and paying the kind of bills don't go through accountants. He'd suffered Jack's rages and ego, the arrogance of the man at the height of his fame and all the prickly denial of his fading light.

Twenty years Harlan suffered. Twenty years putting up with Jack's bad behavior. Twenty years of Harlan excusing every shitty thing Jack did by telling himself it was okay, Jack didn't know. Here it turned out that all this time Jack did know. Every single insult, put down and slight, every drug binge and detox, every single groupie, fan and whore Harlan procured, Jack knew. The whole twenty years, Jack Terrabonne had known Harlan was his son.

Harlan roared in rage and pain. One fist lashed out. The hallway echoed with a booming crash, and Harlan was choking on plaster dust.

That was all over. Bastard was dead, and wasn't nothing going to bring him back.

Even for famous people, dead was dead.

It was time for Harlan to look to the future.

Harlan dragged the back of one wrist across his eyes. They were wet and puffy, and the plaster dust on his cheeks was carved by the watery tracks running down the sides of his face. Every new tear burned like a point of flame.

Alone in the lightless hall, Harlan Winters groaned. That soul-deep sound was half rage, half mourning.

He'd never dreamed he could feel so lost and empty.

***

Beth had the perfect hiding place. She doubted Jack Terrabonne or any of his men even knew where the laundry was.

The laundry room was large and shadowy and silent. There were piles and piles of dirty towels and linen waiting to be washed. Also, the room was on the basement level, with three different exits if Beth needed to run.

The laundry room had one other advantage: The air there was warm and heavy with the perfumed scents of soap and bleach, laundry powder and fabric softener.

It seemed crazy, but Beth couldn't shake the feeling that Harlan Winters was able to track her by smell.

***

Eight kilometers back from the roadblock, Maeve found a side road. This part of the Remarkable Mountains was honeycombed with sheep stations, logging land and old mining camps. Maeve had no idea where this road led, except that it was headed in the right general direction.

The side road was narrow, twisting and treacherous. Maeve was forced to drop her speed to a near crawl. She sat forward in the seat, both hands white-knuckled on the steering wheel, peering through the windshield at the curving white ribbon of smooth snow in front of her headlights.

That old devil nicotine had its teeth in her too. With the stress of the driving, Maeve wouldn't half kill for a fag, but no way Dermott would have her smoking in his pride and joy.

The windshield wipers carved a continuous clear channel across the glass, scraping to the end of their stroke and going back to their own beginning. Maeve listened to their whoosh and chud, whoosh and chud, and tried to chase away the images that returned again and again to her mind's eye.

EIGHTY-ONE

Kane moved like a shadow through Whispering Pines. He held the hammer in one fist and the spiked iron pritchel in the other. The voice of the wind moaned against the walls and rattled the windows, and the house timbers creaked and groaned.

By contrast, the noise of Kane's passage was softer than the pats of snowflakes on the window glass.

He worked his way from room to room, searching for Harlan. After he found the girl's body in the servants' quarters, Kane was keener than ever to find Winters. He was also aware of the danger of letting that man get behind him.

***

Beth worried. What if Chrissy hadn't gotten away? What if she couldn't get the police to believe her? What if she had an accident? What if the police weren't coming because they didn't even know there was an emergency?

Waiting for help was harder than Beth thought. There was nothing to do but sit and think and let her imagination run rampant. Her greatest fear was that she was hiding down here for nothing, that there was no one coming to the rescue.

It was getting late, too. The snow packing the basement windows already darkened the laundry room. The later it got, the darker the room became. And colder. Beth didn't fancy spending the night down here, and she was growing more and more afraid that she'd have no choice.

Email! Mister Terrabonne's study had a computer. A laptop with a battery. As long as it wasn't passworded or something, Beth could get on the net and send for help.

Except the phone lines were down. That was the big question: Terrabonne was certainly rich enough to afford a broadband connection, but did he have it?

Beth debated how safe she really was in the laundry. She debated the merits and dangers of creeping back upstairs to send for help.

She wondered how long she could stay down in the basement, hiding.

***

Harlan ended up back upstairs, in Jack's room. The room was like an icebox, snow blowing in through the broken window. Throughout the suite, shadows grew in the deepening purple light.

Harlan blew his nose on Jack's bedsheet and spat on the floor. The time for sissy crying was past. He pulled the sheets off the bed and dumped them on the floor of the walk-in closet. He hauled the goose-down mattress over, tore the fabric apart with his bare hands and threw big armfuls of feathers on the pile.

One of his trips, Harlan's boot struck what felt like a chunk of pig-iron. The chromed shape of his gun went thumping along the carpet. He must've dropped it sometime around Jack's final flight. Purple and blue lights crawled in the gun's chrome depths, and the metal was cold enough to sting Harlan's fingers, a heavy chunk of lethal ice.

Which reminded him: his steel box still sat on the floor by the doorway. No way Harlan wanted to carry that damn thing around with him, not with two maids still unaccounted for. He heaved the box out the broken window and into the snow. That way, he could collect it on his way out.

The contents of Jack's bedroom liquor cabinet were next. Harlan poured bottle after bottle of single-malt scotch on the sheets and splashed it over the suits on their hangers. One of Jack's hand-painted silk ties went down the neck of the last bottle of scotch.

The one and only bottle of Jack Daniels Harlan saved for himself.

Jack had a lighter in his drawer, a Zippo. It was gold-plated, an engraved present from some other has-been nobody remembered. The lighter started on the first try.

Tongues of flame crawled up the liquor-soaked tie. At the first touch of the Molotov Cocktail's burning fuse, the bedsheets went up with a quick percussive WHUMP, and Harlan felt the skin of his face crisp and tighten in the sudden heat.

In moments the entire closet was ablaze.

Burning goose down floated through the air. Each small feather formed a tiny point of burning light, mirroring and mingling with the snowflakes drifting around the room. Where the snowflakes landed, they left a small spot, wet and frozen. Here and there enough flakes clumped together to start a miniature snowdrift. Where the burning feathers landed, they left a small smoldering scorch mark. Where enough feathers landed together, the fire found new life.

It wasn't long before small fires burned all around the room.

Harlan stalked into Jack's sitting room with the burning bottle. Just three days earlier, the French kids had sat in that room, nervous, not knowing what was coming but certain that it wasn't good. There were no windows in that room. The only light came from the fire in Harlan's fist.

Harlan looked at the love seat those two kids had sat on, and his eyes narrowed.

He cocked his arm back and threw. The flaming bottle struck the furniture and shattered. A fiery blossom flowered and burst, and the love seat was lost in the crackling roar.

Harlan cracked the neck of the Jack Daniels bottle against the wall. . He put the jagged open end to his lips, upended the bourbon and drank.

The bourbon was warm and welcoming. It lit every nerve ending like a Christmas tree. He drank his fill and smashed the bottle against the wall. The liquor burned ghostly and blue.

Harlan stood in the center of the room, reflected flames dancing in his eyes.

EIGHTY-TWO

Twenty minutes later the top floor of Whispering Pines was burning bright. So were half a dozen bedrooms and most everything else Harlan passed on his way down to the first floor.

Light was no longer a problem. Harlan had fashioned a torch from a busted chair leg and one of Jack's three hundred dollar shirts. In each of the boys' rooms and whenever else the notion took him, Harlan ducked in and set the torch to linens and curtains. The smell of smoke was everywhere, but in Harlan's wake those dark cold halls danced with a bright and merry light.

He had one thing left to do. There were still loose ends: those other maids and such, but Harlan wasn't worried. He figured the fire would cover his tracks and take care of most of his problems.

All Harlan had to do was send Jack's farewell email.

He'd keep it short and sweet. Just a few lines, enough to get the cops thinking murder/suicide. It didn't need to be perfect. By the time they sorted anything out, Harlan would be lost in the wind.

***

Beth hunched at the northeastern service stairs, peeking through a crack in the door. The hall was dark and silent. Mister Terrabonne's gold records lined the walls in their frames, neat orderly squares of reflected light.

The air in the hall seemed subtly different. Beth couldn't put her finger on it, but whatever it was put her in mind of autumn leaves and summer barbeques.

The soft tickle at the back of her throat was faintly pleasant and oddly terrifying.

Nothing moved. The hall was deserted. It was now or never.

Beth bit her lip and tried to work up her courage.

***

Kane stepped into the back hall and stopped. Something was wrong. Very wrong.

The air had changed. Kane closed his eyes and concentrated. The smell was there. Subtle yet, but there. It was a scent as old as mankind, and the fear of it was even older, more primal.

Whispering Pines was on fire.

***

Beth stepped softly down the hall. Her throat itched, and she fought the urge to cough.

Mister Terrabonne's study door was still open. Beth moved past the useless phone and went straight for the laptop.

A row of green lights sparked when she hit the switch. Beth listened to the computer's fan and the wind and the fast scared beating of her own heart. She felt like any moment she might pee her pants. The laptop's screen flared to life. Its light was cool and blue and the most welcome thing Beth had ever seen in her life.

Type Your Password:

Beth bit her fist to keep from crying out. Her body shook and rocked, and tears spilled hot and salty down her cheeks.

She struggled to get her body under control. She had to get out of this house, get away from this terrible place, but no matter how hard she tried she couldn't stop crying.

She sat hunched over Jack Terrabonne's desk, her body wracked by horrible silent sobs.

***

Alone in the cab of Dermott's truck, Maeve made a loud triumphant sound. The old logging road met back up with the main road just before the mountain pass that would lead her back to Whispering Pines. From what she remembered, there were a few kilometers more of treacherous and twisting road getting down the mountain, then level traveling through the forested valley. It had certainly seemed easy going that morning, in bright sun and better weather.

Maeve took the turnoff a little too quickly. Despite the snow tires and the four wheel drive, Dermott's truck threatened to skid off the mountain road.

Maeve took her foot off the gas and gently tapped the brake. As the back end slid out to the side, she faced her wheels to meet the swinging bumper. The truck reversed its swing and began to spin the other way. Maeve palmed the wheel in the opposite direction and repeated the process, again and again until the truck stopped skidding and the wheels all faced forward again.

"Too feckin close by half, my girl," she said to herself. "No sense getting yourself killed."

Alone in the cab, her laughter was flinty, cold and bitter.

***

It seemed like forever before Beth's fit passed. She wiped her eyes and tried to swallow the hard knot in her throat. She thought about her next step.

It was easier to think now that she'd got all that fear and despair out of her system. Even the light in the room looked warmer.

The garage. She would head for the garage. If there was another car, she'd be able to take it down the mountain. Beth hated the thought of abandoning Tanya and Jo up here, but it was the only way to be sure of sending help.

The light *was* warmer. The backs of Beth's hands and arms had a distinctly orange tinge to them. As she watched, her skin and the polished surface of Mister Terrabonne's desk grew brighter with a warm and dancing light.

A light that didn't come from the window. Beth smelled smoke and jumped to her feet.

Harlan Winters stood in the open doorway. He held a burning torch high in one hand, its light dancing red and hellish across his face. He looked at her and his eyes narrowed, cold and glittering.

His lips pulled away from his teeth. His gums were dark and mottled, his teeth small and yellow and slimed.

The man's soft laughter was the sound of shovels scraping the earth from a grave.

EIGHTY-THREE

All of Harlan's Christmases had come at once. His favorite little maid stood cowering in Jack's study. She was small and dark, big-eyed and trembling.

On the desk behind her, Jack's laptop sat waiting for its password.

The girl darted for the door. She tried to squeak past him and out into the hall. Harlan stuck one booted leg across the path of those slim and fragile ankles.

The maid landed hard, the wind knocked out of her. Harlan picked her up with one hand gripping the back of her jeans and pinned her facedown against the desk. Her hips were small and slim. Her hair fell loose from its tie to make a soft dark halo around her head and neck.

The girl was powerfully tempting, even if she did smell awful.

"Hell you been doing," Harlan said, "rolling around in laundry soap?"

The girl coughed and choked and squirmed. Harlan took his hand off her back, and she was able to breathe. For a long moment, the crackling torch in Harlan's hand was the loudest sound in the room.

"What are you going to do with me?"

The maid's voice was small and wet and trembling. The sound of it filled Harlan with a dark and dangerous light.

"Well, darlin', that depends on you." He stroked the back of her neck with one big rough thumb. "You want to live, best you cooperate."

Harlan grabbed a handful of hair and lifted. She followed him, hissing and whimpering, around the desk and into Jack's chair. Harlan stood behind her, his left fist still wrapped in her hair. Sitting down like that, the top of her head barely reached his belt buckle.

"Password's *BOOGIEJACKTERRABONNE*, all one word, all in capitals." Like Jack had it in him to think of anything else.

The girl tried to look back at him. Harlan gave her hair a sharp tug. She cried out and put her eyes back down where they belonged.

He had to spell Jack's password out. She touched the keys one at a time to keep from messing up, her fingers were shaking so bad. Harlan moved his thumbnail in small circles over her scalp and halfway hoped she'd disobey.

The burning torch started to get on Harlan's nerves. He wanted both hands free, without that damned flaming stick getting in his way. He threw it away, and he and the maid both watched its flaming arc sail into the leather couch. Dark smoke rose from the place where it landed, and the room filled with a smell like burning skin.

The girl sat frozen at the keyboard. Harlan leaned down until his nostrils brushed the small hairs at the base of her neck. Her sweat was cold, oily and metallic. Soap, shampoo and perfume were all wearing away.

Soon.

Harlan let his hot breath crawl along the side of the girl's neck. She shuddered, and his heart soared.

"You'd best get a move on and call up Jack's email," he whispered, "You don't want to burn to death."

"I'm, I'm trying. The com-computer says it can't make a connection, there's no dial tone. Mister Terrabonne's rich-- he's got satellite TV, why not broadband?"

"God DAMN it!" Harlan threw the girl away from him and kicked the desk. Wood cracked, and the desk top fell slanting to one side. "Stupid cheap backward old man!"

There were more words, but they were lost in Harlan's inarticulate growling rage.

The laptop screen sat there on the off-kilter desk top, mocking him.

Harlan pulled his gun and fired. The screen exploded in a shower of sparks, and the ricochet struck Jack's vintage Dobro.

Down on the floor, the maid screamed.

EIGHTY-FOUR

Kane's footsteps made soft sounds across the marble tile in the entry hall. His shadow flickered in the soft orange light, and the fires burning in the upper stories rumbled with a low muted voice.

Kane didn't want to stay in the mansion. He'd found nothing but dead bodies inside, and Winters was burning the house down around himself. Kane decided to go back to the barn, look after the injured girl and protect the horses.

Snow was blowing in through the open front door. Already shallow drifts were collecting on the cold marble, up to ten feet beyond the threshold.

Kane's shoes were inches from the first drift when he heard the shot. A single gunshot like the boom of a cannon from the direction of Terrabonne's study, followed by the sound of a woman screaming.

The scream rose in pitch and suddenly stopped.

On the other side of the open door, the outside world was clean and cold and purple and gloaming. Jack Terrabonne's mansion was burning down around Kane's head, and for all he knew that woman's scream might well have been her last.

But there was the chance she was still alive.

Kane sighed and tightened his grip on the hammer in his fist.

***

Maeve geared down and corrected out of another skid. She swore softly under her breath more or less nonstop now. Getting back down the mountain was almost as hard as getting up had been. Maybe harder. Dark granite cliffs still rose on one side, and a sheer purple abyss of swirling snow and black pines still waited on the other. The road was every bit as twisty and treacherous as it had been on the other side of the pass, but now it was all downhill.

Maeve had troubles enough without gravity trying to kill her.

She was almost to the bottom when she saw Jack Terrabonne's Porsche among the trees. Or rather, saw one curved quarterpanel, its color that memorable and ridiculous bright blue.

Maeve needed use the handbrake to stop. She angled her wheels and kept the truck in gear to keep it from rolling away, flipped on her emergency flashers and shrugged back into her winter coat.

The Porsche lay on its side, one wheel turned to the icy heavens. Snow clustered between the chrome hubcap and the black rubber tire. A path of broken branches and uprooted saplings led in a straight line from the wreck to one of the road's many sharp turns.

The pine tree was at least a meter thick, ancient and healthy and solid. A few branches and a little torn bark aside, the trunk was unscathed.

The Porsche was not so lucky. Its front end looked like a piece of wadded paper, and drifting snow was well on its way to crawling over the topmost doorsill.

Maeve covered the last few meters to the car with her heart in her mouth. Kane was a hopeless driver, but slow enough to maybe be safe. Jack Terrabonne had been reckless and a showoff. Maeve stumbled in the snow and slid down to the Porsche.

The metal was freezing under her palms. The Porsche's convertible top was crumpled, the black fabric white with frost. The window glass was spiderwebbed with overlapping cobweb patterns of broken glass. Maeve pulled the knife from her boot and stabbed through the ragtop. The two-dollar blade sliced right through the snow-crusted canvas.

The girl inside was not much more than a child. She had blood on her face and broken glass in her hair. She hung in the web of her seatbelt, her face turned to the floor and one arm downward, frozen as though reaching for the duffel bag on the far side of the car, the duffel bag just out of her grasp.

Maeve put two fingers to hollow at the corner of the girl's jaw. There was no pulse, nor did Maeve expect to find one. The girl's skin was already waxy, stiff and cold. Snowflakes blew in through the slit in the roof and clung to the poor thing's cheeks and lips.

Whatever the dead girl stared at, it was no longer on this world.

EIGHTY-FIVE

Kane held the driving hammer in his right fist, cocked high across his body. The spiked iron pritchel he carried left and low. His eyes stung in the smoky air, and the back of his throat felt like it was coated in ash.

Black smoke poured out of Jack's study. Kane thought about and rejected the possibility of a trap. Harlan Winters seemed a man of cunning more than strategy, a creature of impulse.

Kane seized the element of surprise. He charged through the open door.

Eight feet separated Kane from Winters. Two running steps. A quarter of a second.

Winters stood with his back to the door, his left hand raised. Adrenalin burned like holy fire in Kane's body, sharpening his focus, forcing time to crawl through thick blood-warm syrup. He was barely aware of the pale shape cowering on the floor at Winters's feet, and the air seemed blurred and blue at the edges.

Kane's right arm uncoiled. His right foot struck the boards four feet past the threshold.

The hammer head was a shimmering blur. It sliced the air in a fast flat arc, seeking the soft hollow just behind Harlan's left ear.

Winters heard that one step. Felt the rush of air. Detected Kane's presence by scent, body heat or some other sense humanity had long since lost.

Kane's left foot landed. He twisted hard at the waist, swinging for a point several feet beyond Harlan's skull.

The hammer's steel head was inches from its target.

Winters wrinkled his nose. His eyes slit, and his ears seemed to flatten against his skull.

His left shoulder came up. The right side of his body dropped down.

The hammer sailed past the corner of Harlan's jaw.

Winters spun. His left hand struck. An explosion of pain and noise and blinding white light detonated in Kane's body.

The hammer flew out of Kane's hand. It sailed spinning away in the burning room.

Kane moved with the blow. He used the momentum to lash out with his other hand. The foot-long iron spike struck home.

Bone snapped. Muscle ripped. Skin tore. A ragged red line opened from Harlan's brow ridge right across his nose. Blood flooded the wound, syrupy and slow.

The man's roar was distorted, dopplered and slowed. The gun in his hand left a gleaming chrome vapor trail as it rose.

Kane brought the butt of the pritchel down hard on Harlan's thick wrist. Bone cracked and splintered.

The gun went off. Its barrel burned Kane's hand as he stripped it from Harlan's grasp. Winters broke a finger in the trigger loop.

The last thing Kane saw was a fist the size of a human head, rushing toward his face.

EIGHTY-SIX

The girl kicked. The girl screamed. She flailed her legs and beat with her fists and cried.

Harlan dragged her through the burning house anyway.

Whispering Pines was an inferno. Back the way he came, he heard three sharp cracks. The gunshots were rounds from his lost . 44 cooking until they detonated. Flames licked at the walls, flared behind the doorways and consumed the wide double staircase in the entry hall.

Harlan flashed to grim memories of his childhood, and the preacher's sermons about Hell. He remembered the burning shack, and the drifter he hadn't known was inside.

This was better.

The maid was half out of her mind with panic. She tried to twist away and make a break for it. Direction she was running in, getting loose would have sent her running straight into the flames, but the kid tried all the same.

The direction Harlan was taking her was just as fatal, but it was a lot more fun.

Harlan's hand came away from his face sticky. He smacked that broad flat palm down on top of her skull. He didn't want to kill her, just quiet her down some. She was still vomiting when he got her out into open air.

Harlan slapped his hand back over his wounded face. That left eye wouldn't open no matter how hard he tried, and the wound wouldn't quit bleeding.

Worse still, his nose was broken. Every smell and taste in the air was muted and overpowered by the flat iron taste of his own blood.

Harlan would have loved to have taken a little time over that Kane fucker. He'd turned out to be every bit as tough as Harlan had thought. Not tough enough of course, but still trouble.

A crash like a freight train hitting a plate glass window split the night. Jack's chandelier giving up the ghost. Ten thousand German cut-goddamned-crystals hit the slabs of Italian-goddamned-marble and vaporized into ten million pieces of glittering razor-sharp shrapnel.

As Harlan watched through the flaming doorway, the grand double staircase collapsed in on itself. The burning wood groaned with a voice like Hell's own chorus.

Kane was dead. That would have to be enough.

Harlan pulled his stiff lips away from his teeth and grimaced.

Whispering Pines was dying, and it was good.

That fire-glow would be visible for miles. Of course, there weren't that many neighbors to see it, and most of them would be hunkered down inside on a night like this. But one way or another, time was growing short. Harlan knew he had best collect his steel lockbox and get his ass down the side of this mountain and out of this damn country.

Harlan whipped his head around before he realized he'd heard the snow crunching beside him. The maid, running for freedom. Snowflakes gleamed like diamonds in the maid's hair and flew from her heels as she ran for freedom.

He watched her sweet little shape run, masked by curtains of falling snow and lit by firelight.

Harlan had time for this. There was no way he could miss it: it was just too beautiful.

EIGHTY-SEVEN

The sounds of gunshots roused Kane. Three blasts, loud enough to wake the dead, followed by a deep chuckling roar that passed for silence.

Kane coughed and lifted his head. His world was pain. Stiffness and pain.

He fought through it, pushed himself up onto one elbow. Pain, doubled and doubled again, brought awareness. Awareness and memory.

Whispering Pines was on fire. All around him, Jack Terrabonne's study was burning down.

The girl. The teenage maid who'd cleaned his room that morning: Beth, that was her name. Winters had Beth. Kane's head reeled, and for a moment he confused the maid Beth with the young French girl, her mouth full of clay.

But that was wrong. The French girl was dead, killed by Harlan Winters. Beth was still alive.

Deep in the ceiling above him, groaning timbers began to wail. There was a crash, and the fire's roaring voice rose in volume. Kane had to get out.

Heat waves shimmered in front of the picture window. Beyond the glass lay night and snow and safety and freedom.

Jack's chair might have broken the window. Kane was too weak to lift, let alone throw it. He cast around the room on his hands and knees in the smoke, looking for something else. Harlan's gun lay on the floor, a barely recognizable mass of curled and exploded metal. It was too hot to touch.

Finally, Kane saw Jack Terrabonne's guitar. The old Dobro had a bullet hole in its face and a sizable chunk splintered out of the back of it, but it was still in one piece. Kane reached up and took the guitar by the neck.

Out in the hallway, a burning rafter crashed to the floorboards.

Kane swung the guitar with both hands. The wood bounced off the glass with a discordant noise. He swung again, with all his might.

The guitar struck the window with a single loud crack. Long ugly splinters rained down on Kane, but the window held.

That was when Kane remembered the iron tools he'd used as weapons. Groping blind on the floor in the smoke, there was no sign of the hammer or pritchel. His eyes stung and he couldn't stop coughing. He dropped to his belly on the floor, where the air was clear and he could almost see. His only hope was to keep searching.

Finally, under the remains of the broken desk, Kane's fingers brushed smooth cold iron. He grabbed the hammer in both hands and held it tight.

The window wasn't where Kane remembered. The burning couch and burning hall way formed a single flickering orange wall in the heavy smoke, but the window was a dim gray square, barely visible.

Kane lined up to face that gray square. Keeping his face as low to the floor as possible, he took one last breath of clear air, braced himself and rose to his feet. Coughing, choking, dizzy and blinded by tears, Kane threw the hammer with all his might.

Glass shattered. Kane jumped. Oxygen whooshed into the burning building. The resulting plume of flame rose over fifty feet into the air.

The light of the burning mansion blotted out the stars.

Kane rubbed snow over his face and put a handful in his mouth. The taste was cool, clean and welcome.

He picked himself up and staggered away from the inferno. He shook broken glass from his coat and wondered if the hammer would turn up before the spring thaw.

Ten meters away, he stumbled across tracks in the snow. Two sets of prints: small feet in tennis shoes, moving fast. Enormous feet shambling after them, stamping through and obscuring the smaller prints.

The tracks curved off across the wide snowy lawn.

Kane hoped he was not too late.

The girl had run into the treeline. She was somewhere in those dark and hissing pines.

EIGHTY-EIGHT

Harlan swallowed blood and smiled. The girl was quick: So light on her feet, she ran like a deer.

Not that Harlan was in any hurry. He always let his rush get the better of him, that was the problem. This time, this time Harlan was determined to make it last.

This time, it might be perfect.

Besides, the girl's tracks stood out dark clear in the firelit snow. Even with one bloodied eye crusted shut, he was able to see them plain as day. That sweet little thing wasn't going nowhere Harlan couldn't follow.

He trailed along behind her as far as the treeline before he stopped and looked back.

Whispering Pines was beautiful. After all these years of being dragged here, lead dog in Jack Terrabonne's pack of scraggly mutts, Harlan finally got see the old house the way he'd always imagined. The great shambling bulking of it burned red and black, skeletal in the flames.

Harlan stood in the snow and watched with his one good eye.

The top floor, Jack's suite, went first. Whether it was the weakest part of the house or the beams holding it up gave out, Harlan couldn't guess. It was enough that the frame listed inward on itself, paused as though drawing breath and finally collapsed.

The wreckage fell into the second story and brought that crashing down into the first. Harlan's heart swelled.

Two sets of prints curved together over the pristine field: the tight little line of the girl's running feet and Harlan's big messy footsteps. The fire threw dancing blood-colored lights and purple shadows across the snow.

A window popped somewhere on the first floor. A mighty plume of flame, more beautiful than anything Harlan had ever imagined, rose into the air. Spirals of burning sparks blew out across the valley.

Harlan wondered if the trees would burn. He wondered if his boss and father was burning now. He wondered if the girl would tremble all over when he caught her. Harlan knew she would scream.

He touched his lips with the tip of his tongue. One big booted foot smashed down on top of the girl's delicate little footprint.

It was so hard not to hurry.

EIGHTY-NINE

Maeve made the final turn on the road to Whispering Pines. A dirty orange smudge grew closer on the horizon, until the hellish underbelly of the clouds danced with red lights from below. Once, a wild pillar of flame streaked up into the night.

No mistake. There was nothing else in the area. Whispering Pines was burning.

Maeve shook a cigarette out of the deck and fit it to her lips. After so long without nicotine, even the taste of the unlit filter was bloody divine. The lighter wheel rasped, and paper touched flame. Dermott's precious seat leather be damned.

Not ten meters down the drive, the path was blocked. Two snowy white hillocks, the shapes of the trucks underneath just barely recognizable, forming a single piece of impassable geography.

Maeve didn't hesitate. She dropped into a lower gear and turned off the drive into the trees. The truck dipped and jumped over the uneven ground, but the four wheel drive and snow tires were more than a match for the drifted snow and uneven ground.

Dead branches raked the windshield and scrabbled against the sides of Dermott's truck. Maeve lit a fresh cigarette off the butt of the last one and steered a course among the twisted gray trunks. She aimed for the cheery yellow glow coming through the trees.

The glow grew brighter. Soon she drove through a winter fairyland, where the trees threw long and flickering purple shadows and the snow-covered ground seemed to throb with red and orange lights.

Maeve steered for a gap between the two skeletal black silhouettes and emerged into an island of light.

Whispering Pines was indeed burning. It was the most awesome and terrible thing Maeve had ever seen. If Kane or that rich bastard Terrabonne were inside, they were dead. If the truth about Bridey had been in there, it too was lost.

The drive in front of the house had been snowed over. What this morning had been raked gravel and green lawn was now a flat white oval, ragged along one melted edge and pocked with charred debris.

Maeve sat in the cab of the truck and watched the house burn. She didn't trust herself to get out, the pull was too strong. Snowflakes vanished in the flames and melted against the windshield. The heat beat at her face through the glass. She wondered if she walked into that inferno, how close she would get before her skin began to roast and her hair began to burn. She wondered at what point she would burst into flame like a torch.

Maeve shook herself like a dog. Her hand was clamped tight on the door handle, the knuckles hard and white. She forced her hand open, saw that the cigarette between the fingers of her other hand had burned halfway down. She flicked the column of ash into the once-virgin ashtray and dragged smoke deep into her lungs.

The nicotine settled her nerves. There was Dermott's truck to return, and truth be told, Maeve didn't feel ready. She was beginning to fear she might never feel ready.

At the heart of it, Maeve believed the old man. He may have been the last in Mexico to see Bridey alive, but that would be the case too if he put her on that plane to South America. For the first time since that one terrible afternoon, Maeve caught herself doubting the truth of Bridey's death.

She dropped the truck back in gear. The big diesel changed pitch as the clutch engaged, and Maeve palmed the steering wheel to the right, in the direction of the outbuildings. The truth about Bridey might lie in the Andes, or it might lie in the burning ruin of the old mansion, but there was always the chance.

Maeve owed Bridey that chance.

The halogen headlights bleached the walls of the various barns the pale white-gray of old teeth. The truck rumbled to a stop, and Maeve climbed from the warm cab down into the biting cold.

The blazing heat melted the snow a good three or four meters from the house. Where the side garden had been stood the black charcoal husks of rose bushes and shattered flagstones.

A pair of twisted legs stuck out from the edge of the snowmelt. The snow above those legs was a sunken dark slush.

Maeve picked her way closer. The hellish red light made it impossible to tell the color of the suit, but there was no mistaking those tiny feet in those fancy cowboy boots. Her questions for Jack Terrabonne would go unanswered.

"Feck." First she muttered the word, then shouted it to the sky. "*FECK!*"

Maeve shouted again and kicked a clump of snow. A hard shape caught her eye and she kicked again. A corner: enameled black metal.

She bent down and scraped away more snow. The lockbox was a flash item, heavy steel and fireproof. It was also unlocked.

"Dear sweet Jaysus."

It was more money than Maeve had ever seen in her life. Almost too much to be real. And in among the jumbled stacks of American currency, Maeve's fingers found tangled loose strands of what could only be human hair.

"Feck me..." It was all too weird for words.

The box was heavier than Maeve would have thought possible. She had it only halfway back to Dermott's truck when the air itself seemed to crumple and a plume of fire rose high into the night.

That fireball lit the snowy fields up bright as day. In that bright and burning moment, Maeve saw a black and flapping shape vanish into the trees.

NINETY

The girl was left-handed. Most people, if they didn't know how to navigate in the woods, ended up making a big circle in the direction of their dominant hand. Kane saw the girl's tracks and knew that Beth was left-handed.

Which meant he could get out ahead of her. All Kane had to do was arc his own path in the opposite direction.

It was risky. Too big an arc and Winters would catch up to the girl before Kane did. Too small and he'd run into an old trail.

It was a risk, but it was the only chance the girl had.

Kane was in no shape to catch up by running behind. One eye was almost swollen shut. His stomach felt like it was full of broken glass, and every step was a sharp and grinding pain. He kept spitting blood onto the snow.

Kane only hoped it was the busted lip and cut tongue, not internal bleeding.

Off in the distance, Harlan Winters let out a rebel yell. The wild blood-curdling cry echoed through the valley. It also gave Kane a good idea as to Harlan's position.

Kane made his decision and set off. He was able to move faster with his arms wrapped tight around his body.

***

Harlan was excited. Almost too excited. The blood raced in his veins, and the night's pains and wounds and losses were distant, unimportant.

Harlan Winters ran one-eyed and bloody through the night forest. The burning pyre of his father's house lit his way. His hands tore at passing branches and filled the cold air with the sharp scent of pine, and his throat swelled with raw and savage laughter.

***

Kane ran at a stiff and awkward lope. Over the wild voice of the wind in the high pines, he could hear his quarry up in the distance: Harlan Winters chasing down his victim.

The girl, Beth, was tiring. It was hard work, running at top speed through knee-deep snow. The effort was getting to her. The rapid crunching footsteps up ahead no longer came as quickly as they had. By contrast, Winters sounded like he was picking up steam. He crashed through the pines, laughing like a madman, growing louder and louder, seemingly unstoppable.

Kane adjusted his course and put on the steam. The effort made him feel like he'd been sawed in half. Kane bit down on his pain and pushed harder.

It was the girl's only chance.

Kane ran, and listened to the sounds of the chase unfold as he ran. Soon, Winters and his victim were no longer ahead of him. Soon, they were off to his side, with Harlan's wild laughter directly behind the girl.

When he was sure he was in position, Kane stopped with his back to a tree. The pain was a sick and nauseating coil in his belly. His heart raced and his lungs burned for air.

The girl's steps came closer. Kane worried she might not make it. She was breathing badly now, gasping and crying with every faltering step.

Behind her, Harlan Winters was as loud as a freight train.

Kane ignored the pain. He forced his breathing slow and even, willed his racing heart to slow.

He had to be ready.

NINETY-ONE

Harlan loved this moment.

The girl was just ahead. The burning lights winking through the trees gave Harlan glimpses of her sweet pale shape.

There was nothing deerlike about the way she ran now. Her breath came in ragged gasping sobs, and her form was shot, arms and legs flying all over the place in the frantic effort to get just a little bit further away.

To live just a little bit longer.

No longer the deer, she reminded Harlan of something smaller, darker and more fragile. He could almost taste the hot metal of her blood, almost feel the snap of her bones.

There was no chance the girl smelled like soap now.

Harlan threw his head back and let out a mighty yell. It was a cry of triumph, joy and pure love.

The girl looked back over her shoulder. Harlan crouched less than twenty feet behind her. She let out a breathless little scream and put on one last burst of speed.

Her old form was truly gone. The girl ran ten, twelve flailing steps before her exhausted legs collapsed under her.

Snow billowed around her as she went down.

It was perfect.

Harlan charged her down with laughter in his heart.

NINETY-TWO

The girl screamed and ran right past Kane.

She didn't see him in her rush. She didn't see anything in her blind flight. Four steps later, she went down in the snow and lay sobbing.

Winters was hot on her trail. Kane waited until the crashing and the laughter were almost on top of him before letting go.

The pine branch hissed through the air.

Harlan Winters ran full tilt into the ambush.

The wood whipped in a tight circle and caught him square in the chest. Harlan's feet came out from under him, and he flew.

Kane came around from behind the tree. The great furnace of Harlan's breath pumped in shallow and uneven gasps, but he had already struggled up onto one knee.

Kane stepped between Winters and his prey.

Harlan's face was dark with soot and streaked with blood. His left eye socket was a dark and gore-clotted mess. His nose was smashed flat against his face, and burnt hair flew wild around his head.

His one good eye was small, red-rimmed and bloodshot. He stared at Kane in disbelief, spat blood in the snow and slowly smiled.

Snow drifted knee-deep around them. Thick flakes swirled in the air, and the wind in the pines howled with an unearthly voice.

Harlan crouched. His broken hand was swollen, dark and purple. Tongues of steam curled from his clothes and skin.

Kane dropped his weight. His open coat flapped in the wind, and he held his empty hands low and out at his sides. Behind him, the girl Beth wept and tried to crawl.

Winters bared his teeth. His laughter was harsh, scraping and cruel.

Kane flexed his hands and said nothing.

A long wordless roar echoed through the trees, and Harlan Winters exploded from his crouch.

Snow flew into the air. Kane leaned aside from the great dark shape hurtling at him and unloaded a ripping hook into the center of Harlan's body.

It was like punching a wall.

Kane ducked a backhand fist larger than his head and blasted a punch up into Harlan's armpit.

The uppercut never landed. Harlan's leg shot up out of the snow and smashed into Kane with a force he wouldn't have imagined possible. Pain burst red and rotten beneath Kane's ribs, and suddenly he was down on one knee in the snow, a giant bloody-knuckled hand grasping the belt of his jeans.

Kane felt a nauseating lurch as he was lifted into the air. Harlan Winters held Kane over his head with one hand and threw him into the trees.

Kane hit with a loud crash and landed in a rain of pine needles and splintered branches. Feeble wisps of white vapor plumed in the air above his mouth. His head spun, and a strange disconnected sound played in his head, an oddly rhythmic scrutching.

Boots. The sound was boots. Boots in snow.

Kane rolled onto one side and shuddered in pain. The scrutching steps grew fainter, moving away from him. A wave of relief surged through Kane, a wild and absurd joy that brought tears to his eyes.

Until he remembered the girl. Kane wiped his face with his sleeve and saw her. Not twenty feet away, too exhausted to run but still crawling for her life.

And between Kane and the girl, a hulking dark shape lurching in the snow.

Kane forced himself up onto his knees. He spit blood and struggled to his feet.

"Winters!"

Kane's voice was hoarse and shattered. But it stopped that black shape in its tracks.

Harlan Winters turned. His single bloodshot eye gleamed yellow in the wintry light, and the smile on his face was truly terrible.

Kane took a deep breath and prayed his shaking legs would hold.

"You just don't know when to quit, do you boy?" Harlan's voice was broken concrete. "Don't you know I'm gonna take you apart in pieces now? Don't you know I'm gonna make this *fun*?"

Harlan came slow this time. His steps were small and stiff, and he cradled his damaged hand in close to the center of his body. It gave Kane hope his punch had done some damage after all, but it made Harlan no less dangerous.

Size, speed, strength. Pure animal ferocity. Even in Harlan's current state, Kane knew he was physically outmatched.

His only hope was to fight smarter.

Kane circled to Harlan's blind and damaged side. Harlan circled with him, his good right hand weaving and pawing at the air, seeking a kill. The two men's steps crunched in the snow. Their breath billowed away from them in icy plumes that hung still in the air, quickly shredded by the thick falling snow.

Harlan's fist lashed out. Kane leaned in and counterpunched, three short sharp shots to Harlan's broken hand.

Winters yowled. Kane moved into the clawing right hand he knew was coming, caught the bicep on the point of his elbow and trapped Harlan's arm against his body. Winters was too strong to force a joint lock or throw, but at least Kane was safe from those sledgehammer punches.

Harlan reared back and raised his arm. Once again Kane flew off his feet. This time he was ready.

Kane coiled his body into a tight ball. At the height of the lift, Kane smashed both heels down into Harlan's broken nose and ruined eye. The moment of bellowing rage that followed was all Kane needed to hook one leg around the massive bull neck and lock it down behind his other leg.

Kane tightened the choke hold. Pinched carotid arteries stopped carrying blood to the brain. Harlan's roaring cries became a sudden gurgle, and the big man staggered. Unconsciousness was seconds away, if Kane had the will to hold tight.

Winters took three lurching steps and dropped to one knee. Kane kept his back arched against Harlan's good arm and prepared for a fading and desperate thrashing.

Instead, Winters threw his body down onto its side.

The two men crashed to the forest floor together. The impact felt like a block of stone dropped from a great height. It wasn't enough to make Kane lose the choke hold entirely, but it did loosen his grip. Before he was able to lock the arm back down, Harlan Winters had one big hand wrapped around Kane's throat.

The man's strength was horrific. Thick fingers pressed in on Kane's windpipe and black spots danced in his vision. It was a race now, the stakes life or death.

Falling flakes melted on Kane's skin and stung his eyes. The seashell roar in his ears grew louder. He put all his strength into his legs and thought he felt that terrifying grip slacken.

It wasn't enough. The black spots crowded in, and his vision went gray. His limbs felt leaden and dead.

He imagined he saw a dark spirit rush toward him, screaming. Black dreadlocks flew from a bone-white skull. In the hand held high, the gleam of steel.

NINETY-THREE

Kane rolled over. Winter still raged in New Zealand, but here it was summer. The sky was bleached the color of bone, and the waters of the Aegean were a deep and impossible blue. The sun was hot on Kane's chest and stomach, the stones warm against his back. For some reason, his scars seemed to feel the heat more. Each one burned like constellations, tiny points and lines of ruby light.

"Kane?"

"Hm?"

"What is it you're thinking?"

"Nothing."

Kane looked over at Maeve. The stone deck was private, and her body was sunwarmed, bare and brown.

"You're thinking about it again, aren't you."

"No," he lied.

Maeve rolled over onto her side. Her nipples were dark against the pale caramel color of her breasts. She looked at him, her eyes slanted and green, shadowed behind the blue-black tumble of her dreadlocks

"I think about it," she said. "All the time."

Kane raised up on his elbows. Maeve traced a pattern on the warm stones with one finger. The scars on her forearms were bright against her tan, and the fine hairs caught the sun like gold wire.

"You can't second guess yourself." Kane took her hand, twined her fingers in his own. "You do your best and don't look back."

"Easy for you to say."

"Not really."

"I still see Bridey," she said. "Not all the time, mind. But sometimes."

Kane said nothing. Maeve closed her eyes, shuddered and bit her lip.

"I thought... ah, never mind."

She moved closer. Her mouth moved along the side of Kane's throat to the hollow below his jaw. Soon, they moved together in rhythms as ancient as stone and sea.

***

Maeve and Kane made love often, all through the summer. In truth, they did little but make love and swim in the blue and blood-warm waters of the Aegean Ocean. Some days, after the flat hammering heat of the afternoon had faded from the sky, they took the little motor launch into town.

Kane had a few words of Greek, and he soon picked up more. Maeve used the internet connection in the town hall to hold the gathered threads of her wide-flung life. She had friends all over the world.

Together they drank in the taberna and ate fresh fish in the town's single restaurant. Whenever an old Jack Terrabonne song came on the radio, the singer in death popular again, Maeve's eyes clouded with pain and Kane left the room.

Kane healed quickly. His strength was slower to return. Even after his body was once again hard and brown and heavy with muscle, his eyes remained wounded, alive with pain. Whenever Jack Terrabonne's posthumous hit single, *Bad Angel Blues*, came on the radio, Kane's face closed, dark and grim.

The song played a lot that summer.

***

One day in town, Kane wandered the sun-baked streets alone. He ended up, as he always did, in the taberna.

The old men were at their usual table. Kane wished them *geia sou*, passed the time of day in his halting Greek and took the place offered him at their table. From time to time the old men spoke in French or English for his benefit, but for the most part Kane was content to let the sea-change melodies of spoken Greek wash over him.

The cafe was cool and smelled of damp stone. The Mavrodafni was the deep shadowed color of ripe plums. It tasted of chocolate and caramel, and of the sunblasted hills on which it grew.

For now, for Kane, it was enough.

He was on his second glass of the dark sweet wine when Maeve returned from the town hall's internet terminal.

She brushed her fingers across the back of Kane's neck and sat down. A single familiar gesture, and the owner of the taberna brought Maeve's glass of ouzo, already turning cloudy, opaque and white as it mingled with the ice.

Maeve drank of half her glass at a gulp. She rattled her ice, and the air filled with the smell of licorice.

Kane watched in silence.

"They found Harlan's body."

Maeve's eyes were hot and witchy. She held his gaze and continued.

"They finally found him," she said. "An early thaw this spring. Twas all there on the New Zealand Herald's website."

Kane looked down into the glass of blood-dark Mavrodafni between his palms. The memory lay there between them, Maeve on Harlan's shoulders, his blood a bright spattered apron steaming in the snow.

Maeve's empty glass made a loud click against the scarred wood.

Kane's face remained closed, locked down. Maeve ordered a second round, and a third.

That night, they skipped dinner and took the early launch back to their island.

***

Summer lasted a long time that year. Long past the point it should have. As a boy, Kane called that kind of season an Indian Summer, and it was welcome.

This summer, every extra warm day was a wire twisted in his heart.

One day, summer ended. By the time the first cool winds blew out of the north, the days were already growing short.

Maeve found him sitting on the stones outside their cottage. He had his tattered old coat from New Zealand draped around his shoulders and his harmonica in his hands. He sat without playing, staring out at the wine-dark sea.

Maeve stood beside him. She bumped him with her hip and turned so that her breasts touched the solid heat of his shoulder.

"If he'd lived, he never would have paid."

Kane looked at her, his eyes as sad and ancient as the sea beside them.

"You didn't have to murder him, Maeve."

"And risk that *thing* one day walking free?" Her eyes flashed in the gloaming. "No."

Maeve ruffled her fingers through his hair. Kane took her hand and kissed the inside of her wrist.

"You're a good man, Kane. The finest."

The setting sun lit Maeve's skin like burnished bronze, and her dreadlocks fell softly around her face and shoulders. It was an image Kane knew would stay with him for the rest of his life.

"You don't have to go."

"You're wrong about that."

"Bridey will leave you alone one day. You just have to let her."

Maeve's smile was a sharp twist of pain.

"That's what I'm afraid of." Maeve twined his fingers in hers. "Play for me, one last time?"

Kane's eyes clouded with pain. After a long silent moment, he nodded.

He played her the *Bad Angel Blues*.

In the morning Maeve was gone.

Kane knew the cottage was empty when he woke. She left behind a folded sheet of paper and four banded packets of US one hundred dollar bills.

Maeve's note was five words long: *We'll meet again one day.* Kane dropped the paper and the money in his pack and left the cottage. There was no more reason to stay.

That afternoon, one of the old men from the taberna took Kane in a fishing boat to the nearest harbor town. He told Kane that the woman headed north, to Athens and the airport. Kane thanked the old man but asked to go west. From the harbor town, the ferry would take him to Igoumenitsa and the daily boats to Italy and Marseille.

Kane wasn't ready for Paris. Not yet. The French kids had been from the south, the Languedoc. A couple hundred dollars for their iPod might have saved Chloe and Emil from Harlan Winters. Now forty thousand dollars was all he had to give their families.

As the boat tied off in harbor, Kane wished the old man one final *yassou*. The old man told him *Andrōn epiphanōn pasa gē taphos*. Something about how certain men have the whole earth for a tomb.

The ferry didn't leave for a couple of hours. Kane found a cafe with a polished brass espresso machine and a marble countertop grooved by years of use. He sat down at a tiny table on the cobblestones and brought out his Oskar.

Kane had a tune in his head. He thought it might be a new song.

THE END

AFTERWORD

In the autumn of 2006 I saw the Otago for the first time. I had lived on New Zealand's South Island for some years by then but spent my time on the Canterbury Plains, or in the beachfront, seaside communities of Nelson and Kaikoura. Nothing prepared me for what I found as I descended the snow-covered pass out of the Southern Alps.

The forests were a riot of reds and golds and deep masses of tall dark pines. Rivers roared white and frothing over the rusted skeletons of abandoned mining equipment, and ghost towns rotted and crumbled in forgotten valleys. Hiking those hills, it wasn't unusual to find a crumbling section of what had been a stone wall or a few feral fruit trees in what had once been a small orchard. People had come here chasing gold and, in that wilderness, left graves marked only by wildflowers.

In the center of it all sat Queenstown. Playground for the rich and a magnet for tourists. Scruffy poor backpackers sharing the sidewalks with movie stars and well-fed college kids griping at the tops of their voices about blowing out their parents' charge cards.

Before I knew it, I was researching my next book.

Work on the manuscript was slow. The story I had plotted wasn't the story I was telling, and I wasted months and tens of thousands of words trying to force it. My 3x5 index cards said the story need to go one way, but my characters all wanted to go another. Some of them wanted to leave the story altogether. In the end, after a horribly vivid dream of two men in deep snow swinging on each other with black chains, I surrendered.

I started over. Jack Terrabonne's right hand man changed from an oily manipulator and blackmailer into something far worse. Jack himself became the sleazebag he'd been trying to be all along, and his much more talented wife quickly became his ex-wife, prospering without him with her younger lover, her pregnancy, her awards and album sales and greater celebrity. Beth and Tanya, two very different young tourists living in the backpacker community, became Kiwis working as maids at

Whispering Pines. Kane's original girlfriend disappeared. The two never got along, and their lives were headed in different directions.

Maeve stepped onto the scene, just as she is.

The work flowed then, though not what anyone would call fast. With so many files, so many false starts on my hard drive, I couldn't type yet another. Instead I wrote by hand-- something about slowing my hand speeded up the words. When things got rough in the middle (things *always* get rough in the middle of a story), I even resorted to using a dip pen. Dip. Write. Dip. Two words, three. Dip. Half a sentence. Dip.

The pace was painful, but I got through it. And the story picked up momentum. Typing in the pages I'd handwritten every day, I found myself going past them, a few sentences, a paragraph or two, eventually whole scenes. By the time I reached the final act I was back to typing like a madman. The final quarter of this book was written over the course of five white-hot days, words flying out of me as fast as my fingers could bang the keys.

A year and a half after I wrote the first words, I was finally able to write the last....

Christchurch, New Zealand

May 2013

ABOUT THE AUTHOR

Steve Malley is a former American making his home in Christchurch, New Zealand. An awful lot of his time is spent painting, writing and playing with his cats. You can check out his day job at *http://inkspot-tattoos.com*

You can write to him at *stevemalley@live.com*, or if you happen to see him around and about, just say hi. :)

Look for the next Kane adventure in 2014.